BOOKS BY HELENA NEWBURY

Helena Newbury is the *New York Times* and *USA Today* bestselling author of sixteen romantic suspenses, all available where you bought this book. Find out more at helenanewbury.com.

ROYAL GUARD

HELENA NEWBURY

For Chris.
Who was always one of the good guys.

PROLOGUE

If I stared into his eyes, I could forget about where we were.

I could forget about the freezing, brutal wind. I could forget about the terrifying nothingness that began less than a foot away.

I could forget about what they were going to do to us.

I stared up into eyes that were blue like the Texas sky, too honest, too *good* to belong here. He belonged in America, not in this vicious, backstabbing place I'd brought him to.

My hip was pressed against the chill metal of the safety rail, all that stood between us and the drop. It was so dark, I couldn't see the water as it roared over the dam. But I could feel the spray as it rose and soaked us, plastering the dress to my body, soaking the fabric of his uniform. And I could hear it: a sound like constant thunder, so loud that I could only make out Garrett's voice because our faces were inches apart.

"I'm sorry," he said.

I shook my head viciously. This wasn't his fault. None of this was. He'd done so much, protected me like no one else could. But they'd beaten us. I knew I was meant to be brave, facing death. That's the royal way: noble and courageous to the end. But all I felt was sickening fear. And regret, regret that we hadn't had more time together, that so much had kept me from this amazing man for so long. This *couldn't* be the end.

I pressed myself against him and he locked his arms around me. The wind dropped away as that huge, muscled body sheltered me and I closed my eyes and pressed my cheek into his chest. "Please tell me you have a plan," I said, my voice cracking.

I felt him shake his head. His chin pressed against the top of my head and his arms tightened around me in a final embrace.

"Him first," said a voice from the darkness. "Then her."

Garrett tensed minutely and I knew they'd put the muzzle of the gun against his head.

"You can kiss her, if you like," said the one holding the gun.

I started to panic breathe because no, this couldn't be *it.* There was so much I wanted to tell him. I had to thank him. I had to tell him I was sorry. I had to—

I felt his chin lift. I tilted my head back just in time to meet his lips as they came down on mine. I was panting, desperate. He was slow and deliberate and fueled by rage, arms cinching tight to crush me to him while his lips owned me, claimed me, made me his and the hell with tradition. I sobbed and clutched at his shoulders, molding myself to him. The tip of his tongue teased mine in that forbidden way that made me go weak: if we kissed hard enough, shut out all thoughts of everything else, maybe this would all go away—

"Enough," said a voice.

I drew back from him, my vision swimming with tears, my chest tight with fear.

The one holding the gun to Garrett's head, cocked it. Pushed the muzzle even tighter against his scalp.

Garrett drew in a quick, tight breath and I felt his arms tense: my first warning that he was about to do something. His eyes met mine and he gave a tiny nod. I saw it then, in that split second. He'd made a decision. One final sacrifice, after all the others he'd made. One final attempt to protect me.

He threw his weight to the side, pulling me with him.

We tipped over the safety rail.

The gun boomed as it went off.

And then we were falling towards the water three hundred feet below.

1

GARRETT

One Week Earlier

I woke to darkness and that tiny, unsettling trembling of the floor that reminds you you're in a plane. For a moment, I thought I was back in Iraq, strapped into the back of a C-130: my hands actually groped for my rifle. Then I looked down and saw my plaid shirt and jeans and remembered where I was.

The cabin was still dark and everyone was asleep so I figured we were still a way from Los Angeles. I'd been asleep since New York and now I ached all over: my economy seat wasn't built for someone six foot six. I felt like a bear crammed into a dog kennel and about as good-tempered. All I wanted to do was land, scrape together the bus fare to my apartment, and crash for the rest of the day. But I knew that instead, I had to go job hunting again. *Dammit!* I let out a low growl.

The guy sitting next to me opened one eye, saw me, and quickly pretended to be asleep again. In a few hours, I'd be a story to tell the guys at his office. *I got the red-eye from New York and you wouldn't believe the guy they sat me next to. Two-fifty pounds and the scariest son-of-a-bitch you ever saw.* But until then, he was keeping his head down.

I don't like scaring folks. It's just the way I'm built.

I needed to take a leak. I squeezed out of my seat and stood bleary-eyed, looking up and down the aisle. I dimly remembered the cabin crew pointing out where the restrooms were. Some were at the back but weren't there some up front, just beyond that curtain?

I was so half asleep that I'd pulled aside the curtain and was three strides beyond it when I realized something was wrong. The seats here were bigger, big enough that they'd have fit even me. And the lighting was soft and moody, more like a fancy bar than an airplane. And there was so much space: there were less than ten seats in the whole cabin. *Aw, hell.* I'd wandered into First Class. I turned around to go back: I didn't want to get thrown out. And that's when I saw her.

One time, up in the mountains in Iraq, my buddy rousted me out of my tent at five a.m. and got me to come look at the sunrise. For a full half hour we'd just stood there in silence, drinking it in, imprinting it into our memories because we might never see anything like it again. This was the same. I was rooted, feet pointed back towards economy class, but upper body frozen in place, turned towards her.

She was far and away the most beautiful thing I'd ever seen in my life.

It was her lips that got me first. Softly pink and pursed together into a pout that was both innocent and...something else. Something that meant I couldn't look away. It was in the set of her delicate jawline, too, even in sleep: she held herself with a sort of authority, but totally different to the officers I'd known in the Marine Corps. I frowned, but I couldn't figure it out. The closest I could get was statues of emperors I'd seen on field trips to museums when I was a kid. *Imperious.* And yet at the same time, her lips were so pure, so soft and untouched.... The thought made me exhale through my nostrils like a bull. She looked to be in her early twenties, but *goddamn*, it looked as if she'd never been kissed.

Something about her drew me in: I wanted—*needed* to reach down and touch her cheek, just to make contact. But I couldn't: it felt like I'd break some spell if I did, like trying to catch a soap bubble.

She was *magical.* And there was something else: a feeling deep in my chest that was like something had been caught by the wind. I knew I'd felt it before, but I couldn't figure out where.

All I knew was, I was in the presence of something special.

There was a fineness to her. Sure, she was a lot smaller than me, but then most people are. But someone had built me using bulldozers to push mountains of earth and rock up into a person, and then shaped it with a wrecking ball. She'd been sculpted out of marble by some artist who'd spent days on the lines of her cheekbones, weeks on the tiny details of her eyelashes.

The blanket had fallen half off her and I thought at first she was wearing some sort of thin, silky sweater. It was the rich, deep red of expensive gift wrap at Christmas. It was only when I saw the airline logo stamped in gold that I realized she was wearing pajamas: a luxury perk they must give you in first class. And her seat had been folded down flat, like a bed, so I was gazing down at her like some prince gazing at Sleeping Beauty.

Her long hair spilled out over the pillow in a glossy chestnut halo. Her breasts made two full, perfect mounds in the soft fabric, rising and falling as she breathed. Nothing was actually on show, but just the sight of them under the fabric had me instantly hard in my pants. And as I watched, she shifted a little in her sleep and some of the hair fell away from her neck. God, her skin was so pale, so different to my deep tan. Like she'd never been outdoors. My mind started running riot, imagining the body that must be hiding under those pajamas, creamy-white skin and light pink nipples, and all the things I'd like to do to her—

And yet at the same time, I felt guilty for it, like I was tainting her just by thinking those thoughts. Like she was above all that. In fact, something about her made me want to just scoop her up in my arms and...*protect* her. Even though she'd be like a doll in my big paws. Even though my palms would be rough as hell against that silky hair. Even though I had no business being near something so beautiful.

Someone else thought so, too. A body slammed into me from behind, carrying me forward a few feet before I stumbled to a stop.

I looked over my shoulder and saw a guy in a deep blue suit glaring up at me. To his credit, he wasn't scared off by my size, even though I was a good six inches taller than him. He was in his sixties, fit for his age, his silver hair meticulously styled and his posture ramrod-straight. I got a military vibe from him.

"*What are you doing in here?*" he said in a furious whisper. He glanced at the slumbering woman and I realized he was trying not to wake her. "*You're not supposed to be in here!*"

His accent was British, like a butler. And as he looked me up and down his lip curled in distaste. I didn't belong in First Class. Hell, from his expression, I didn't belong anywhere except in a cage.

Another guy in a blue suit hurried up and stood behind him. He was as young as the first guy was old, early twenties at most, and he was built like a pro wrestler, not as tall as me but *wide,* a wall of solid muscle. He didn't look as hostile as the first guy, but he wasn't messing around.

And now I made out gold trim on their lapels.

"*Lakovia!*" he hissed.

Princess? I blinked a couple of times. Princesses were something from fairy tales. But it suddenly all made sense. That look she had... *regal* summed it up just right. I looked down at that sleeping face and I had absolutely no doubt I was in the presence of royalty. No wonder she looked so finely sculpted, so perfect. No wonder I'd felt like she was special. A *princess.*

The old guy tried to shove me towards the curtain again, but this time I resisted and he found out that I'm a pretty difficult person to move. I didn't want to cause trouble. I just couldn't stop staring at that sleeping face. I'd never seen anyone like her. I was goddamn entranced.

I'd heard of Lakovia somewhere, but I couldn't remember where. All I knew was that it was somewhere in Europe. I wondered what she was like awake. *Probably a spoiled, selfish, champagne-glugging brat.*

I frowned. That didn't feel right. Somehow, I couldn't imagine her being like that.

"*Go!*" hissed the old guy, raising his voice a little.

The Princess stirred in response.

The old guy bit back a curse and shoved me forward again. This time, I let my feet move. I didn't want to cause trouble. Folks always think I must be spoiling for a fight just because I'm big, but all I want is to be left alone. I craned around as I stumbled through the curtain, holding onto the view of her for as long as possible. Then the curtain closed and she was gone. I sighed.

Just as I was about to move off, a female voice drifted through from first class. "Who was that?" it asked sleepily.

Damn it if I didn't catch my breath, just hearing that voice. She sounded British too, but where the old guy sounded like a butler, her accent was full-on upper class. Clear like glass, polished smooth: it made me want to arch my back like a goddamn cat and rub up against it. It had weight and solidness, a quiet authority. It took all that slow-burning anger that glowed at my core and cooled it, like rolling an ice-cold can of Coke against your forehead on a hot day. I could have listened to her voice all day.

And then the old guy sniffed and said, as if he was discussing something he'd cleaned off his shoe, "No one, Your Highness."

I closed my eyes. They got that right. *No one.* Just a big, dumb ground pounder. Born in a barn, only been good at one thing my whole life. And then they'd taken even that away from me.

I went all the way to the back of the plane, used the restroom and went back to my seat. I slumped down and tried to sink into deep, black sleep, the sort so deep there aren't any nightmares. I figured I'd sleep until Los Angeles.

But when I woke up again, the cabin was still dark. And I wasn't half-awake, this time, I was bolt upright and alert, pulse racing. I'd heard something from behind the curtain. A muffled scream.

Her scream.

I punched my seatbelt release and started running.

2

KRISTINA

At first, it was just a nightmare. The same one I have every night. Suffocating blackness, damp stone walls under my fingers. Total silence... and then the only thing worse: the sound of their boots as they came down the steps to get me.

Some tiny sound coaxed me out of the dream and up towards waking. It used to be that I'd scream as I woke up, my body's way of releasing all the horror I'd just relived. I'd wake up half the palace. But I found that if I really, really focused as I came awake, I could clamp down on the scream and stop it before it started. That's why people think the nightmares have stopped.

So as I swam up through the blackness, I concentrated hard on where I was. *You're safe. Thousands of miles from where it happened. In a plane. And you're in America!* A little thrill of excitement at that. I'd always wanted to see America and now I was finally getting to, even if it was just little glimpses through the windows of limos. *You're safe. No one's trying to hurt you.*

I opened my eyes.

It was dim in the cabin. I could see Emerik and Jakov, the two guards who'd been on duty when I went to sleep. They were my favorites: one old and experienced, one young and dutiful. It was a pity they hated each other.

I frowned. I had a hazy memory of someone asking who I was in a deep, slow, American accent, and Emerik being annoyed with him. Had that really happened?

Emerik and Jakov were asleep in their seats so the other two guards must have taken over. I looked around for them—

Movement in the shadows caught my eye. One of my guards seemed to be standing to attention, his body rigid and straining. Then he suddenly fell like a puppet with his strings cut and I saw the blood gushing from his throat.

Oh Jesus.

A man appeared from behind him, all dressed in black. He stepped over the dead guard and now I saw the second body beside it. Both the guards who'd been on duty were dead. And now the killer turned towards the sleeping Emerik and Jakov. *No!* Not them! I opened my mouth to shout a warning—

My head was suddenly tugged back against my seat. I screamed, but a palm was pressed tight over my lips, muffling it. I looked up into the eyes of another man. He was dressed in black too, but his skin was bone-white, so pale it almost glowed in the dark cabin. His eyes were as coldly gray as a gravestone and he was staring down at me with absolute hatred. Not the way a person hates another person. The way a person hates cockroaches. I'd never seen hate like it.

Wait. My stomach twisted. I'd seen it once. Five years ago. *God, no. It can't be!*

He moved around in front of me and pressed my head back even harder into the softness of my leather seat. I felt my neck stretch, my throat exposed. A knife flashed in his hand and I grabbed his wrist with both hands to keep it away from me. I was panic-breathing, now, but I could barely move air beneath that smothering hand. And he was strong, his forearm solid muscle and his hatred and fury making him even stronger.

Inch by inch, the knife descended towards my throat. The edge gleamed, dipping and trembling as we struggled, but always moving inexorably downwards. I screamed, sobbed and pushed, but now it was so close I could feel the breeze on my skin each time it moved. Then the first touch of it, ice cold, but scoring a line of fire across my throat—

A huge shape loomed behind the man in black. A monster, surely: too big to be a person. The man with the knife was suddenly lifted... and *hurled,* like he was nothing more than a toy. There was a thump as he hit the bulkhead at the front of the plane and slid to the floor.

The shape moved forward into the light. God, he was *huge,* not just tall but wide, his shoulders twice the width of mine, his chest so solid and broad he put me in mind of a bull about to charge. He had thick, black hair, shaggy and unkempt, and his cheeks were dark with stubble. As soon as you saw him, you knew he'd been put on this earth to do one thing: fight.

Brute. That's what my mother would have called him. He was exactly the sort of man she'd always warned me about. I should have been terrified.

And yet... his eyes. He was staring down at me and his eyes were as blue and clear and honest as a summer's day. There was a hunger in those eyes, but there was more, too. Fury, that someone had tried to harm me. And a desperate need to stop it ever happening again.

"You're gonna be okay," he told me in that strange, heavy American accent I'd half-heard in my sleep. Alien to me, and yet familiar. An accent that crept in through my ears and rumbled down through my body, going off like a hot bomb when it hit my groin. It was like an earthquake dipped in honey. It went with his face: God, he was *gorgeous. Hard* beautiful, not soft beautiful. Like a storm cloud or a mountain. His looks were totally unlike the men my mother had introduced me to: the princes with their looks refined through umpteen generations of *proper breeding,* all long noses and weak chins. Or the politicians and industrial tycoons with their broad, pink faces made soft by years of liquid lunches. This man was peasant stock, his heavy jaw stern and unyielding, his features hewn from granite. I pegged his age at about thirty. His strong brows set off those clear blue eyes, balancing out their tenderness. And his lips.... Wide and powerful, hard and yet gloriously soft. My eyes locked on that full lower lip and a tremor went through me. If *he* kissed you, you'd stay kissed.

Then I glimpsed movement behind him and drew in my breath in fear. The man he'd thrown had gotten to his feet. He picked up his knife... and ran right at my rescuer.

3

GARRETT

I WAS PANTING, heart pounding from how close she'd come. I didn't even know her, but the thought of something bad happening to her made my stomach knot. She was still terrified, staring up at me, eyes huge. I heard myself tell her she was going to be okay and she gave this tiny, almost imperceptible nod. Like she trusted me.

Like she wasn't scared of me.

That feeling I had when I first saw her was back. Like something inside me had been caught and lifted by the wind. What *was* that? And the attraction... I'd felt it before, but now, looking into her eyes, it was ten times stronger, a force of goddamn nature. When I looked at her, I couldn't stop. Those fine, delicate features. The lips, so soft, the creamy skin—

Across her throat, I saw a hair-thin line of red where the knife had pressed. He'd marred her.

I wheeled around with a growl, just in time to see the guy run at me, knife outstretched. Hot rage boiled up inside me and I took two big steps forward, my body filling the aisle, a protective wall between him and her. As he reached me, I roared right in his face and slammed a right hook into the side of the head. *Get away from her!*

I knew this was risky. The memories were right there, hanging above me like a thousand ton weight, ready to descend. Fighting like this could bring them down on me and then I'd freeze and this bastard would kill me.

But the only other option was to walk away. And I wasn't going to let her be harmed. No way. I gave a low growl, dodged the knife, and thumped him again.

The guy went staggering back, but stayed on his feet. He was tough: there weren't many guys who'd still be standing after a punch from me. He wasn't as big as me, but he seemed to be all lean, wiry muscle. And he knew how to use a knife. I saw now that he had a buddy, over on the other side of the cabin. That guy was struggling with the two guards I'd met earlier. Another two guards lay dead on the floor.

This wasn't some crazy guy with a knife. This was a professional hit. They'd waited until she was on a commercial flight, the one place her guards weren't allowed to carry guns. Then they'd bided their time until the middle of the night, when half the guards could be silently killed in their sleep. Someone had planned to kill her. A vicious, cowardly attack... but well planned. It would have succeeded, if I hadn't heard her scream. And the assassins were well trained. My eyes narrowed, an unsettling thought scratching at the back of my mind.

The guy I was fighting stabbed at me again. I swayed back out of the way and as he stepped under a light, I got my first good look at his face. His skin was weirdly pale and stretched tight over his cheekbones. His dark hair was slicked back and plastered to his scalp with gel: it made him look almost skeletal.

I landed a good hit on his ribs, feeling my training coming back. He panted in pain and his lips drew back in a snarl. "Who are you?!" His accent was thick, something guttural and European.

I risked a glance at where the two guards were fighting the other assassin. The young guard had him in a headlock and the old guard had pried the knife from his fingers. "No one," I muttered.

There was one other person in first class, a woman about the same age as the Princess, her blonde hair pulled back in a ponytail.

Out of the corner of my eye, I saw her run over to the Princess, unfasten her seatbelt and help her up out of her seat. They started backing towards the curtain that led to economy. *Yes. Good. Get her out of here.* The guy I was fighting was tough, but I was holding my own. Once the Princess was safe, I should be able to take him down.

The guy I was fighting could sense the tide turning. He looked at his buddy, already restrained. He looked at me and the murderous rage on my face. He looked at the Princess, backing away to safety....

He pulled something from his belt and threw it. It hit the exit door in the side of the plane and stuck there. It was only when I saw the red light flashing on it that I realized what it was.

I turned and ran at the Princess. Launched myself at her and bore her to the floor even as I screamed at her to *get down!*

The force of the explosion knocked me forward, heat scorching my back. Then I was being pulled backwards by a howling, gale-force wind.

I craned my head around and saw the ragged hole where the exit door used to be. The hole everything was now being sucked out of.

4

KRISTINA

WE FORGET. We sit in our cozy, pressurized cabins, insulated from sound and wind and cold, and it slips our minds that *that's the sky, out there.* Air so thin you can't breathe, so cold it freezes your lungs. A place humans can't survive. And now, suddenly, the sky was *right there*, twenty feet away, reaching in through the gaping hole to claw everything warm and living out into the blackness.

I'd wound up on my back in the aisle, my head towards the hole. My hair was streaming out, sucked so hard that the roots screamed in protest. My airline pajamas were rippling in the wind, the fabric snapping and jerking as if a giant was plucking at it. The air was getting thinner and what little there was was rushing past so fast, it was hard to snatch a breath.

All around me, anything not bolted down was tumbling across the floor and shooting out of the hole. Life jackets, newspapers, pillows... a coffee cup flew across the cabin, clipped a seat and shattered, raining down fragments. There was a flash of silver as a fork shot past, missed the hole and embedded itself in the bulkhead like an arrow.

But I didn't move an inch. Because *he* was pinning me to the floor like a rock on a leaf. He was taking some of his weight on his forearms, so as not to crush me, but he had enough of his muscled form—

I swallowed. *On* me...that I wasn't going anywhere. His chest was pressed to my chest and *god,* it was like rock, not an inch of fat on him. My fingers and toes were already going numb from the cold, but the front of my body, where it touched him... that was *so warm.*

Everything my mother had always told me to fear: a commoner and a huge, brutish one, more beast than man, with his threadbare clothes and dirty boots, pushing me down on the ground. Her voice in my head, *men like that only want one thing*—

I looked up into his eyes and I saw it there. He *did* want that. And I wasn't ready for the answering flush that started in my face and went right down through my body, a need I hadn't even known I had, suddenly awakened. But that wasn't all he wanted. Those blue eyes were burning as he glanced between me and the assassin who'd tried to kill me.

He wanted to protect me. A different kind of warmth flooded my body. I reached up and instinctively clung onto his shoulders and it was like tethering myself to a sun-warmed rock. As long as I stayed there, I knew I'd be alright.

Movement made me glance towards the hole. The assassin took three running steps towards it and then flung himself through. Just as he jumped, he looked right at me. That glare of pure hate again: I was nothing, an inferior species. Then he was gone, lost in the blackness.

"Just hold on!" The man who'd saved me had to yell over the howl of the wind. "It'll get easier as we go lower!"

I nodded. He was right: we were descending, the floor tilting at a steeper and steeper angle. The pilot was taking us down to where the air would be thick enough to breathe. One assassin was gone and Emerik and Jakov had the other pinned to the floor. Just another few minutes and we'd all be alright—

A scream split the air. I looked over my rescuer's shoulder and my stomach lurched. Caroline, my maid, was clinging onto the top of a seat, her body entirely horizontal in mid air, flapping like a flag. And her grip was slipping. As I watched, her fingers failed and she shot past us, straight towards the hole. *No!*

One of her feet clipped an overhead luggage bin and she spun sideways... and jerked to a stop. Her leg had wedged between two seats. But the wind was sucking at her, clawing her free, and her leg was sliding between the smooth leather. First her hip was gripped, then only her thigh, and she was slipping faster and faster. "*Kristina!*" she screamed, terrified.

Caroline is twenty-two, the same age as me, and she's been my maid since we were both teenagers. We've grown up almost like sisters. When I was fifteen and someone spiked my drink with vodka at a party, it was Caroline who got me out of there safely. When she was sixteen and knocked over and chipped a Ming vase on a visit to the French President's house, I lied and said it was me. She's the one person who tells me things straight, who doesn't bow and scrape. She's my only true friend. And now she was going to die because someone wanted to kill *me*.

I started to wriggle out from under my rescuer. He looked down at me, horrified, and grabbed my shoulders. "*No!*"

I twisted, breaking his grip and slithering out from under him. Immediately, the wind clutched at me, threatening to grab me and suck me straight out. I grabbed hold of the nearest seat and checked Caroline. Oh God, her leg was slipping between the seats: they only gripped her calf, now. Very cautiously, I got to my knees.

That was a mistake. The suction got ten times worse. For one horrible second, my knees actually lifted off the ground.

I slammed myself face-first, flat on the floor, heart thumping. Then I started to wriggle down the aisle towards Caroline. When I glanced back, the man who'd saved me was trying to crawl after me. "No!" I yelled over the ear-splitting screech of the wind. "Stay there! I'll pass her to you!"

He stared at me, face taut with worry, then reluctantly nodded. He'd realized the same thing as me: the suction got worse, the closer you were to the hole. He needed to stay where he was, so he could haul Caroline to safety: I'd never be able to pull her *and* fight the wind.

I checked Caroline again and my stomach lurched. Her leg had slid through the seats to the ankle. Only her foot wedged her in place. I moved as fast as I could, but the air was thinner here: I could feel myself getting light-headed and every movement felt like an Olympic effort. Oxygen masks had dropped from the ceiling, but they hung tantalizingly out of reach. If I risked standing to grab one, I'd likely be sucked out. I gritted my teeth and kept going, bracing feet and hands against the seats, trying not to think about the howling, sucking hole or how it would only take one slip—

There. I'd made it. I reached for Caroline's leg—

The wind twisted her slightly and her foot slithered through the gap—

I screamed and shot forward and suddenly all I could see was the back of a seat. I was mashed up against it and I couldn't see Caroline at all. *I've lost her!*

Then I became aware of the burning pain in my fingers. My arm was buried between the seat backs, right up to the shoulder, and I couldn't pull it back. Something was pulling on my hand. Two of my fingers had curled tight around something thin and soft that bit into my skin. I gripped it even tighter and then braced my knees on the seats and *heaved.*

My arm gradually emerged. And when it reached my hand, I saw that I'd hooked my fingers around the ankle strap of Caroline's shoe. Using both hands, I grabbed her foot and pulled her in, then wrestled her over the seat and down to the floor where the wind was tamer. We lay there for a moment, panting. If I hadn't reached for her *right then.* If she'd been wearing different shoes....

I helped her out from between the seats and up the aisle until my rescuer could grab her wrist and pull her to safety. When she was safely behind him, I let out a huge sigh of relief. Then I started pulling myself towards him, bracing myself on the seats so that I didn't slip backwards. I was shaky and exhausted but I could do it. His outstretched hand was only a few feet away.

And that was when the pilot must have decided we weren't descending quickly enough, and pushed the nose down into a steeper dive.

The floor tilted crazily under my feet.

I grabbed for a handhold, but my oxygen-starved muscles were weak and slow. I fell backwards, tumbling head over heels. The wind grabbed me.

And I was sucked out through the hole and into the dark sky.

5

GARRETT

I WASTED precious seconds staring at the hole. Behind me, the blonde woman was wailing, yelling Kristina's name over and over again.

Think! Not what I'm good at. But I had to think of something because if I couldn't, she was dead. And I wasn't willing to accept that.

I thought about the explosive the assassins had used. This must have been the plan all along: kill the Princess, then escape by blowing the door and jumping out.

Which meant the assassin I'd fought, the one who'd jumped out, had been wearing a parachute.

Which meant the other one must be wearing a parachute, too.

I half-slid, half-scrambled down the aisle, my heavier body, making it easier for me to fight the wind. I hauled myself over to where the old guard and the young guard had restrained the other assassin. They were pretty much sitting on him, the only way they could pin him down and still have hands free to cling onto something themselves. Both of them were staring in horror at the hole. "*Move!*" I snapped.

They were too shell-shocked by what had happened to argue. I wrestled the assassin onto his front. Bent over him and strained my eyes against the wind. Was it just a backpack, or.... *Please be right, please be right—*

Yes. A parachute.

I pushed a knee into his back to pin him down, undid the buckles and wrestled the thing off him. He let out a yell of pain as I bent an arm the wrong way in my hurry, but I really didn't give a damn. I got to my knees so that I could pull the parachute on. As soon as I took my weight off the assassin, the wind snatched him away. He shot across the cabin, pinwheeling in the air, and disappeared through the hole.

I stood up and ran, still fastening the parachute's buckles. Within a few steps, the wind took me and feet left the ground. As I was sucked towards the hole, I curled myself into a tight ball.

And then I was outside in the vast, freezing sky. The plane shot away from me, shrinking to a speck in a few seconds. Meanwhile, I was falling towards the earth at a hundred miles an hour.

I straightened my body into a dart, arms behind me, and pointed myself at the ground. And I willed myself to go faster.

6

KRISTINA

I FELL.

I was a leaf in the wind, tumbling and pinwheeling, one second belly-up, the next face down. The air dragged out my limbs until I was starfished and the joints burned and screamed. I thought they were going to be ripped from my sockets. The air screamed as it passed my ears and felt like a concrete block where it hit my face: if I opened my mouth even a little, it punched its way down my throat and tried to balloon my lungs. Yet however much air I gulped, there wasn't enough oxygen.

As my eyes adjusted to the semi-darkness, I realized dawn was breaking. Sunlight was rapidly spreading across the sky, lighting up the clouds above me... and the ground below.

I saw a patchwork of gold and green squares that had to be fields, hair-thin lines that must be roads. And they were rushing up to meet me with horrible speed. It was that same sick feeling you get when your foot hooks into something and you feel yourself trip: a stomach-clenching, cold sweat moment... except this one didn't end. The fear just kept building and building as the ground expanded. Wispy strands of low cloud whipped by me and with each layer I cleared, the fields grew clearer, more real. *This is how I die.*

I closed my eyes, but the not knowing was worse than the knowing. I opened them just as the wind flipped me face-up again....

And saw a darker speck against the lightening sky. At first, I couldn't make out details: it was so solid, so unwavering, I thought it might be a piece of debris that had fallen from the damaged plane. Then I made out fabric, snapping and flapping at the edges. A plaid shirt. Dark hair. My rescuer from the plane, diving down towards me.

I stared up at him in disbelief. *How did he—Why is he—*

He drew nearer, near enough that I could make out his eyes. He was staring right at me with a look of single-minded determination.

I held my breath. Looking upward, it was as if we weren't moving at all. I could have been just lying there, floating, as he drifted slowly towards me. Only the itching between my shoulder blades reminded me of what was rushing up towards me from behind. I reached up a hand towards him. *Come on. Come on!* I didn't even know what his plan was. I just knew that I didn't want to be alone.

He drifted closer, almost within touching distance. Then the wind caught him and spun him off to one side. He dropped a shoulder and veered towards me again, steering himself like a diving bird of prey. He moved across above me, grabbed for me—

Missed.

The noise of the wind had changed. It was easier to breathe and it was warmer, too. And all those things were bad because they meant the ground must be getting very, very close. I knew I shouldn't but I couldn't help it. I looked below me—

The fields had grown fences and telephone poles. The roads had fattened, like feasting snakes, and white lines had erupted up and down their backs. I could see little oblongs of color moving along them.

I snapped my gaze up, towards him. He was approaching again, fast, this time. *Oh please, PLEASE—*

His chest slammed into mine and the impact sent us tumbling. I instinctively clutched him, wrapping my arms around him. The feel of him again: so *big,* so solid, after having nothing around me but air. His heart pounding against mine. He was so *warm.*

My searching fingers found the bulky pack attached to his back and I suddenly realized what his plan was. I clung onto him harder than I've ever held anything in my life because I knew he'd be jerked away from me, *hard,* and if I slipped out of his arms....

I needn't have worried. He'd already locked his arms and legs around my body in a death grip. He wasn't letting me go.

He pulled the ripcord and my stomach slammed into my feet as our downward rush slowed. The scream of the wind dropped away and there was just the creak of fabric and cords above us.

"*Roll!*" he said. My face was pressed against the curve of his pec. I had to look up to see his worried eyes. "When we hit, *roll.*"

When we hit?

I looked down and saw a dusty road. A field filled with trees, dark green and—Oh, God, I could make out the oranges hanging from their branches. We were *that* close. And I realized my stomach was still in my feet: we were still slowing. We were coming in too fast.

"*Roll!*" he told me again.

I opened my mouth to speak and then everything happened at once. We hit the ground in a sort of sideways swoop, he released his grip on me so that he didn't slam down on top of me, my legs turned to jelly as the impact went up them and, at the last second, what he'd said registered and I let my knees go slack and rolled, curling into a ball and wrapping my arms over my head.

I must have closed my eyes. When I opened them, all I could see was an orange tent, the fabric moving softly in the breeze. As I uncurled myself, I felt like one big bruise. But I was alive.

The ceiling of the tent rose and jerked. I felt heavy footsteps through the ground and then *he* was there, scrambling over to me on his knees, flinging the parachute fabric back over his shoulders as he moved under it. He stopped right next to me, his knees brushing my side, his big body hulking over me. "Are you okay?" he blurted, eyes wide with concern.

I nodded. I wasn't capable of speech, yet. My fingers were still pressing into the dirt, reassuring myself that I was on solid ground. I just looked up at him, huge and strong and... I caught my breath. For the first time, I had a chance to drink in just how gorgeous he really was. Gorgeous in a way I'd never seen before, rough and primal and dangerous—

A big hand encircled my upper arm: God, I was like a doll, next to him, his fingers easily encircling my bicep. His palm was gloriously warm through my thin pajamas. He squeezed and I got just a hint of the power in those hands, how he could easily crush the life out of someone. But he squeezed with such care and tenderness, it made my chest contract. He swung a knee across me and started mimicking the process with my other arm at the same time. He squeezed my upper arms. Forearms. Wrists—

For just a second, he was astride me with one of my slender wrists in each of his hands. A hot rush went through me: I told myself it was the aftershock, the adrenaline wearing off. But every filthy fantasy I'd had since I was a teenager was suddenly slamming through my head, everything about the idea of a rough, strong, common man, pushing aside all my suitors in their finery and just throwing me down and *taking* me—

My cheeks flared red. The heat rippled down my body and exploded in my groin. *He's just checking you for broken bones! Control yourself!*

He released my wrists, moved down my body and started again at my ankles. Calves. Knees.

Thighs.

He froze there, fingers pressing into the back of my legs an inch from my ass, thumbs pressing the fronts of my thighs, just barely below my panties. His eyes had locked on something.

I looked down. My pajama top had ridden up, exposing a slice of bare midriff, my navel slyly winking up at him. And just visible above the waistband of my pajama trousers was a narrow strip of black lace: the tops of my panties.

He exhaled, that massive chest contracting. His face was so close, his hot breath wafted across my bare skin, little currents and eddies of warm air rippling outward and making me catch my breath.

"You're fine," he announced. And stood up, his head and broad shoulders lifting the parachute. Then he gathered up the fabric and suddenly daylight flooded in. I blinked up at him, blinded for a second, then reached up and gingerly took the hand he offered. He hauled me to my feet and we stood there face to face. Or rather, face to chest. God, he was so *big!* Did they just build them big, in America? He tossed the bundled parachute down and then there was utter silence.

I gazed around. We'd come down by the side of a two-lane road in the middle of absolute nowhere. On one side, there were fields of orange trees, stretching on for miles. To the other, nothing but scrubland and desert. The sun was just rising, painting the sky pink and gold. And it was already warm, the air fragrant with the scent of oranges. During my whole trip, I'd been nowhere but air-conditioned hotels, limos, and then the plane. I'd forgotten it was summer. I wondered how hot it got here at midday.

I quickly tugged my pajama top down to cover my midriff and pulled the bottoms up a little. Now that the parachute was gone, now that we weren't private, I was suddenly self-conscious of my reaction to him. *What's the matter with me?* I looked at the horizon while I got myself together. Then, finally, when I was ready, I dared to look up at—

I gulped. It hit me all over again, a physical reaction. My head only came up to the top of his broadly curving pecs: it didn't help that I was in bare feet. I had to look up just to meet his eyes and when I did, he was looking back at me with such raw, unchecked lust that it was like standing in front of an open oven door.

I was suddenly aware of every inch of my body, basking in that heat as if my pajamas weren't even there. The curve of my breasts, the peaks of my nipples, the soft mound of my pubis.... And what shocked me was what was happening inside, as my eyes flicked around his face, over those clear blue eyes and hard lips. It was as if I'd found my exact opposite, the perfect shape I was meant to fit against. I had this crazy urge to just press myself to him, my softness to his hardness, my small form to his huge one, everything that was meant to be so shiny and precious about me rubbing up against all that roughness.

I tore my eyes away and looked at the landscape again. That helped to hide what I was feeling, but, as I stared at the wilderness, my stomach started to knot. We really were in the middle of nowhere. I'd never known it to be so *still:* I'm used to a bustle of people, chatter and negotiating and planning. And I'm used to my guards around me, never any fewer than four. The nearest person I knew was on the plane, already miles away and disappearing further into the distance with every second. I was alone, vulnerable, in a country where people were trying to kill me. I dug my nails into my palms, trying to control the fear, but it was turning to panic—

And then I looked at him again and the fear melted away.

I couldn't explain it. I didn't even know him, but something about him made me feel safer than any number of my guards. He fit here. In his plaid shirt and jeans, and those dusty boots, he was almost part of this place. And that triggered a memory in my head. That heavy accent of his. I couldn't place it, but it fit here, too, with the desert and the big skies. "What's your name?" I asked, the first time I'd managed to speak since I'd left the plane.

He gave me a long look. I was reminded of an animal again, a big hulking beast, unsure whether to trust me or not. I almost wanted to hold out my hand, palm up.

"Garrett," he said at last in that slow, rumble. "Garrett Buchanan." And now I finally placed the accent. My head filled up with all the American movies I'd watched as a kid: men galloping on horses, steam trains and sheriffs and everyone in Stetsons. *Texas.* He was from Texas. And the name fit perfectly: a rancher's name, a cowboy's name, a hero who'd sweep some woman in a big dress off her feet and carry her off on his horse as she swooned. I swooned just a little bit myself. *Garrett Buchanan.*

And then he added, "Ma'am."

And I remembered who I was. Daughter of the King. Heir to the throne. *The Jewel of Lakovia,* as the tabloid press had nicknamed me. Every lecture my mother had ever given me flashed through my head.

People like me don't get to fall in love. We don't choose who we marry.

I drew in a calming breath and tried to lock everything down. I tried to become icy and regal, like my mother. "Thank you, Mr. Buchanan. For everything you did."

He nodded just once. "Weren't nothing," he muttered, as if embarrassed.

I looked around. "Do you know where we are?"

"California." He rubbed at his jaw and it was so quiet, I could hear the rasp of his stubble. For a second, I imagined how that stubble would feel against my neck if he kissed along my jawline. Then I dug my fingernails into my palms. *Stop it!* "Figure we follow the road," he said. "Should be able to pick up the interstate, then get you a ride to LA."

I nodded quickly. "Good. Yes. Thank you." And I smiled at him. And then wished I hadn't because, instead of smiling back—I wasn't sure this man *could* smile—he just gave me such a look of urgent need that I actually heard myself gulp. It wasn't just the simple, hot lust I'd felt before. It was deeper, and even more intense.

Don't be stupid. I was just as different and strange to him as he was to me. He probably didn't think of me that way at all. Not a *princess.* His world was big skies and thick steaks cooked over campfires. He was used to women who square-danced and hollered and wore tiny denim shorts and had names like Mary-Sue. The polar opposite of me. He wouldn't want someone who was all tied up in rules and tradition, someone so...

I flushed. *Innocent.*

And yet, no matter how many times I broke eye contact and looked away, when I looked back he was still there, looking at me. *I'd give a fistful of silver to know what he's thinking.*

7

GARRETT

STOP LOOKING AT HER.

Stop goddamn looking at her. Right now.

But I couldn't.

Up there, in the glamorous first class cabin, she'd fit right in. Now she'd fallen like an angel from heaven and she was standing there in the desert, *my* world, with that pretty hair all mussed and her fancy pajamas already dusty and sand between her toes and somehow, she looked even better. All the dirt and dust and roughness just showcased her beauty even more.

There was a smudge of dust on her left cheek. Resisting the urge to reach down and wipe it off that smooth skin was the hardest thing I'd ever done.

Instead, I forced myself to look down at her bare feet. "We got a long way to walk," I said. I could see for at least a few miles in each direction and wherever the Interstate was, it was beyond that. "You can't walk like that."

I thought for a minute and then grabbed hold of the left cuff of my shirt and tugged it until the stitches at the shoulder tore free and the whole tube of fabric slid down my arm and off. I knelt down beside her. "Give me your foot—" I broke off. I knew there was probably some fancy term I was supposed to be using. Didn't seem right that I kept calling her *ma'am*. "What am I meant to call you?"

I looked up at the same exact moment she looked down. Her eyes were that lush, verdant green you never see in the desert, the green of thick forest. Our eyes locked and all that attraction just hit me again, like a wave slamming into me from behind and lifting me right off my feet. The temptation to just stand up, bury my fingers in that chestnut hair and pull her down for a kiss.... I couldn't remember the last time I'd fantasized about kissing a woman. Not fucking her: *kissing* her.

She parted those perfect lips. Started to form a syllable that might have been *Kr*— Then she bit it back and swallowed. Straightened her spine and lifted her chin. "Your Highness," she said firmly.

I stared at her for a beat and then nodded. I got it. "Give me your foot, Your Highness." The term felt weird in my mouth, like drinking champagne. But it reminded me of who she was and who I was...and that was a good thing.

She lifted her foot into my offered hands and I used the sleeve of my shirt to wrap it like a bandage. I tried not to think about how soft her skin was, like she'd never walked barefoot her entire life, or how elegant her ankles and calves were, like some finely-carved statue. I tore off the other arm of my shirt and wrapped her other foot. *There.*

As I stood up, my dog tags clinked under what was left of my shirt. In the absolute quiet of the desert, even that tiny sound carried.

The Princess's eyes locked on the chain around my neck. "You're a soldier?" she asked.

"*Was* a soldier," I muttered. The memories gathered above me, storm clouds made of lead. I felt myself tense—

I forced them back and nodded at the road. "We should start walking, Your Highness, before the sun gets too high."

She nodded and we walked. Well, I did what *I* call walking, shambling along like Bigfoot. But she...she *glided*. Even with bits of cloth for shoes, even on the asphalt that soon got to be baking hot, she was as graceful as if she was on ice skates. Was that something they taught princesses, when they were kids?

And that stereotype of her being spoiled and selfish didn't hold up at all. She didn't complain once about the rising heat, or wanting a drink, or how much her feet hurt.

I thought about how scared she must be. Knowing that there are people out there trying to kill you...hell, that had been my normal, in the marines. But for *her*....

It didn't help that we were out in the wilds. I didn't know much about Lakovia, but my image of it was trees and mountains, mist and snow. It sure as hell wasn't like *this*. And she was used to being in a bulletproof limo, or in a hotel suite with lots of those guys in blue suits to protect her. Not out here, exposed, with a complete stranger. I wanted to reassure her but that meant talking and I've never been much good at that. Even if I was, I sure as hell didn't know how to talk to a princess. And when I felt like *this* about her—

There was a growl, off in the distance. The Princess drew in her breath and took an instinctive sideways step...towards me.

That protective urge swept over me. I just wanted to put one big paw on her shoulder and pull her in until she was resting against my chest, my body sheltering her from everyone and everything. Assassins, animals...I'd take them all on. My fingers actually *flexed,* reaching to do it—

Instead, I said, "Cougar. Probably coming back from a night hunting. It won't bother us."

She swallowed and nodded. "We have wolves in Lakovia."

I nodded. But she must have seen something in my eyes because she cocked her head to one side. A little of the fear left her eyes and, for the first time, I saw just a hint of teasing humor. "You don't have any idea where Lakovia is, do you?"

I felt my neck and ears go hot. "Uh...Never was that good with places, Your Highness. Except for the Middle East. They never sent me to Europe."

She nodded. And as we walked, she told me about Lakovia. It *was* in Europe, right in the center, wedged between all those places like France and Italy to the west and all those former Soviet states to the east. It was proudly traditional, and a little suspicious of outsiders.

And it was unusual in one other way. "We're one of the few actual monarchies left," she said.

I let that roll around my head for a second. A real, full-on monarchy. The King's—her dad's—word was law: no parliament, no prime minister. Her family weren't just figureheads, they actually ran the country. Which meant she was a politician, just like the guys who'd taken everything from me.

So why did I like her so much?

As I thought it, I got that feeling again, the one I still couldn't place, like the wind had caught hold of something inside me and filled it, made it fly like a flag. It went way beyond just being attracted to her.

I stayed quiet and let her keep talking. Partly because it seemed like it was helping her to relax, partly because it meant I got to hear her voice. She told me about their silver mines—the reason Lakovia was so rich—and their weird, old-fashioned currency of silver coins. She told me how the King had sent her to New York for a preliminary meet and greet to see about joining the UN. I could have listened to her for hours. Every word was like a little teardrop of glass, cool to the touch, that smoothed its way over my brow and scalp and then slid all the way down my spine. It was the antidote to all the hot, smoky anger I carried inside me. It calmed me, it settled me, it made me *listen* and forget everything else. And when it reached the base of my spine, all that class, all that refinement, did something else to me. Something so wrong, it made my damn ears burn all over again. She was just so *posh,* so...*clean,* that I couldn't stop thinking about what it would be like to hear her say something filthy. Like *fuck.* Or, hell, to hear her say my name, right when she was shuddering and clutching at me and—

I pushed the thought away and we walked on, mile after mile. It was the most peaceful I'd felt in years. Then she told me about Garmania, the country that bordered them to the north. The one that invaded her country five years ago.

My boots hadn't stopped moving in a couple of hours: marching is second nature to me, I don't even notice I'm doing it. But when she said that, my stride faltered. *Aw, hell.* Now I remembered where I'd heard of Lakovia. I'd seen hazy, smoke-filled images of it on CNN: buildings half-demolished by shelling, occupying soldiers moving through the streets, sobbing civilians. A nasty, bloody war that had shocked the world. But not enough that the world had actually done a whole hell of a lot to stop it. Lakovia had won, eventually, and pushed Garmania out, but a lot of people had died. Like everyone else, I'd shaken my head and muttered about how awful it was, but it had all seemed so distant, a country I'd barely heard of, thousands of miles away. Finding out it was *her* country made my stomach churn. I just wanted to grab hold of her and hug her tight.

"We're at peace with them now," she said. Her voice was too light, too casual: I'm not a subtle person, but even I could hear the pain she was trying to hide. "And we've rebuilt. But..." She swallowed. "There was a lot of damage."

Her eyes were distant. I wondered if she'd lost someone. I knew what that felt like and I wouldn't wish it on anyone.

"The guys on the plane: you know why they were trying to kill you?" I asked.

She opened her mouth as if about to say something but then bit it back and shook her head again. "...no."

I marveled at how the wind caught her fine chestnut hair. Every time a strand of it billowed across and stroked my bare forearm, my whole body went tense. I was close enough to inhale her scent and it was incredible. Warm female skin, some sweet, citrusy perfume and...something else. Something that calmed me and cooled me even under the blazing sun. It was like she was made of mountain mist.

God, I was like some lovesick kid walking the prom queen home. "Nobody's threatened you?" I asked.

She shook her head again. "I get threats from crazy people occasionally, but nothing that would explain this. It's my father who rules. I'm not even important!"

My head snapped round and I almost glared at her. I knew what she meant, but...she *was* important, dammit. She caught my eye and blinked in surprise. Then her cheeks colored and she watched the ground again. "What were you doing in New York?" she asked.

I gave her the sanitized version: how I'd been living in LA, working as a bouncer for a bar. How I'd gone to New York for a job, but it hadn't worked out. I didn't get into the details of how I'd wound up in this state, or how I'd lost the bouncer gig, or what had gone wrong in New York. No need for her to know my whole history. Once I got her back to civilization, I'd never see her again.

That was the first time I'd thought about saying goodbye to her. I wasn't ready for how it made my stomach twist.

"So what will you do now?" she prompted.

I shrugged. "Find another job, I guess." *Something where they need dumb muscle.* "Or try another city." I stared at the horizon because I didn't want to see the look of pity on her face. "I move around a lot."

"Do you like being on the move?"

The answer, when it came, surprised me as much as her. I just kind of blurted it out. She was easy to talk to, dammit, and it had been a long time since I'd talked to anyone. "No," I said. "Just haven't found a home, yet."

A half hour later, a blue pickup truck at least forty years old rattled up behind us. An entire family was crammed into the cab while three farm workers lounged in the cargo bed. We flagged them down and I started trying to talk them into letting the Princess have a seat in the cab but she wouldn't hear of it. So we rode in the cargo bed with the workers, the Princess balancing a chicken in a cage on her knees.

They took us as far as the interstate and then we thumbed a lift from a truck driver who took us right into LA. I grabbed the first cab we saw and told him to take us to the FBI.

The Los Angeles FBI office was chaos. Every available agent was either investigating the assassination attempt or coordinating the search for the missing princess.

So when we walked through the door there were cheers, prayers and cries of disbelief. Then she was mobbed by her two surviving guards and the blonde-haired woman from the plane. I didn't get the same welcome. Agents quickly separated me from her and, while they didn't actually point guns at me, they had their hands on their holsters. I didn't blame them: when a missing VIP shows up with a big, unshaven guy in a ripped shirt and jeans, they aren't going to take any chances. But it was a reminder of just how different we were.

"We've got your luggage from the plane, Your Highness," the blonde woman told her. She pointed to a huge pile of bags. At first, I figured the pile was all the luggage from the whole plane and wondered which suitcase was hers. Then I saw that everything matched: cream suitcases, bags, little round boxes, all with the gold royal crest. *All that's hers?!*

The Princess glanced up and saw me, smiled, and gave me a little wave. I awkwardly raised one big paw in the air, just in time for one of the FBI agents to thrust a shabby military kit bag into my arms. *My* luggage. In fact, everything I had in the world.

The Princess ran off to get changed while two agents sat me down in a small room and had me go over everything that had happened about fifteen times. I was finally rescued by the head of the LA office, a Director Gibson. I distrusted him on principle because he wore a suit. But he chased away the other agents and he brought me the first cup of coffee I'd had all day, so I figured he couldn't be all bad. I rose to shake his hand and he automatically backed up a little before he caught himself. I forget that my size can be kinda…intimidating.

We sat. "You figure out who those guys on the plane were?" I asked between mouthfuls of coffee.

He shook his head. "I can tell you who they *weren't*. They weren't passengers. We've accounted for everyone on the passenger list."

I froze. "Then how the hell did they get aboard?" With airport security so tight these days, it would be flat-out impossible for two assassins to sneak onto an aircraft.

Unless they had help.

I started to get an itch, right between my shoulder blades. It was like when you feel there's someone right behind you, only a thousand times worse. I knew that feeling. I'd had it on my last day as a marine. That feeling that there's something huge going on, a plan that's rolling forward, unstoppable, and you're nothing more than a bug in its path. And maybe, so was the Princess.

I frowned. There was something else, too. Back on the plane, there'd been something familiar about the way that guy fought. He hadn't felt like some extremist, trained in a cave and full of religious zeal. I'd fought those. This guy had been schooled by experts. He'd felt like a soldier.

The more I thought about the whole thing, the less I liked it. *Who the hell is after her?*

While I'd been thinking, Director Gibson had started leafing through a file. It was only when he started talking that I realized whose file it was. "Four tours in the Marines. Afghanistan. Iraq. Two Purple Hearts, two Silver Stars and then you were just *gone*. Discharged, but it doesn't say why. The whole thing's redacted."

I stared silently back at him.

"Must have been something big. With your record, they wouldn't discharge you without a damn good—"

"I hit a guy for asking too many questions," I growled.

He tried to look tough but I could see the way he paled. He nodded and put the file down. "Well, whatever the reason you left...I'm glad you were on that flight today. She would have been dead, without you. You did a good thing."

And he held out his hand.

I sat there staring at it for a second. It was a hell of a long time since anyone had praised me, longer still since someone had wanted to shake my hand. I slowly took his hand and shook it. For a suit, he wasn't so bad.

When we went back into the main room, everyone was on their

feet looking at something. It took a while for me to press my way to the front and then, as the crowd parted....

She'd changed into a dress—

No. *Dress* wasn't right. She'd changed into a gown.

I'd heard stories of women spending thousands of dollars on clothes. I'd never understood how a few handfuls of fabric could possibly cost that much...until I saw this. It probably cost a year's rent on my apartment and it was worth every damn cent.

It was a warm white, formal but approachable, somehow. It clung tight on her top half, following every curve of that gorgeous body. It wasn't low cut—it was carefully respectable, in fact—but it revealed just enough cleavage and hugged her just closely enough to spark a whole chain reaction in my brain about what she looked like underneath. It nipped in tight at the waist and then flared out into a huge, circular skirt that went right down to the floor and must have been four feet across at the bottom. The whole thing was embroidered with gold thread but the pattern was so delicate, it didn't look gaudy or flashy. It looked...*beautiful.* I hadn't realized princesses still dressed like...well, *princesses.* But then I remembered how fiercely traditional she'd said Lakovia was. And I loved it. She looked like a princess *should* look.

But the dress was only a frame. What mattered was her. That long, shining chestnut hair wasn't mussed now: it hung in soft waves over her shoulders. There wasn't a trace of dust or dirt on her pale skin and the fear in her eyes had gone. She wore a gleaming silver tiara, each point holding a tiny, sparkling jewel.

She'd been gorgeous on the plane, asleep in pajamas. She'd been gorgeous in the desert, dirty and disheveled. Now she was the Princess of Lakovia again and she took my breath away.

She'd been moving around the room, thanking the FBI agents for their hard work. They were grinning and doing their best to bow and curtsy. I recognized the look in their eyes because I'd felt it, too: surprise at how friendly and down-to-earth she was.

And then she turned, saw me and walked towards me. The entire room turned to watch. I felt like a teenager again, watched by the whole school as the prom queen approaches. She stopped right in front of me. "I need to thank you," she said.

I swallowed. When had my mouth gotten so dry? "It was nothing."

She just looked up at me and I saw in those big green eyes just how grateful she was. More than she could say. And I had that feeling again, like the wind had grabbed hold of something inside me, ballooning it, tugging me into action. I stood up straighter. My arm kinda *twitched* like it wanted to do something but I didn't know what. *What is this?*

I settled for just nodding. But partway through, I caught her eye and a crazy idea blew through me like a tornado. I'd remembered something from old stories my mom used to read me when I was a kid. Knights who saved princesses and what they said afterwards—

I wanted to say, *the only thing I ask for is a kiss from you.* The words were actually on my lips. I could hear the blood pounding in my ears. *No, you idiot! No!*

She was too beautiful, too special. I wanted—*needed*—to just scoop my hand under her butt, pick her up and tilt her back and—

My mouth opened. I drew in a breath. *No! What are you doing?!*

And I saw her draw in her breath, too. Not horrified. Anticipating. Her cheeks colored but her eyes flicked down—*did she just look at my lips?* Everyone was still watching us but they'd all faded into the background. They didn't matter anymore.

And then someone stepped between us. The old guard from the plane, his silver hair as perfectly coiffed as ever. "*All of us* are grateful," he told me. His voice was smooth but his eyes bored into me like lasers.

I felt my face go hot. *You big idiot! Like she wants you kissing her.* I'd been kidding myself. She'd been horrified, not excited.

And then the Princess glanced up at me and blushed.

Guiltily.

I forced a smile onto my face. "You're welcome," I told the old guard.

"This is Emerik," said the Princess. "He's been my guard since I was a baby." Then she nodded at the young guard, the one who was all muscle. "And that's Jakov: he's much newer."

I nodded respectfully at them both. Jakov grinned at me but Emerik just glowered.

"And I'm Caroline," said the blonde-haired woman, running forward, a huge smile on her face. "The Princess's maid."

The Princess was still blushing every time she looked at me. "Please, come with us. I need to call home and Aleksander will want to meet you."

I nodded and fell in beside her as she walked—in the floor-length dress, she seemed to glide. "Aleksander?" Too many names, most of them with that strange, Lakovian sound.

"The chief advisor to the royal family. He handles communications with the media and other nations...we couldn't operate without him." She showed me into a side room. A laptop was open on a desk and she started a video call.

Almost immediately, a white-haired man in an expensive suit answered. He was sitting at an old-fashioned desk and behind him was a tall, very narrow window, almost like something you'd get on a castle. Then it hit me that he was probably in the palace. *It really looks like that?* Through the glass, I could see a deep valley lined with trees. Lakovia was beautiful.

"Thank goodness," said Aleksander with a deep sigh. "The FBI have been sharing all their data with us in real time. We knew you survived but it's so good to see your face!" He smiled and the Princess beamed. It reminded me of a kindly uncle and his niece. "The FBI say they can get you on a flight in a few hours. Your parents are flying home from Paris: they'll be back before you arrive."

The Princess nodded. Then she grabbed my hand and tugged me into shot. "This is Garrett Buchanan. He's the one who saved me."

I shuffled my feet and gave Aleksander what I hoped was a respectful nod. It occurred to me that maybe I should have gotten changed as well. I was still wearing the shirt with the torn-off sleeves.

But Aleksander leaned towards the camera, warm and

welcoming. "The whole of Lakovia owes you a great debt," he said with feeling. I gave him another nod.

"Aleksander...." The Princess's voice had changed. "There's something I need to tell you. I haven't told the FBI yet. I haven't told anyone." She threw a quick, guilty look at me. "But you need to know. The men who tried to kill me...I heard one of them speak. And I'm sure his accent was Garmanian."

There was a sudden intake of breath from everyone in the room. Caroline turned pale. Emerik looked as though he wanted to punch something. And then, weirdly, he glared at the young guard, Jakov, who was staring at the floor. What was *that* all about?

Aleksander nodded gravely while he thought. "You were right not to tell anyone," he said. "If it gets out that someone from Garmania tried to kill you...."

"...it could restart the war," whispered the Princess.

I felt my hands tighten into fists. I'd seen way too much of this when I was a marine. Even when there's peace, grudges carry on for decades, through generation after generation. There's always some nutjob who says things like *never forget* and wants vengeance for their grandfather. With a few acts of terror, the whole thing can erupt again, like blowing on the embers of a fire. And the war between Lakovia and Garmania ended less than five years ago....

"I'll have our intelligence services investigate," said Aleksander. "And I'll ensure any mention of Garmania stays out of the press."

"I'm sure they were just a couple of extremists," said the Princess. "Nothing to do with Garmania itself." We could all hear the emotion in her voice. She *needed* that to be the case. I wondered again if she'd lost someone in the war.

"You're probably right, Your Highness," said Aleksander. "But we have to be certain."

The Princess nodded and ended the call. At the same time, Director Gibson knocked on the door and then tentatively opened it. "Your Highness?" he asked. "We've organized a convoy to take you to the airport."

The Princess nodded and her entourage filed out. She turned and looked up at me. "Will you be coming with us?"

By now, we were alone. I opened my mouth. Hesitated, the *yes* already on my tongue. I'd do anything just to spend another few minutes with this woman.

But that was crazy. *Maybe* she'd wanted me to kiss her but she was royalty, for God's sake. For a few hours, our paths had crossed. Now it was time for both of us to get back to reality. She had the FBI to protect her, now. She didn't need a dumb grunt. Hell, I wasn't even a soldier anymore. I'd been damn lucky to make it through that morning without a flashback: if I'd frozen up at any point, she'd have been dead.

And the longer I spent with her, the more chance she'd ask questions. She was too damn easy to talk to. And I couldn't relive what happened or let her see what a wreck I was inside. Not when she was so perfect.

"No," I said at last. I gazed down at her, trying to drink in as much of her as possible so I could remember her forever. "You're in good hands, now."

She tilted her head to one side for a second and her eyes were hurt. *What did I do wrong?* The urge to reach down and lay my big paw on her cheek and tell her *nothing* and pull her in and kiss those sweet lips was almost more than I could take—

But then she gave a quick little nod. "Well, then I suppose this is goodbye." She drew in her breath. "Thank you, Mr. Buchanan. I won't forget you."

I'd never heard my name said that way, with respect. And the sound of that upper-class accent sliding over all the hard consonants, like smooth glass coating the pebbles in a creek...it was addictive. But I just nodded.

She held out her hand towards me and I went to shake it. But she was holding it palm down, not palm sideways. A hazy memory from old movies filled my mind....

I took a half step back and bent at the waist in what I hoped was a bow. I brought one big hand up under hers: God, her fingers were so slender and cool, next to mine. And then I pressed my lips to the back of her hand. Her skin was soft and so *smooth*...For a second I stayed there, my hand pressing into hers, my lips hot against her, my heart racing. I couldn't let go.

I was goddamn crazy for this woman.

I forced myself to straighten up. Halfway there, we locked eyes and I froze. I could see the need in her, the reflection of that pull I was feeling. I could hear her breathing quickening, matching mine. All I had to do was tug on her hand and pull her in for a *real* kiss—

She's a goddamn princess!

I straightened fully and looked away. Immediately, she looked away too. And then she was hurrying out the door.

All the FBI agents were occupied organizing the convoy so I wandered to an upstairs window to watch. Three big black SUVs were standing by the curbside. *This is it, then. Goodbye.* I'd only known her a handful of hours but the idea of not being there to protect her was chewing away at me. Even though she was with the FBI now. Even though the danger was probably passed. I still had that itch between my shoulder blades. Something about this wasn't right.

Or maybe I just didn't want to let her go.

The Princess's entourage were getting into the center car while FBI agents got into the front and rear ones. *See? Lots of protection. I did the right thing.*

They got the Princess to climb in last, so she was exposed as little as possible. *Smart. They know their stuff. I did the right thing.*

She had to bundle up the skirts of the huge dress like a bride on the way to her wedding. Her pale skin gleamed in the dim interior of the car, her chestnut hair shone—

I did the right thing.

An FBI agent slammed the door and—

Suddenly, I was running. Jumping down the stairs. Grabbing my kit bag. I burst out through the doors, ran over to the Princess's car and jumped in beside her. "I'll come with you as far as the airport," I told her breathlessly.

A delighted smile spread across her face, so wide I could see her fighting to control it. She looked down at her knees for a second, then back to me. "Very well, Mr. Buchanan."

I looked around for the first time. The back of the car was huge, with three seats facing backward and three facing forward. The Princess sat directly across from me, with her two guards next to her. Emerik was giving Jakov another of those long, venomous stares. What was it between those two? Sitting next to me was Caroline...and in the final seat was FBI Director Gibson. I was surprised that he'd come along but it gave me even more respect for the guy.

The convoy moved off. For the first few minutes, I just soaked up how beautiful she looked. With the door closed, the tinted windows made it even dimmer inside and her pale skin and the cream dress seemed to shine. I felt...*lucky,* just to be near her.

But by the time we reached the highway, the silence had become uncomfortable. I realized the entourage were used to this: they'd sit there quietly while the Princess chatted away to some prime minister or president. Now *I* was that guest, sitting right across from the Princess, and they were all waiting for me to say something. I felt my neck getting hot. *Goddamn it, I'm no good at this stuff.* The Princess gave me a desperate look—

"Your English is real good," I muttered.

She beamed, relieved. "English is actually our official language."

I blinked. They spoke English in Lakovia?

"It's a funny story," said the Princess. "About three hundred years ago—"

Movement just outside the window caught my eye. A red SUV was pulling alongside us, its window open. I caught a glimpse of a black-clad figure and the gleam of a gun barrel—

"*Get down!*" I yelled. I lunged forward, hooked the Princess around the waist and threw us to the floor, my body covering hers, as bullets ripped through the car.

8

KRISTINA

MY FACE WAS PRESSED into the floor: all I could see was clean, charcoal-gray carpet, still with that new-car smell, and polished leather shoes. Then there was a deafening sound I remembered from the war, like a thousand firecrackers being set off right inside my eardrums. The windows didn't break, they exploded, thousands of little pebbles of safety glass tinkling as they cascaded down.

But they didn't hit me. A huge, warm body was pressed to every inch of me, coming up over my head and reaching back past my feet. I could feel the hard bulges of his biceps as they pressed my arms to the floor. I could feel his hot breath on the top of my head and the beat of his heart as his chest pressed into my back.

I was utterly terrified. But it was the safest I'd ever felt.

When I was a child, the President of Italy bought me a teddy bear. A huge, ludicrous thing, much bigger than me - it was almost five feet tall and incredibly soft. I named it Barnaby and used to curl up in its lap and fall asleep cuddling it. But what I used to dream about, what I used to try to simulate, by wrapping its paws around me, was *it* cuddling *me*. Even before the war, my mother never really seemed to do that.

When I was ten, I came home one day to find that my mother had thrown Barnaby away. He was childish, she said. It was time to grow up. And of course I had to be brave and not cry because I was a princess. But I'd lost that feeling of someone wrapping me up and holding me close and I'd been missing it ever since.

Until now.

I squeezed my eyes closed and, despite the danger we were in, there was a part of me that just wanted Garrett to keep holding me that way.

There was an explosion that I realized must be a tire bursting. I felt us swerve and then suddenly the car was rotating in a way it wasn't supposed to. My legs tipped up, my head down and the road noise dropped away completely. My stomach lurched and my fingers clawed at the carpet. All four wheels must be off the ground: we were flipping.

The ceiling became the floor and then we landed hard on our roof. Garrett fell first and then gave a soft grunt as I fell onto his chest. The car skidded along on its roof, orange sparks flying. I was lying face up on top of Garrett. Above me, I could see the others still strapped into their seats. *Oh God! They didn't get down on the floor! What if they—*A drop of something warm and wet hit my cheek. *Blood! One of them's bleeding!* But it was too dim and everything was rattling around too much to tell who.

The movement of the car slowed. Stopped. We came to rest, rocking slightly.

"Who's hurt?" I said, my voice tight with panic. "Caroline? Emerik? Jakov? Mr. Buchanan?"

One by one, they called that they were okay. Everyone was panting and shaken and trying to figure out how to get out of their seats while still buckled in upside down. Beneath me, Garrett gently eased my head to one side so that he could look around.

Then I remembered there was one more person in the car. "Director Gibson?!"

Nothing.

Garrett tried. "Gibson?"

Silence. Then, "I'm—"—a pained intake of breath—"I'm okay. Bleeding but okay."

I let out my breath. Everyone was alive. Then I started to think about what had just happened and a cold sweat broke out right across my body. *It isn't over. They tried to kill me again.*

Garrett suddenly stiffened beneath me. "We have to move," he snapped.

I looked around in panic. Was the car on fire?

Then I saw what he'd seen, in the car's wing mirror. Four men, dressed in black and carrying assault rifles, were approaching the car.

9

GARRETT

I WRENCHED on the door release and then shouldered the door open. Lifting the Princess off me was easy—she was just a little thing. I eased her up while I slid my body from under hers.

I emerged into a nightmare. The highway was blocked by crashing cars, both in front of us and behind. The other two FBI cars were wrecks, peppered with bullet holes. One was on fire. I didn't have to check them to know no one inside survived. Thick black smoke was being whipped up by the wind and rolling across the highway. It kept blocking my view of the guys advancing on us. Each time it cleared, they were closer.

By now, Emerik and Jakov were out and were helping Director Gibson. I reached for the Princess, but she insisted on pushing Caroline out first. Then she emerged and the sight of her: so perfect, so beautiful amongst all the smoke and fire and twisted metal, made my chest close up. She just looked so painfully vulnerable: I wanted to pull her to me and spirit her the hell away from all this.

And I wanted to kill the guys who were putting her at risk. I got everyone to hunker down behind the car. Then I ran around to the driver's seat. The driver was dead, but I found a handgun in a holster under his jacket.

When I ran back to the others, Director Gibson was taking out his cell phone. He'd gone very pale and was bleeding heavily from a long gash down one side of his face. He nodded at the gun. "Have you even fired one of those things, since you left the marines?"

The answer was *no*. But my hands seemed to have a life of their own, checking the magazine, chambering the first round, making sure the safety was off. The training was taking over. *I can do this. I can do this.*

Or at least, I *could*. Before the desert. I looked at the Princess. *Please. For her sake: don't have a flashback.*

"Call for backup," I grunted to Gibson.

"Doing it," he said. And started issuing orders over the phone. Emerik and Jakov had guns out, too: I was right, they'd only been forced to disarm for the flight. With four of us, we might just be able to hold them off until help arrived. With a foreign VIP and an FBI director under fire, half the agents in California must be racing towards us.

At that second, the first bullets ricocheted off the car. I instinctively grabbed hold of the Princess and shielded her body with mine. She gave a yelp of fear and pulled Caroline tight to her, making sure she was protected, too. The guards stood and returned fire, one at either end of the car. Those two might not get on, but together they were formidable.

Gibson ended his call. "Three minutes," he told me breathlessly.

I stood and returned fire while the guards reloaded. More bullets picked away at the car. The gunmen were close enough now to make out faces and I spotted the pale guy with the slicked-back hair giving orders. I watched as they spread out, trying to encircle us. I was sure, now: these guys had military training.

We weren't going to last three minutes.

"We have to get out of here," I muttered. But I couldn't see anywhere to run.

I heard Emerik curse. Jakov was running towards the assassins, firing, trying to push them back. *Goddammit!* The kid was brave but he was going to get himself killed.

Even as I thought it, the gunmen returned fire and he had to hunker down behind a crashed minivan. Now he was trapped, out in the open. And the gunmen would be on him any second. *Idiot!*

I growled and charged out into the open, firing wildly. I grabbed Jakov by the collar and hauled him along the ground and back to safety. "*Stay together!*" I snapped. He nodded, chastened.

There was a scream from Caroline. I looked round and froze.

I'd thought there were only four gunmen, but I'd missed the fifth. While I'd been rescuing Jakov, he'd silently circled around and sneaked in from the side. Now he'd grabbed the Princess, one arm around her waist and the other holding a gun to her head.

I stopped firing. I felt as if someone had his hands around my throat and was choking me. I knew I couldn't point my gun at him before he killed her. He'd got the drop on all of us.

I saw his finger tighten on the trigger. My heart leapt up into my mouth: I've never felt fear like it. "*Don't,*" I said desperately, as if that would stop him.

And then the Princess did something incredibly quick with her hand, like a cobra striking. She jabbed him under the arm and he let out a cry of pain and dropped his gun. Immediately, the Princess pulled away from him and ducked.

Emerik, Jakov, Gibson and I all raised our guns and fired. The guy staggered back and crumpled to the ground.

We all hunkered against the car again as the gunmen started shooting. They'd crept even closer while we'd been distracted. But all I could do was stare in disbelief at the Princess. I'd thought she was vulnerable, defenseless. What was *that?!*

She stared back at me, defiant. And just a tiny bit proud. I shook my head: I'd get her to explain later. Right now, we had to get out of there before we were overrun. I looked around again but this time, I thought to look down. The highway rose to form an overpass just ahead. Below us was a grassy embankment that sloped down to a construction site. "*There!*" I yelled, pointing.

But then I looked at the Princess and a chill went through me. No way could she run in that huge dress.

She caught my look and looked down at herself. "Wait," she said quickly.

I stood again and fired at the gunmen. They were dangerously close, now. Behind me, I could hear the sound of fabric being frantically ripped. Out of the corner of my eye, I saw Emerik glance down and his eyes widen. Then he quickly focused on the gunmen, his face red. *What the hell?*

"Okay." The Princess's voice. I ducked back behind the car and—

The skirt was gone, thousands of dollars of silk and netting reduced to a long snake of cloth that now lay in the dirt. Below the waist, the Princess was now just in—

I had a glimpse of long, shapely thighs and elegantly curving hips. White panties—

I tore my gaze away. A second later, one white high-heeled pump was tossed onto the asphalt. Then another. "Ready," she said.

I nodded, still keeping my eyes averted. "Emerik first, then you, then Caroline, Gibson, Jakov. I'll go last. *Go!*"

Emerik wasn't the fastest and he was panting a little by the time he reached the barrier, but he vaulted it and slid down the embankment. The Princess was next, bare legs flashing as she sprinted to safety. By the time it was my turn, the assassins were almost on top of me. I ran for the barrier and had to dive headfirst as a hail of bullets chewed up the asphalt. Then I was bouncing and rolling down the grassy slope, to come to rest at the Princess's feet.

I lay there for a second, panting. I couldn't help but look: those amazing, long legs were a foot from my face. Gorgeously shaped, athletic but feminine. *Goddamn*, I wanted to run my hands all over them. And then at the top, those simple white panties, pure and innocent—

Emerik grabbed hold of my hand and jerked me to my feet, his eyes burning with rage. I felt my neck go hot. *What is he, her dad?* The old guy seemed to be one part bodyguard, one part butler and one part moral guardian.

I pushed it out of my mind and looked around. The construction site seemed to be deserted. Five huge concrete pipes, each one easily six feet wide, were poking out of the side of the embankment, leading off into darkness. *In there!* The gunmen wouldn't know which pipe we'd gone into. And long before they had time to search them all, backup would be there.

I picked a pipe at random and got everyone inside. We passed a pile of sacks of concrete, left inside the mouth of the pipe to keep it out of the rain. I got everybody past the pipe's first turn, so they were out of sight, and hunkered down in the shadows at the corner to keep watch.

Footsteps approached and then the gunmen appeared outside, checking behind dumpsters and underneath the parked construction equipment. They glanced at the pipes but, like I'd hoped, they weren't sure if we'd gone in there. And if we had, they didn't know which pipe. *We're going to be okay.*

Then I saw one of them walk right up to the pipes. It was the guy from the plane, the one with eerily pale skin. He pulled out a cell phone and started talking.

And then he did something that sent ice water right down my spine: he glanced up at the sky.

"Oh, *shit,*" I mumbled. I knew that look. I'd done the exact same thing myself, hundreds of times, in war zones.

It's the look you do when you call for aerial surveillance. You lose track of the bad guys so you call back to base and wait for someone watching via satellite to rewind the footage and tell you where they went. You can't see the satellite, of course. But you still glance up, while you wait. I do it. All soldiers do it.

But if *these* guys were doing it, it could only mean one thing.

The guy listened, nodded and put his phone away. Then he called to his buddies and started moving forward. Right towards our pipe.

I ducked around the corner and almost collided with the Princess, who'd crept up beside me while I'd been watching. "They're coming!" I whispered. She paled. "Go! Get as far down the pipe as you can!" I glanced down the pipe and wanted to weep. After the corner, it ran straight. Just smooth concrete walls with no hiding places. The assassins would cut them down as soon as they turned the corner. There just wasn't enough time.

Not unless someone held them back.

I looked at the Princess. My eyes met hers in the darkness and—

It took hold of me, stronger than anything I've ever felt. *I need to protect this woman.* I wasn't going to let her die here, scared and alone in the dark. And it wasn't just about how beautiful she was, how much I wanted to grab her waist and pull her to me and kiss those sweet lips. There was a whole other level to it: that feeling in my chest, like the wind filling a sail—

I suddenly realized where I'd felt it before: at the recruitment office. And at my passing out parade. And when we'd been called in after one of our embassies had been bombed and I'd seen the Stars and Stripes lying on the ground, shredded and burning.

I hadn't recognized it before because it had been so long since I'd felt it. Loyalty. Duty. That feeling that there's something much more important than you. Something worth giving your life for. I wasn't just entranced by this woman. I was loyal to her.

Before I knew what I was doing, I'd reached out and grabbed her hand. I squeezed it: so delicate, so slender in my big, clumsy paw. I let go, but just as I moved back, *she* grabbed *my* hand and crouched there staring up into my eyes, her mouth open as if there was something she needed to say.

"Go, Your Highness" I said hoarsely. And then I ran around the corner towards the assassins.

The four of them were just approaching the entrance, still in the light, and they didn't see me in the shadows for a second. I fired twice and got one of them in the chest: he went down but kept moving: *dammit, body armor.* These guys were well-equipped, too.

They started to fire into the pipe: they could barely see me in the darkness, but they didn't have to, they could just spray and sooner or later, they'd hit me. I ducked behind the pile of concrete sacks, panting, then rose and fired a few more times. My jaw was set, grim determination powering me on. I didn't have to hold out forever, I just had to slow them down until backup arrived.

A burst of fire hit the sacks of concrete and powder spurted into the air. The gray cloud enveloped me, filling my nose and mouth. I tried to breathe and sucked it straight down into my lungs.

And I felt the flashback coming straight for me with the speed and force of a runaway truck. I braced myself, tried to grapple with it, tried to slow the impact and hold it back—

I was back in the desert, the sand scouring my face and working its way under my eyelids. The sandstorm had turned everything into a featureless gray-brown void. I couldn't breathe and I couldn't see.

In the back of my mind, I knew that I must be still in the pipe, probably standing there vulnerable. But that all seemed so distant. The desert, that was real. *I have to find him!*

Pain exploded in my leg. I cried out and fell to one knee, then went down on my ass, my big body making a hell of a thump as it hit. I heard my gun clatter across the concrete floor.

"*No!*" A woman's voice, echoing off hard walls. The Princess.

I was back in the pipe, blinking through the concrete dust. I'd taken a bullet in the leg while the flashback had me frozen. Now I was sprawled on the floor of the pipe with no gun and the gunmen were coming in. I looked around. Dammit, the Princess had run back to the corner and was standing there watching me, panting with fear. Emerik had hold of her arm and was trying to drag her away but she was resisting with everything she had.

They were going to kill her.

I groped for my gun but I couldn't find it. The gunmen advanced, guns raised. Another few feet and they'd see me through the dust. I gave a growl of fury and clambered to my feet, wincing in pain. I'd run at them. Even if all I did was soak up some bullets, if it kept her alive another few seconds—

A wail outside, rising and falling. A siren. And then another and another, and the pounding clatter of helicopter blades. Backup had arrived.

The assassins took one more step towards me...and then turned and vanished into the dust.

Seconds later, armed FBI agents filled the pipe. I put my hands on my head so that no one would shoot me and let Director Gibson take over. I was too busy choking on the concrete dust to answer questions anyway. And inside, I was beating myself up for that flashback. They'd all nearly died because I was weak, because I was too much of a screw up. Then it got worse: I heard that the assassins had gotten away. My heart sank.

The FBI took us outside and I was finally able to breathe again. The Princess was sitting on the tailgate of an FBI truck, a blanket wrapped around her. They got me to sit down next to her and a medic dressed the wound on my leg. The bullet had only nicked the flesh: it hurt like a son of a bitch but I could still walk.

"The area's secure," Director Gibson told the Princess. He was holding a gauze pad against the gash on his cheek. "We'll put together a fresh convoy to take you to the airport. But the important thing is, you're safe now."

Her glossy hair was dull with concrete dust, her legs bare under the blanket where she'd ripped her dress away. There were two big spots of blood on the front of the bodice where someone, maybe Gibson, had bled on her. She must have been terrified but she didn't cry, didn't complain, just nodded her thanks.

It killed me to do it. But if I wanted to protect her, she had to know.

"She isn't safe," I said in a low voice.

"What?" asked Gibson, frowning. "This whole area's crawling with—"

"How did they know about the convoy?" I growled. "How did they know exactly where to find us on the highway, and which car she was in?"

Gibson's mouth opened and closed soundlessly.

"These guys aren't crazies," I spat. "They're trained soldiers. And someone's feeding them information. You had satellite surveillance of this whole damn thing, right?"

"Of course," said Gibson. "Standard protocol."

"Well someone's leaking it to the assassins. I saw them call someone up and ask which pipe we'd gone into."

Gibson's eyes flashed with fury. "If there's a leak, it's not in my office!" He pointed towards the highway. "I've got eight agents dead!"

I glared at him. But I believed him. A leak at the FBI would explain a lot, but not all of it. It wouldn't explain how the assassins smuggled two guys onto a plane. And Gibson seemed like a good guy.

Wherever the leak was, though, the result was the same. I looked at the Princess. "As long as the leak's there, she ain't safe. You put her in a convoy, they'll hit it. Take her to the airport, they'll put a bomb on the plane. They've been one step ahead of you from the start."

"Well, what would you suggest?!" Gibson snapped.

I glared back at him. Thing was, I didn't know what to suggest. I was way out of my comfort zone. International conspiracies? Traitors, assassinations? I'd never felt more like a big, dumb, ground-pounding grunt.

But then I looked at the Princess again. She'd turned and was looking up at me, terrified. Those big green eyes were begging me to take it back, to tell her she was going to be okay. I nearly did. I could feel the muscles of my neck pulling, ready to shake my head. *Ah, forget it. I'm sorry. I'm probably wrong.* But—

But I wasn't wrong. I could feel it in my gut, like I had in Gibson's office. Something was rolling forward here, something huge and powerful that wanted to crush the Princess like a bug. *The system.* Politicians, governments, forces you can't fight. Just like when I'd been kicked out of the Marines. And it was bellowing for me to *get out of the way.* These people had already killed eight FBI agents and put a plane full of passengers at risk: they'd kill me without a second thought. But it was her they wanted. All I had to do was shake my head, let the FBI take her, and I could head back to my life.

And tomorrow, I'd hear about her death on CNN.

I felt my jaw set. *The hell with that.* I looked at her, nostrils flaring with fury, and felt the sudden swell of loyalty and the *pull* towards her hit at the same time. Even like this, even filthy and dressed in ragged clothes, she was so beautiful it hurt. The need to protect her welled up inside me, unstoppable, and then it tightened down to a tiny, diamond-hard nugget of Texan stubbornness.

I didn't care if the system wanted her dead.

I didn't care that I was just one guy.

I wasn't going to let it happen. Not to her.

The words were out before I knew what I was going to say. "I'll do it. I'll protect her."

10

KRISTINA

I'd BEEN SINKING FAST into the cold, dark place that haunts me in my nightmares. *If the FBI can't keep me safe, who can?!* Suddenly, America, which had seemed so exciting just last night, was a terrifying, alien place. I just wanted to be back in the palace, sinking into a steaming bath scented with oils, with guards outside the door and more down the hall and thick stone walls and a perimeter and my parents and—

And then he said he'd protect me.

And I drew in a shuddering breath.

"What?!" said Director Gibson. "Are you *nuts?* I can't let her go off with you! What would you even do with her?"

"Get her off the grid," said Garrett in that deep, Texan rumble. "She's gotta disappear. Only way she'll be safe. Then I'll figure out a way to get her home."

My breath caught and a big swell of emotion made my eyes prickle with heat. He'd already done so much for me. Now he wanted to put himself at risk to save me. But...could I trust him? I'd known him less than a day.

I looked at Jakov and Emerik. They'd protected me so well, back in Lakovia. Emerik was like an uncle. His obsession with etiquette and tradition could be frustrating but I knew he was only trying to look after me. And Jakov was like a hot-headed, protective brother, scarcely older than me and ready to body slam anyone who threatened me into the dirt.

But they were outnumbered. And this strange country wasn't their home. It was Garrett's.

I wavered...right up until I looked into Garrett's eyes. I gasped when I saw the fire there, the protective fury. It wasn't like Jakov's, quick and hot, impulsive. It wasn't like Emerik's, a steady flame held in a gilded lantern for decades. Garrett's was like looking into a volcano: a never-ending supply of scalding determination. He *would* protect me. No matter what.

I nodded. "Mr. Buchanan, I accept your offer."

Director Gibson's eyes bulged. "What?! I can't allow this! You're coming back to our headquarters."

I could see him nodding at other FBI agents to come over. He seemed like a good man. He was only trying to do his job. But Garrett was right: someone on the inside was helping the assassins. And the FBI was part of that system.

Agents surrounded me. A hand landed on my shoulder and I was coaxed to stand. They were going to lead me away, away from Garrett—

No they weren't.

I was terrified but my father had taught me to never let people see you're scared. I drew myself up to my full height and did my best attempt at what I call my mother's *queen voice*. "I have done nothing wrong," I said. "And you have no right to detain me."

The hand disappeared from my shoulder. All the agents took a step back and looked at Director Gibson, their faces pale. Garrett took a step forward and put his body between me and them.

"How the hell are you going to make her disappear?" asked Gibson. "She's a *princess!* She walks into a hotel, it'll be all over the newspapers!"

"We'll be discreet," rumbled Garrett. That voice. It seemed to vibrate through my whole body, leaving me thrumming and tight-breathed. *Oh God, what have I done?* I was dangerously attracted to this man. Every time he gazed at me in that raw, heated way, I felt my body's answering call, shockingly strong. I wanted to run and press myself to that big, hulking body and tilt my head back for his kiss. I wanted to feel those big hands on my back, on my ass, sliding up under my breasts and parting my thighs. I wanted to writhe against that strong chest and those hard abs, clawing at him as he tore my clothes apart.

Now I was putting myself in his care: we'd be together constantly. How the hell was I going to control myself?

Emerik elbowed his way through the agents. "Your Highness! I must protest! You're entrusting our safety to—"—he lowered his voice to a harsh whisper—"to a *common soldier!*" Then he glanced at Garrett. "No offense."

"None taken," growled Garrett. "Never been ashamed of being a soldier."

I glared at Emerik. He was treating Garrett the same way I'd seen the FBI agents treat him when we'd first arrived: like a beast. People were polite with Garrett, but only because they were scared of him. They talked down to him. With the FBI agents, it was because he wore threadbare clothes instead of a suit. With Emerik it was because he wasn't the right social class. And all of them treated him as if he was stupid. Well, I wasn't going to stand for it anymore. "That *common soldier* saved all of our lives!" I told Emerik tightly. I looked at Garrett. "What's the plan?"

"We'll need one of your cars," Garrett told Director Gibson. "And I need a gun."

Gibson looked incredulous. "I can't give a civilian an FBI firearm! Do you know what—"

"If you want her to live, give me a gun!" snapped Garrett.

Gibson glared at him...and then motioned for the nearest agent to hand over his weapon. Garrett took the holster, too, which he had to adjust to fit his big frame.

"Now what?" I asked.

Garrett met my eyes and then his gaze rolled down my body, head to toe. I was a complete mess...but the look in his eyes didn't say that at all. He looked at me as if I was the best thing he'd ever seen and that sent a warm glow right through me.

"Now," he said, "you disappear."

Garrett got behind the wheel of one of the FBI SUVs and drove us back up to the highway. Director Gibson got agents to collect my luggage and load it into the back. I grabbed a moment alone in the back seat to change. After rummaging through my suitcases, though, I realized I had a problem. I needed to be inconspicuous, but how do you do "inconspicuous" when everything you own has been picked out by the palace stylist to look good for the crowds? Half of the clothes were fiercely traditional, like the dress I'd worn that morning, and the other half were one-off designer pieces. I eventually pulled on the white business suit I'd worn at the UN, but I knew it still wasn't right. I still looked like *me.* It would do for now, but I had to do better. I'd put enough people in danger already.

Emerik, Jakov and Caroline got back in and we sped off. Garrett's first stop was a strip mall. He got me to draw as much cash from an ATM as my card would allow. "After this, no credit cards," he told us over his shoulder as we climbed back in. "And everyone throw their phones away."

"Our *phones?!*" squeaked Caroline. She's addicted to her phone, usually messaging some guy. But she along with the rest of us dutifully dropped our phones into a trash can as Garrett drove past it.

"You really think they're tracking us like that?" I asked, my voice shaking a little.

"Your Highness, I don't know *what* the hell is going on," said Garrett. "But I'm not taking any chances, not with...you." On the last word, his eyes met mine in the rear view mirror and locked there, and I felt that pull, stronger than ever. Then he looked away as if embarrassed, and I nodded and looked at my lap, face flushed.

And next to me, Caroline nudged me in the ribs and gave me a *tell me everything* look.

I gave her an innocent shake of my head, as if nothing was going on.

We had to ditch the SUV, Garrett said, because the FBI could track it. So our next stop was a used car dealership called *Honest Al's*. Most of the cars had rust patches and the dealer...well, maybe I didn't understand American humor but he didn't *look* honest.

I gazed up at the sky. It was just past noon and it was *ferociously* hot. Emerik was scowling but I loved it. The sunshine in Lakovia always felt somehow distant. Here in America, the sun touched your exposed skin, its warmth soaking into your body. It made me want to strip everything off and bathe naked in it. I flushed at the thought and tried to look innocent.

Garrett looked around for a few minutes and eventually settled on a car. There was a lot of negotiating, some handshakes and then a few extra bills changed hands. "Alright," said Garrett when it was done. "He's going to 'forget' to put the paperwork through for a few days."

Emerik stared at what he'd bought. "You can't be serious."

But I was staring for a different reason: I loved it. For a second, I forgot my fear.

It was a white pickup truck that had once been red: the paint still showed through in a few places. There were dents and chips on almost every surface and the wheels were thick with dried dirt. I'd never seen one up close before. Immediately, I was in some American movie, with small towns and high school proms and skinny dipping in the lake and—

Before anyone could stop me, I'd climbed into the passenger seat. *Oh, wow!* This was even better. It even smelled different to a limo. They smelled of chemicals and plastic. This smelled of wet earth and freshly-chopped wood. When I slammed my door, it went *clank,* metal on metal, not the dull *whump* of an expensive car. I couldn't help it: I grinned.

Garrett climbed into the driver's seat. Straight away, he looked more comfortable than he had in the expensive SUV. When he saw my grin, his heavy brow knitted. "What?"

I flushed. *A princess is meant to be reserved,* I could hear my mother saying. *Not excitable like a child.* "Nothing," I muttered. "I've just never been in a pickup before. And I've never sat up front before."

He nodded in understanding. "Except to drive."

I flushed even deeper.

He blinked. "You don't...drive?"

Emerik and the others were climbing into the back seat. "A princess is *always* chauffeured," he said. He looked disapprovingly at how close we were sitting.

"My mother learned," I said. "In fact, she used to race cars when she was young, before she met my father. But I never did." Hot embarrassment flooded my face. *The pampered princess who doesn't know how to do anything.* "You must think I'm so stupid," I muttered. I stared hard out of the side window.

"No." Garrett's voice was both gentle and firm. I slowly turned to look at him. "I don't think that," he told me. "Not for a second."

I swallowed. Those gorgeous, clear blue eyes were suddenly all that existed in the world. And then my eyes were drawn inexorably down. That hard upper lip. That full, soft lower one. I drew in a breath and it was tight and shaky. And then we were leaning in towards each other, a fraction of an inch at a time....

"Perhaps we should get going, Mr. Buchanan," said Emerik from the back seat.

I jerked back. *Stupid! What are you doing?* And did Emerik *know*? Was I that obvious? *Of course you are, you're behaving like a love-sick child!*

I scooched a little further away from Garrett, and stiffly reached for my seat belt. Then I folded my hands demurely in my lap and nodded, and Garrett started the engine. It wasn't until we turned back onto the highway that I risked a look at him. And then only a quick look, barely a glance, just enough to take in that rugged jaw, his blue eyes so serious, so determined, the tan bulges of his shoulders and biceps, revealed by his ripped-off shirt sleeves—

I realized I was staring again and forced myself to look away.

And we roared off down the highway.

11

GARRETT

I HEADED EAST, out of Los Angeles and then out of California. I didn't have a firm destination in mind, just wanted to get her as far from the assassins as possible. We needed to be *lost*.

Driving's a lot like marching: just point your nose in the right direction, turn off your brain and *go*: perfect for a dumb grunt like me. It figured that the Princess had never learned. She had a hell of a lot more to offer the world. But staring at that white line gave me plenty of time to think.

Why the hell did I do this? The assassins were well trained, well armed and they had satellite surveillance and God knows what other help. And we were just three guys: one past retirement age, one barely old enough to be out of training and *me*: thrown out of the Marines, can't even hold down a job and a goddamn liability if I had another flashback.

My knuckles turned white on the steering wheel as it all surged up inside me. Rage first, at what happened, at the system I used to be so loyal to, at the whole goddamn world for not giving a rat's ass. Guilt, for what I'd done. And hot, biting shame that I'd let it mess me up. What good is a soldier who can just freeze at any time?

People say you need to let stuff out, but that means remembering and it's just too much damn pain. I'm not facing the memories again, not for anyone.

Besides, I couldn't talk about it even if I wanted to: I get so mad at myself, when I think about it, everything just slams closed and I can't speak. I don't want a belly full of pills. The only thing that ever calmed me worth a damn was being around horses and it's been a long time since I had the chance to do that.

So I did what I always did: I wrestled all that pain and hurt back down. I buried the memories of sand and screams. And when I could breathe again, I took a look at the Princess.

And immediately, I knew the answer to my question. *Why the hell did I do this?*

Because someone had to.

Because letting her be harmed...that wasn't an option.

The Princess had changed into...a power suit, I guess you'd call it. It was pure white, all hard lines and sharp angles, but the fabric looked as soft as freshly-fallen snow.

If an angel had needed a suit for a meeting with Beelzebub to thrash out the rules for heaven and hell, *that's* what she would have worn.

Not many people could have carried it off but on the Princess, it looked right. It was as if she was made from different stuff from the rest of us. We were getting close to Arizona, now, the dusty scrubland giving way to barren red rock cooking under a fierce sun. The battered pickup fit there. Hell, *I* fit there. But the Princess looked as if she'd stepped down off one of the fluffy white clouds that dotted the huge, blue sky. She was breathtaking.

The way she looked around in wonder at the landscape only made her seem more otherworldly. When she saw me watching her, she blushed. "Sorry, I'm just not used to..."—she waved her hand at the landscape. "When I thought of America, I thought of cities I'd seen on TV. New York. Washington. I didn't know about all this." She gazed at the vivid red cliffs. "Look at the colors!"

I glanced around, seeing it all with fresh eyes, and grunted in agreement. It *was* pretty, if you liked rough and rugged. "Ain't got nothing on a Texas sunset, though," I muttered. And for a crazy second, I had this deep hankering to show her one.

I'd never felt anything like this attraction before, not with the girls I'd known before I joined the marines, not with the girls in Texas I'd met on leave. I only had to hear her voice, see that face, and I was helpless. She was my exact opposite, as smooth and pristine as I was rough and dirty. So why was I so taken with her?

And it was more than just lust. Sure, I was having all sorts of filthy fantasies involving pulling the Princess down into the bed of the pickup and slowly stripping off her clothes, running my hands up and down her body until she begged me to fuck her. But I also couldn't stop thinking about kissing her. Just kissing her.

But she was royalty. And even before what happened in the desert screwed me up, I was just a jarhead, son of another jarhead. My dad used to say we were born with boots on our feet. The marines, or breeding horses...that's all any of us Buchanans have ever done. *A princess isn't going to want me.*

And yet I kept looking up and catching her looking at me. At my bare arms, at the denim stretched tight over my thighs. And then she'd quickly look away. And then I'd look at her, and *she'd* catch *me* and I'd jerk my gaze back to the road. I could feel something building, growing with every mile we spent together. After two solid hours, I had to grip the steering wheel hard to stop myself from doing something crazy...like slamming on the brakes and skidding to a stop by the side of the road. Taking her cheeks between my hands while she was still gaping in surprise and bringing my lips down on hers....

My foot actually twitched against the brake pedal. I had to break the silence or I was actually going to do it. "What was that thing you did with your hand?" I asked. "When the guy had a gun to your head."

"Rans Tagaka," she said.

I glanced at her, frowning. "Rans *what?*" It sounded like a character from *Star Wars.*

"It's the royal martial art."

I blinked. "You have your own martial art?"

"One of my ancestors invented it, hundreds of years ago. A last-ditch defense, in case we're attacked." She looked down at her lap. "Being one of the royal family has always been dangerous."

I tried to imagine growing up, knowing people wanted to kill you simply because of who you were. What a life. And she hadn't asked for this, hadn't stood for election or got to make a choice. She'd been born into it. I softly shook my head. Everyone thought she was so lucky. They didn't see this part. That protective instinct hit me again: I just wanted to take her away from all this: not just the danger she was in but take her away from *being a princess*. Like that made any sense.

I drove right through the afternoon. By the time the sun started to set, we were well into Arizona. The interstate was a narrow strip of black cutting through bare desert and walls of red rock. As the sun went down, our headlights became the only light for miles and the sky above turned from blue to black to a shimmering carpet of stars stretching from one horizon to the other.

I figured we'd run far enough.

The next time I passed a sign for a motel, I turned off the interstate and followed the signs. When I found the place and killed the engine, it was so quiet I could hear my own breathing. For the first time all day, I relaxed a little. No one was going to find us out here.

The motel was a little single story place with only about ten rooms. But it looked clean enough and there was a rib shack next door for dinner. There were strings of colored light bulbs strung along the paths to light your way. A good thing because it was dark as hell. "Watch your step, Your Highness," I murmured.

"Holes?" she asked, looking down.

"Snakes," I told her gently.

I got us some rooms and told everyone to rest up for a half hour, and then we'd get some dinner. I needed time to figure out how to get her back to Lakovia undetected.

In my room, I dug out a fresh shirt to finally replace the one I'd torn that morning. Then I hesitated, looking in the mirror at my dust-streaked face and matted hair....

I took a long, hot shower and shampooed my hair. Tried to comb it into some sort of order. Then I caught myself trying to scrub the dirt from under my nails, where there's *always* dirt. *What the hell are you doing? Trying to impress her?* I felt my neck color. *You big idiot.* I threw down the soap and pulled on the fresh shirt.

There was a creak of floorboards, just outside my door. I could see the person's silhouette in the blind that covered my room's window: a woman. I saw her raise her hand to knock, then put it down again. She did it a second time. A third time.

Was she...*nervous?*

I covered the distance to the door in two big strides and pulled the door open. The Princess yelped in surprise and jumped back, her hand still raised to knock. "Oh!"

I just stood there and stared.

"I wanted to check this was okay," she said, glancing down at herself.

I couldn't reply. She'd finally found some normal clothes. Jeans and a top, with heels. Except....

Except *oh my God.*

I'd only ever seen her in expensive clothes. Normal clothes didn't make her look normal, they just showed off how different she really was. They made her *glow.* She'd pulled all that chestnut hair back into a ponytail to try to look less glamorous but all it did was expose more elegant, pale neck. My lips actually prickled, imagining the feel of that soft skin against them: the warmth of her throat, the beat of her pulse as I kissed down the length of it.

Her tank top was the dark red of ripe cherries. On another woman I wouldn't even have noticed it. But on the Princess, the dark red set off the pale skin of her arms. Her arms! I hadn't seen them bare, before, hadn't realized how beautiful they were, feminine but toned. Something about her naked shoulders made me want to wrap one big arm around her back and pull her into me, like we were teenagers at the movies, my fingers rubbing over that soft roundness.

Goddammit! Since when was a shoulder so sexy?

My eyes roved lower. The tank top hugged the curves of her

breasts, showing me the shape of her in a way the dress and the suit and even those fancy pajamas hadn't. Soft and yet pert...*majestic.* Watching her breathe was hypnotic.

Her blue jeans were faded and distressed. In a few places there were actual holes, little windows that gave tantalizing glimpses of pale skin. And the way the denim clung to her...I wanted to put my hands under that firm ass and lift her, pull her against me—

"So will I blend in?" she asked.

"No," I growled. I could hear the lust in my voice. Blend in? Every man in the restaurant was going to be staring at her. She wasn't just beautiful, she was...*glorious.*

And *royal.* I kept telling myself that. *She's a princess.* Except...the more the attraction grew, the more that idea changed. I'd been worried about tainting her, somehow, with my blue collar ways. Now, I was so drawn to her, all I could think about was getting that noble perfection very, very dirty.

"It's perfect," I managed.

She gave a shy smile and looked down at herself again. "Thank goodness. I borrowed everything from Caroline. It's not too, um..."—she blushed—"tight?"

I looked down at those lush curves again and that was it. My mind tipped over the edge and became a runaway train on a downhill slope. I needed to take hold of her cheeks, tilt her head back and taste those royal lips. I needed to hook my thumbs under that tank top and hook it up over that magnificent chest. I needed to lift her and pin her against the nearest wall, those long, denim-clad legs wrapping around me, and—

I took a step forward. Now we were staring at each other from six inches away, her on my doorstep and me filling the doorframe. She tilted her head way back to look up at me.

Suddenly, all I could see were her lips.

"Mr. Buchanan?" She sounded nervous...but there was an urgency there, too.

I leaned down to kiss her.

12

KRISTINA

THOSE GORGEOUS LIPS COMING CLOSER, the sheer size of him scary and wonderful as he leaned down. God, he was everything my mother had warned me about, big and brutish and definitely not of royal blood. I could see it in that hard, curving chest, in the sculpted shape of his forearms. He was made to till fields and ride horses and fight his country's enemies. Real work, not signing documents and endless talking. He was my polar opposite, as rough as I was refined and *God,* I wanted him.

And then suddenly he stopped. He put both his hands on the doorframe above our heads with a heavy *thump thump.* His knuckles turned white. He was grabbing it so that—

So that he wouldn't grab *me.* God, the look in his eyes, a man on the very edge of control: was *I* doing that to him?!

He let out a low growl that vibrated right through my body...and draw back from me. *Why?*

There was something in his eyes, something I'd glimpsed back in the desert when I'd asked about his dog tags. Pain so deep and jagged he couldn't hide it. My chest ached for him. *What happened to this man?*

He looked away and the spell was broken. Reality came rushing back and I flushed scarlet. He was from a different country...and a whole different world. I could hear my mother's voice in my head. *What on earth came over you?* That was the part that shocked me most: I'd been as out of control as him. And *now* what? What did I say to him?

"Your Highness," said Emerik, emerging from the darkness. I jumped about a foot in the air. He has at least a thousand different ways of saying *Your Highness*. This was his *I'm onto you and I disapprove* tone. He'd used the same one when I was seven, and he'd caught me sneaking jelly beans from the palace kitchen. I carefully avoided his eyes and I didn't dare look at Garrett, either.

Jakov and Caroline joined us and we headed towards the restaurant. There was a line to get in. Emerik looked at it in bemusement, then in exasperation. Like me, he'd never had to wait in line to get into anywhere. But I joined the end of the line, then gave him a look. *We'll wait politely like everyone else.*

"I can't call you *Your Highness* in there," muttered Garrett after a few moments. He didn't look at me as he said it. Both of us were still stumbling and awkward after that nearly-kiss.

"Kristina will be fine, Mr. Buchanan," I told him. "But I have to call you Garrett."

Now he turned to look at me, blinking in shock. "Aw, hell. You don't need to—"

"I insist." I tried it out. "*Garrett.*" I nodded to myself: I loved the way it sounded: so strong, so...*cowboy.*

He looked down at his boots for a few seconds, as if no one had called him by his first name in a long time. But then he rallied. "Kristina," he said in a low growl.

I flushed and caught my breath. I hadn't thought about how my name would sound in his throaty rasp. When people announce me as *Princess Kristina,* it sounds light and clean, like snowflakes falling on a Danish village. But when Garrett said it, he rolled the *r* in a way that sent a shiver right down my spine and then rasped out the *tina* so that it throbbed right in my groin. *That* Kristina wasn't snowflakes and innocence.

I swallowed, throwing glances up at him as we neared the restaurant door. The tension between us was back, every tiny brush of his shirt sleeve against my arm making my skin throb and prickle. He'd pulled back from the kiss but both of us were still one touch, one word away from just grabbing the other.

I took a deep breath...and we went to dinner.

I had no idea what a rib shack was but, as soon as we got inside, I loved it. It was loud and dark, lit only by dangling bulbs and the occasional neon beer sign. The tables and chairs were bare wood, the floor was bare boards and everyone was gnawing meat from shining bones, dripping with dark sauce. The most amazing smell filled the room: succulent pork and beef and the heady tang of that dark sauce. My mouth started watering immediately.

"Your Highness," whispered Emerik in my ear. "I'm not sure that this establishment—"

"Don't call me *Your Highness*," I told him. "And it'll do perfectly well."

Caroline whooped and pointed. "*They have a jukebox!*" We pooled our loose change and she queued up a full hour's worth of American pop. She loved everything about this country. While I'd been getting changed, she'd hit the tiny store next to the rib shack and loaded up with US candy bars and magazines.

We ordered groaning platefuls of steaming ribs, sticky with sauce, bowls of French fries and mac 'n cheese, coleslaw and grilled corn, all washed down with icy, crisp beer. None of us had eaten since dinner on the plane, the previous night. We demolished everything.

It was the first time we'd been able to relax and all of us needed it. I saw Garrett's broad back lose a little of its tension and even Emerik relented and unbuttoned the top button of his collar. Caroline, who seemed to see this whole thing as an adventure, laughed and chatted and spun a story to a neighboring table about us being tourists from Italy. It made me wish that I could be as free and fun-loving as her. The whole experience was a reminder of everything I'd missed out on in life: food and beer with friends, being able to just wander about casually and enjoy life, without having everything pre-planned and security checked and assessed by Aleksander and his PR people.

I was on the run. But in some ways, it was the freest I'd ever been.

Garrett looked amazing. The new shirt he'd put on was blue and black plaid and it set off his tan skin and those amazing eyes. He'd rolled up the sleeves and my eyes kept being drawn to his thickly muscled forearms as they rested on the table. Every time I looked at them, I imagined myself being lifted right off my feet—it would be so easy for him. Lifted and pressed up against a wall, or tossed on his bed, my jeans peeled down my legs—

I forced myself to look away but it was no good. If I looked at his collar, I imagined myself sliding my hands down under his shirt, tracing the hard slabs of his chest. If I looked at his wide shoulders, that brought home the raw size and power of him, how he'd loom over me, blocking out the light as he lowered himself between my thighs. And if I looked up into those clear blue eyes....

If I looked into his eyes, I was lost.

What had nearly happened in his doorway had changed everything. All my fantasies had gone super-high-definition, so real they left my heart racing and my breathing tight. Worse, I knew it could have happened. Could still happen, if I just—

No! Garrett belonged in this world of pickup trucks and ribs and beer and friends. I had to keep reminding myself that I was only visiting. "Do you have any ideas for getting us home?" I asked.

Garrett shook his head. "Nope," he rumbled. "But now you're safe, I'm thinking on it." He dropped his eyes as soon as he'd said it, as if the idea of him thinking was ridiculous. My chest contracted in sympathy and then hot anger flared up inside: people had been underestimating this man for so long, seeing him as a big, dumb brute, that they'd even gotten *him* believing he was stupid.

Caroline grabbed my wrist. "Dance!"

I was still saying *what* when she hauled me out of my seat and pulled me stumbling into the open space by the bar. "Dance!" she said again.

And she started dancing to the music from the jukebox. I stared.

It wasn't like any dancing I was used to but then I'd only ever danced at formal balls.

"What?" asked Caroline. "This is how they do it here."

I watched at her circling hips and thrusting ass. "Are you sure?" But I joined her. The opportunity was too good to miss. I never got to dance at home. Certainly not like *this*.

"So. Garrett." Caroline's eyes were gleaming expectantly.

I flushed down to my roots. "What about Garrett?" I loved the sound of his name.

"Don't 'what about Garrett' *me*, you've been looking at him like you wanted to hoist up your skirts and climb on top of him."

I went even redder. "Don't be ridiculous."

"What happened out in the desert?"

"Nothing!"

"Has anything else happened?"

I thought of that moment in his doorway. "No," I lied.

"He's from Texas," said Caroline dreamily. "That's like America, only more so."

"What about you?" I asked, desperately trying to change the subject.

She gave me a sly look.

"Someone back home?" I asked, excited. I ran through the possibilities in my head. I hoped it wasn't Jakov, because I'd seen him looking with puppy-dog eyes at Simone, one of my father's maids.

"Maybe," she said airily. And we both grinned. This is what I love about Caroline: she makes me feel normal. She has to call me *Your Highness* when other people are around but when we're in private she's like a sister.

Then I glanced at Garrett...and swallowed. His eyes were locked on my hips as they gyrated, on the denim stretched tight over my ass as it thrust back and forth. I'd never seen him look quite so...*hungry*. And I felt the answering swell of heat in my core, sliding down to my groin to turn into slick wetness.

"That doesn't look like 'nothing,'" whispered Caroline in my ear.

I flushed again and led her back to the table. Garrett's eyes tracked me the whole way, the heat of his gaze burning through my clothes and melting my core. I'd never been looked at that way before. Most men didn't dare to lust after a princess so openly, or they thought I was too noble, too innocent and sweet.

Garrett looked at me as if I was special, as if I was up in the clouds. But underneath there was that fierce, lashing heat that wanted to grab me and drag me right down to earth, pin me with a kiss and rip my dress off and—

Our eyes met. Locked. I caught my breath. We stared at one another for one, two, three beats of my racing heart. Then we finally managed to tear our eyes away.

Garrett leaned across the table towards Emerik. "So...you've guarded Kristina for a long time?" His voice was still gruff, but I could hear him trying to sound friendly. He was doing his best to get along with the older man, and I gave Emerik a sharp look: *play nice!*

"I've been with her family for three decades," said Emerik. "It's a great honor." He still sounded a little stiff, as if a conversation with Garrett was beneath him, but he couldn't stop the emotion creeping into his voice on the last few words. It really *was* a great honor for him.

"And Jakov joined us just a few months ago," I told Garrett. "Graduated top of his class in the army. The youngest ever to qualify as a royal guard."

Jakov flushed, nodded his thanks and excused himself to go to the bathroom. I sighed as I saw Emerik's hate-filled gaze follow him all the way there.

Garrett saw it too. "What am I missing? He seems like a good kid."

Emerik gave him a disparaging look. He was too polite to speak his mind, of course. So, with another sigh, I explained.

"Jakov was born in Lakovia," I said. "But his parents are from Garmania. Jakov was one of the first people with Garmanian heritage to enroll in the army. And the first to become a royal guard. It was hard for him: he had to train alongside men whose families had been killed in the war with Garmania. He still gets hate mail, every day, from people who see him as the enemy. But having him guard me is such an important symbol. It sends a message that it's time to move on."

Emerik scowled, got up and stalked away.

"But a lot of people aren't ready to move on," Garrett rumbled, watching him.

I nodded. Emerik never said anything openly against Jakov but everyone could feel the hate and distrust bubbling away just under the surface. They were rarely paired together: it just happened that they were on shift at the same time on the plane and now they were the only two guards left. "We can't go back to all that," I muttered, half to myself. It was warm in the rib shack but my skin suddenly felt chilled by memories of cold, damp stone. "I just want all of us to live in peace." Then I shook my head and gave a tired laugh. "Sorry. I didn't mean to get preachy."

But Garrett shook his head. "Didn't sound preachy. Peace is good."

I could hear the pain in his voice. Peace was good...because he'd seen enough of the alternative. Our eyes met and he quickly looked down at the table. He already knew what I was going to ask him.

"Everything you did on the plane and on the highway...you must have been a great soldier. Why did you quit?"

He still wasn't looking at me. "I didn't quit. They discharged me," he said at last. He spoke as if there was a huge weight pressing on his chest.

Without thinking, I reached out and put my hand on his. I couldn't stand to see him hurting like that. "What happened?" I whispered.

"A mission went wrong," he said. "We lost some people." Then he shook his head: *enough*. His eyes flicked up to meet mine and there was such anger there I actually drew back, shocked. But it wasn't flaring out at me. It was all turned inward, tearing away at himself. And I could feel how his whole body had locked up tight with emotion.

It wasn't that he wouldn't talk about it. He *couldn't* talk about it. God, there was so much going on under the surface of this gentle giant, so much people didn't see. "I'm sorry," I said.

He nodded. Looked away, unable to meet my eyes.

I thought of darkness and cold stone. My own memories of war and the nightmares they still brought. Garrett was my opposite. But what if we were more similar than either of us had thought?

That night, I lay in bed unable to sleep. I tried one of the trashy magazines Caroline had lent me but eventually I slapped it down on the bedside table, nearly knocking over the lamp. There was too much going around my head: the plane, the attack on the convoy, Garrett....

I squeezed my eyes shut. *No! Don't think about him sitting on the bed behind you, the mattress creaking under that big body. Those strong arms wrapping around you, making you feel safe. His lips at your ear, that deep Texas rumble as he tells you what he's going to do to you....*

I opened my eyes and saw my pile of suitcases in the corner, each with their royal crest. When all this was over, I had to go back to the palace and be the Princess my people needed. I had to help my father, learn from him and, one day, take the crown and rule. I'd marry some man my mother found for me, someone *suitable*. That was my job.

I glanced at the bathroom. What I *really* needed right now was a bath but the motel room only had a shower. At the palace, I had a big corner tub that I could happily spend a full hour in, the room lit with candles and the water fragrant with a special scented oil a local craftswoman made.

I closed my eyes but, as soon as I saw darkness, I started to feel the cold stone under my hands, the damp in the air wetting my skin. That feeling of being utterly and completely alone. It becomes overwhelming in my nightmares but it's there even when I'm awake. It's *always* there. When I'm standing on a balcony, waving at a crowd. When I'm giving an interview on TV. Even when I'm in a room full of people.

Except today—God, was it really only a day since I first woke up on the plane? Today, for a brief time, when he'd held me in his arms...I didn't feel alone.

After a long time, I slept. The nightmare came, as I knew it would. I was in the cell, running my fingers over the rough stone again and again just to give my mind some texture, some stimulation, in the absolute blackness. The lack of sound was the worst. No birds, no wind in the trees, *nothing*.

I began to panic, the sound of my own frenzied breathing bouncing off the walls and reflecting back at me, making me panic even more. But this time...something was different. I was taking huge gasps, my mouth wide, but I wasn't getting any air—

I woke up and looked straight into the face of the man from the plane. I'd fallen asleep with the lamp on and its glow lit up his pale, tight skin, his hate-filled gray eyes.

It isn't over! Somehow, he'd found us again. I screamed...but nothing came out.

He was straddling me, his weight on my chest and his hands wrapped around my throat. His thumbs were crushing my windpipe. I couldn't breathe...or make a sound.

I heard something outside. Voices. Garrett and Emerik, right outside my window! *Help me!* I thrashed with my arms and drummed my heels on the bed, but it made almost no noise.

Garrett and Emerik kept talking, oblivious.

I *screamed* but still nothing came out.

My head started to feel light. I was dying.

And they didn't know anything was wrong.

13

GARRETT

MY PLAN WAS to get some sleep for a few hours, then go and relieve Emerik on guard duty. But I spent the time tossing and turning. I told myself it was because the motel bed wasn't big enough: my feet were almost hanging off the end. But in the corps, I'd learned to sleep anywhere. It wasn't the damn bed. It was *her*.

In a way, she was the opposite of everything I'd expected. I'd never met a politician before who was so genuinely passionate about peace. Most of them are happy to send thousands of grunts off to die just to make themselves look tough and get a boost in the polls. And I'd never expected someone from her background to be so down to earth and caring.

But in other ways, she was exactly what I'd expected. She was everything a princess should be: beautiful and noble and... *better*. Better than the rest of us, in a way that makes you want to be better, too. I was crazy about her. Obsessed. That's why what happened in my doorway was still spinning, nonstop, in my mind. I'd nearly tasted those sweet lips.

But I couldn't. I couldn't get close to her, or she'd find out what a mess I was, inside. From now on, I'd make sure to keep my distance. I'd protect her, but that was it.

To distract myself, I tried to figure out how to get her home while staying off the radar of whoever was trying to kill her. I sure as hell couldn't put her on a commercial flight. Her name would make ten thousand computer screens light up at the FBI. Whoever was leaking information to the assassins would tell them, they'd sneak someone onto the plane again, and she'd be a sitting duck for eight hours. Or they could just plant a bomb on the plane. Three hundred passengers meant nothing to these people.

It took me over an hour of wracking my brain, but finally, I got it. Barney. Barney could do it. It meant getting her to New York, a two thousand mile drive. But it would work.

The downside of figuring it out was that my brain went right back to what happened in the doorway. What *would* have happened if I'd kissed her. The scent of her, warm and sweet, but with that coolness of mountain mist. The soft push of her breasts as I crushed her to me. Her panting as I pinned her up against the doorframe and unbuttoned her jeans. I'd slide a hand down the front, under her panties, and cup her. She'd moan and toss her head, that chestnut hair lashing my face—

Under the covers I was achingly hard. The temptation to just keep thinking about her, to slip a hand down there and—

No! Jesus, I wasn't going to jerk off to her! I wasn't some teenage kid and it didn't seem right, with her sleeping just a few rooms away. I sprang out of bed and pulled on my clothes. If I couldn't sleep, I might as well go relieve Emerik early.

Outside, I walked down the line of rooms to where Emerik stood outside the Princess's door. "Go get some rest," I told him. "I'll watch her, then Jakov can take a shift."

Emerik didn't move. "I'm fine," he said. "It's my duty. *You* get some rest."

I frowned at him. Sure, he was loyal, but I'd never known anyone argue with having their shift cut short. "Seriously," I growled. "Go."

"Seriously," he echoed, "No."

I frowned again and then tensed, staring at the Princess's door. "Did you hear something?"

He went silent for a moment and then shook his head. And I didn't hear anything more, either. I relaxed. *Just my imagination.*

"Go back to bed, Mr. Buchanan," said Emerik. "I'll be fine until Jakov takes over." He glared at Jakov's room.

"You think she's wrong about everyone living in peace, don't you? You don't trust him."

He looked me right in the eye. "I lost two nephews in the war, Mr. Buchanan. So, no. I don't trust any Garmanian. No matter where they were born."

I shook my head sadly. I was trying to figure out what to say to the poor guy when I thought I heard a faint noise again. I put my hand on the door handle. "I'm going to check on her," I told Emerik.

He grabbed my wrist. "You most certainly *are not!* It's forbidden for a commoner to be in the Princess's room!" I opened my mouth to argue but he cut me off. "There's only one door and one window in her room and I've been standing in front of them all night! She doesn't need you!"

I didn't miss the way he said that last part. We glared at each other, our faces only a foot apart. But I could feel my neck going hot. He *knew.* Of course he did. *Did you really think you were the first guy to fall for her? He probably sees this all the time.*

I dropped my eyes to the door handle. Had I really heard something? Or was I just looking for an excuse to open the door and see her again?

I let go of the handle and stepped back. "Fine," I grunted. "I'll see you in the morning."

And I walked off towards my room.

14

KRISTINA

I WAS DYING. My vision was narrowing, a circle of light that darkened to gray and then to cold, empty black at the edges.

I tried to hit the man who was strangling me. But he was bigger than me, his arms longer. My fingers scratched and clawed the air an inch short of his face. I tried to pry his hands loose from my throat, but they were iron-hard, trembling with the power he was putting into killing me. The power and the hatred. I could see it in those gray eyes: I *disgusted* him.

I thought I heard the handle of my door move and my heart lifted. They were coming in! But then to my horror it went quiet again.

My eyes searched for something, anything that would make a noise. I was so woozy now, my vision lagged and lurched. *The lamp!* But it was out of reach of my straining fingers.

Muffled voices outside. I was hysterical, now, pleading in my mind. *Come in! Please!* But then I heard heavy footsteps walking away. *Garrett! No! I need you!*

My fingers brushed something on the nightstand, smooth and glossy and thick. *The magazine!* My muscles were going limp, but I summoned all my strength and shoved it as hard as I could. It hit the base of the lamp and sent it skidding towards the edge....

The assassin heaved me by the throat, pulling me away from the bedside table so I couldn't do it again. My eyes locked on the lamp. It slowed and came to a stop half off the edge, rocking back and forth.

The assassin froze on top of me, his eyes on the lamp too. If he released me to catch it, I'd scream. The lamp teetered. *Come on, please!*

It fell to the floor with an almighty crash.

I heard running footsteps outside. But the assassin was squeezing my throat even harder, desperate. My vision narrowed until all I could see were his eyes. My stomach lurched. *They're going to be too late.*

Everything went black.

15

GARRETT

I HURLED THE DOOR OPEN, my stomach knotted. I was praying that I'd find the Princess half-awake, frowning sleepily at something she'd knocked over in her sleep. I'd apologize, close the door and—

She was limp on the bed. Unmoving. A dark figure knelt over her, his hands locked around her throat.

I bellowed a wordless cry of rage and surged across the room, fists already coming up. *This is my fault!* Twice, I'd heard something, but I'd second-guessed my instincts because of my own selfish feelings for her. Never again. If she could just be okay, I'd happily bury those feelings forever. *Just let her be alive!*

I lowered my shoulder to ram the bastard off her—

And suddenly *I* was knocked sideways. I slammed into the wall and went down. And looked up into the face of the second guy, the one I hadn't seen, hiding in the shadows.

I managed to get back to my feet, but he grabbed me and swung me against the wall again. I felt the cheap plaster crack. These guys were tough, definitely military.

Emerik ran in, dived and tackled the guy on the bed, carrying him down to the floor. The Princess's body was tugged sideways for a second and then, as her throat was released, she flopped back like a rag doll. *Oh Jesus, no!*

I punched my attacker in the guts, then in the face. He was a big guy, but I was *pissed* and my fists had all my anger behind them. He went staggering backwards, then recovered and came at me again.

I didn't have time for this. I had to help her. I pulled the gun out of the back of my waistband and shot him twice in the chest, and he crumpled to the floor.

Emerik was on the floor on the far side of the bed, tussling with the assassin. I saw the old guy take two good punches in the ribs: he was holding up well, but it was obvious he was losing and I couldn't shoot, not without risking hitting him. I waded in and kicked instead, hooking my boot right into the assassin's chest, and he tumbled backwards. Jesus, it was the same pale-faced guy from the plane, the one who'd parachuted out!

I raised my gun to fire. But the assassin was too quick: he grabbed a vase of flowers off a side table and hurled it at me. It hit the gun and my shot went wide. The vase shattered on the wall to my side, spraying me with fragments. The assassin dived across the bed —*Jesus,* he was fast—and raced through the open door.

I took a single step after him... then I looked towards the bed. I didn't know if she was alive or dead, but no way was I leaving her alone again.

I jumped onto the bed and fell to my knees, straddling her. She was still silent and unmoving, her head turned to the side, her long hair covering her face. I brushed it back out of the way, but her eyes didn't open. "Your Highness?" There was no response. "*Your Highness! Please!*"

16

KRISTINA

My eyes opened slowly and *he* was there, his big form looming over me, his hands warming my cheeks. I saw those blue eyes open wide as I woke up and the elation, the sheer joy and relief on his face as he saw I was alive sent a huge, warm throb through my chest.

Then two huge hands slid underneath me and I was being lifted off the bed and clutched to him like a child. My head was against his, my chin on his shoulder, and every part of me from neck to ankle was pressed against him. His life and warmth soaked into me, bringing me back from the edge.

It was the best thing I'd ever experienced. I'd never felt so safe.

I heard other people running into the room. Jakov cursed. Caroline gave a cry of fear. I couldn't see either of them. I had my eyes firmly closed, focused on just breathing. It felt like my bruised throat was the width of a drinking straw and it was terrifying. The only thing that made it bearable was Garrett.

It wasn't just that he was so solid, a wall of muscle between me and those who'd harm me. It wasn't just the knowledge that he'd smash anyone who threatened me.

It was the way he held me.

He held me like he'd never let me go. His whole body was tense against mine, almost trembling with rage and emotion. Everyone else in the room was silent. I knew Emerik must be there, but even he didn't say something about this being inappropriate and I knew why. He didn't dare. No one in the world would have dared try to separate Garrett from me, right then.

At last, my breathing started to ease. Slowly, reluctantly, Garrett put me back down on the bed and I opened my eyes. The others gathered around me. Jakov looked furious. Emerik was pale, sick with fear or... guilt? Caroline was biting her lip, tears in her eyes. And Garrett was looking down at me with an expression of raw, vengeful fury that was growing by the second. His gaze was focused on my neck. They were *all* looking at my neck.

I turned to Caroline. God, even turning my neck hurt. I tried to speak, but that was a mistake: it sent me into a fit of coughing that closed my throat up completely and brought tears of pain. Caroline grabbed my hand and held it and Garrett held my other one and all of them watched helplessly until I recovered. *"Is it bad?"* I rasped to Caroline at last.

She looked at my throat and tried to force a smile onto her face. "No, Your Highness," she lied. Then, more firmly, "Nothing make-up won't cover."

Emerik turned away, still looking guilty, and started to pick something up off the floor, something made of pottery that was in pieces.

"No!" Garrett told him. "Don't touch that!"

I expected Emerik to make some scathing comment, but he just nodded meekly and moved away. *What's wrong with him?*

I drew in my breath when I saw the body in the corner. Garrett searched the man's pockets. "No ID," he said. "Nothing." He fetched a towel from the bathroom and used it to cover the body.

Jakov picked a latex glove up from the bed, then found its partner on the floor. "The bastard wore gloves, so he didn't leave prints breaking in," muttered Garrett. "So why would he take them *off?"*

I thought, and when I got the answer, I wanted to throw up. "Because he wanted to feel it, as he was strangling me." I said, my voice a weak rasp. Everyone looked at me in horror. "I saw his eyes. He *hated* me. He wanted to feel me die."

And that's when it really hit me: *it isn't over.* For a few glorious hours, I'd felt safe. I'd felt normal. I thought we'd escaped, but we hadn't at all. The assassins were still after me. Sick fear crept up my body and I turned cold despite the night's heat.

"How did they get in?" Caroline asked.

Everyone looked around. There was only one door and one window next to it and Emerik had been on guard right outside. Then Garrett pointed: one of the ceiling tiles was ajar. He was tall enough that he could reach up and lift it, and we saw a dark crawlspace above. "They must have picked the lock on your door, while we were eating dinner."

That whole time I'd been lying in bed, unable to get to sleep, they'd been up there waiting. When I was asleep and defenseless, they'd crept out like spiders and—I shuddered.

"I need to speak to you alone," said Garrett.

Again, Emerik didn't argue. "We'll go and patrol," he said. Then he grabbed Jakov and pulled the younger man with him. *That* hadn't changed, then, just how he interacted with Garrett. Caroline followed them out and closed the door.

Garrett sat down on the corner of my bed. For the first time, I remembered what I was wearing: a traditional, lacy nightgown that was very pretty, but not at all substantial, and the comforter had fallen down to my hips when I sat up. I felt his eyes track down my body before he managed to tear them away and they left a smoldering trail in their wake.

"We have a problem," he said. "The FBI didn't know we were coming here. *No one* knew we were coming here. I paid in cash and we all threw our phones away so they're not tracking us that way." He looked at the body on the floor. "But these guys still managed to find us."

I swallowed. "How?"

Those hard lips pressed together. "One of us is working with the assassins. You trust Caroline?"

I gaped. "Caroline's my *best friend!*"

"Then one of your guards is a traitor."

17

GARRETT

SHE'D BEEN brave all the way through this: on the plane, on the highway, even having been strangled half to death. Now, for the first time, she looked truly shaken. The idea that someone so close to her could betray her, hit her right where she lived.

"You're wrong," she croaked. I could hear the pain from her bruised throat every time she spoke and it lit a white-hot anger in my chest. I was going to find the man who'd done this and tear him apart. "There's got to be another explanation."

"There isn't," I said.

Tears shone in her eyes. She trusted those two guards completely.

I tried to pick my words carefully, wishing I was better at this stuff. I've always been about doing, not talking. And it didn't help that I was mad at myself for failing to protect her. "Your Highness, Jakov—"

She shook her head. "I know what you're going to say and—"

"We can't just ignore—"

"*No!*"

"You said one of the assassins sounded like he was from Garmania!" I hated snapping at her but she needed to hear it. "Jakov's folks are from there."

"Jakov's completely loyal. And we don't know for sure that the assassins are anything to do with Garmania. We've heard one man's accent, that's it."

I stood up and started pacing. I was completely out of my depth. *I'm a soldier, not a damn detective!* "Then it's Emerik," I said at last.

"That's even crazier! He's been protecting me since I was a kid!"

I shook my head in frustration. We had to figure it out. As long as we had a traitor with us, my plan to get her home via New York was useless: the assassins would set a trap there, or put a bomb on the plane. "One thing I do know," I told her. "We gotta leave. We got a dead body and folks heard those gunshots. Cops are probably on their way. If they arrest me, that leaves you alone with the guards. Can you travel?"

She nodded—even that small movement made her wince in pain —and climbed out of bed so that she could get dressed. I swallowed. She was wearing some sort of nightgown, half Victorian, half Victoria's Secret. It had a high neck and long sleeves and the hem reached down to her ankles. But it was gauzy and, when all the frills stretched out and the light hit it the right way, you could catch glimpses of...*everything.*

Then I saw the vivid red finger marks on her neck and I ground my teeth so hard in anger that they ached. My fault. I'd been right outside the goddamn door and I hadn't come in because I was second-guessing myself. My feelings for her had almost gotten her killed. *Never again.*

She grabbed some clothes and ran to the bathroom to get changed. I put my head out of the door and told the others we were leaving, then ducked back inside to wait. I wasn't leaving the Princess's side, not tonight.

"Ready," she said. She'd thrown on a loose green sweater and the dark jeans. Then she stopped dead. "Wait...if you're right, if one of the guards is the one working with the assassins...then the FBI are in the clear! *They* can protect me. They can put me on a flight home!"

I thought about it, then sighed. "No. Maybe one of the guards told the assassins about the convoy, but they couldn't have sneaked them on board the plane, or fed them satellite data to help find us in the pipes." I ran my hand over my face, the exhaustion catching up with me. "We've got *two* problems. Somebody high up, in the FBI or connected to them. And another person, right here in our group."

"Someone really wants me dead," said the Princess in a small voice.

She suddenly looked so vulnerable. My hands itched with the need to grab her and fold her into my arms. "I'm not gonna let that happen," I told her. *Shit!* Was that sirens, in the distance? "Let's go."

But halfway to the door, my foot nudged a piece of the broken vase. I stopped, frowning.

"What?" the Princess asked.

I held up my hand: *let me think.* I felt like there was something important about it. That's why I'd stopped Emerik from tidying it away. But what?

"What is it?" she asked. "Don't we need to hurry?"

I nodded. I was getting frustrated with myself. *Dammit, why aren't I better at this?* In our unit, I was the big, dumb guy. Doing the thinking was Baker's job. But tonight, all my size and strength hadn't been enough to protect her. I needed to be more than just a grunt. So I *thought.* Until, suddenly....

"When he picked up the vase, he'd already taken the gloves off," I said with great satisfaction. "He left fingerprints, and they'll still be on these pieces. We can find out who the bastard is!"

The Princess drew in her breath and smiled, delighted, and I felt my chest swell with pride. It was the first tiny piece of good luck we'd had. But now we had to get the hell out of there before the cops arrived. I opened the door, hustled her out—

And my eyes fell on the towel I'd thrown over the body. Blood was soaking through the white fabric in two places, splotches of red merging together into one big stain—

Suddenly, it wasn't a towel anymore. It was a bandage around Martinez's torso. He was lying on a wooden table, howling, begging for relief from the pain, and Felton, our medic, was holding him down. "I can't give you anything else!" he snapped, and I could hear the raw emotion in his voice. "We're out! There's nothing left!"

The gunfire from the militia was getting closer, no more than fifty feet away, now. I needed to go back out there and help Baker but I was still slumped against the wall, coughing and choking. The dust was blocking my nose and coating the inside of my mouth. It was down in my lungs—

A hand gripped my arm. One of them was inside the house! I spun around and grabbed the arm, muscles already tensing to break it—

But the arm felt wrong under my fingers. Soft. Slender.

Her.

And suddenly I was back in the motel room. I had the Princess's arm gripped in both hands, so tight it must be hurting. I released it as if burned, the nausea rising in my throat. *Jesus, I was about to break her arm!*

She was looking up at me with huge eyes, terrified. But there was sympathy in her expression, too. It made my chest tighten but it sent a hot wave of shame and anger washing through me.

The sirens were much closer. How long had I frozen for? Seconds? Minutes? I'd put us all at risk again.

"Come on," I growled. "We gotta go."

18

GARRETT

WE TORE out of the motel parking lot just as the whole place lit up red and blue. I drove a few miles, then pulled over at a gas station and called Director Gibson. I didn't trust the FBI with our safety but I could at least let them help figure out who the assassins were. I filled him in and told him about the prints on the broken vase.

We sped on through the night, our pickup the lone car moving on the deserted highway. The guards and Caroline were dozing in the back, the Princess up front with me. The guilt built and built in my chest until I finally broke the silence. "I'm sorry, Your Highness," I muttered.

"For what?" That beautiful voice, glass-smooth and gentle. It seemed to glow in the darkness, lighting up the dark places.

"Grabbing you like that."

She didn't answer, but I could feel her looking at me. I stared hard at the road. I knew what was coming. I felt myself tense, felt all that anger and shame rise up and lock me down.

"It looked like maybe you were remembering something," she said carefully.

My forearms flexed. The steering wheel creaked. But there was something about that voice. It coated my mind like cool running water, calming me. Everything was still locking down, but more slowly.

"What was it?" she prompted.

I owed her an explanation, but I couldn't let those memories out. I couldn't handle reliving it all, or seeing Baker's face again. And I didn't want her to see what a mess I was. Bad enough that she must be terrified of me, now.

"Nothing I want to talk about," I muttered.

She bit her lip and nodded, then turned to stare out of the window. *Aw, hell.* My stomach twisted. She'd only been trying to help.

I sucked in a breath and hardened myself. Getting close to her had just put her in more danger. From now on, I had to keep my distance. And if I wanted to keep her alive, I had to figure out which one of her guards was the traitor. I looked in the rear view mirror.

Emerik was sitting with his arms primly crossed, his back ramrod straight even in sleep. He'd tried to stop me going into her room. To protect her from me? Or to protect the assassin? He'd claimed he hadn't heard anything. Because he was in his sixties and his hearing wasn't as sharp as mine? Or had he heard the same sounds I had and flat-out lied? Afterwards, he'd looked guilty as hell. Because he'd messed up? Or because he was in league with her attacker?

Then there was Jakov. *Everything* pointed to him. He was new to the job. His parents were from a country that was still Lakovia's enemy, even if the fighting had stopped. The same country the lead assassin seemed to come from. He could have been placed as a sleeper agent. Or someone could have turned him, or blackmailed him into helping them.

I sighed. It could be either of them. The only way to know was to test them.

Just outside Phoenix, I pulled into a gas station and roused everyone. "Use the restroom, grab a drink," I told them. "We're heading for Tucson."

Jakov just nodded politely but Emerik spoke up. "How long will that be?"

"Two hours, maybe a little less."

He hurried off in the direction of the restrooms. A few moments later, he was back. *Just long enough for him to pull out a secret cell phone and tell the assassins where we're heading.*

I reached the off-ramp for Tucson before I announced, "Changed my mind. We'll head on to Benson and stop there. Less people, less chance the Princess will be recognized. It's only another hour."

Emerik's face fell. "Are you sure, Mr. Buchanan? Why not just stick to the plan?"

Yeah, I thought, furious, *because your buddies are waiting for us in Tucson, aren't they?*

"Mr. Buchanan knows this country better than us," the Princess told him. Benson will be fine."

I saw Emerik look forlornly at the lights of Tucson as we sped past. And he got more and more agitated as we drove on. Soon he was checking his watch every few minutes and I could see sweat gleaming on his forehead. My chest tightened. I was sure, now. *Yeah, you need to call and tell them where we're really heading, don't you?*

As we drove on, I could see him constantly watching Caroline and Jakov. When it looked like both of them were dozing, he reached into his pocket. I stared in amazement. He was so desperate, he was going to try to send a message right there, from the back seat. But then Jakov stirred and Emerik quickly pulled his hand back.

We pulled into Benson just after dawn. I found a diner and we all trooped inside. I could feel my heart pounding. *This is it.*

Right on cue, Emerik said, "I need to use the restroom." And he was gone, almost running towards the door.

I told the others I'd be back in a minute and marched towards the restroom, the anger building with each step. That son of a bitch. The Princess had trusted him for years, since she was a child. And he'd betrayed her in the worst way possible.

I silently opened the restroom door. Four stalls. One occupied. I couldn't hear him talking to anyone, so he must be texting. I took a step back, gathered myself and smashed my boot against the door. It flew open, crashing against the wall. And there sat Emerik, with—

What?!

With a syringe in his hand.

For a second, we just stared at each other. Then I grabbed him by the throat, lifted him into the air and slammed him against the wall. "You're a *junkie?*" I yelled. "*That's* how they got to you? They got you hooked, then they blackmailed you?"

"*What?*" he croaked. "*Who?!*"

"The assassins! You ran in here to tell them where we were! Just like you called them to tell them we were going to Tucson!"

The confusion in his eyes turned to shock, then anger. "You think I'd betray her?" He closed his eyes and sighed. "I'm *diabetic!*" He said it as if it was some huge confession. "No one knows."

I blinked. And replayed the last few hours in my head.

Me rousing him in Phoenix. Him running off to the restroom to check his glucose levels in secret. Asking how long until we got to Tucson. Figuring that he could inject there, in two hours. Then being trapped for an extra hour in the car, getting pale and sweaty, unable to inject without revealing his secret....

Shit! It all made sense. I released him and he dropped to the floor. "Why keep it a secret?" I demanded.

"I'm past retirement age!" he snapped. "Any physical weakness and I'd be gone, and—" He looked down at his polished shoes for a second. "And protecting her is my life," he said quietly.

All the adrenaline drained out of me. It wasn't him. I could hear the emotion in his voice and you can't fake that kind of loyalty. I cursed and leaned back against the wall of the stall. Then I filled Emerik in on the leak, and how I'd narrowed it down to the two guards.

"It's Jakov," he said immediately. "I never trusted him."

It made sense on paper, given Jakov's heritage, but he didn't *feel* like a traitor. *Goddammit, I'm no good at this!*

I marched back to the table and asked the Princess for a moment alone. Then I told her everything that had happened, leaving out Emerik's diabetes. She was furious that I'd tested him, but relieved that he was cleared. "So now what?" she asked.

It had to be Jakov. But I couldn't accuse him without evidence.

And until I figured out how to prove it and neutralized him, the assassins were going to follow us wherever we went. *Dammit!*

We went back to the table and I gave the waitress twenty bucks to let us make a call on her cell phone. FBI Director Gibson picked up on the second ring and I put him on speaker.

"The guy who left his prints on the vase is Silvas Lukin," Gibson told us. "I'm looking at his photo right now. Mean-looking son of a—" —he caught himself when he remembered who was listening—" Sorry, Your Highness. Anyway, he was an officer in the Garmanian army."

The Princess looked up at me, her eyes huge with fear. Emerik said nothing, but his shoulders had set hard with tension. Jakov was staring at the phone as if willing it to unsay what it had just said.

"*Was?*" asked the Princess.

"He was jailed for war crimes. He ran a special ops unit tasked with operations behind Lakovian lines. Very efficient: he was awarded a whole slew of medals. But his unit also got a reputation for cruelty. They were sent to assassinate a Lakovian strategist and they tortured his wife in front of him first. They were told to destroy a weapons plant and, instead of just letting the civilian staff escape, they rounded them up in the cafeteria and executed them. But the worst one was in a town called..."—he struggled with the pronunciation—" Thoreeny? Thorina?"

"*Thorine,*" whispered the Princess.

I'd never heard her sound so scared. Raw horror, something so bad it was buried in her psyche forever. Something she'd give anything to un-know. I reached under the table, grabbed her hand and squeezed it tight.

The others were having the same reaction. "That was *him?*" muttered Emerik. Caroline looked as if she was about to start crying.

"What happened in Thorine?" I asked helplessly.

"It was a town Garmania took over early in the war," said Gibson. "Lakovia had finally liberated it. Lukin and his team sneaked in to...to get revenge, I guess. They went to the town's main church and—" He broke off. When he spoke again, his voice was thick with emotion. "Oh. Oh Jesus."

The Princess was squeezing my hand like that was all that was holding back the tears. "It was where we'd taken all the children," she whispered. "To keep them safe."

"Lukin's team used gas,' said Gibson. "Three hundred and sixty-seven children. Dead. Lukin said at his trial that he didn't want them growing up into more Lakovian parasites. They sent him to a military jail for life, but he escaped four months ago. And it's not just him. The guy you shot, at the motel? One of Lukin's old unit. My bet is that all the assassins are. Lukin's put his old special ops team back together."

We still didn't know if these people were operating on their own or with the backing of the Garmanian government. But at least we knew who we were up against: a special ops team, used to sneaking behind enemy lines, lead by an absolute psycho who detested Lakovians.

And now their mission was to kill the Princess.

I reached under the table with my other hand and clasped the Princess's hand in both of mine. *Not if I have anything to do with it.*

"What do we do?" asked the Princess. It was the most shaken I'd seen her.

I sighed and tried to think. We couldn't risk going to New York until we got rid of the traitor: we'd be sitting ducks on a plane.

I needed somewhere I could protect her. Somewhere safe. Somewhere familiar.

The answer came to me and I closed my eyes and let out an exhausted sigh. *No!* I couldn't. I couldn't face him. Couldn't put him in danger.

"What?" asked the Princess.

I opened my eyes. I couldn't let *her* be in danger, either. I made up my mind.

"We're going to Texas," I told her. "We're going home."

19

KRISTINA

I WATCHED open-mouthed as the landscape changed. I'd been blown away by Arizona with its vivid orange rock and sweltering heat, so different to Lakovia. But Texas was different *again*. Texas was huge, rolling plains and a sky so big it took my breath away. We drove all day and I watched the odometer count up: miles and then tens of miles and then hundreds of miles and we were *still in Texas*. Lakovia is not a big country. My whole sense of scale was being redefined. *Even Garrett probably seems small in this place.*

I stole a quick glance at him. No. Not even Texas could make him seem small. But he did fit here, more than he had even in California or Arizona. This was his home.

My quick glance was turning into a stare. I knew that behind me, Emerik would be scowling at my obsession. But I couldn't stop. Couldn't tear my eyes from that jawline and those hard lips. My own lips tingled from the imagined feel of brushing his and the feeling spread, kisses tracing over my chin and down my neck. I felt his breath hot on my skin and his stubble scraping against me. Felt the softness of his hair as it twisted between my fingers and the hot shock of his tongue on my nipple—

I was becoming addicted to him. It was more than just the

physical. It was having seen how far he'd go to protect me. I'd been guarded my entire life, but no man had ever made me feel safe like this. And it was the way I felt every time I was close to him. Bring us within six feet and there was this...*craving* I felt down the whole of my body, a need to be pressed up against him, to have his arms around me.

It made no sense. I was meant to be soft and graceful and refined and I'd always assumed that the man I'd fall for, when it happened, would be similar: I imagined him slender and quick, a man who wore an immaculate suit and knew how to dance. But my soul-deep yearning was for the exact opposite: for thick, sculpted forearms that crushed me to a hard chest, for a stubbled chin that rested against the top of my head, for thighs and ass that were all about brute power. I was soft but I wanted grit. I was pure, but I wanted—I flushed—to be pinned and spread by that muscled body.

I pressed my thighs hard together looked away. But as soon as my eyes left him, I could feel his eyes on me. Gliding down over my cheek, my neck. Over the thin cotton vest top I'd stripped down to, caressing my bare shoulders, smoothing over my breasts as if with big, warm palms. I actually felt my nipples pucker and tighten. Being this close was torture.

I forced myself to focus on the landscape. He was right: the sunsets here *were* amazing. The sinking sun turned the clouds from gold to amber to deep, boiling red, until it looked as if the sky was lit by glowing coals. Just then, I saw my first enormous herd of cattle in the distance, and got my first glimpse of cowboys on horses herding them, just tiny silhouettes against the glow of the sun. I drew in my breath and watched, transfixed. I tried to imagine their lives: riding under that massive sky, the quiet around them, the solitude. Compared to the bustle of the palace and the city—"They look so... free," I breathed. Then I blushed. "That probably sounds really stupid."

I heard the jingle of his dog tags as he shook his head. That deep rumble, gentle and sincere. "Nope. Don't sound stupid at all."

When we turned off the highway, I felt his mood start to change.

Those powerful shoulders rose with tension and his whole body hunched over the steering wheel. What was it about this place that freaked him out? Wasn't this his home?

We turned into a long driveway, rounded a corner screened by trees and suddenly screeched to a stop. Everyone *oof*ed against their seatbelts. The hood of the pickup was an inch from a closed gate.

Garrett got out, opened the gate and climbed back in. "Sorry," he muttered as we drove through. "That wasn't there, last time I was here."

"How long has it been?" I asked.

He was silent for a moment. "Two years."

A farmhouse came into view ahead, old but still beautiful, with walls the color of buttermilk and an eggshell-blue roof. A man was walking towards us across the grass, thick curls of white hair visible under his Stetson. At first, he wore a frown. Then, as he saw Garrett, his eyes widened.

Garrett pulled up and switched off the engine. The sudden silence was deafening. He climbed out and walked slowly towards the older man.

I leaned forward, entranced. The man was just as tall as Garrett, his body loaded with muscle despite his age, and he still had that ramrod-straight, military posture. He had the same heavy jaw and hard cheekbones as his son, but his skin was weathered by a life outdoors and crinkled by smile lines. *I'm getting a look at what Garrett will look like, when we grow old together.* And it was good.

Then I realized what I was thinking and crushed those thoughts down inside. *Stupid!* My only future was back in Lakovia. I'd be back there within days... or I wouldn't live that long.

As the two men drew closer, Garrett walked slower and slower, almost trailing the toes of his boots on the ground like a reluctant child. That fear had reached its peak: *this* is what he was scared of.

"Hi Dad," he grunted.

20

GARRETT

It got harder to move forward the closer we got. Two years of shame and guilt heaved me back. *Just get in the pickup and go!*

But if I did that, she was dead.

I lifted a boot that felt like it weighed a million pounds. Took a hesitant step towards him. But I couldn't take another. There was so much on that craggy face: shock and sadness and hope and pity. *I don't want your pity.*

And then I didn't need to walk any further because *he* took two big steps forward and crushed me in a hug. Being hugged by my dad is like being grappled by a bear, big and warm and strong and you ain't getting out of it. I took a deep, shaky sigh, closed my eyes and relaxed into it. And for a moment, at least, everything was okay.

When he finally decided to let me go, I looked towards the car. The Princess quickly jumped out, followed by everyone else. "This is Princess Kristina of Lakovia," I told him. "And her maid and her guards. We need your help."

Dad looked me in the eye just once to check I wasn't yanking his chain. I gave him a solemn nod.

"Well, I'll be," muttered dad. And then he turned to the Princess and, despite being a Jarhead, ground-pounding hayseed himself, he whipped off his hat and did a very good approximation of a bow.

Dad still ran the place with the same military discipline and attention to detail he had when I was a kid. Probably what had kept him going since mom died. He got the others settled in the living room and then took me into the hallway so we could talk.

"Always figured you'd show up one day with a girl," he said. "Never figured it'd be a princess."

"It's not like that." I felt my neck go hot. "I'm just protecting her until I can get her home." And I filled him in on everything: the plane, the highway, the motel, Silvas Lukin and his special ops team. "I'm way out of my depth here. This is some sort of conspiracy. I'm just a grunt."

"Grunts are the ones who win the war," said Dad. "Always have been." He took me over to the gun locker, unlocked it and swung the doors wide. "How much trouble you figure we're in?"

I gazed at the wide array of guns and then took out an assault rifle, just like the one I'd used in the marines.

Dad stared at me. "That much, huh?" He took a pump-action shotgun for himself.

"We've got another problem," I said, and told him about the traitor in our group. "I think it's Jakov. His folks are from Garmania."

Dad gave me a look. "I didn't raise you to think bad of someone on account of where they're from."

"I know. But it's the only explanation that makes sense. Can you help me watch him?"

"He can take tonight's guard shift with me. You can go with the one with the stick up his ass... Emerik."

I let out a breath I didn't realize I'd been holding. Ever since this started, I'd been trying to do this on my own. Having someone to share the burden with felt amazing. But my stomach still knotted when I thought about the danger I was putting him in. "We need to be careful. These guys are trained killers. They came all the way to America to kill her."

"Well...." Dad racked the slide on his shotgun. "They come to Texas, they're going to find out they made a mistake."

I had to smile at that. I laid a hand on his shoulder. "I'm sorry for bringing this to your door."

He scowled at me. "Son, if I'd heard you'd had this kind of problem and you *hadn't* stopped in here, I'da whupped your ass." He looked at me for a long time. "Sure is good to see you."

And suddenly all the tension between us was back. I wanted to explain why I'd been away so long. I wanted him to know I hadn't abandoned him. I just hadn't been able to face him, after getting discharged. I'd felt like a damn failure. And then the flashbacks, and being unable to hold down a job. How could I explain all that? *He'd* managed a whole career in the marines without ever suffering PTSD or anything like it.

After dinner. I'd talk to him after dinner. For now, I just nodded. "You too, dad."

Dinner was steak the way it should be, a slab that fell thick and heavy to your plate, charred lines crispy and tangy on the outside, the meat juicy, pink and full of flavor on the inside. Nestled up against a mountain of creamy mashed potatoes and the whole thing drowned in rich gravy. The Princess's eyes widened as her plate was set before her, but she proceeded to devour the whole thing. "Don't they feed you, where you come from?" asked Dad.

"Not like *this!* It's amazing, thank you!" She looked at me. "You may have to roll me home." It was strange, hearing the smooth glass of her accent in the farmhouse I'd grown up in, where everything is rough-edged and functional. It didn't fit... and yet, in some ways, it felt right at home.

My dad chatted with the Princess as easily as if she was some long-lost daughter, telling her about the ranch and what I was like growing up. It was relaxed and...you know, *warm*, like any family meal. But it made the Princess grin and her eyes go bright with wonder...almost as if she didn't have that warmth, back in Lakovia.

Since Dad and I had cooked, the Princess insisted on washing up, despite our protests. She roped Jakov, Emerik and Caroline in to help and they formed a production line. Dad and I leaned against the door frame and peeked in.

The Princess rolled up her sleeves, filled a bowl with hot water... and then carefully read the instructions on the back of the dish soap. It hit me that she'd never washed dishes before. Not once. She'd only ever seen people do it in commercials. But she was trying. She'd been attacked, shot at, sucked out of a plane, she'd endured hundreds of miles in a pickup truck... anyone else would have curled up into a ball and cried, or flounced off to her room and treated us like servants. But she was still going and still treating us like equals. *That's what makes her a princess.*

I felt that swell again in my chest, that feeling like a flag being caught by the wind. She was someone I'd follow into battle. "We can't let anything happen to her," I mumbled, my throat tight with emotion.

When I glanced at my dad, he was giving me the same look he'd given me back in high school, when I'd told him about Katie Wagner in my math class.

"It ain't like that," I told him, pulling him away from the kitchen so they wouldn't hear us.

"The hell it ain't. I saw the way you were looking at her. Saw the way she was looking at *you.*"

I flushed right down the back of my neck. "I'm not the sort of guy she should be with. She's *royalty.*"

"Maybe you should trust her to judge for herself."

"She doesn't know enough about me to judge! If she knew—"

Dad crossed his arms and waited.

I wanted to tell him. I wanted to tell him about the desert and

Baker and Felton and Martinez and Drummond. I wanted to tell him about the guilt. I wanted to tell him about the flashbacks and ask if he'd ever had anything like that. But I couldn't. He was my dad. I wanted him to be proud of me.

So I walked away.

He'd kept my old room, hoping I'd come back. Even my damn framed football jersey was still hanging on the wall. I'd been a linebacker in high school. That whole small-town life came flooding back to me: harvest time and the state fair and trips to Gold Lake to see the rodeo. Good times. And so utterly different to what her childhood must have been like. Where do princesses go to school? Some place in Switzerland surrounded by the children of presidents and sheikhs?

We had nothing in common. Dad was wrong.

A wave of guilt hit me as soon as I thought of him. I had to talk to him. Hell, if I couldn't tell him what happened in the desert, I at least had to tell him I loved him. But talking's not my strong point. *Tomorrow. First thing.*

We'd agreed over dinner that he and Jakov would take the first watch and Emerik and me the second. I'd barely slept in three days: a few hours on the plane, then a couple of hours at the motel the night before. I changed the dressing on the wound on my leg, then flopped onto my bed and immediately fell into a troubled sleep. I woke up still feeling sand scouring my face and smelling blood on the wind.

I stumbled out into the darkened hallway. Jakov was standing right in front of the Princess's door, so motionless that he looked like a huge granite statue. Only his eyes moved, scanning the hallway constantly. He gave me a cheerful grin when he saw me and it made my stomach knot. He still had no idea I suspected him.

My dad clapped me on the shoulder and then, as Jakov wandered off to bed, he nodded towards him and shook his head. He hadn't seen him do anything suspicious. Was I wrong? Or was Jakov just biding his time?

Emerik arrived. His suit was as immaculate as always, his shirt gleaming in the darkness. *Does he sleep in that thing?* We settled in for our shift. This time, though, I couldn't resist silently cracking open the door and checking on the Princess. She was sleeping peacefully, chestnut hair trailing down over the edge of the bed, one arm thrown up over her head.

When I turned back to Emerik, he was scowling at me. He'd been a lot less of a pain in the ass, since we'd had our run-in at the diner. But whenever he saw me looking at her, he went right back to hating me. I sighed and looked away.

Then, in the darkness, I heard, "I only want to protect her."

I turned that over in my mind. Thought about how attached to her he must have gotten, guarding her since she was a child. I softened towards him a little more. "I'd never hurt her," I muttered.

"That's not what I mean."

I felt my shoulders rise defensively. I was glad of the darkness because I could feel my damn neck going red. "Yeah, well don't worry. I know my place."

"It's not that simple," said Emerik. "I think her highness has feelings for *you*."

I tried to let nothing show. But inside, I could feel my heart slamming in my chest like I was some kid in high school being told the head cheerleader was sweet on him. Even though I knew nothing could ever happen. I grunted. I was going to leave it at that, but I didn't like the way he was babying her. She was the smartest, bravest woman I'd ever known: why did he think she needed him watching out for her? "Even if that's true, I figure she can make her own decisions," I muttered.

Emerik gave a frustrated sigh. "Don't you understand? She's a princess! Unmarried!"

"I know what she is."

He was getting more and more worked up. "Lakovia is a deeply traditional country. A princess, until she's married, remains...." He'd gone red. "You know...."

I just looked at him blankly.

He waved his hand at me, exasperated. "You're treading on unbroken snow."

I opened my mouth to tell him I had no idea what he was talking about.

And that's when I heard her scream.

21

KRISTINA

Blind panic.

I was alone in thick, suffocating darkness, my fingernails cracking and splintering as I clawed at the rough wood of the door. If I focused hard enough, strained my eyes, maybe they'd adjust. Maybe I'd at least be able to see *something*. But there was no light at all in this place. Nothing except rough wood and cold stone. I was gasping, hyperventilating—

And then there was something warm. Big hands, cupping my shoulders. A voice that didn't belong to *them,* low and rough and yet sweet like honey. A voice I recognized. "Your Highness!"

But the fear had me. I was a scared girl locked in a tiny room—

"Kristina!"

My eyes opened. The lights were off, but after the darkness of the nightmare, the moonlight streaming in through the window made it seem like noon. It silhouetted Garrett as he hunkered down over my bed, his chest only a foot from mine, his lips inches away.

"Nightmare," he told me. But he didn't say *it was only a nightmare,* like my mother would have. He said it with the sympathy of someone who knew their power. He said it with his voice choked with anger and worry at what I was going through.

And suddenly I was clinging to him, my arms wrapped around him, my body pressed to his. My back was up off the bed and I hung from him, but he took my weight easily, not budging even an inch. He just pressed his stubbled cheek to my neck and held me tight.

But even he couldn't change the past and the memories were still owning me, wrapping around me like tendrils and tugging me down into the darkness. It *wasn't* okay because *it really happened, it could happen again oh God, if we go to war, it could happen again*— I could still feel the horrific closeness of the stone walls around me and it made me want to scream. I was panting, sweating, breathing so hard I was barely aware of the tears running down my cheeks.

My body was tight against him, but it wasn't sexual: this was far beyond that. I needed *him*. I just knew, on a gut level, that he was the one person who could protect me. And he was the one person who'd understand what fear like this was like. He'd understand that I was so scared I couldn't move or speak. He'd understand that he had to get me out of it because I couldn't on my own.

And he did.

Those big hands scooped me up and cradled me like a child and then we were walking through the bedroom door and out into the hallway. I heard someone step aside—Emerik? —but Garrett ignored him, just kept walking, carrying me as if I weighed nothing. Down the stairs. Out of the back door and into....

I drew in my breath as the cool night air hit us. I was soaked in sweat, the thin nightgown plastered to my body, and it should have felt freezing. But just being in the open air, able to breathe again, felt *so good*. And he didn't allow me to become cold: his thick biceps pressed into me and his strong chest was like a warm wall against me. It was better, but I still couldn't stop panting, couldn't shake the fear's grip.

I could hear the scrunch of him plodding through the grass. I knew the wound on his leg must be hurting him, but his stride never faltered. We passed a big building to one side: a barn? And then we came to a long, low building. No lights were on inside. Where was he taking me?

He shifted me to one arm while he opened the door, then carried me inside. "I know what you need," he muttered, and took me further into the gloom.

He gently let me down and I felt straw under my bare feet, scratchy and soft. In the moonlight I could just make out a big, rounded shape in front of us. *What's... Where's he brought me?*

He took my hand in his and guided it. My palm touched soft hair and then a solid, warm body. A body that shifted under my touch. And then I heard it snort and toss its head.

Horses.

22

GARRETT

I DIDN'T KNOW if it would work. I was going off gut instinct and what worked for me.

After the desert, when I'd come back here for a spell, I'd found the horses were better than a thousand therapists. I only had to lay my hand on one and the pain and anger seemed to drop back a little inside me.

And I could feel it working for her, too. I still had my body pressed against hers from behind because I wasn't sure how steady she was on her feet. I could feel the tension in her muscles slowly ease as she calmed. I didn't say anything. Sometimes, nothing's all that needs to be said.

I put my hand between her shoulder blades and felt her breathing slow. But it was still too early to talk about it. She needed to get well clear of the fear, so it didn't grab her again. So I said, "Always did prefer horses to people. Most folk, anyway. Horses don't need you to talk to them."

She turned a little, laid her cheek on the horse's back and let out a long sigh. She reached up along his neck and scratched him just right, just where they really like it, and he gave a little snort of pleasure. "Horses are loyal," she told me. Her voice was still shaky, but it was getting stronger. "They'll never stab you in the back, or manipulate you, or cut you up in the press."

I frowned. It felt like she knew horses, but how could that be? Horses, in my mind, were for country folks. Rich folks don't like getting their hands dirty. And royalty: didn't they just go from air-conditioned jet to air-conditioned limo?

She glanced up and caught my look. "I love horses," she said softly. "I used to ride, until my mother said it was too undignified."

Well, I'll be. Maybe we did have something in common.

She looked up at me, her cheek still pressed to the horse's back. "Thank you," she said. "I feel better."

And then suddenly she wouldn't meet my eyes. I knew that feeling, the shame that follows a flashback or a nightmare. She was feeling exactly like I did after I froze in the motel. "Hey," I told her, taking that delicate chin in my hand and turning her to look at me. "You don't have to be embarrassed." She looked doubtful, then tried to turn away again. "Look, you already figured out... I got some of that stuff in my head too. From the war."

When I said the last word, she looked right at me, eyes huge and liquid.

Aw, hell. I'd known that was a rough time for her country but I'd imagined she'd been protected, locked away in a palace miles from the front. "Something happened to you, didn't it? In the war with Garmania?"

She gave a jerky nod.

Before I knew it, my hands were on her shoulders, pulling her trembling body against mine. Her breasts were pressed against my chest and that soaked, filmy nightdress might as well have been tissue paper. But it wasn't about wanting her, right then. It was about something deeper, truer. It was about letting her know she was safe, now.

I cursed whoever had hurt her. I wanted to run off and find them and tear every one of them apart with guns and knives and my bare hands. I was *good* at that stuff.

But it wasn't that easy. She didn't need a soldier.

What she needed was something I wasn't any good at. But if I wanted to help her, I had to do it anyway. I pressed my chin into the top of her head. "You want to talk about it?"

I felt her nod. Then, "But I need to be outside. This place is too dark. Too small." She hesitated. "But it's going to be too cold out there. And I don't want to be back in the house, where people will hear."

I rubbed my hands over her shoulders. "I know a place."

I took her by the hand and led her out across the field to the barn. Held the ladder for her while she climbed up into the hayloft. It was mostly empty, a cavernous space, but sheltered from the wind. Moonlight trickled in through a million little gaps and chinks between the wooden boards and tiles. She looked around in wonder and then nodded. *Perfect.*

I sat down with my back against a hay bale. She came and sat between my legs, her back against my chest.

And she told me what happened in the war.

23
_____

KRISTINA

MY MIND COULDN'T GO THERE, at first. Even with Garrett's comforting
warmth against my back, even with the pinpricks of starlight shining
in through the cracks in the roof, reminding me that I was above
ground. I had to work up to it.

"There was a time when I loved being a princess," I said. "I mean,
every little girl wants to be a princess. Can you imagine actually
living in a palace? The *dresses?* It was wonderful. Magical. As I got
older, it got harder. Being a teenager's rough anyway, but when the
press are analyzing *every little thing you do:* have you gained weight,
have you lost weight, is your make-up perfect, have you kissed a
boy....my mother protected me from the worst of it but she couldn't
stop it completely. And I still got hate mail. Do you know what it's
like, at fourteen, to get a tweet saying you're a disgusting whore and
you should just fucking die? And the fan mail, some of that was even
worse. Men two, three times my age who started off saying I was
pretty, but then they'd get into...." I shuddered. Garrett wrapped his
arms around me, his biceps going hard against me in his rage.

"The war started when I was eighteen. We knew Garmania's new
president was a hard-liner, but we never expected them to invade. It
just all happened so fast: troops swarmed across our borders, tanks

rolled into our cities. Then the shelling started. At first we assumed other countries would do something. I remember my father making phone calls all through the night, talking to the UN. To Britain. France. But they didn't want to get caught up in a foreign war. Then he called *your* president, begging. But he was told *no.*"

Garrett didn't say anything but I could feel the wave of shame that rippled through him. I didn't blame him, or the US. Even the countries closest to us hadn't wanted to get involved.

"By the time we managed to counterattack, Garmania had already taken a huge portion of our country. Our army was more powerful but theirs was dug in, now. They couldn't move forward, but we couldn't move them back. It turned into a brutal, messy war. Towns captured and occupied. Hospitals running out of medical supplies, people starving. After nearly a year, it was still going on. We'd gone from being a rich country to one where people were sleeping in the rubble and washing in the water from broken pipes. In the cities further away from the front, people were trying to live their lives as normal: go to work, go to school... but every night there'd be air raids, apartment blocks just... *gone,* hundreds of people just wiped from the face of the earth. You can't live like that. No one can."

I sighed. "I was working at a refugee center. Miles from the front, my parents figured it was safe and there was no way I was staying in the palace when our people were dying. But then soldiers broke through our lines and by the time we got the warning they were *there,* kicking down the door. A few of us managed to hide in a storeroom. But I could hear them rounding people up. Telling them to stand up against a wall and—" I swallowed. "I heard the gunshots. I heard the first bodies fall to the floor. They were going to wipe everyone out. Unless—"

I closed my eyes.

"Unless I gave them something better," I said.

I was back there. I saw myself open the storeroom door, the woman who'd been hiding with me grabbing at my sleeve, trying to pull me back. I could feel the cracked linoleum under my feet as I walked along the hallway, trying to stop my legs from shaking. I was repeating, over and over in my head, something my father had taught me when I was very young. *Being royal isn't about doing what you want. It's about doing what your people need.*

The soldiers couldn't hear me approaching. They were already raising their guns to execute the next batch. I had to call out to get their attention. Then I flinched as all the guns swung round to point at me. I put my hands in the air and told them who I was.

They didn't believe me at first. I'd been helping in the kitchens and I was dressed in an apron. But then the officer in charge took a closer look at me, cursed and got on the radio. It worked: they were far too busy talking about capturing me and the promotions they'd get to worry about the remaining civilians.

They pushed me into a chair to wait. I was hoping—praying—that our army would reach us in time. I knew they must be on their way. And then, through the window, I saw distant black dots in the sky. Helicopters, racing towards us. *Yes!*

But there was something wrong. The noise was too loud for them to still be that far away. I twisted around....

A Garmanian helicopter was landing, right outside the refugee center. My whole body went cold, my stomach a tight, hard knot. I was marched outside. I tried to delay, to stumble and trip, but they knew they had to hurry and they all but carried me to the helicopter. I was strapped in. The helicopter lifted off just as our helicopters arrived.

The last thing I saw of my country was the horrified face of one of our pilots. He was hovering just fifty feet away, but he couldn't fire, not with me on board. And then we were racing away towards Garmania.

They wanted to use me as a bargaining chip. But it wasn't enough for me to just sit in a cell. They wanted me to suffer and they didn't want anyone to know where I was, to avoid my father mounting a rescue mission. So I was taken to what I later learned was an ancient, abandoned prison, over three hundred years old. It had been built up and up over the years and I was led down into the very depths of it, where the steps changed from concrete to stone, and then to stone worn smooth through centuries of use. We were well below ground: no windows and no light, except for flashlights.

Finally, the stairs stopped and there was a silence like I'd never known, a kind of pressure in your ears from it being so quiet. I was led along a hallway and we came to a door. I'm not tall, but even for me, the top of the door was only at eye level. People were smaller, hundreds of years ago.

The soldiers opened the door. The room inside was just bare rock: it hadn't been built, it had been carved out. The space was about the size and shape of a bathroom on a plane, but with a ceiling that meant you had to stoop.

They nodded me inside.

"No," I said stupidly. "No, I—Not in *there!*" I was trying to be brave, but my voice cracked on the last word. It was the lack of windows. There wasn't even a window in the door. The idea of being shut in there, trapped—

They pushed me inside.

I was still catching myself on the back wall, the rock scraping my palms, when the door slammed closed and the key turned. Immediately, I was in almost total darkness. There was a hair-thin slit of light at the bottom of the door and a tiny circle of light coming from the keyhole. Both were faint and growing fainter as the soldiers moved away with their flashlights. "No!" I yelled with rising panic. "No! Don't!" I shoved my face against the door and put my eye against the keyhole, but already, I could barely make them out: they were nearly to the end of the hallway and there was another door there. "*DON'T!*"

They closed the door. And the darkness was suddenly total. I couldn't see where the keyhole was, or detect anything under the door. Just... black.

I strained my ears, trying to hear over the sound of my own frantic breath. I could just make out their boots, walking away. I was beyond being brave, now, beyond pride. "*Don't leave me here!*" I screamed. "*Please!*"

And then there was silence.

24

KRISTINA

I HAD no way to measure time. There was no night and no day, no change in the temperature. I had to go on hunger and how many times I'd slept. Based on that, they left me for forty-eight hours, the first time.

By then, I'd been through every possible emotion. I'd cried, I'd cursed, I'd beaten on the wooden door with my fists. I'd fallen asleep and woken thinking it was all a nightmare, then tried to struggle out of bed and felt only damp rock under my hands.

I didn't realize the significance of the walls being wet. Not then.

I'd learned every inch of my cell. The ceiling was low enough that I couldn't stand up. The length was just too short for me to sit with my legs outstretched, but too narrow for me to sit cross-legged. The floor was as rough-hewn as the walls, lumpy and jagged: there was no way to comfortably lie, even curled up. When I slept, it was through pure exhaustion.

When I heard someone coming, I thought I might be hallucinating it. So many times, I'd convinced myself I heard helicopters, or footsteps hurrying to rescue me. But this was real: two sets of boots approaching. Just to hear something other than my own breathing and sobbing was glorious. And then I saw their flashlights under the door: only a faint glimmer but my eyes were straining so hard, it was blinding. The door opened and I staggered forward, convinced I was being rescued.

It was the same two Garmanian soldiers. But at least I was being taken somewhere else. Maybe my father had negotiated for my release. Maybe the war was over—

They shoved me back in.

Something metal clanged on the floor. Something else was tossed into the corner. Then the door shut and locked again. I was so frantic not to be locked in there again, I forgot about the height of the cell and cracked my head against it as I leapt forward to hammer on the door. I screamed that I'd do anything, but their footsteps kept walking away. I didn't understand. Why would they come all the way down here and just put me back in?

When the precious light and sound had faded away, I crouched down and felt around to see what they'd thrown into my cell. The metal thing was a bucket. There was a plastic bottle of water and four slices of bread.

Realization sank in. This wasn't a temporary thing. They were intending to keep me there for as long as they needed to. Weeks. Months. Years.

For a few hours, my mind refused to accept it. I couldn't believe that they'd treat a human being like this. But they didn't come back. This was real.

My life turned into darkness, broken only by their visits. They seemed to come every three days, leaving just barely enough food and water for me to survive, emptying the bucket and then locking me up again. I tried to reason with them, to befriend them. I spent all my time alone planning what I was going to say to them. But they never spoke, never looked at me with anything other than contempt.

I had no idea how much time passed. I tried to keep track but it was impossible. I couldn't make marks on the wall: I couldn't even *see*. Instead, the things that broke the routine began to stand out. The time I rolled over in the night and crushed the water bottle: half of my water ration squirted over the floor and by the time they came back, I was delirious from dehydration. Or the time a nightmare made me kick over the bucket.

I had no idea what was going on in the outside world. Had it been weeks? Months? What if we'd lost the war and my parents were dead and I was going to be there forever?

Then, one day, the soldiers didn't arrive.

I triple-checked that it had been three days. But I was right, I'd finished off the last of my bread and water the night before. *What if...what if they've forgotten about me?* I'd only ever seen those two soldiers. I knew they'd want to keep my location secret, to make rescue more difficult. How many people even knew I was here?

What if this was it, and I was going to starve to death down here?

The fear was so real, so visceral, that I shut down. I just froze there, on my knees. I'd never felt so utterly alone. Something broke inside me, at that moment. Some vital connection was severed.

The next day, just one of them showed up, stinking of alcohol. As best as I could figure it, they'd gotten drunk the night before and simply not bothered to check on me. It was chilling: I was completely at the mercy of these two men. What if they got ill, or had an accident? What if Lakovia won the war, took the building and shot them, and no one thought to come down into the ancient cells to check for prisoners?

It went on like this for weeks, the visits growing less and less reliable, the soldiers becoming sullen and unshaved.

And then it rained.

I didn't know it was raining, of course. I didn't know that Garmania was experiencing the worst storms for a decade. Or that the ancient prison had been built close to the river, which had burst its banks. I didn't know about the flood water washing three feet deep over the ground outside.

I only knew that the walls went from damp to wet, and then I could actually feel the water moving under my fingertips, every surface coated, a million tiny waterfalls. I couldn't see where it was coming in: tiny cracks in the rock above my head, I presumed, because no matter where I pressed my palms, I couldn't stop it. It started to pool on the floor: the first time I heard my feet splash, I nearly threw up with fear. Then, within minutes, it was creeping *over* my feet.

I threw myself against the door. "*Help!*" I screamed. "*HELP!*"

But there was only silence and blackness. The soldiers weren't even due to visit for another two days. Would they realize the danger? Or were they passed out from drink upstairs? Were they even *here?!* For all I knew, they didn't even stay in the building between visits. They might be twenty miles away, far too far to reach me in time.

The water was up around my knees. I started kicking the door. I know it was futile: I'd tried to break it many times in the first week, before hunger sapped my strength. But there was nothing else to try. I slammed my foot against it again and again but the wood didn't even bend. And then the water was up around my hips and kicking became impossible. "*Help!*" I yelled. "*Please!*"

The water was freezing, making me pant with cold on top of my fear. The ceiling meant I had to bow my head and the water rose horribly fast towards my face. It passed my waist, my breasts...I arched my back and pressed my face to the ceiling, nose and lips scraping against the rock. "*Please!* Oh God, *please!*"

The water washed into my ears. It lapped at my chin and brushed my lips. "*HELP ME!*"

The door opened.

I fell through the doorway, the water rushing over my head and half-drowning me. Hands were on my wrists, pulling me along, and lights were shining in my face. I was hysterical, babbling, begging them not to lock me up in there again. It was only when we got upstairs that I saw the badges on their uniforms and realized they were Lakovian special forces. I was being rescued.

They flew me home. A ceasefire was declared two weeks later and a week after that, the war officially ended. Lakovia had been winning for months. We'd captured one of their command centers and that's what had finally given the military my location.

I'd been imprisoned for five months. Almost half a year of my life.

I went on TV and gave speeches, praising the brave soldiers

who'd rescued me, celebrating our victory, reassuring the people that it was all over. I was okay, I told them, and we should all look to the future.

Except...inside, I *wasn't* okay. Something had broken inside me that went beyond just the nightmares. I'd been alone on some deep, indescribable level. And now, even in a room full of people, I was still alone. And I'd be alone forever.

I finished my story and opened my eyes. Garrett had been silent throughout but his arms, locked around me, had given me the strength to keep talking. I could feel the tension in his body. His pain, at what I'd gone through. I was spent, emotionally exhausted. But telling him had helped. The wounds had been re-opened but maybe they had a chance to heal, now. And however weak I was, there was something I had to tell him.

"I was alone until I met you," I whispered.

And his arms cinched even tighter around me, a steel wall that nothing could penetrate. And we just sat there in the starlight and we knew. We didn't have to say it. We knew how we felt about each other.

And we knew it was the cruelest trick fate could play. The one man who made me feel protected, who made me feel not alone: and it was someone I could never be with. Someone I'd be saying goodbye to within days or hours. The one man I ached for and he'd never kiss me. But at least I could be not alone, just for a little while. I pressed myself back against his chest, letting his warmth soak into me.

"When I heard the assassin's accent on the plane, I couldn't believe it," I said. "I thought it was all over. Now it could all start up again. It's not just about what happened to me. It's my whole country. All those people who died. We can't let it happen again."

I felt him nod. He was sick of war, too.

Something came out, then, that I'd never told anyone. "I told myself, after the war, that I didn't hate them. I told myself we were all the same. I couldn't judge a whole country just by the actions of its leader, or what he ordered his troops to do. I told myself they weren't bad people. But...what if I was wrong?" I twisted around so that I could look into his eyes. "What do you think?"

He looked helplessly back at me. The anger and pain flared bright in his eyes. "I'm just a soldier, Your Highness."

"You're a lot more than that. You've been to war. Did you hate them?"

"I want to say no," he said at last. "Like you said, it's a minority, not the whole country. But I guess I did, at times."

I hung my head. "After I was rescued, in those last few weeks of the war...sometimes, late at night when I was crying in bed...I wanted my father to just launch everything we had at them. Every plane, every missile. I wanted him to *wipe them out*. Does that make me a bad person?"

"No," he said. "That makes you human." He pulled me even tighter to him and for a long time he just held me like that as silent tears rolled down my cheeks.

When he eventually broke the silence, his tone was lighter. "Got a little good news for you. Didn't get a chance to tell you last night, but I got a plan to get you home. There's a guy called Barney, in New York. A pilot. Met him in Iraq, he flew us on missions a whole bunch of times. Anyway, when he came home, he set up a cargo freight business, flying packages from the US to Europe. And...well, not everything he does is completely legit."

Hope was slowly rising in me. "A smuggler?"

"He bends some laws," Garrett allowed. "He'll be able to sneak you onto a plane and make a stop in Lakovia. But we can't risk going to him until we know we've got rid of the traitor. If the assassins get wind of this, they'll just wait for us at Barney's place. Hell, they could shoot the plane down. So we gotta deal with this first, but I *will* get you home."

The last of my tears dried and I nodded. "Thank you," I whispered. But even as I said it, my stomach twisted. Home. Back to Lakovia where I belonged.

Without him.

I decided something, in that moment. If we had to say goodbye soon, there was something I had to do first. I twisted around to look at him again. "You helped me," I whispered. "You saved me. You make me feel not alone. I want to help you. Something happened to you, too, didn't it? Something you can't forget."

He looked away.

"Tell me," I begged. "Let me try and help."

He still wouldn't look at me. "Don't deserve that," he mumbled.

"You're a *good man!*"

"Your Highness," he said tightly. "You don't know what I am."

"Then *tell me!*"

He finally looked at me. I could see the indecision on his face but this was more open than I'd ever seen him. "*Please,* Garrett!"

He opened his mouth to speak. And froze, listening. "Do you hear that?" he asked.

I listened. I *did* hear it. A sound I'd heard before, in the war, but it made no sense *here*. It was a whistle, rapidly descending through the scale. We stared at each other, eyes widening.

The sound of incoming artillery, falling through the air straight towards us.

25

GARRETT

FOR A SECOND, I thought I was having a flashback. That made more sense than incoming artillery *here, now,* in Texas. But the Princess could hear it too. She'd grabbed hold of my shirt in both fists, terrified. I didn't know how, but war had found us both again, and it was going to steal her from me—

I grabbed her and threw her down in the hay, then covered her body with mine. The whistle became a scream. I braced myself and closed my eyes—

The round hit the roof right above our heads but there was no explosion. Just a dull *whump. What the hell?* I rolled over and looked up.

The cracks in the roof had turned a blinding white, so bright it hurt to look. As I watched, something fell through one of the cracks. No, not fell: *dripped,* each drop trailing fire.

It landed in the hay and erupted into flames. More drips were falling all around us. The Princess rolled out of the way, breathless, as one of them just missed her. Fires were starting everywhere. "*What is it?!*"

Another long whistle. Another *whump* above us, then another.

"Some sort of incendiary rounds." The roof of the barn was on fire, above us, and the hay in the hayloft was going up fast. "Come on!"

I grabbed her hand and ran with her to the ladder, then pushed her down ahead of me. By the time we were down, the hayloft was a roaring inferno. And now the lower level was starting to catch. The ceiling above us wouldn't hold for long: everything was tinder-dry, this time of year, and the barn was old and rickety. We only had minutes.

We raced towards the door...and stumbled to a stop as we saw the scene outside.

The incendiary rounds were barely visible, black against the night sky as they fell in long arcs from somewhere near the road. But wherever they hit, they exploded in a blinding flash, long trails of flaming liquid spraying out to start countless new fires. It wasn't just the barn they were aiming at. The fields were on fire in several places and every few seconds another fire would erupt. They were tracking back and forth across our ranch, making sure they hit everything.

Out by the side of the road, the assassins had a mortar. Just a simple metal tube, like something you'd launch fireworks from, but absolutely devastating in the wrong hands. One guy would be kneeling beside it, dropping in a round every few seconds, and another one would be watching the ranch with binoculars, helping him adjust the aim.

The ceiling creaked. We had to get out of there *now*. I grabbed the Princess's hand and ran through the door—

There was a feeling. Call it the ground pounder's instinct, the one you get from being cannon fodder for so many years. I hurled myself down, pulling the Princess down too—

A bullet hissed over my head, so close I could feel its heat.

We hit the ground and I grabbed her and dragged her back inside the blazing barn. "Sniper," I panted. Suddenly, I understood the assassin's plan. There was a third guy out there with a rifle. They were smart. They knew we'd have guns, on a Texas ranch. So instead of storming the house, they were going to burn all the buildings and shoot us as the fire forced us outside.

We stared at each other, panting in fear. The air was scorching our lungs, now, and even with the open door the barn was filling up with choking clouds of smoke. *"What do we do?"* coughed the Princess.

There was a creak and then a splintering crash: something falling, up in the hayloft. I shoved the Princess away from me, then fell back the other way. A roof timber crashed through the ceiling and slammed into the floor with a ground-shaking thud, right where we'd been standing. Liquid fire rained down all around it and the Princess screamed as her nightdress burst into flames.

I was on her in seconds, slapping at the flames with my hands. She tried to grab my wrists to stop me but I knocked her hands out of the way and smothered the flames, flattening my palms over her stomach even though it made me wince. Then I grabbed hold of her nightdress and hauled it up, baring her. The pale skin of her stomach was flawless, untouched. *Thank God.* She took hold of my wrists, looking at my burned palms but I shook my head. *I'm fine.*

There was a creak above us, loud enough to drown out the roaring flames. It went on and on: the building's death rattle. Now that one of the big roof timbers was gone, the whole place was collapsing in on itself. The air singed the little hairs in my nose and scorched my throat. "We can't stay here," I rasped between coughs. "How fast can you run?"

She followed my gaze to the door. I saw her go pale as she realized what I was suggesting. "Quite fast," she said weakly.

"You gotta run faster than that. Faster than you've ever run in your life. And you gotta run *random*, not in a straight line."

She shook her head. "No." There was real fear on her face: she'd probably seen snipers at work in the war. She knew what they could do. "I can't!"

There was another creak from above. Another timber fell, and liquid fire trickled down after it. I could hear the whole building moving, now, boards cracking and splintering as they bore loads they were never meant to. We had *seconds*. "It's sixty yards to the house.

You can sprint that in ten seconds. He'll have time for maybe three shots. We can do it."

She shook her head, terrified.

I took her face between my hands. God, she was so beautiful. So special. "You can do this," I told her. "I know how brave you are. And you're not alone anymore."

She stared back at me...and nodded. I took her hand.

The barn creaked...and this time, the noise didn't stop. I didn't dare look up.

"One," I said, bending my legs. "Two. *Three!*"

We ran.

The night air was shockingly cold after the fire, like jumping into a lake. And the night was black, after the blinding brightness of the fire: the only light was from the blooms of fire as mortar rounds hit the fields around us. We ran flat out, legs pumping, lungs heaving, and we covered ground fast. For a glorious few seconds, I thought maybe I'd been wrong. Maybe the sniper wasn't watching, maybe he'd changed position—

There was a tug on my shirt as a bullet passed through the flapping fabric. I cut left for two steps, then right—

The Princess screamed. I looked at her in panic: was she hit? But she was still running: the bullet had just passed so close, she'd heard it. Twenty yards to the house. I jinked right, then left. Ten yards—

The bullet was meant for her but it passed between us, clipping my left thigh. I grunted and sprawled on my face, my leg exploding into pain. My hand was torn from hers and she ran on a few steps...then slowed.

"*No!*" I yelled. "Keep going!" I was scrambling to my feet but my leg didn't want to cooperate. "Keep going!"

She was nearly safe. But she turned and ran back to me.

I imagined the sniper lining up his next shot. But before I could stop her, she'd hauled my arm over her shoulder and was helping me heave myself to my feet. I couldn't speak: I was too scared for her, too focused on the bullet I knew was coming—

It hit the ground an inch from her right foot. We stumbled the last few yards....

And then we were hidden by the house. We fell heavily against its wall, panting. I wanted to kiss her. I wanted to kill her for putting herself at risk for me. In the end, I just said, "Thank you."

I felt my leg, wincing. The bullet had just clipped the flesh: it would slow me down, but it would be okay as long as I got a dressing on it.

There was a subtle change in the whistle of the mortar rounds. I glimpsed one arcing overhead, followed it down....

It hit the roof of the house and erupted into flames. I froze, staring up at it in horror. A few seconds later, another one hit the end wall. Flaming liquid bathed the house from roof to ground and the flames roared as they took hold. *Oh Jesus...Dad is in there!* I took a step towards the door, then stopped.

I couldn't leave her alone. But I couldn't leave them to die in there.

I turned to the Princess. "Stay here," I ordered. "Stay right here! I have to help them." Then I remembered Jakov. *Shit!* This might all be part of the plan: the assassins attack and their man on the inside kills her while everyone's looking outward. "If you see Jakov, don't trust him!" I told her. "Don't let him near you!"

She nodded.

And I ran.

26

KRISTINA

HE RAN TO THE DOOR, stumbling a little each time he put his weight on his wounded leg. Then he was inside, the screen door swinging closed behind him. Another mortar round hit the house and I heard one of the upstairs windows shatter as another room erupted into flames. *No!*

I looked around me, tears flooding my eyes. It looked like hell had come to the ranch. The barn was just a seething mass of flame, only a few skeletal timbers still standing. The fields were rolling seas of orange. Even the trees were burning. Now the Buchanan's family home was on fire. *And this is all my fault. I brought this down on them!*

Another mortar round flew overhead, but this one didn't hit the house. It went further, arcing down to hit a distant building that had been unscathed until now. Flaming liquid spread along the roof, letting me see the shape of it. Long and low. The stables.

A sound carried on the wind: snorts and desperate hooves, whinnies of fear. My chest contracted. *Oh my God: the horses!*

The stables was in the lee of the house, hidden from the sniper. I looked once towards the house, remembering Garrett's order to stay put....

And then I ran.

27

GARRETT

I burst into the house. Down on the first floor, everything looked almost normal. But I could hear the roar of flames from upstairs and white smoke was billowing down the stairs. I pounded up them, gritting my teeth at the pain in my leg. "Dad!"

No reply. The second floor was filling up with smoke, lit up orange by the flames. One whole end of the house was ablaze and it was spreading fast. Worse, the whole roof was creaking and once it came down, nowhere would be safe. "*Dad!*"

I heard a curse from one of the bedrooms, then he stumbled into me, coughing. Both of us bent over, trying to suck in the cleaner air down near the floor. "Princess safe?" he managed between coughs.

I nodded.

"Jakov...not in room," he croaked, nodding at the room he'd come from.

Shit. I'd have to worry about that later. First, I had to get everyone out. I stumbled forward, hunched low, trying to see through the smoke. This was worse than the barn: the smoke couldn't escape and we were upstairs, where it was concentrated. "Emerik!" I yelled.

The first roof timber fell, slamming into the floor a few feet in front of us. Flames spread outward and the floor bowed and creaked worryingly under its weight. "Emerik! Where are you?"

He emerged out of the smoke on the far side of the fallen timber, a limp, blonde-haired bundle in his arms. *Caroline!* She wasn't moving. Unconscious, or...*God, no.*

Emerik looked to be in a bad way, wheezing and choking, but he marched on determinedly. He was halfway to us when the timber crashed through the floor leaving a splintered hole ten feet wide. I pointed him towards the back of the house. "Go around!"

Dad and I circled around to meet him. That meant going through the worst of the fire and it was an inferno, flames creeping up the walls and meeting in the ceiling. Framed photos on the walls made popping noises as their glass shattered and the precious pictures inside curled and blackened. My mom's needlework poem about *Home* was on fire, dripping hunks of burning thread as it was consumed. We went past my mom and dad's room and I saw his medal case fall from the wall. Our whole history was being destroyed. *Those bastards!*

I was worried Emerik wouldn't make it but when we reached the landing he was there, coughing and choking but still clutching Caroline. His beloved suit was charred and smoking from where he'd protected her from the flames. He might be uptight but he was a brave son of a bitch when it counted.

We started down the stairs. We were on the third step when the staircase gave way in front of us. *Shit!* It was really bad, now: the air was filled with embers and it was so hot, it felt like we were breathing the fire itself. More timbers were falling from the roof. The whole house was collapsing and we were trapped upstairs.

Dad was coughing too badly to speak but he pulled me over to a window and hauled it open. We were just above the rear porch. He pushed me out first and I helped Emerik get Caroline down to the porch. Then I climbed down to the ground and he passed her down to me. "Dad!" I yelled, looking back at the blazing house.

He barely made it out in time. Tiles and flaming boards were falling from the roof, raining down around him as his ass hit the porch. He didn't waste time trying to climb, just slid off the roof and tumbled to the floor. I grabbed him and hauled him to his feet. "Dad?"

He was fine. A rush of relief went through me. If anything had happened to him....

Emerik was kneeling over Caroline. The fresh air had brought her around and she seemed to be okay. But—

"Where's the Princess?" I asked, panic rising in my chest.

Everyone looked around but there was no one in sight. Emerik clambered to his feet. "I'll help you look," he wheezed. Then he started coughing and couldn't stop. He'd inhaled a lot more smoke than the rest of us, saving Caroline.

"You stay here," I told him. "You did good." I looked at Dad. "There's a sniper, somewhere in the trees, that way." I pointed.

He nodded and raised his shotgun. "I'll circle around and take care of him. You save your princess."

He ran off into the darkness. I spun around and around, searching for her...and finally saw a figure in the distance, silhouetted by the burning stable. I put my assault rifle up to my face and used its scope. *Yes!* It was her.

But just as I lowered my rifle to run, I saw someone else. A big, squat shape, running towards the stables. *Jakov.*

I ran. But he had a big head start and the wound in my leg would slow me.

I knew he'd get there first.

28

KRISTINA

I SKIDDED to a halt outside the stable door. The whole roof was on fire and the interior was a solid mass of white smoke: I wouldn't be able to see more than a foot ahead of me.

A terrified whinny came from inside. I plunged in.

I had to shuffle through the hay with my hands out in front of me. It was even worse than I'd thought: flaming liquid and bits of timber were raining down from above, threatening to set my nightgown on fire again, and the moving horses cast confusing shadows everywhere. I couldn't see where I was—

A horse suddenly reared in front of me, its front hooves almost hitting me in the head. It had broken out of its stall but it was as lost as I was and it was liable to kill me in its panic if I wasn't careful. "*Shh,*" I told it. "*Shh, shh,* it's okay." I'd slipped in through the side door but the stable had big double doors, too: if I could open those, the horse could get out. But getting to them meant getting past it. "*Shh.*" It reared again and I had to fall back against the wall. The back of my neck lit up in scalding agony and I screamed and slapped at it, smelling burning hair. I approached the horse again. "*Shh.* Trust me, *please!*"

I reached out...and managed to pet it. It snorted at me,

uncertain...but it stopped rearing for a second. Heart pounding, I slid past it, lifted the bar that held the doors shut and pushed them wide.

Immediately, the horse shot past: I barely darted out of the way in time. Clouds of smoke followed it and the stable cleared a little: I could see the other horses now, still trapped in their stalls. I ran to the nearest one and started along the line, opening door after door. One by one, the horses ran to freedom. But I could see the roof sagging dangerously. The whole place was going to come down.

I freed the last horse, looked up...and Jakov was standing in the doorway. "Your Highness!" he panted. "Come on!"

I looked around. There was no one else there. He could say anything happened. Hit me over the head and leave me to die in the fire.

The roof groaned. *"Your Highness!"* yelled Jakov. "Please!" He held out his hand.

What if Garrett was wrong?

What if Garrett was *right?* I searched around for another way out, one that didn't involve going through him. But he was between me and both of the doors. "Back off," I told him, my voice shaking. "Just back away."

"It's not safe here!" he yelled over the flames. "Come with me! Now!" And he raced forward and grabbed my wrist.

There was a splintering crack from above us.

We looked up just as the roof collapsed.

29

GARRETT

I GAVE a strangled cry as the stable roof collapsed. I was running flat out, but my wounded leg kept making me stumble and I had to keep dodging the horses as they galloped towards me out of the smoke.

When I reached the stables, the walls were still standing but inside it was just a pile of burning debris. *"Kristina!"* I howled. A burning timber had fallen diagonally across the door, blocking it. I grabbed it, snarling in loss and fury. I could feel my already-burned palms blistering as I gripped the wood but I didn't care. I heaved it aside and staggered through the door.

Nothing. Just a sea of tiles and timber, all of it burning. The heat scorched my face. *"Kristina!"*

Then movement. Tiles sliding down from a pile that was slightly higher than the rest. Something *big* started to shift....

I watched as a timber as thick around as my waist started to inch into the air. Jakov was crouched beneath it: he had it on his shoulders and he was heaving it into the air like Atlas lifting the earth.

And lying between his straining legs was Kristina.

Jakov pushed all the way up to standing. He had both hands on the timber, steadying it, and he was using every ounce of strength he had to bear its weight. *"Take...her,"* he spat through gritted teeth. *"I can't move."*

I raced forward, flames licking at the cuffs of my jeans. Kristina was semi-conscious and groaning. I grabbed her and threw her over my shoulder, then looked up at Jakov. The timber was alight in several places, the flames licking at his clothes. He was dripping with sweat, his face contorted with effort. *"Go!"* he grunted. "I can't hold it!"

I ran outside. Emerik was just arriving, still coughing and wheezing but pushing through it. Caroline was following behind him, weak and shaky. I handed Kristina to Emerik.

And then I ran back inside.

Jakov glared when he saw me. "Get out of here!"

But I wasn't going to leave him to die. Not after being so wrong about him. I ran forward, stood next to him and got my shoulders under the timber, too. If I could just lift it off him....

But it was much, much heavier than I'd thought. And Jakov's legs were failing, putting even more of the weight onto me. The damn thing just weighed too much: there was no way to safely get out from under it. If we let go, it would fall and smack into our spines before we could move out of the way. "You idiot," panted Jakov. "Now we're both going to die."

My knees began to shake and I couldn't stop them. My back began to bend. I couldn't catch my breath: there was too much smoke, too much heat. My head swam. And with every second the timber seemed to get another hundred pounds heavier. He was right. We were going to die here. I exchanged a look with Jakov. *I'm sorry. But at least we saved her.*

Movement at the door. Emerik stumbled in, still wheezing. He looked at Jakov and their eyes locked....

And then the older man ran across to us and got *his* shoulders under the timber. For the first time, we managed to raise it a half inch.

"Lift it and roll it back," croaked Emerik. "On the count of three."

All of us were shaking, our muscles close to giving out. I could hear the sweat dripping from me and hissing in the flames. But if we died in here, there was no one to protect her. She needed us. She needed all three of us.

"One," said Emerik. *"Two. Three!"*

And we damn well lifted. We got it just high enough that we could roll it back off our shoulders like he said. We staggered forward and it missed our backs by an inch. We had to support each other just to make it to the door: our legs were like wet rope.

We collapsed just outside, panting and gasping. I've never known exhaustion like it, every muscle screaming.

Kristina was on her feet, coughing a little from the smoke but okay. She ran between us, checking us over, and for a second I just let myself lie back and rest. Emerik, Jakov and I exchanged glances. We'd done it. We got everyone out safe.

Then, in the distance, I heard a shotgun boom three times. Everyone looked round.

And then there was silence. We'd all gotten so used to the whistle of the mortar rounds passing overhead that it was eerie when they suddenly stopped. My dad had done it. Three shots from his shotgun: the two men working the mortar and the sniper. I let out a long sigh of relief. It was over.

Then another shot echoed through the night. Not a shotgun. A handgun.

Dad hadn't been carrying a handgun.

"Dad?" I could hear the fear in my voice. "Dad?"

Kristina reached for me but I was off and running across the fields. My legs would barely support me between the aching muscles and the wound but I had to get there, had to know.

I reached the trees and started searching. "Dad!"

I found the mortar team first. Two men, like I'd thought. Then another man, a rifle next to him. All dead.

"I got 'em," said a weak voice.

Dad was sitting with his back against a tree. I stumbled over to him and fell to my knees beside him. That's when I saw the glistening wet patch on his shirt. I could smell burned fabric. Someone had shot him point-blank in the guts and left him there to die.

"Never saw the fourth guy," wheezed Dad. "Not 'till it was too late. He's fast. Pale, creepy-looking son of a bitch."

Silvas Lukin. My hands tightened into fists. I could feel tears slipping down my cheeks. There was so much I had to tell him. That I was sorry I was away for so long. That I loved him. "Dad!"

"You do whatever you have to," Dad said. "But you keep that bastard away from her."

And his eyes closed.

30

KRISTINA

WE ALL WORKED as a team to get Garrett's dad loaded into the pickup. Then we tore out of the ranch and off towards the nearest hospital. Emerik and I were frantically trying to stop the bleeding, pressing wads of torn-up shirt against the wound, but they kept soaking through.

When we screeched up outside the emergency room, Garrett took his dad's shoulders and the guards took a leg each. We carried him in like that, with Caroline and me running alongside and pressing on the wound. Doctors surrounded us and helped us lower him onto a gurney, then raced him into a trauma bay.

"Outside!" snapped a doctor. "Let us work!"

Garrett, Caroline and the guards moved reluctantly away. I went to step away too, but suddenly a hand gripped my wrist. I looked down. Garrett's dad had opened his eyes. He'd been drifting in and out of consciousness since we got him in the pickup but just for a few seconds, he seemed lucid.

"He's a big lunk," he croaked, staring up at me. "But he's got a good heart. He just needs something to fight for."

I nodded, tears rolling down my cheeks.

The doctors put a mask over his face and his eyes closed.

I walked into the hallway just in time to see Garrett slam his fist against the wall. His whole body had gone hard, every muscle taut with helpless fury. A nurse arrived to dress the wound on his leg and managed to coax him into a chair, but he barely seemed to know she was there. He just sat in silence as she worked, the anger and guilt rolling off him like a physical force, pushing all of us away.

"It's not your fault," I whispered when the nurse had gone. I put a hand on his back but he twisted away. He blamed himself for his father's injuries, but if it was anyone's fault, it was mine. *I should have died on that plane,* I thought bitterly. How many people were going to die, or be injured, protecting me?

And then I saw the police officers talking to the nurse at the reception desk.

I looked at Garrett. I knew what I needed to do but...God, I couldn't. I looked at the guards. They shook their heads. Neither of them dared approach Garrett, not when he was going through this. It had to be me.

I swallowed and walked around in front of him. He was staring at the floor and didn't even acknowledge me.

"Garrett?" I said hesitantly. "Garrett, I can't believe I have to ask you to do this but...the police are here. There are three dead bodies at the ranch. They're going to take us into custody, all of us. We know there's still a leak, high up. Sitting in a cell somewhere, we'll be vulnerable."

He finally looked up. The anger in his eyes almost made me step back. But I met his gaze: after all he'd been through for me, I could take it.

At last he dropped his eyes, marched past me and out of a fire exit. The rest of us raced to catch up. Seconds later, we were in the pickup, roaring away.

We'd lost everything. All our luggage had been in the house when it burned down. Our clothes were singed, tattered rags, our faces stained with smoke. Worst of all was the fury in Garrett's eyes. I'd done the right thing but that didn't make it okay. *If his dad dies, if he's not there....*

The miles rolled by in silence and I watched Garrett's anger harden and focus. His brow furrowed, just like it had back in the motel room when he'd spotted the broken vase. He was figuring something out, working through the possibilities.

And finally, he came to a conclusion.

I let out a scream as Garrett stamped on the brakes and the pickup went skidding sideways along the highway. He swerved us off the asphalt and onto the dirt. We bounced, leaned, and finally lurched to a stop facing the wrong way. Everyone was panting and cursing in fear.

Garrett was out immediately. He stalked around to the rear door and hurled it open. Then he reached in, grabbed Caroline by the neck and dragged her around to the front of the car. She screamed as he threw her down in the beam from the headlights.

Then he drew his gun and pointed it right at her head.

31

KRISTINA

"*Stop!*" I flung open my door, jumped down and ran to him. "*Stop! What are you doing?*"

The barrel of Garrett's gun never wavered. "Someone told the assassins we were at that motel," he growled. "Someone told them we were at the ranch. It wasn't Emerik. It wasn't Jakov. She's the only one left."

Caroline was sobbing, hysterical. "*This is crazy!* I'm her friend! I'm her *best friend.*"

I nearly grabbed Garrett's arm but I was too scared the gun would go off. "Garrett, she's right!" I told him.

He wheeled to face me. "Your Highness, *let me handle this!* If you want to help, search her!"

"Garrett, it's *not her!* She's my friend!"

"We all threw our phones away," he said. "She must have another phone, or a radio. Some way of contacting them."

I raised my hands in defeat. Doing it might placate him. "I'm sorry," I told Caroline. "It'll be okay." I helped her stand. She was still wearing the jeans and t-shirt she'd fallen asleep in and I passed my hands gently over them. Nothing. Of course there was nothing. It was crazy to even think—

Wait. What was *that,* deep in her back pocket?

When I pulled out a phone, I nearly dropped it.

"It's not what you think," said Caroline.

I wanted to throw up. *Caroline?!*

"It's not for the assassins!" she sobbed. "It's for Sebastian!"

The world seemed to stop. I stared at her, incredulous. "Aleksander's assistant?!"

Her eyes were full of tears. "We're in love," she whispered.

"Why keep it a secret?" asked Garrett. "Why have a second phone?"

"Palace staff aren't allowed to fraternize," I told him. "If anyone found out, they'd both be fired." I stared at Caroline and felt my face fall as I figured out what had happened.

"What?" she demanded. "Look, it's not the assassins! It's just Sebastian! And I know I should have thrown it away along with my main one but no one's tracking it! I bought it for cash and I only use it for him! He's the only one who even knows I have it!"

Garrett and I exchanged looks. My stomach knotted. *She doesn't realize. Oh God, we're going to have to tell her.*

"*What?*" Caroline begged.

"You send this Sebastian guy a message?" asked Garrett. The anger had gone from his voice. His gun swung down to point at the ground. "You tell him we were at the motel?"

"Yes," said Caroline uncertainly. "He was worried about me."

"And did you tell him we were in Texas?" I asked gently. "Did you tell him we were at Garrett's dad's ranch?"

I could see the realization start to form in her mind. "Yes...but..." She gave a choking, hiccoughing sob. "But..." She looked around at our faces. "But that doesn't mean that...."

I bit my lip and nodded sadly.

"But we're *in love!*" She stared wildly at me, willing it to be true. And then her face slowly crumpled and she went sickly pale. "Oh God. Oh my God. *This is all my fault!*" She took a stumbling step towards Garrett. "Your dad...oh my God, I'm so sorry!"

Garrett just shook his head and turned away. He thrust his gun back into his waistband and let out a long, bitter sigh.

I ran to Caroline and threw my arms around her. "It's not your fault," I told her. "You were used. You had no way of knowing he was one of them." Inside, I was shaking with rage. *Sebastian! That utter bastard!* He'd exploited a naive young woman's feelings and he didn't care about her at all. She'd nearly died in that fire.

We all climbed back into the pickup. For a second, we just sat there in silence. I still felt the anger rolling off Garrett in waves but it was directed outward, now, at the assassins and Sebastian, not inward at our little group. For the first time, we knew we were all on the same side. And that meant we could finally go to New York and get me home.

"Send a message to Sebastian," said Garrett. "Tell him we're on our way to Chicago. By the time he realizes we're not there, you'll be on a plane."

I nodded and started tapping in the text message. "I'm going home," I thought in wonder. Then I realized I'd said it out loud.

Garrett slowly nodded. Then he looked at me and I drew in my breath when I saw the sadness in his eyes.

That's when it hit me. I was going home and I'd never see him again.

32

GARRETT

AT THE FIRST gas station we passed, I pulled over and called Barney in New York. We hadn't spoken in over a year and it took a while to convince him I wasn't kidding about the Princess. But he agreed to help. He had a cargo flight going to Austria that he could sneak the Princess onto, and it could make a stop in Lakovia. Only problem was, it was leaving at ten the next morning. That gave us only twenty-four hours to get from Texas to New York.

So I *drove,* for hour after hour. I couldn't stop thinking about my dad. I called the hospital from each gas station we passed but each time, he was still in surgery. Finally, around noon, I managed to get one of the surgeons on the phone. Hunched over a payphone, trying to shut out the roar of passing trucks behind me, I closed my eyes and focused on his voice.

"We got the bullet," he said. The poor guy sounded as exhausted as me. "But it really tore him up inside. Heart, one lung, nicked a kidney. Whoever shot him knew exactly where to aim for maximum damage. He'd be dead, if he wasn't such a tough old coot. It's going to be touch-and-go for the next few days."

I thanked him and hung up. I had to resist the urge to smash the handset to pieces against the side of the payphone. *Silvas Lukin.* That son of a bitch. If I ever got my hands on him....

Footsteps behind me. I whirled around and the Princess was there, hands nervously twisting in front of her. "How is he?"

That glass-smooth voice was like a cool palm placed on my forehead. I drew in a shuddering breath. "Alive," I said.

"I'm sorry. Not just for what happened with Caroline but...everything." She looked down at her feet. "You must wish you'd taken a different flight."

It felt like my chest contracted into a tiny black hole. I closed the distance between us with one big stride. "Hey!" I growled. "Hey!" I took her chin between thumb and forefinger and tipped it so she had to look at me. "No. Don't say that."

She nodded but her eyes were shining with tears. I had to show her I wasn't mad at her. And then I remembered something, something I'd been meaning to ask her since that very first day.

"That Rans Tagaka stuff," I said. "When you took out that guy on the highway. Can you teach me?"

She squinted through the tears: *Really?* Then she sniffed and looked away, blinking. Her chin was still in my hand and a few warm tears fell in my palm. "You were a marine," she said. "You know much more about fighting than I do."

"I don't know *that,*" I said. "And my squad leader always said, when you stop learning, you start dying."

She bit her lip and, instantly, that deep *pull* towards her took over. *God, don't do that! Not when your chin's in my hand. Not when I could just lean down and kiss you—*

Her breathing went tight and I realized I was staring at her lips. We both looked away.

"Alright," she said, a little breathlessly. "Stand behind me."

I ambled around behind her. Emerik had lent her his suit jacket to wear over the nightgown. It meant she was halfway decent but her long legs were still tantalizingly visible through the gown's gauzy fabric.

"Put an arm around my neck," she ordered.

I stepped closer and the scent of her filled my senses. I hooked my arm around her neck. My sleeve was rolled up so it was skin on skin, her touch like silk.

"Like you're going to hurt me," she said, her voice trembling a little.

I could never hurt you. I cinched my arm tighter and felt her swallow. Her body was in contact with mine all the way from neck to ankle, her ass just grazing my crotch. There was a lull in the passing traffic and suddenly it was very quiet, the only sound the wind whipping our clothes.

"You have to form your hand into a point, like this," She pressed her fingers together into an arrowhead. "And then with your middle finger you have to strike just the right point...."—she reached up under my armpit—"...*here*. It's only about the size of a...what are those coins you have? The tiny ones? Nickels! So you have to be precise." She pressed very gently, then twisted around to check I'd understood.

I nodded, but...when she'd turned, it had made one cheek of her ass press right against my crotch. And now my arm had half-dropped from around her neck and the underside was just kissing the top of her breast. Every time she inhaled, I could feel its soft warmth pressing against me. "That's it?" I asked. I was trying not to get lost in her eyes again. "It doesn't *feel* very dangerous."

I glimpsed something I'd never seen before: a wicked little smile. Her hand pulled back and then flashed up, faster than I could follow, and—

My fingers twitched and then went loose and floppy: I couldn't have closed my hand if my life depended on it. The feeling traveled up my arm in the time it took me to blink. It slid from around the Princess's neck and just *hung,* dead weight. I couldn't even stop it swinging back and hitting me on the leg and, when it did, I couldn't feel it. It felt like a side of goddamn beef hanging in a meat locker. *"What the hell?!"* I grunted.

She giggled. It was the first time I'd heard it: a beautiful, musical sound like water flowing over jewels. "I didn't do it very hard," she said. "The feeling'll come back in a few minutes."

I gave her a mock-scowl and she grinned, and my heart just lifted. I was so relieved that I'd made her feel better. *I did that. Me.* Just for a second, it was like we were a couple.

And then I remembered this was our last day together. Tomorrow, she'd remember she was really a princess. And I'd remember I was really a burned-out jarhead who was lucky to get a job tumbling drunk assholes out of clubs.

It didn't matter how good she made me feel. Tomorrow, she'd be gone.

33

KRISTINA

I WAS BUYING road snacks before we hit the highway again. I'd discovered that America did road snacks better than anyone else in the world: big bags of crunchy, salty chips, candy in every flavor from strawberry to cola and ice-cold soda to wash it all down with. I was so absorbed trying to choose between grape and watermelon candy, I bumped into Jakov, which was like bumping into a wall. His big fists were full of a selection of candy and he was glaring at it, trying to decide. All of the packets had one thing in common. I grinned: I'd never known that about him. "Cherry's your favorite flavor?"

He looked up, startled, and blushed.

I frowned. What was embarrassing about that? Unless...I drew in my breath. "Is it *someone else's* favorite flavor?"

He looked everywhere except my eyes.

"My father's maid?" I asked, my voice rising in excitement. "The one with the long red hair?"

He was flushing down to his roots. "Simone," he mumbled. I'd never seen him embarrassed before. It was adorable. And after all the horror of the last few days, it was a relief to hear about something sweet and positive. "I thought she might like a gift from America," he said.

"That's a *great* idea. Buy all of them!" I pushed him towards the checkout.

But he shook his head. "I haven't told her how I feel."

"Why? Tell her!"

"For one thing, it's against the rules."

I sighed. That stupid rule. If Caroline and Sebastian hadn't had to creep around in secret, we would have known she was messaging him a lot sooner. "I'm going to talk to my father about getting that rule lifted," I told him. But then I frowned at his expression. "It's not just that, is it?"

He shook his head. I could see the doubt in his face: he wasn't used to sharing his problems with me, or maybe anyone. But this whole experience had brought us all closer together. "It's her father," he said. "He's in a wheelchair." He met my eyes. "Since the war."

"Oh, Jakov..." His guilt over what Garmania did to us in the war was something he carried around all the time, a crushing weight on his shoulders. But now it was cutting him off from the person he wanted to be with. "Talk to her," I said gently.

"What if she hates Garmanians?" He was staring off across the store, unable to meet my eyes. "A lot of people do." He swallowed. "I've liked her for so long. If I talk to her and I find out she hates us...."

I nodded slowly. I understood. The whole vision of her he'd built up would be destroyed. I didn't know what to say. But there was something I *did* need to say and now was as good a time as any. "Jakov, I'm sorry. I'm sorry I thought you were the traitor."

He nodded. "It's not your fault. It made sense, with my heritage."

I put my hand on his arm. "I won't ever doubt you again."

He shook his head. "Thank you, Your Highness. But it's not you who's the problem. It's everyone else."

And he tossed the cherry candy back onto the display stand and walked away.

I watched him sadly until he'd gone. Then I gathered up the cherry candy and bought it. I might not be able to fix everything between our two countries but I was damn well going to help this one man be happy.

34

GARRETT

THE AFTERNOON PASSED in a blur of miles. We were a team, now, and Jakov, Emerik and Caroline all took a turn at the wheel. I could see a storm rolling towards us in the rear view mirror, but as long as we kept moving, we'd stay ahead of it. By sundown, it was my turn again. I blinked and strained my eyes and tried to focus on the white line. I hadn't slept properly in days. None of us had.

"When are you going to stop?"

The Princess's voice made me jump and swerve. I'd thought she was asleep, like everyone else. I regained control. "I'm not," I told her. "We've got enough gas to reach New York. Should be another five or six hours."

"Garrett, you're exhausted."

When had it become *Garrett* instead of *Mr. Buchanan?* Hearing it did something to me: I felt like the shy kid in high school, noticed by the prom queen. I felt *special.* And my name...it's a good old-fashioned name, never had a problem with it. But it's a working name, a name to be bawled across a field or shouted over the din of machinery. *Garrett* sounds like tools and rope and dirty hands, just like *Kristina* sounds like snowflakes and sweet-smelling petals. And yet when *she* said my name, it sounded different. It sounded respectable.

My chest ached like something vital was being wrenched out of it. *God, I'm going to miss her.*

"I'm okay," I lied. But my eyelids felt like they were made out of old, gritty sackcloth. Blinking felt *good*. I just needed a good *long* blink—

"*Garrett!*"

I'd wandered into the oncoming lane. *Shit!* I wrestled us back onto our side. "I'm fine."

"Let someone else take a turn!"

I looked in the rear view mirror. Emerik was asleep, hands carefully folded. God, even the man's snores were prim and proper. Jakov had his head thrown back and his arms and legs spread wide, taking up half the back seat. Caroline was dozing with her head on his shoulder, frowning and muttering in her sleep, working through the guilt. I knew how that felt.

"There is no one else," I told the Princess.

"Teach me," she said.

"What?!"

"Teach me to drive."

I glanced across at her to see if she was serious.

She flushed. "Look, I'm not stupid! I just never learned!"

"I know you're not stupid, Your Highness," I looked at her, so she could see I meant it, and our eyes locked. *Tomorrow, she'll be gone....*

"It's a long, straight, empty road," she said.

I looked. She had a point. Aside from the odd truck, we were the only thing moving.

"*Please,*" she said. "I don't want to be useless."

"You're *not* useless," I told her firmly. I sighed. "Okay. Get over here."

I'm not sure what my sleep-starved brain had in mind. I knew she'd be sitting in my lap, but somehow I hadn't thought about what it would be like to have her—

She slid onto me with a rustle of fabric, a gentle waft of that exotic scent, and a brush of her hair against the front of my neck. Then her soft ass was on my thighs, twisting as she hooked her feet into the footwell, and I had to fight to keep from groaning. She was still in that gauzy nightdress and Emerik's jacket. That meant her ass was only covered by a pair of panties and lacy fabric about as substantial as a spider web. The slit up the side of the nightgown had fallen open and those long, shapely legs were nude as they pressed against my jeans.

Suddenly, I was wide awake. "Take the wheel," I grunted.

Her fingers wrapped around the rim right below mine, her thumbs brushing my pinky fingers. Immediately, that *pull* rolled through me like thunder across a Texas sky. Up through my arms, into my chest...and when it hit my heart, god*damn!* I had to crush the wheel in my hands to stop myself wrapping my arms around her and pulling her to me. With every breath, I inhaled her scent. *She's there! She's right there in your lap and tomorrow she'll be gone!*

Tomorrow, she'll be back home with her kind. With princes and lords and billionaires.

She wiggled her legs, trying to get comfortable. The problem was, I'm pretty big. There wasn't much room between my thighs and the bottom of the steering wheel. Not unless she scooched herself....

...all the way *back*. The firm cheeks of her ass nestled against my crotch. If the *pull* was like thunder, deep and resonant, the lust was like lightning, blinding bright and scorching hot, arcing and crackling. Any second, it would strike just the right spot and I'd be helpless to stop myself lunging for her. It would be so easy, so *goddamn easy* to just slide one big forearm around that slender waist and jerk her back hard against me, her back pressed to my pecs as my hand roved up under that jacket and palmed her breasts—

"Okay," she said. I could hear that tension in her voice, that urgency. She was on the edge of control, too. "What do I do?"

I opened my mouth to speak but I couldn't focus on the road. All I could focus on was her neck, pale and soft and perfect, locks of that chestnut hair drifting silkily across it as she swayed atop me. I needed to lean forward and brush the hair out of the way, kiss all the way down to the lace on her shoulder, then all the way up her throat to her chin, twisting her around in my lap so I could reach her lips—

I could feel myself getting hard. *God, no. Not with her sitting right—*

I thought of all the reasons why we couldn't be together. The gulf between us. The parts of me I was hiding from her. Most of all, the need to protect her. I couldn't guard her if I was too busy imagining—

That ass, so fine and pert and toned from riding, bouncing on top of me as my hands traced up her sides. Her twisting to kiss me, groaning as my rough fingers found her nipples—

It was no good, I was rock hard, the bulge under the denim pressing right between those cheeks. "It's an auto," I said with difficulty. "So you don't have to worry about shifting gears." I pressed my right thigh against hers. "Try giving it a little gas."

I lifted my foot off the pedal and let her slide hers on. She hesitantly pushed and the car surged forward. Her ass pushed harder against my crotch and my whole body tensed. Her head was right next to mine and I was drunk on the scent of her, driven crazy by the silken brush of that hair on my neck. *Just kiss her!*

"Now the other pedal," I told her. "Gently.."

She braked, harder than she meant to. That was when I remembered that she didn't have a safety belt on. My arms came up before I was even aware of it, criss-crossing over her waist, hauling her back against me, just like I'd been fantasizing. We swerved a little, then she released the brake and we straightened out.

But I was still holding her tight. I could feel every breath she took, every beat of her heart. *Goddamn it, I am crazy about this woman.* And then I felt the soft warmth against my forearms and realized they were pressing against the underside of her breasts.

I swallowed. She'd gone rigid atop me, her breath shaky with anticipation. I brought my lips close to her cheek, closed my eyes—

"You got it," I forced myself to say. "You'll be fine."

I opened my eyes and met hers in the rear view mirror. I nodded. *It has to be this way.*

And after a moment, she nodded too.

She lifted herself and I undid my belt and slid out from underneath her and across to the passenger side. Halfway there, I saw Emerik watching me in the mirror. When had he woken up? How much had he seen?

His warning stare told me: *enough*. Sure, we were getting on much better, now, but when it came to the Princess, he was still viciously protective. Too protective for it to just be about me being unworthy of her—which I was. It felt like there was something I didn't understand. All that *unbroken snow* stuff....

I shook my head. Maybe there were still things about Lakovia I didn't understand.

By the time we reached New York, we were all ready to drop. The storm was close behind us, black clouds shutting out the stars. I automatically started searching around for a cheap motel but the Princess shook her head. "It's my last night in America," she told me. "I insist."

And she took us to one of *those* hotels. The ones where there's a guy playing the piano in the cocktail bar, where bellhops load your suitcases onto those fancy polished carts. The guy at the reception desk looked at me like I'd crawled out of a drain, but he changed his tune when I booked a suite and paid with a thick wad of the Princess's cash.

Upstairs, in the suite, I looked around in astonishment. My bedroom had a carved wooden bed the size of a boat, with sheets so smooth and soft it felt like I was going to slip right off them. My room alone was bigger than my whole apartment back in LA.

To the others, of course, it was all normal. Emerik was grinning like a man who'd just stumbled out of the jungle after a month lost. Caroline was on the phone to the concierge, giving careful instructions on what clothes she needed him to run out and buy for us. And the Princess had fired up the room's huge flat-screen TV and was placing a video call to....

The screen lit up. I didn't recognize the man who answered but I recognized the thick chestnut hair and the imperious jawline.

"*Kristina!*" breathed the King. "Thank God!" He laid his hand on the screen and the Princess did the same, touching their palms together. Then he glanced around the room. "Caroline. Gentlemen."

"*Your Majesty,*" the other three all said in unison.

Then the King looked at me. "And you must be Mr. Buchanan. Thank you for looking after my daughter."

I felt that fluttering in my chest again. The same surge of loyalty I always felt around the Princess. He wasn't anything like the slimy politicians I'd met. I felt...*humbled.* But not talked down to. "You're welcome, Your Highness," I mumbled.

The Princess told her father that Sebastian, Aleksander's assistant, was a traitor. He nodded gravely. "I'll have him arrested and interrogated. Hopefully, he can give us a lead on the assassins."

There was a tiny sound behind me, a barely audible moan. When I turned, Caroline was standing there, her dress twisted in her hands, her eyes brimming with tears. She bolted from the room. *Poor kid.* I knew what it felt like to be betrayed. But this was worse, in some ways, than what had happened to me. She'd been in love with him and those feelings don't just switch off. She didn't want to think of him chained and interrogated.

"The FBI found the three men killed at your father's ranch, Mr. Buchanan," said the King. "All Garmanians, members of Silvas Lukin's squad in the war."

The Princess caught her breath and drew her arms tight around her. All I wanted was to march over there and sweep her into my arms, pull her tight against my chest and make sure nothing could ever get to her. But I forced myself to stand still.

"They could be an extremist group: men out for revenge for the war," said the King. "But we can't ignore the possibility that they're backed by the Garmanian government. Their Prime Minister denies all involvement but Aleksander thinks he's lying."

"If Garmania ordered my assassination, it could restart the war," whispered the Princess.

The King leaned forward. "I am *not* going to let that happen," he said. "Have a safe flight. I'll see you tomorrow." And the screen went black.

We called down for room service and wound up ordering about half the menu: we hadn't eaten properly in almost two thousand miles. I took a long, hot shower, changed the dressings on the wounds on my legs and then the clothes Caroline ordered arrived. I dressed in a fresh pair of jeans and a shirt, and, damn, it felt wonderful. I wandered out of my bedroom to check on the Princess and—

Stopped.

She was just coming out of her room wearing one of those big, white, fluffy hotel bathrobes. Her skin was freshly-scrubbed and gleaming, her hair still damp. She was stripped of her fancy clothes and shoes and tiara and it didn't matter. She'd have looked like a princess in a sack.

She caught my gaze. Held it. I'd taken three steps towards her before I realized I was moving, called to her by something I couldn't explain or fight. I finally got my feet under control and stopped just before I reached her. But I still couldn't look away.

"I can't believe I'm here," she said at last. God, that voice, like having every aching muscle in my body caressed by smooth, cool glass. She turned to look out of the window. "New York City. When my father said I had to attend a meeting here, I was so excited. In the end, I didn't get to see anything except the inside of a limo and a few meeting rooms at the UN. She walked over to the window and put her hand on the glass. "Tomorrow I'll be back in Lakovia. Even once your FBI catch the assassins, I doubt my father will ever let me come back to America again. It's too dangerous here."

I nodded. I couldn't speak. I'd known this was goodbye but hearing her say it...*I'm never going to see her again.* I felt...blessed, just having had her in my life, even just for a few short days. I knew that, my whole life, I'd never again know anything this special. And it made me want to do something for her.

"Come with me," I said.

I took her hand and led her out of the suite and up to the top floor, then hunted around until I found a stairwell that led up to the roof. When we stepped outside, the rain clouds were right overhead. The storm was going to break any second but we were okay for now.

"Do you trust me?" I asked.

She nodded immediately.

"Close your eyes."

She closed them. I walked behind her, my hands on her shoulders, threading her through the maze of air conditioning ducts, telling her when she needed to step over a pipe. My eyes were locked on her bare calves, where they emerged from beneath the robe.

We reached the edge of the roof. I helped her step up onto the parapet, wrapping an arm around her waist in case she swayed, and then said, "Your Highness: open your eyes."

She drew in her breath. New York was laid out before her, glittering canyons of skyscrapers with rivers of glowing white flowing between them. The Flatiron building, the Chrysler building, the Empire State, all dressed in lights.

"Figure we haven't given you the best welcome," I said. "Wanted you to see the good in this country, before you go."

She looked down at the arm wrapped around her waist. "I've seen the good in this country."

I stayed silent.

"When we get home," she said, "I'll be giving the guards medals for their service. I wish I could do something for you. Obviously, you'll be rewarded—"

"I didn't do it for money."

She craned her head around to look at me. With her up on the parapet, we were eye-to-eye. "Anything you want."

Suddenly, it was difficult to breathe. I remembered standing in the FBI office, thinking about that old line from the stories. *All I ask for is a kiss from you, Your Highness*—

But life ain't no damn fairy tale. I said nothing. And after a second she gave a sad little smile and a nod and looked back to the city. I could see the lights reflected in the tears in her eyes. "I'm going to miss America, Mr. Buchanan."

My mind was screaming at the wrongness of it. I knew I was

doing the right thing, knew I wasn't the sort of guy who could be with her. Knew I was just a big lunk with dirt under his fingernails, a jarhead and a damaged one at that. I've never been ashamed of what I am. But dammit, in that moment I would have given anything to be some duke or prince. I tried to force my voice to be level, but it shook a little. "America's going to miss you, Your Highness."

She pressed her lips tight together and nodded. Then she stepped down off the parapet and we started towards the stairs.

I held her hand to guide her and just that tiny contact sent energy pulsing up my arm, right to my chest. There was something about the feel of her delicate hand in my much bigger one. *What if this is the very last time I ever touch her?*

We reached the stairwell door. I released her hand but my fingers didn't want to let go: they tangled and caught at hers. She looked up at me, eyes huge, breath coming quick. I quickly looked away. *Don't be a damn fool, Garrett.*

I hauled open the door. Looked down the cold stairs that led to a polite goodnight, an early start, then her getting on Barney's plane. I caught her eye again and saw the tears there. Looked away and nodded to myself firmly. This was the right decision. The *only* decision.

I stepped forward.

Only *she* stepped forward, too. My hip brushed her hip: soft terry robe and hot flesh just beneath; damp chestnut hair flicking against my neck as she gasped and turned in surprise, the scent of her warm skin—

Every man has a goddamn breaking point.

I slammed her up against an air conditioning duct and kissed her as hard as I could.

35

KRISTINA

I'D BEEN DREAMING about this kiss for so long. At least since that moment in the FBI office when he'd stared down at me and I'd silently prayed that he'd ask to kiss me. Maybe since the first moment I'd seen him on the plane.

It was everything I'd dreamed it would be.

His lips came down on mine, hard and possessive. Not just wanting me but *needing* me as I needed him. I could feel days of lust stacked up behind the kiss like an invading army. He pressed, twisted, brutal against my softness. He tasted me and his growl of satisfaction rumbled right through me.

I was panting, lips together but nostrils flaring. My whole body was quaking against him. God, the feel of him, the hardness of his body, made me go weak. He was all around me: his denim-clad leg, thick as a tree trunk as it pressed against my bare thigh. His broad, curving chest, mashing against my breasts. Those big hands, cradling my back and tugging me even harder into him. His lips were rhythmic, now, each press slow and deliberate but sending an earthquake of raw pleasure down through me. My legs trembled and I went limp in his arms, the pleasure turning hot and scarlet-black as it reverberated up and struck my groin. The kiss was the drumbeat of a conqueror's army, a thunderous hammering on my gates.

I opened and his tongue traced the soft 'O' of my lips, teasing me, luxuriating in my submission. Then he plunged inside and I moaned: nothing mattered except the kiss. Every press of his lips sent another wave of pleasure shuddering down my body, so strong it might break me apart. I felt as if I was riding him, my whole body moving with his as we twisted and pushed and entwined together. My hands found the muscles of his back and I clung to him.

He grabbed my ass through the robe and crushed me close. My breasts pillowed against his chest, nipples rubbing against the hard muscle but the sensation tamed by the soft fabric between us. My whole body had suddenly gone burning hot: I was a writhing, twisting, naked mass beneath the robe, desperate to shed it and be naked against him. He was forceful, almost brutal, in the way he pinned me in place. But what overwhelmed me was my own reaction. Everything I'd been feeling for him, these last few days, was rising up inside me in a hot, dark gusher, filling my muscles and stealing control. If I hadn't been so firmly held, I would have been tearing at our clothes.

His lips parted from mine and for the first time I could hear my own urgent panting. His hands roved up my back, then down my front. Down to the belt of the robe. *Does he realize I'm naked underneath?*

He hooked his fingers under the ends and jerked the knot open. The robe fell apart a little way but that wasn't enough for him. He grabbed both sides and rammed it apart, so wide that it folded back on itself at the shoulders, trapping my arms. I was bare all the way down my front, the warm night air whipping across my skin.

His eyes tracked down my body and then came back up more slowly. I squirmed, turned on but shy. *What if he doesn't like me?*

But when his eyes met mine again, the furnace heat there told me everything I needed to know. His face was glowing with unrestrained, lustful joy that sent a hot wave of pride through me: I'd never been so simply, gloriously *appreciated* before.

His hands slowly lifted my breasts, thumbs working to squeeze the pale flesh just a little. Then he brushed the nipples, his huge hands more gentle than I'd have thought possible. He was almost reverent in the way he touched me...but I could see that powerful chest rising and falling as he panted. I was being worshipped...but by a man who any second was going to—I flushed—*fuck* me and *pound* me and *ride* me and all those other things a princess was not supposed to think about.

He moved closer, so close his big body blocked the wind that was starting to gust across the rooftop. So close that I could feel the hard bulge at his groin kiss my inner thigh, the warm denim rasping over my soft skin and then—I caught my breath—brushing across my soft curls of hair.

He stared straight into my eyes. His hands came up to cradle my cheeks, thumbs brushing over my lips. When he spoke, I felt it through the vibration of his chest against my breasts as much as I heard it. *"Beautiful,"* he rumbled, his accent pure Texas gold.

His hands slid down my neck, over my shoulders and traced the shape of me as if sculpting me from clay, his eyes on my breasts. *"Beautiful."*

He crouched, his eyes locked on my groin, his mouth so close to me that I felt the word on my folds. *"Beautiful."*

I drew in a shaky breath. My eyes were half-closed, hooded with lust. I was only distantly aware of the lights of the city and the storm clouds overhead, didn't care that I was naked on a rooftop, or that someone might see. All I cared about was him.

He put his hands on my hips, then used his elbows to nudge my legs apart. That's when I realized what he was going to do and the thought of it, of those hard lips *there,* sent a ripple of heat straight down to my groin. I spread my legs, the concrete warm against the soles of my feet. He moved closer and then, as if he couldn't resist, he stood for a second, towering over me, reminding me of his size, and laid a trail of kisses. He started at my lips and moved in an *S* down my body, snaking from breast to breast, over my stomach, my pubis, my thighs. Then, when I was gasping, he knelt between my open legs and—

Ah! I instinctively closed my legs at the first brush of his tongue against my lips, only to find them blocked by his hulking shoulders. He went slowly at first, teasing me, caressing each millimeter of sensitive skin with the tip of his tongue. I closed my eyes and for long seconds there was just my panting and the feel of him licking along my lips, following them up and inward to the hidden nub at their apex, running his tongue around and around and *across*—

I sunk my hands deep into his hair as thunder rolled overhead. He went *back* and *across* and then in an *X*. My hips were following him, now, dancing and swaying, urging him on. I could feel my lips growing heavy and soft, could feel myself opening to him as I got wetter and wetter. But he held back, teasing with just the tip of his tongue. The pleasure was strumming through me, my whole body writhing with it. I was soaking, aching...but still he teased, prolonging it, savoring me. Only when the pleasure climbed all the way up inside me to my throat and I begged, *"Please!"* did he give me what I needed.

I cried out as his lips pressed hard against me and his tongue thrust up inside. I rocked and twisted, my thighs clamping tight on his shoulders, the pleasure rocketing skyward. His upper lip found my clit and his hands squeezed my ass, his tongue rough and hot and perfect. I rose up on my toes, rocking there as he fucked me with it. I was panting helplessly, the pleasure lashing and pulling at me, the dark core of it growing and tightening.

The realization hit. He wasn't going to stop. He wasn't going to stop until I—

His lips rubbing over my throbbing clit, the pleasure tightening and tightening—

Until I—

That hard jaw pressed up between my thighs, his tongue splitting my folds, diving and twisting—

Until I—

He sensed I was close and his growl of victory vibrated right up through me.

Oh God!

I screamed and arched my back, rocking and shuddering against him. My legs failed and I had to grab hold of the air conditioning duct behind me as I panted out my climax, my fingers twisting in his hair.

When I was finally still, he stood and kissed me. Then he eased me away from the duct and slid his hands under the robe, pushing it back off my shoulders so that it fell to the floor. I was still so weak and sensitive from pleasure that just the feel of his rough hands on my skin made me tremble. I could barely stand. But that wasn't a problem because he bent and scooped me up, naked, and hoisted me into the air. I hung there naked in his arms, still panting.

He grabbed the robe in his free hand and walked to where there was a clear area of floor. He spread the robe out and gently laid me down on my back. I lay there looking up at him, stars twinkling in the darkness behind him.

He began to unfasten his shirt as more thunder rolled overhead. Each button revealed more of him: the curving slabs of his hard chest, the pink, dime-sized nipples I'd only imagined until now. Then the hard centerline leading down between the ridges of his abs. I wanted to touch him more than I've ever wanted to touch anything: my fingertips tingled with the need to strum across those hard peaks and valleys. I was already thinking about how they'd feel under my lips.

He unbuckled his belt and kicked off his boots. Shucked down his jeans and with it his shorts and—

My eyes locked on his cock as it rose up against his belly, the head thick and gray-purple, silky smooth, the shaft the same rich tan as his body. I swallowed, fear and shameful excitement twisting together, staring at it as he rolled on a condom. I'd known he was big, of course: he was big all over. But it was thick and long and *heavy* and God could I really—

He knelt slowly between my ankles. Moved higher, nudging my legs apart. I looked up at him, suddenly breathless. *This is really happening.*

His eyes were clouded with lust. He moved higher still and I felt the first touch of his cock, hard and *God* so hot against my inner thigh. *God it's really going to happen*—I was panting, crazy for him, but my eagerness was edged with nerves.

He must have seen it in my eyes because he slowed. Stopped. Frowned cautiously at me.

I tried to brazen it out. My hands grabbed his shoulders, fingers tracing his muscles....

But it was too late. "Your—" He broke off. He'd almost called me *Your Highness,* out of habit. "*Kristina.* You've—Wait—"

We both stared at each other for a second. I could see the growing certainty on his face.

"This is your *first time?!"* he asked.

I flushed scarlet and looked up at the stars. "It's...the tradition. I'm meant to wait for my prince."

When I dared to look at him again, he was shaking his head in shock. "Suddenly, a lot of stuff Emerik said makes sense," he muttered.

I blushed even harder. And then to my horror, he started to sit up. "*Wait!"* I grabbed his shoulder again.

"Kristina..." God, that honeyed rumble. It got me every single time, that one man could be so big, so gentle and so powerfully sexual, all at the same time. "You're meant to wait for—"

"My prince," I said seriously, looking right at him.

Now *he* flushed. "I'm not..." He looked down at himself. "I'm just—"

"You're not *just* anything, Garrett."

He met my eyes, shocked.

"I want it to be you," I said firmly. "I want to be—" I felt my face redden and I sort of nodded: *you know.*

That last part had an unexpected effect. The lust of a moment ago came back into his eyes. He knelt back down. "No," he said. "Say it."

Say it? I'd never once said that word, my whole life. It's about as far from a princess's vocabulary as it's possible to get. "I want to be...*fucked*...by you." My cheeks blazed as I said it.

But it worked. Something about hearing my accent wrapped around that dark, forbidden word. His whole body seemed to go hard with excitement. He roughly spread my thighs, his cock heavy and rock hard against me. "Say it again," he growled. "*Princess.*"

I gulped. I was shocked to find *I* liked saying it, too. The filthiness of it was like rough iron chains tightening around the pleasure and squeezing it so it glowed even brighter. "I want you to fuck me," I panted. This time, the words spilled out easily. "I want you to fuck me, Garrett."

And with a growl his hands pushed my shoulders down to the floor and his cock parted my folds and—

I drew in my breath as he *pushed*...and slid inside me. Not deep. Not yet. But God, the feel of him, thick and hard inside me, every tiny movement sending fresh ripples of sensation through me. My fingers played over his back, nervous, uncertain. Knowing I wanted more but afraid.

He was supremely gentle with me, his self-control incredible. He moved so slowly that it was almost a rocking, just a millimeter more of him at a time. The deeper he went, the better it got: my whole body seemed to be clutching at him and everywhere we touched there were new explosions of pleasure. I could see the aching lust on his face: he wanted to go fast, wanted to full-on *ravish* me but he was holding back for my sake.

And then, with a final slow push of his hips, he drove all the way inside me. I lay there gasping, staring up at him, and he gently brushed my hair back off my forehead, leaned down and kissed my lips. "Okay?" he asked.

I swallowed, still getting used to it. To the feel of him, so hard, so deep, so hot. *"Um-hm,"* I managed.

And he began to fuck me.

It was a slow rhythm at first, gentle waves that made me close my eyes and bite my lip as the pleasure built and built and I got hotter, wetter. Then faster, his strokes getting longer and I gasped: the pull and drag of him sending streamers of silver pleasure crackling through me. He groaned and I realized I'd begun to circle my hips around him. He lowered himself to his forearms so he could touch his hands to mine and our fingers interlaced. I arched my back up off the robe, meeting his body as he moved against me. Each forward stroke made his chest stroke against my upraised nipples and we gasped at the contact. We were both panting, our bodies gleaming with sweat.

The heat inside me was gathering, tightening into a glowing center, throwing off streamers that made me gasp and jerk. My eyes opened: I needed to see him. The sight of his tanned ass, rising and falling between my legs, was the hottest thing I'd ever seen. Right up until I looked into his eyes and saw how much he wanted me.

He was slamming into me, now, our bodies slapping together. The heat inside me tightened, cinching tighter and hotter with every thrust. I felt the first drop of rain hit my cheek, deliciously cold against my heated skin.

He propped himself on his elbows and took my breasts in his hands, squeezing, rubbing his thumbs over my nipples. He was being careful not to hurt me, not to let his muscled body crush me, but a little more of his weight started to rock between my thighs and God, I loved it. I loved that he was so big, pinning me down on the roof. I pressed myself up to meet him, gasping, just as another drop of rain hit my leg.

His head came close to mine, his ear to my mouth and suddenly I was saying things, words spilling out in fevered pants. *"God yes. Yes, like that. Fuck me like that."* I shut my eyes, caught my lower lip with my teeth but it was no good, it had to come out. *"HARDER!"*

I felt my face burning but Garrett growled, loving it. His hands grew rough at my breasts, sending dark ribbons of heat shooting down to my groin. His body rose and fell, his cock pounding me, owning me. Making me his. *God,* this was so much better than the pleasure I'd coaxed my body to, alone under the covers. The heat tightened down to a pinprick inside me, as hot as a star, then expanded, rushing out to fill me. My hands went wild on his back, sliding over his muscles, clutching him to me, *"God, yes!"* I wailed.

The sky released the rain and it bathed us, washing away who we were and the gulf between us. All that mattered was how much he wanted me and how much I wanted him. His thrusts became a blur, his cock silk-wrapped steel inside me. I wrapped my legs around him, arching my back and shouting my climax as I spasmed and shook around him. He rode me through it, the pleasure stretching out and out, and then groaned and shuddered atop me as he released.

I remember lying there for long minutes, the rain hammering down on his back, me safely sheltered beneath him as I panted and trembled and finally lifted my head to kiss his chest. I remember him picking me up and carrying me to the stairwell and then down the stairs to our suite. I remember being laid down on soft sheets. And then nothing.

36

KRISTINA

THE FIRST THING I felt was him. A glorious presence behind me in the bed, a warmth that pressed against my back all the way from shoulders to ankles. I tried to nestle back into him and it was wonderful. *This is what it's like to wake up with someone.*

The second thing was the change in me. Not just the warm, pleasant ache between my thighs or the way my breasts still throbbed with the memory of his hard fingers. I'd done it. That moment I'd been thinking about for so long had happened. It had been completely different to the way I'd imagined it: a four poster bed and Egyptian cotton sheets and some earnest, well-bred man atop me. And so, so much better.

The third thing I couldn't figure out at first because it was something that was missing. I lay there trying to figure it out for a few minutes and then sat up, frowning.

Garrett sat up, too, and kissed my bare shoulder. Then he got up and ambled across the room and started making coffee. His naked ass made it difficult to concentrate, but this was important. What was it that was missing?

Then I got it, and drew in my breath. I hadn't had the nightmare.

"Something wrong?" Garrett passed me a cup of coffee and sat down on the bed.

I shook my head and smiled a shy smile. *No!* Everything was so very *right!*

But he turned and glanced at the door that led out to the suite. Where Emerik and Jakov and Caroline and reality were waiting. Then he looked towards the window. I followed his gaze and my stomach filled with cold dread.

It was dawn. In just a few hours, we'd have to go to his friend's airfield. Then I'd get on a plane. Without him.

"No," I said tightly. "I want to stay."

"It's dangerous here—"

"I don't care."

"Kristina—"

"This is the first time," I blurted, my voice cracking, "that I haven't felt alone!"

He lowered his eyes guiltily. I didn't want that. I grabbed his hand and, when he looked at me, I leaned forward and slowly kissed him. I needed him to know that I didn't regret it.

He nodded. But from the way he squeezed my hand, I knew his heart was breaking, too.

"We could make it work," I whispered. But I knew it wasn't that simple. I'd had so many years of the *them and us,* commoner and royalty mentality from the palace staff, from Emerik, and especially from my mother. I didn't agree with it. But I wasn't naive enough to think I could just ignore it, either.

And it wasn't just that. "You deserve better than a grunt," Garrett told me. "Especially one who's...." He lowered his eyes and let my hand fall through his fingers.

I grabbed his wrist. "*What?* Tell me?" He shook his head. "Garrett, please! You helped me. I want to help you, too."

But he shook his head again. It was almost as if us being split apart had locked that door for good. *He wants me to remember him strong.*

He stood and started to pull his clothes on. I sat there slumped and despondent until he'd nearly finished. He leaned down and lifted my chin so that I had to look at him. "I gotta go back to my world," he told me. "You gotta go back to yours."

It was everything I should have wanted: back to Lakovia, my parents, my people. A world I understood, a world I was safe in. *Back to being a princess.*

Except, without him, I didn't want that anymore.

But my father taught me a long time ago that being royal isn't about doing what you want. It's about doing what your people need.

So I nodded, then stood and pressed myself to him in a full body hug. His arms wrapped around me and pulled me in tight and we stood there silently for long minutes.

"You'll find a prince," he whispered.

"I already did," I whispered back. I pulled out of his arms and turned away. I kept my back turned to him while I picked out some clothes because I was already blinking. I hurried into the bathroom, turned on the shower and only then did I let myself slump against the door and sob my heart out.

When I emerged, the bedroom was empty. I found everyone in the living room, killing time until our flight by watching TV. It only took me a split second to realize that *everyone knew.* It must have been obvious as soon as the guards went to relieve Garrett during the night. They'd have found his room empty and my bedroom door closed and....

Emerik was sitting with his hands neatly folded, radiating silent fury in Garrett's direction. Jakov carefully avoided my eyes. Caroline looked awestruck and excited: *tell me everything!*

And Garrett just stood by the door, as vigilant and watchful as ever. But when he glanced in my direction, I could see the raw pain in his eyes.

I had to do something or I'd start crying again, so I sat next to Caroline and focused on the TV. It was a news channel and my father was on the screen, standing at a podium at the front of a packed hall.

"He's in Zurich," said Caroline. "A speech about our social program."

I nodded. He was encouraging other countries to do what we'd done: scale back their military and spend on the poor, instead. I leaned in to listen. I was always in awe of the way he could inspire a crowd. Someday, I'd be expected to do the same and I had no idea how.

And then I saw him. Just for a split second, as the camera cut to a different angle. I jumped to my feet.

"What?!" asked Garrett.

"I—" I blinked uncertainly at the screen. *No. I couldn't have.* "I thought I saw...." But it was crazy. He was *here,* in America, not in Zurich. It was just my mind playing tricks on me.

And then I saw him again, and this time I let out a scream. It was *him.* Dressed in a suit like the other dignitaries, standing at the back of the room. I'd never forget that pale face with its snide, downturned mouth. *Silvas Lukin.* "*He's there! Lukin is there!*"

We all looked at each other. Everyone made the connection at the same time.

We'd been wrong about this thing the whole time. It wasn't about just assassinating *me.*

"*Get him out of the room!*" I screamed at Emerik. "*Call someone!*"

But we'd thrown all of our phones away. Emerik had to waste vital seconds manually dialing on the hotel phone. "I'm calling Aleksander," he muttered as the number rang. "He'll be there."

All of us were staring at the screen, scared to watch, scared to look away. I was dimly aware that I'd grabbed Garrett's hand and was squeezing it.

"*Code red!*" snapped Emerik into the phone. "*Assassin in the room! Evacuate the King!*"

He put the phone on speaker and we could hear the rustle of cloth and muffled voices. Long seconds ticked by. "*Hurry!*" snapped Emerik.

"I'm sorry!" Aleksander sounded out of breath. "I'm in a crowd, trying to get to a guard!" More muffled voices. I imagined him trying to fight through the tightly-packed bodies. *Hurry! Please hurry!*

And then we saw the guards on stage suddenly jerk to attention and run to my father. Aleksander must have finally delivered the message. They grabbed the King under the arms and rushed him away from the podium—

A crimson flower erupted on his chest as a gunshot echoed through the room.

37

GARRETT

KRISTINA GAVE a strangled moan of horror. Her legs buckled and she would have fallen if I hadn't looped an arm around her waist. I held her as we stared at the screen. The King was being carried off stage, his body limp. Then the news program cut to a white-faced news anchor in the studio.

I realized Aleksander, the advisor, was still on the phone. We could hear him saying *Oh my God, oh my God,* over and over again. Then he said he'd call from the hospital and he was gone.

And then we had to wait, powerless and desperate. I sat Kristina down on the couch and gripped her hand. I couldn't imagine what she was going through. At least I'd been able to rush my dad to the hospital, to *do* something. She was stuck thousands of miles away.

After ten minutes that felt like ten weeks, Aleksander called. The King was alive and in emergency surgery. The shooter had somehow slipped away, but they'd found his rifle. "It was my fault," he kept saying. "I was too slow."

Kristina hushed him. "You did everything you could."

Almost an hour went by and then the screen lit up with a video call. I knew the woman must be in her fifties, but she looked no more than forty. Not a single strand of gray dared to break the pitch-black of her shoulder-length hair. Her blue business jacket and skirt were immaculately styled and cut to show off her ruthlessly-toned figure. I could see traces of Kristina in her eyes, although the princess looked much more like her father. But even if the resemblance hadn't been there, I'd have known who she was from the way everyone bowed. *"Your Majesty,"* they all said in unison.

"He's still in surgery," the Queen told Kristina. Unlike the King, she didn't bother to acknowledge the staff, or me. "I've had the top specialists flown in but it'll be a while before we know anything." Her voice barely trembled and, though I could see a hint of tears at the corners of her eyes, it was as if they were imprisoned behind glass. She would not allow herself to show weakness.

The Queen glanced at me and her eyes narrowed. When I followed her gaze, I realized she was glaring at our joined hands. *Shit!*

"Mother, this is Mr. Buchanan," said Kristina. "The man who's been protecting me."

The Queen's nod was quick and sharp as a scalpel. "Thank you," she said, but her eyes seared into me as if she wanted to burn me off the face of the earth. When she ended the call, my stomach was knotted. *She knows. Or suspects.* And it wasn't like the distrust I'd felt from Emerik. The Queen seemed to actually hate me, just because I was a commoner. It was a brutal reminder of the gulf between me and the princess. I glanced at Kristina's troubled face. She was so much more like her father, trusting and kind. I tried to imagine what it must have been like, growing up with a mother that cold and hard. Had she always been like that?

My stomach lurched. What if she hadn't? What if becoming queen had done that to her? Was that what Kristina would be like, when she eventually took power?

We had to wait another hour for the next update. This time it was Aleksander and, after the Queen, it was a relief to see his friendly face. But the news he had wasn't good. "The bullet only clipped his heart: he moved just in time to save him. And the surgery went well. But..." He sighed. "He's lapsed into a coma. The doctors don't know when he will regain consciousness...."—he pressed his lips tight together—"... or even if he will."

Kristina nodded, her lower lip trembling.

"What *is* clear is that this isn't some simple act of revenge by an extremist group. They tried to assassinate you, now they've moved on to your father. This is an act of war by Garmania. They're trying to wipe out the royal line, to destabilize our country."

"To what end?" croaked Kristina. From the way she said it, she already knew the answer.

"So that they can invade again," said Aleksander.

Kristina nodded and ended the call. Then she hunched forward in her seat, almost curling herself into a ball, and began to sob. I reached for her, but she shook her head: *give me a minute.* I retreated to the hallway.

And found Emerik standing there, arms crossed. It was the first time we'd been alone together that morning and I recognized the look he was giving me. It was the same look Katie Wagner's brother had given me in high school when I'd asked her out. *You hurt her,* it said, *and I'll kill you.*

I gave him a slow, deliberate nod to show I understood. Then I made a pot of coffee for everyone. They were doing their best to hide it, for Kristina's sake, but they were shaken: this was their *King.* He seemed like a really decent guy, despite being a politician. Hell, I'd only spoken to him once and even I liked him.

While the coffee brewed, I called the hospital for an update on my dad. No change. The bullets had done so much damage that, at his age, he'd be in critical condition for days or even weeks. *I should be with him, dammit.* But I couldn't leave her, not now.

I tried to figure out what we should do. We knew now what the assassins had done after we'd finally plugged the leak and lost them in Texas. They'd flown to Lakovia to assassinate the King. They must have false passports, or the FBI would have stopped them at the airport. More evidence that someone high up was helping them.

With them in Lakovia, Kristina should be safe in the US for now. If I could keep her off the grid, maybe she could wait this whole thing out. I just had to take her somewhere we could disappear. Someplace with plenty of tourists, where no one would look twice at a woman with a British accent. *New Orleans!* We'd rent a cheap room somewhere and just vanish.

I handed out the coffee and marched through to the living room to tell Kristina. "Grab your stuff," I told her. "We're going to—"

"I'm going home," she said.

I blinked. *"What?"*

"Back to Lakovia."

I could feel my face falling. "Lakovia is the most dangerous place in the world for you right now! The assassins are there, waiting for you!" I stepped closer. "I know you want to be with your dad, but there's nothing you can do right now. You'll be safe in the US and—"

"You don't understand," she said, standing. "My father's incapacitated. I'm next in line. Garrett... *I'm now Queen!*"

My jaw dropped. I'd been so busy thinking about her as a person and how upset and scared she must be, I'd never thought about that part. "But they'll kill you!"

"My people need me. Our country can't be without a ruler, not if Garmania's about to invade."

She looked up at me and *God,* the fear on her face. This whole thing was taking her back to what happened to her during the war, to being left alone in that black, bare stone cell. And yet that imperious jaw was set firmly. She was doing this for her people, even though she was terrified. Even though she was years from being ready to rule. Even though it would probably mean her death. That fluttering in my chest, that swell of loyalty: I've never in my life respected someone so much. It only took me a split second to make my decision.

"If you're going," I told her, "I'm coming with you."

She looked at me, incredulous. "Garrett, you can't!"

"I'm not letting you go back there unprotected."

"I'll have my royal guards."

"They couldn't protect the King."

Emerik, Jakov and Caroline had drifted in, drawn by our raised voices. Kristina looked embarrassed and lowered her voice. "Garrett...

Lakovia is a different world. You know how traditional we are. There are barely any foreigners. You wouldn't fit in."

"I don't give a damn."

"You wouldn't be allowed. The only people allowed to protect the Queen are the royal guards and—"

"Then make me one."

She froze and stared at me.

"Make me a royal guard," I repeated.

She held my gaze for another second and then lowered her eyes to the floor. "Give us the room, please," she said, then waited while they left. When they'd gone, she took my hand. "Garrett... I'm the Queen, now." Her voice was shaking. "Even if there was a way we could be together before, we can't be now. The people, the media... they're deeply distrustful of outsiders. If you come with me, *we can't be together*."

I knew she was right. Knew this would be even harder than before because I'd have had her and lost her. Hell, I'd be right next to her, all the time, but unable to hold her, touch her, kiss her. It would be torture.

But not being able to protect her... that would be even worse. I looked her right in the eye. "I understand," I said, "Your Majesty."

Her eyes were filling with tears. Her throat moved, but she couldn't speak, not without losing it completely. She just nodded.

"Tell me what I have to do," I said.

She bit her lip. "Kneel," she managed.

I went down on one knee before her, like I'd seen them do in the movies.

"Repeat after me," she croaked, barely holding back the tears. "I swear allegiance to my Queen."

I looked her right in the eye. "I swear allegiance to my Queen."

"I promise to pro—to protect her from all dangers, foreign and domestic."

My deep Texas growl filled the room. "I promise to protect her from all dangers, foreign and domestic."

"I will guard her to the end and sacrifice whatever my duty

demands, even if—"—she gulped, sobbed, recovered—"even if it demands my own life."

"I will guard her to the end," I repeated. "And sacrifice whatever my duty demands, even if it demands my own life." That feeling I'd had, ever since I first met her, was filling my chest. I'd never thought I'd find something worth giving myself to, after the marines. But her? My Queen? Hell yeah, I'd die for her.

She nodded: it was done. I was a royal guard. I could see her trying to form *thank you* with her lips, but she'd started crying too hard to get it out. Instead, she reached down, placed her hand on my head and knitted her fingers into my hair. I nodded and gently rested my own hand on top of hers.

It was time to go to Lakovia.

38

GARRETT

THE CARGO FLIGHT from New York to Lakovia was long and uncomfortable: we spent it strapped into the fold-down crew seats, passing around a thermos of coffee. But it got us there safely and with the time difference, we arrived early in the morning.

As we came in to land, I saw snow-capped mountains sweeping down to rich, green valleys and acre after acre of thick forest. It was beautiful...but it was as different from Texas as she was from me.

When we stepped off the plane, I shivered. It was cold, despite it being summer. A fresh, crisp kind of cold I'd never felt before: the air tasted so *clean*. Off in the distance, I could see the white turrets of what must be the palace. They poked up through a mist that seemed to shroud the whole country. It gave Lakovia a storybook feel. I half expected to see a dragon.

"It's the altitude," said Emerik, next to me. "Lakovia is so high in the mountains, we're almost in the clouds." He was having the opposite reaction: he was almost bathing in the frosty air, glad to be home.

"You'll get used to it," Jakov told me. He clapped me on the back and we started down the steps. A lot had changed in the last few days.

When I'd first met the two guards, I'd been nothing but suspicious and Emerik had downright hated me. Now, after everything we'd been through, I'd trust them both with my life. In this strange place, they were the only friends I had.

Kristina stopped for a second when she reached the top of the steps and stood there, eyes closed, the breeze blowing her hair out behind her, as she took a big, grateful breath of mountain air. She fit here, I realized, in the same way I fit in Texas. She was home.

As we reached the bottom of the steps, we were surrounded by royal guards. For days, they'd been stuck here in Lakovia, helpless, while their princess was in danger in a foreign land. Now they finally had her back. Couple that with the fact she was now queen, and their King being shot, and they weren't taking any chances. We were ushered straight to a heavily-armored SUV and the convoy was moving almost before the doors were closed. For a second, I wondered if I'd done the right thing. *Maybe she's right. Maybe she doesn't need me, with all this protection.*

But these men hadn't been able to protect the King. I looked across at Kristina and my jaw set. I was right where I needed to be.

We'd barely left the airport when we heard an explosion in the distance. "What was that?" asked Kristina.

"Bombs, Your Majesty," said the driver. "In the city. They started going off just before you landed."

It was warm in the SUV and Kristina had slipped off her coat and laid it across our laps. She grabbed my hand under the fabric and squeezed. I squeezed back, trying to reassure her, but I was shaken. First her father being shot, now bombs? We'd spent days trying to get her home, where she'd be safe, but this place wasn't safe anymore.

"You have a video call, Your Majesty," said Emerik. "It's the President of the United States."

Kristina and I looked at each other in shock. Then she swallowed and nodded to a screen. "Put him through." She took a deep breath, her face pale. I felt my chest ache in sympathy. She'd probably never spoken directly to a world leader before, certainly not our President, and never as the leader of a country herself. She was being thrown into this job long before she was ready—

She remembered something and quickly pulled her hands out from under the coat and folded them in her lap.

... and I can't even hold her hand.

The screen lit up with the Presidential seal. And then it was *him,* sitting behind that famous, huge wooden desk, his face grim. I tried to work out how I felt. *Awed,* partly: I mean, it was the President, dammit. President Matthews is a Texan, like me, and I've always liked him: even more so after that whole thing with his daughter and the threat to our country. But he's also a politician, part of the system that betrayed me. I couldn't trust that system ever again.

"Your Majesty," said the President. "I was so sorry to hear about your father."

Kristina nodded stiffly, as if afraid to trust her voice.

"I wanted to apologize for what happened to you in my country. I want you to know that the FBI is working non-stop to get answers and they'll continue to share all their information with the palace."

"The men who attacked me weren't American, Mr. President," said Kristina.

"But it happened on my watch," said the President. "You were a guest in my country and someone hurt you and for that I apologize."

I was stunned. I'd never heard a politician speak from the heart like that.

"If there's ever anything I can do for you," said the President, "I hope you'll ask. One more thing: I understand you have a Mr. Garrett Buchanan with you?"

I froze. Then swallowed and leaned slightly so I was in shot. "Yes, Mr. President?"

"Mr. Buchanan, you did a good thing. And I'm a big believer in second chances. Just... bear in mind that you're representing America over there. Okay?"

I nodded. Awe was winning out over my distrust, and easily. "Yes, Mr. President," I managed.

He ended the call. A moment later, everyone started craning their necks to look at something on our left, just becoming visible through the trees. "What is it?" I asked.

Kristina's voice was thick with emotion. "We're home."

39

KRISTINA

I'VE ALWAYS LOVED the palace, with its slender towers and pointed roofs. When the sun hits the white walls it almost glows, pure and bright, like nothing bad could ever happen there. Now, though, it was different. Only one of my parents was going to be waiting to greet me. *Don't cry, don't cry.*

To my relief, Garrett distracted me. "What's *that?*" he asked, pointing to what looked like a massive stone wall in the distance.

"A dam," I told him. "It generates the power for half the city. My father had it built, just after the war. He wanted to send a signal that it was time to scale back the military and look to the future." *And it looks like he was wrong. And now I might have to take my country to war.* Suddenly, the palace didn't seem welcoming. I was terrified. *I'm not ready!*

As I stepped nervously down from the SUV, the palace guards bowed low and then swung open the doors. My mother was waiting just beyond them and I ran to her. We hugged... well, *I* hugged; she stood there stiffly. But I've learned to accept the way she is now. I still remember what she was like before the war, when she smiled and laughed and *loved,* and that helps. I know that she's still in there, somewhere.

"What's *he* doing here?" she asked as soon as she saw Garrett.

"Mother! He saved me!"

"And he'll get a fistful of silver, or pounds, or whatever they have in America. But it's not appropriate that he's here. Only the roy—"

"He *is* a royal guard. I made him one."

She gawped at me, then crossed her arms and glanced at Jakov. "It was bad enough when you and your father insisted on hiring a Garmanian to guard you. But an American?" She narrowed her eyes. "What's going on, Kristina?"

I felt myself flushing and prayed it wasn't visible. "Nothing!"

Garrett arrived behind me and bowed politely. My mother just glared at him, then wheeled around and stalked off.

Aleksander ran over and embraced me. He, at least, was capable of giving me a real hug. He turned to greet Garrett, too, but faltered when he found himself eye level with Garrett's chest. He recovered fast, craning his neck back to meet Garrett's eyes and warmly shaking his hand. "I'm sorry, Your Majesty," he said, "But there are things you must attend to. As soon as your maid has had a chance to dress you in something more appropriate—"

I held up my hand. "Before anything, I need to see my father. Where is he?"

Emerik took Garrett off to find him a guard's uniform. Aleksander led me to an elevator and took me down. Due to the bitter winters in Lakovia, people have always built down into the earth. The palace has several floors of cellars, including the palace dungeons and a medical facility.

Dr. Glavnic, the head of the palace's medical staff, showed me into a private room. He was in his sixties, a bear of a man with a thick silver beard, and he'd been looking after our family for decades. He even helped to deliver me. "There's no change," he said sadly. "But talk to him. There's some evidence that it helps."

He and Aleksander left me alone and I walked slowly towards the bed. My father looked so peaceful: aside from the bandages on his chest, he could have just been sleeping. But the shrill beep of the machines made it impossible to pretend.

I ran to him and threw my arms around his neck. And once I started to cry, I couldn't stop. It was the first time I'd been alone since I became Queen. When would I next be able to let it out?

So I sobbed. I cried until the sheet covering him was damp. "I don't know what to do!" I whispered to him. "I'm not ready to rule, not even close! And there's no one I can talk to, not one person—"

The door creaked behind me.

I turned around.

The dark blue of his royal guard uniform was like the very last light of the day, just before true dark. And its gold braid, when it caught the light, was like the first kiss of dawn. I'd been around royal guards my whole life but I'd never seen the uniform look like *this* before, the snow-white shirt stretched tight over a chest so broad. He was born to wear it. His shoulders were so strong and wide as they pushed out the jacket, his waist so tight and muscled above the leather belt. I knew that Emerik would have tried to tell him that all royal guards are clean shaven, but Garrett had clearly drawn a line because his cheeks were still dark with stubble. Strong, honorable... and *rough.* Willing to break the rules, if that's what it took to protect me.

I'd been wrong. There was still one person I could talk to, even if we couldn't be together. I ran to him, threw my arms around him and he hugged me into his chest for long minutes. We only separated when we heard Aleksander's footsteps in the hallway.

Aleksander took me upstairs to my bedroom—as my chief advisor, he's one of the very few staff who is allowed in my private chambers—and waited outside my room while Caroline helped me in a dress. It was a relief to be back in more traditional clothes, but—I looked sadly at the American clothes I'd just taken off—sort of a shame, too.

"If you're ready, Your Majesty," Aleksander called from outside, "we should go. They're waiting for you."

I rushed outside. "What? *Waiting* for me? Who's waiting for me?"

"Your other advisors. The commanders of your armed forces.

Representatives of the treasury, the courts, the intelligence services and the police—"

"You just said there were some things to attend to!" I said, hurrying down the stairs. "Why didn't you tell me there were people waiting?!"

"Well... because you're the Queen, Your Majesty. They'll wait all night, if necessary."

I stopped dead on the stairs and stared at him. That's when it really sank in. *I was the Queen.* And this was the moment I had to start ruling.

Downstairs, Garrett rejoined us and fell into step beside me. Aleksander led us to what we call the Great Room, where my father has all his meetings. The doors are twenty feet high and Aleksander walked ahead of me, nodding to the guards to open them.

I stopped. *I'm not ready!* I didn't know tactics or political maneuvering like my father. I couldn't give inspiring speeches, and I couldn't do that voice my mother did that made people obey: my version was just a pale imitation. "I can't do this!" I whispered to Garrett.

"Yes you can, Your Majesty," he told me in that honeyed rumble. He grabbed my hand and gave it a secret squeeze behind Aleksander's back. "I believe in you."

I took a deep breath and moved forward into the room.

There were at least a hundred people there, rows and rows of them arranged around a circular table that held the most senior ones. As one, they all stood and bowed.

I tried not to let my legs shake.

My father's huge, ornate chair was waiting for me. I slowly sat down. My feet *almost* touched the ground.

Everyone waited.

I swallowed. "The bombs," I said. "Tell me about the bombs."

"No deaths yet, Your Majesty," said the head of the security services. "But a lot of destruction: famous storefronts, monuments, some public squares. All well-known places. They're trying to spread panic and it's working: people are terrified. No group has claimed responsibility. We're analyzing the explosives they used. We're guessing they'll turn out to be Garmanian."

"It's a classic tactic." Everyone turned to look at General Novak. He was a big, round man with thick white hair and mustache. "Eliminate the leadership, then spread panic among the population. When you have absolute chaos: invade."

Novak had been in charge of our armed forces for twenty years and had guided my father through the war. He hadn't wanted the peace deal: he'd thought we should have pressed our victory and wiped out Garmania completely. My father always described him as a big, loyal attack dog who had to be kept on a tight leash. They'd argued, especially over cuts to the military, but my father had always trusted him. And now it looked like Novak had been right all along. Garmania was going to invade us again. *Oh God, please no.*

"The Garmanian Prime Minister continues to deny any involvement," said Aleksander.

"Is it possible he's telling the truth?" I asked. "Could Silvas Lukin be doing all this on his own?"

"I don't see how," said the head of intelligence. "He has access to military-grade weapons, like the mortars he used in Texas."

Garrett ambled forward out of the darkness. A few people eyed him suspiciously, but his imposing size made them listen. "There's something else. Someone high up, someone who has access to all the information coming out of the FBI, is helping them out. If Lukin's just some lone nutjob on a cause, I can't see how he'd get that kind of help. But if a government's behind it, that makes a whole lot more sense."

Novak nodded gratefully. Then he turned to me. "Since the war, your father's been scaling back our military. The Garmanian forces outnumber ours. If we wait until they attack, we'll lose."

My stomach sank through the floor. "You want me to attack *first?!*"

Novak slammed his fist on the table. "They attacked *us!* They shot your father! They tried three times to kill you! They've put bombs in our capital city! If that isn't an act of war, I don't know what is!"

The room seemed to spin around me, a carousel going way too

fast. *This can't be real. I can't have millions of lives in my hands.* "I won't go to war without more evidence," I managed. I looked at Aleksander. "And make sure nothing leaks to the media about these attacks maybe being connected to Garmania. *Nothing.* Not until we're sure."

"At least let the Air Marshal ready our bombers," said Novak. "Then we can launch immediately if things change."

I hesitated... then weakly nodded. All of ten minutes in power and I was discussing going to war. All the horrors I thought we'd left behind us... they were all going to come back. I was scared and if *I* was scared..."The people must be terrified," I said aloud.

"Yes, Your Majesty," said Aleksander. "You should address the nation and tell them to be brave. I'll arrange a broadcast—"

"No," I said. "That's not what my father would have done. He wouldn't have sat here, safe in the palace, and told people to be brave while there were bombs going off. And if this *does* turn into war, I'm going to have to ask mothers to send their sons and daughters into combat. I can't ask them to do that if I'm cowering in here myself." I thought for a second. "What's happening with my coronation?"

Aleksander looked shocked. "With the threat to your life, I was thinking we'd just do a small, private ceremony—"

"No. Do what we'd normally do. The whole thing. A parade. Show the people that these bastards don't scare us."

There was shocked silence. Then, "Of course, Your Majesty. We'll make plans right away."

I met Garrett's eyes across the room. He looked furious that I was putting myself in danger... but he slowly nodded. He understood why I was doing it and he'd protect me.

Just gazing into those clear blue eyes made my heart feel like it was being slowly torn in two. I needed him to protect me, but I needed so much more than that. I needed to feel his arms around me again. I needed to wake up to the warmth of his chest against my back. I needed *him*. And I knew, looking into his eyes, that he needed me, too.

Those feelings weren't going away. We were just keeping them buried.

And I wasn't sure how long we could.

40

KRISTINA

TWO DAYS LATER, the lights went out.

I'd known it was going to happen at some point. There'd been another bombing: like the others, it hadn't killed anyone but it had been carefully calculated to spread panic and disruption by taking out the high-voltage lines that led from one of our power stations. Half the city was without power, including the main hospital. I'd ordered that the palace's supply be diverted: the patients were more important than we were. But it was still a shock when the room suddenly went dark, enough to make me cry out.

Garrett burst in, then slid to a stop when he saw I was okay. By then, though, he was almost touching me. I felt the tiny hairs on the back of my arms stand to attention and I caught my breath. God, I *ached* for him.

With shaking hands, I lit a candle. The flickering light threw his shadow onto the wall, making his huge form seem even bigger. We stood there gazing at each other. He looked *amazing* in the guard's uniform, even better than he had in his plaid shirts and jeans. Something about all that expensive dark blue and gold stretched over his tan skin. Formal on the surface, rough underneath. He looked... *right* in a uniform.

His wounds were healing up well and he was adjusting to palace life. I'd heard him taking lessons from Emerik on etiquette: he was learning all the proper terms of address, when and who to bow to, even some of our traditions. He was completely out of his element: he'd been thrown into this just as I'd been thrown into ruling, but he was determined to be the best royal guard he could. I loved that about him.

"If everything's alright, Your Majesty," he said in that honeyed rumble, "I should be outside."

Technically, he wasn't supposed to be in my chambers unless there was an emergency. And I knew we should stick to that, to avoid temptation. Just walking around the palace with him was hard enough. Every brush of his hip on mine, every touch of his hand as he steadied me when I tripped... we'd look at each other and I'd feel it flooding through me: we were a *hair's breadth* from diving at each other and we both knew it. Being alone like this was foolish. Downright dangerous.

But....

But I'd been in meetings with General Novak all day, my stomach twisting as he talked about casualty projections measured in the millions. Now it was dark and in another few hours I'd have to go to bed. And then the nightmare would come. I'd be back in that stone cell, all on my own, the water rising. I'd wake up, soaked with sweat, stifling a scream, and have to dig my fingernails into my hand and bite my lip to resist calling Garrett, knowing that all it would take to banish the nightmare forever would be to give in and be with him again. I couldn't. I knew that. Seeing Lakovia and my mother again, taking the throne... it had reminded me of my responsibilities. *Princesses don't get to choose who they love.*

I missed America, too. I missed the scenery and the horses and especially the food. The day before, I'd asked the palace chef to make ribs for dinner and looked forward to them all day. But when they'd arrived, it was a plate of four tiny bones, artfully arranged in a square, with a small pot of barbecue sauce on the side for dipping. With silver cutlery, so that I didn't dirty my hands. I'd thanked him politely but it wasn't the same.

Mainly, though, I missed him. I needed him there. Just for a little while. Even with the candle, my bedroom was too dark, too like the cell. If I had to be there on my own, I'd go insane. And I couldn't ask Caroline: she was still broken-hearted over Sebastian. We'd barely talked, since we got back to Lakovia. *Does she blame me for what happened?*

Something glinted in the candlelight and I saw the excuse I needed. I set the candle down on the table next to the chessboard. "Do you play?" I asked.

He ran one big hand through his hair, embarrassed. "Ah... I've played a little. Felton, in my squad in Iraq, he had it on his phone. He taught me how, but I ain't much for strategy." He looked closer. "Are they *solid silver?*"

I nodded. "The pieces and the board. From our silver mines. I always thought it was a bit over the top. But I keep it set up because my father likes to play with me." I caught myself and bit my lip. "I mean... he did."

He gazed at me across the board... and slowly nodded. He pulled out a stool and sat, and we began.

"Any word on your father?" I asked after a few moves.

He shook his head. "Still critical. No better, no worse."

God, if he dies.... I bit my lip. "Garrett, he needs you—"

"You need me more." Our eyes met and a big, hot bomb went off in my chest. There was no argument to be had, here. He *would* protect me, no matter what the personal cost. *I can't be worth all that,* I thought helplessly. But God, he made me feel safe like no one else.

"Heard you've been getting up early," I said, dropping my eyes to the board. "Caroline keeps seeing you walking the halls, before anyone else is about."

He grunted. "Been trying to learn my way around. All the damn doors look the same, Your Majesty. And nothing leads where you'd expect."

I nodded and grinned: the first time I'd smiled in days. Just being in his presence was relaxing. "You haven't even seen all of it yet," I told him. "There are secret passages, too."

He moved his knight and then gave me a sideways look, unsure if I was joking.

"There *are!* Three of them." God, it was so good just to talk to him. "One of them leads from the dungeon out to the gardens: there's a door hidden behind some white camellia. That was for if the royal family were ever captured and locked up in their own dungeon and needed to escape. The other two lead from different places direct to bedrooms. They were for smuggling in lovers."

I caught his eye just as I said the last word and suddenly flushed. I tried to look away, but I couldn't: our eyes were locked. I could feel my cheeks and then my ears turning red. Lovers... like us. The Queen and her guard. *Stop thinking like that!* I had to forget New York ever happened. I fumbled for a piece and made my move.

"Checkmate," he rumbled, placing down his knight.

I blinked at the board in amazement. His knight had my queen pinned in a corner. *What?!*

When I rewound the game in my mind, I saw it. I'd been playing tactically, like my father had taught me. Sacrificing pawns, faking out my opponent, always thinking three moves ahead. Like a queen in charge of an army. But he...he hadn't sacrificed a damn thing. He'd protected his soldiers. He hadn't tried to outwit me. He'd just powered through with sheer grit and determination... like a marine.

And that's when it overwhelmed me. God, I loved this man. He was my exact opposite... and that was exactly what made us work so well together.

He stood to go, but I stood, too, without consciously willing it, that *pull* between us linking me to him. He drew in his breath. "Your Majesty...." he said warningly.

"I know." But I took a step towards him. I couldn't help it. I knew in my head that we couldn't allow anything to happen, but my whole body was aching for him. My heart was slowly tearing with each millimeter he moved towards the door and I knew that all I needed to do to fix it was touch him. My skin was alive, prickling and sensitive, ready for the brush of his fingers, the press of his body. My ears hurt from the silence. I needed to hear that deep Texas growl.

I took another step towards him.

He glanced at the closed door behind him and drew in a shuddering breath. I could see the muscles of his chest standing out under his shirt: his whole body had gone hard with tension. "We can't."

"I know." But I took another step.

"*Stop, damn you!*" he grated.

I finally stopped and we stood there staring at each other in the darkness, only a foot apart.

"You don't know how close I am to grabbing hold of you right now," he growled.

"Yes I do," I whispered.

There was a loud knock at the door and we jerked apart like startled cats, hearts pounding. It took another knock before I got my breath back and told them to come in.

Aleksander was standing there, along with the head of the intelligence services. I showed them in and they sat at the table. Garrett loomed silently out of the darkness and both of the newcomers jumped in shock: like most people around the palace, they found Garrett's size intimidating and they hadn't expected him to be in my chambers. Aleksander glanced curiously between Garrett and me. But if he suspected something between us, he was polite enough not to say anything.

"Your Majesty," said the intelligence chief, "I'm here because we're not making any progress with Sebastian. He claims he wasn't passing Caroline's location onto anyone. He claims he's genuinely in love with her."

I nodded slowly. "Well... I'm sure you're doing the best you can."

He and Aleksander stared expectantly at me.

"I'm sorry," I said. "I'm not sure what else you want me to say."

The intelligence chief leaned forward. "Your Majesty... conventional interrogation techniques aren't working."

And then I understood. I heard Garrett's intake of breath from the darkness as he realized, too. "You want me to authorize torture," I said slowly.

They nodded. Aleksander looked grim. *God, Sebastian's his assistant! They've worked together for years!*

"No," I said firmly. "Absolutely not."

"It would be strictly off the record," said the intelligence chief in a low voice. "Only a few people would ever know. "

My jaw dropped. "You think I'm worried about getting *caught*? Reported to the UN? You think *that's* my problem with this?!"

Garrett stepped closer and that low Texas growl filled the room. "Your Majesty... they may be right. It might be the only way to catch the assassins. They wouldn't hesitate to do much worse to you."

I held his gaze for a moment. Those clear blue eyes were full of concern: he just wanted me to be safe. But—

"No," I said. "And that's final. I won't sink to their level."

Aleksander bowed. "As you wish, Your Majesty." And he and the intelligence chief left. Garrett gave me a careful bow, then stepped towards the door to leave as well.

"Garrett!"

He stopped.

"Do you think I made the right decision?"

He turned to face me and I could see the sympathy in his eyes, the way his big hand was crushing the door handle. He was fighting the urge to grab me and pull me into his arms. "I'm just glad I'm not the one who has to make it," he said at last.

"My father always said this was the loneliest job in the world," I told him. "I'm just starting to understand what he meant."

He looked down at the floor, breathing hard. I could sense the battle going on inside him because I felt the same way. "We can't be together," he said at last. "That doesn't mean you're on your own."

My eyes went hot and I had to press my lips together hard. I nodded.

"Will there be anything else, Your Majesty?" he asked.

I shook my head, my voice cracking. "No, Garrett. There won't be anything else."

He backed out of the door and closed it. I slumped against the heavy oak, then slid down it to the floor as the tears started.

41

KRISTINA

"It's time," said my mother.

I stood... and nearly fell, my legs were trembling so much. Caroline grabbed my arm and steadied me.

My mother put her hands on my shoulders. On the surface, she was as controlled as ever, her make-up perfect, but for once I could see the genuine emotion in her eyes. "I know this isn't the way we wanted it to happen," she said. "But this is *your* day. Try to enjoy it." She squeezed my shoulders. "I'm so proud of you."

I couldn't speak. Between the fear of messing this up and the danger I would be in, I was so scared I thought I might throw up. So I just nodded. My mother stepped back and, ahead of me, the doors to the square creaked open.

The sunlight was so bright that I couldn't see anything. It felt as though I was walking forward into a fiery doorway that would just consume me. Then, as I got outside, my eyes adjusted and—

Thirty thousand people lined the balconies of the historic square: five floors of them, towering above me. Some of them had stood in line for a full day and night to get a spot. My steps faltered. *I can't—*

Then my eyes locked on Garrett, standing to attention just beside the throne. For this ceremony, they'd added a peaked cap to his uniform, its polished brim glinting in the sunlight. The shadow it cast made those blue eyes shine even more. He gave me a tiny nod. *You can do this.*

I walked to the center of the square, where the head of the church was waiting. I sat slowly on the throne, my hands tightening around the golden arms.

"I crown you Queen Kristina," he said. "May you reign well."

The crowd started its cheer before he'd finished speaking and the volume only increased as the crown slid onto my head. *God, it's so heavy!* I carefully stood, heart thumping, petrified I was going to drop it. The crowd was deafening, now: I had no hope of hearing what they were saying, but the roar lifted me up and carried me. I looked up and waved to them and it got, if possible, even louder.

For a second, the crowd's joy swept everything else away and my heart swelled. *I am Queen.*

Then the responsibility hit me again. *Please God, don't let me let them down.*

But I was so glad I'd insisted on having the ceremony. Every face in the crowd was joyous. They needed this, after the bombs and the assassination attempts. And I needed to remember what I was fighting to protect. *I can't let all this be destroyed by war again. I can't.*

I walked the short distance to where the royal carriage was waiting. Six well-trained white horses were harnessed and standing patiently, despite the roar of the crowd. Garrett gave me his hand to help me climb up. They'd given him white gloves, too.

"I'll be right behind you," he said. And squeezed my hand.

I drew in my breath. God, the temptation to just lean forward and kiss him....

Ten million people are watching on live TV. I gave him a prim little nod and climbed up into the ornate carriage. It was like climbing into a golden jewelry box.

The parade set off. Police motorbikes at the front, two SUVs full of guards, my carriage and then another two SUVs. We crawled along at walking pace through streets lined twenty deep with people, all applauding and cheering. *My people.* I waved until I felt like my hand was going to drop off. *I'm just... me. I don't deserve this.* But feeling that outpouring of love was amazing. I was a mess of emotions: ecstatic and awed and humbled and terrified, all at once.

And then the bomb went off.

It was somewhere off to my left: I saw a flash and then the whole carriage was lifted and tilted to one side. I was sprayed with tiny, hard nuggets of something: they rained down all over me, glinting like jewels. I realized the safety glass in the windows had been blown out. But I was okay. The carriage slammed back down onto its wheels. We were alright—

There was a chorus of terrified whinnys. *Oh God, the horses!* They were rearing and stamping, terrified. The crowd was in uproar, too, everyone running and screaming, and that was panicking them even more. The driver was frantically trying to calm them. The parade had stopped and I saw guards scrambling out of the SUVs, guns drawn to protect me.

Then the second bomb went off, this time to my right. The horses reared again—

And bolted.

I was thrown back in my seat as the carriage shot forward. Boxed in by the SUVs, the horses picked the one clear path left to them: sideways into the crowd, through the space that had been cleared by the first bomb. We bounced over curbs and flower beds. They were galloping at full speed and all I could do was hang on.

When I glanced behind me, my heart sank. The convoy was in complete disarray: the guards had all jumped out of the SUVs when we stopped, not expecting the carriage to shoot off. There were too many people running and screaming for them to drive after me and we were moving faster than they could run.

I was on my own.

Ahead, the street was blocked by crowds. It was chaos: people had run to try to escape the explosions, but now the horses were bearing down on them. The carriage was jolting and bouncing as we clipped parked cars. We were going far too fast—

And then the horses slewed to the side. The carriage couldn't turn that sharply. I felt it tilt—

No!

....and roll. I screamed, desperately trying to cling onto something. There were no safety belts. The windows were gone and I was terrified I was going to be thrown out and crushed beneath the carriage when it landed.

We crashed down on our side, spun and slid and then grated to a stop.

I lay there panting for a moment, disoriented. Then I got to my knees and gingerly peeked out through the front window. All I could see was legs: thousands of people running past the carriage in blind panic, so many that it kept jerking and rocking as their bodies banged against it. Another explosion shook the street, then another. Each one whipped the people faster. I saw people falling and being trampled. *Oh Jesus....*

And then I heard gunfire. No more than fifty yards ahead of me, and getting closer.

The assassins. They were coming for me.

I ducked down, wedging myself into a corner. And then I heard someone climbing up the carriage and clambering onto the side that was now the roof. I shrank back, terrified....

Garrett leaned down through the window and stretched out his hand. His cap was gone and his chest was heaving. He must have sprinted flat out to catch up to me. "Take my hand," he said.

I've never been so glad to see anyone in my entire life. I grabbed his hand and he hauled me off my feet and *up, up, up*—

I gasped as I saw the scene. The carriage was a tiny island in a sea of rushing people. Everyone was surging down this street to get away from the bombs and we were trapped in the middle of it. And I could hear the gunfire coming closer and closer. "We can't stay here," said Garrett.

I looked back the way we'd come. The SUVs couldn't get any closer, not without mowing down the crowds. And the flow of people was too strong for the guards to force their way through on foot.

"Listen," said Garrett. "I'll lower you down first—"

"Into *that*?" My voice cracked. The crowd was made of normal, rational people, people who'd been cheering me just moments ago. But now they were running for their lives and, with so many of them, the crowd was like a living thing, a surging river that was sucking down and drowning anyone who didn't keep up.

"I'll be right behind you," he told me. "Just stay right beside the carriage. Do *not* move."

I nodded breathlessly. He took my hands, then crouched and lowered me over the edge. People tore past me, inches from knocking into me, but I managed to stay in the lee formed by the wheels. Then my feet hit the ground and I pressed myself up against the underside of the carriage.

"Good! Stay there! I'm coming!" He scrambled to the edge and started to jump down—

A man sprinted past me and his elbow caught me. I spun, stumbled in my heels...

"*No!*" yelled Garrett.

And the crowd swept me away.

42

GARRETT

I'VE NEVER KNOWN fear like it. The crowd carried her off like a twig tossed into rapids. Inside of a second, she was gone.

No! There! A glimpse of her white and gold dress. I jumped down off the carriage and was running as soon as my boots hit the ground. My height let me see over the crowd and keep her in sight: *just*. All around me, people were pushing and shoving but I just dropped my shoulder and ran like I was a linebacker again. The hot fury was building inside me: I could see people on the ground and lost children crying for their parents. These bastards didn't care how many innocents they hurt. And the gunfire was getting closer: they were coming for her.

They weren't going to get her. I surged forward, battering people out of the way. I kept catching glimpses of her up ahead and I was gaining. *Just stay on your feet, Kristina. Another few seconds.*

And then the smoke from one of the explosions rolled across the street. It missed Kristina, up ahead, but it surrounded me. I'd been sucking down big lungs of Lakovia's crisp, clean air as I ran, but suddenly my lungs spasmed, shaken by acrid fumes. All I could see was white and I could feel ash and cinders hitting my face, some of them still hot enough to burn. My part of the crowd slowed and broke up, everyone stumbling in different directions. *Shit!* I had to pull up short to avoid tripping over a fallen woman and then I couldn't figure out which way I'd been going.

I turned in a circle, coughing. The smoke thickened and—

I felt the memory bearing down on me. I closed my eyes, tried to shut it out but—

It slammed into me. The sand scrunched under my feet as I fought for grip against the wind. I was fumbling along the side of the house, rough concrete under my fingertips. Then there was nothing to follow: I was lost, buried in sand and dust, the air as solid as the ground. I could see nothing, not even my own boots. I staggered on, gun out in front of me, struggling to breathe. And then the man ran out of the dust. Only feet away and heading straight for me—

Cool, damp mountain air bathed my face. The wind was whipping the smoke away. I was in Lakovia, on the street. The crowd was picking up speed again as more explosions sounded in the distance but—

I couldn't see her. I couldn't see her anywhere.

Oh Jesus. How long had I frozen for? *Oh God, please no.* My eyes searched the crowd.

But I'd lost her.

43
***
KRISTINA

I WAS LIFTED AND CARRIED, scrambling to stay on my feet. All I could see was shoulders and necks and black, screaming mouths.

Another bomb went off, this one close enough that the world jolted and rocked and, when it stabilized again, there was no sound. I looked back for a second and, to my horror, the carriage was like a toy in the distance. Then smoke hid even that.

The crowd ran until it hit the end of the street, then pooled and twisted, splitting to rush down side streets. Someone pushed me in their panic and I slipped and went down. I saw backs and then—

No!

Running legs and—

No!

Feet.

I screamed and curled into a ball as I was trampled.

44

GARRETT

IT'S MY FAULT. My fault for being weak, for being a mess. If something happens to her—

I forced myself to push it all aside. Now that the smoke had cleared, I could get my bearings. I sprinted in the last direction I saw her, overtaking the rest of the crowd, barging them aside. But I still couldn't see her. Up ahead, the street ended and split into a maze of side streets. It was a swirling mess of people. I was taller than most of them but—my stomach knotted—if she was down on the ground....

I jumped up onto a parked car and from there onto a parked truck. That let me climb up onto a hotel balcony and then, finally, I could look down from above. Still nothing. I glanced around, frantic: was there a better vantage point?

And then I froze.

Silvas Lukin was on the balcony two along from mine, a radio raised to his mouth. We stared at each other in shock for a full second. Then the rage hit me and I started sprinting along the balcony towards him. *My dad! Kristina! All those children you killed!* I was going to rip his *goddamn head off!*

I was just jumping across to the next balcony when I saw him snap an order into the radio and point to a spot in the crowd. I followed his finger.

Kristina! My throat closed up. She was lying on her side, unmoving. Her white and gold dress was stained red with blood.

Then I saw the men moving through the crowd towards her. Lukin's men, dressed in black and armed with rifles. That's what he was doing up on the balcony: he'd been directing them as they searched for her. And now he'd found her.

I took another step along the balcony. He was six feet away. I could reach him: I could end all this.

But not before his men killed her.

With a howl of fury, I vaulted over the side of the balcony and landed hard on the street. Legs screaming, I put my head down and charged through the crowd to where Kristina lay. I dropped to a crouch as I reached her and touched her shoulder....

She didn't move.

My stomach lurched. I didn't have time to check if she was alive: Lukin's men would be on us in seconds. I picked her up and tossed her over my shoulder, praying nothing was broken. Then I looked for somewhere to run.

The first gunman burst out of the crowd and pointed his rifle right at Kristina. I roared in anger, grabbed the barrel of his gun and heaved, hurling him aside.

I battered my way onto one of the side streets. It was quieter, there, easier to move, but almost immediately another gunman burst out of a cross-street ahead of us. I had to hold Kristina to my shoulder with one hand while I pulled my gun and shot him with the other. Then I looked around, panting. *Shit!* They were surrounding us. I was outnumbered and it would be a while before the rest of the royal guards found us. Where could we go? *Think!*

Then I looked down.

I set Kristina gently down on the street and then heaved up the heavy manhole cover. Someone was watching out for us because Kristina chose that moment to stir. My heart lifted. *She's alive!*

We didn't have time for the ladder. I took her hands and lowered her down. She was groggy but she had just enough awareness to stand when her feet touched bottom. Then I scrambled in myself, pulled the cover over my head and dropped down to join her.

For long seconds we stood there in darkness. Had one of Lukin's men seen us? I pointed my gun up at the cover, waiting for it to lift....

Nothing. I finally let out a long sigh and then wrapped Kristina into my arms. "Are you okay?" I whispered. "Are you hurt?"

She mumbled something, still groggy. I pulled out the new phone Emerik had given me and used its screen as a light. Her delicate face was smudged with dirt and there was a red mark where she'd taken at least one kick in the cheek. Her dress was covered in footprints and when I gently ran my hands over her she winced at the bruises. But I couldn't feel anything broken and the blood on her dress was on the outside. Someone else's.

I took her hand and we hurried through the ankle-deep water, the noise of the crowd fading behind us. When she couldn't run anymore, I carried her. I eventually stumbled to a stop at a grating. Beyond the bars, I could see the sun sparkling off the river. We were at least half a mile from the assassins.

We were safe.

I called Emerik and told him where we were. Then I took Kristina in my arms and we clutched each other harder than we ever had before. I'd come so close to losing her. As long as I was holding her, she was safe.

But after just a few minutes, I heard sirens approaching. Then doors slamming and running boots. Kristina's mouth was by my ear. Even so, I could barely hear her voice, it was so weak. "You have to let me go," she said.

I savagely shook my head and tightened my arms around her even more.

"You have to," she rasped. "They can't find us like this. You have to let me go, Garrett."

I closed my eyes. And let her go.

45

GARRETT

WHEN THE DOORS of the palace opened, Aleksander was there to meet us. He gave a huge sigh of relief when he saw Kristina. "Thank God," he said, embracing her. Then, over her shoulder, "Thank you, Mr. Buchanan."

When he released her, he shook his head. "From now on, Your Majesty, I must insist you don't leave the palace. This is the only place we can guarantee your safety. I've also asked General Novak to put soldiers in the palace, to supplement your royal guard."

"I'm safe in here," said Kristina bitterly. "What about our people, out there?"

I felt that flutter in my chest again, the rush of loyalty alongside the love. She'd nearly died and her first thought was for her people.

"They're terrified, Your Majesty," Aleksander allowed. "And there's something else: a few news sites have started running stories about Garmania. How the attempts on your life were by Garmanians, how this is likely a prelude to war."

"*What?!*" Kristina went pale. "How did that get out there?"

"I don't know," said Aleksander. "But it's out there now." General Novak joined us and stood silently listening. "There have already been some attacks on Garmanian communities in Lakovia. Vigilante 'justice.' There may be rioting, once the sun sets."

An intake of breath beside me. Jakov had walked in and was standing there, fists balled. God, of course: his parents lived in one of those communities. I patted the big guy on the back.

"I'd like to put troops on the streets, Your Majesty," said General Novak. "To patrol those communities and quell any riots."

Kristina closed her eyes. "If that's what it takes... very well."

"Also, Your Majesty," said Aleksander, "the Garmanian Prime Minister wants to speak to you."

"I'll call him right away," she said. Then she swayed on her feet and I had to grab her arm to stop her falling.

"He can wait," said Aleksander tenderly. "Let's get you cleaned up and let the doctors take a look at you." He led her to the elevator. As the doors began to close, I stared into her tear-filled eyes. I had to force myself not to run to her, haul the doors open and gather her into my arms. I sighed and headed off to call the hospital and check on my dad.

"*Mr. Buchanan!*"

I'd know that voice anywhere. I winced and turned around. Jakov had disappeared and even General Novak had slipped away. It was just me... and the Queen. Or as she was now known, the Queen Mother.

"Your Majesty," I said with a bow. "What can I—"

Her voice was a dagger shaped from ice. "Did you really think I wouldn't find out?"

Shit.

She stalked closer to me, her heels echoing on the marble floor. "Emerik denied everything. But I eventually got it out of Jakov. I know what happened in America. In *New York*!" She spat the last two words.

I lowered my eyes to the floor and said nothing. I didn't blame Jakov for talking: the Queen Mother was intimidating as hell. But I was glad to hear that Emerik had tried to cover for me.

"How *dare* you?" she said. "You're a soldier. A hired thug."

She spat the word *soldier* as if it dirtied her mouth. For a second, I couldn't understand the hatred. Then I remembered Kristina's horrific imprisonment at the hands of Garmanian soldiers. *Dammit.*

"She was grateful to you for protecting her," snapped the Queen Mother. "So you took advantage of her. You took her to bed and mounted her like a cheap wh—"

Hot rage boiled up inside me, unstoppable, and my head snapped up. The anger in my eyes stopped her dead. I wouldn't let her speak about Kristina like that. I fought to get the words out, to tell her how I felt about her daughter—

But I didn't have to. The Queen Mother's expression changed: first shock, then horror, and then she just looked tired. "You stupid, *stupid* man," she breathed. "You're in love with her."

I braced myself... and nodded. She closed her eyes and sighed. "Aren't you going to ask if she loves me?" I asked.

"No, I am not. Love isn't for people like us, Mr. Buchanan. It's for you, the common folk. A queen marries for power, for security, for peace. That's the way it's been for hundreds of years. She *cannot be with you*, Mr. Buchanan."

"I don't care," I growled. "I'll protect her, for as long as she needs me."

"And what about when the courting starts?" asked the Queen Mother. "The romance? Are you ready to hold the door open for her suitors as they arrive? Will you chauffeur them, watching in the rear view mirror as they kiss in the back seat?" She leaned closer, each syllable a vicious little stab. "Will you stand guard outside her bedroom door, knowing he's fucking her inside?"

I stood there helpless. I was furious, but I had no words to fight back with.

"Spare yourself, Mr. Buchanan." She said my name as if it tasted bad. "And if you don't care about yourself, spare her. She has enough to worry about, with Garmania about to invade again. Can't you see the pain you'll put her through: the man she can't have, right there in her sight every day? You're condemning her to misery."

I marched off, raging. I walked the halls trying to calm myself, but there was a hurricane blowing inside me. I felt like a goddamn bull in a china shop: my heavy footfalls set vases rocking and suits of armor rattling. I was too big, too unrefined for this place.

I finally came to a stop under a row of life-sized paintings of the royal family and their ancestors. They were arranged by date and in the most recent one, Kristina stood there in a white dress and tiara. She was beautiful. She was special. She *fit* in this place.

She was up there in the clouds and I was down in the mud, where soldiers always are. Even if I wasn't, even if I had a magic lamp and a genie who could make me a goddamn prince, it didn't change what was inside me. It didn't change what I'd done.

I made a decision. And went to find Kristina to tell her.

46

KRISTINA

DOWN IN THE MEDICAL FACILITY, Dr. Glavnic checked me out. I had some scrapes on my shins and calves that he carefully cleaned, a lump on my head where I'd been kicked and plenty of bruises, but there'd be no lasting damage. "You were lucky," he told me.

"I had Mr. Buchanan," I told him.

I checked in on my father, but there was no change. I slowly climbed the stairs up the tower to my room. Just lifting each foot was an effort: I was exhausted. *Everything's such a mess.* Garmania about to invade us. My own people close to rioting. I'd seen Jakov's face when he heard about the vigilante justice. All his fears were coming true. I'd hidden the cherry candy I'd bought in America away in a drawer. I knew I wouldn't be able to convince him to give it to Simone, not when things were like this.

In my bedroom, I fell into a chair. The sun was low and the room was a mass of shadows.

Something moved out from behind the drapes. A figure. I let out a half scream and dived for the door. *There's someone in here!* I turned on the lights—

"Sorry," said Caroline absently. "Didn't mean to scare you."

I wilted, panting, my hand to my chest. "*Jesus!* What are you doing in here?"

"I just wanted to be alone," she whispered.

She looked thin and drawn. *Is she eating?* "Caroline..."

She shook her head and tried to push past me. I had to grab her arm to stop her. "Talk to me!" I demanded.

She was close to tears. "You have a country to run," she said.

So *that* was why she hadn't been talking to me. Being Queen had even messed up things with my best friend. "Oh, Caroline!" I gathered her into my arms. "I *always* have time for you."

She hiccoughed. Her face crumpled. And suddenly it all came out, all the tears she'd been holding back since we discovered Sebastian was a traitor.

"I'm just—" She sniffed. "I just want to see him. Even after what he did. I just—Why can't everything just go back to the way it was?"

"I know," I whispered, stroking her blonde hair. "I know."

She shook her head viciously. "You *don't* know," she said. She pulled back and looked at me. "Kristina, I thought he was the one!"

She threw herself against my chest again and started sobbing. My chest ached for her. I'd had no idea it was that serious. No wonder she was heartbroken.

"They have him in a *cell!*" she sobbed. "And everyone's—"

She broke off, but I frowned. "Everyone's *what?*"

"I heard some of the other maids talking. They think I must have known. Or that I'm stupid for not realizing."

My arms tightened around her. I was going to have some very stern words with those maids. "He was very convincing," I said gently. "I liked him too. He had us *all* fooled. He's so nice." Shy, in fact. That's why I'd been so surprised at the idea of him and Caroline together.

"That's what I like about him," croaked Caroline.

I released her from the hug so that I could look at her.

"Other men just want to..." She looked down at her feet. "You know. They think I'm blonde, and a maid, and they want me for... *fun.* But Sebastian, he treats me like I'm something special." Her lower lip trembled and she looked up at me. "He makes me feel like—"

She broke off and started sobbing again, but it didn't matter: I knew what she meant. I've always known that it must be hard for her, being best friends with a royal.

Sebastian had made her feel like *she* was the princess.

I hugged her close. "I'm sorry," I told her. "I'm sorry all this happened."

She shook her head. "It's not your fault," she managed.

But that didn't stop the guilt that was welling up inside me. It was me they were trying to kill. All the casualties of this thing: the dead FBI agents, Caroline, Garrett's dad... I felt responsible. I held Caroline for a long time, until she'd cried herself out.

"Do you want to do something, when all this is over?" she asked, sniffing.

I nodded. "That spa in the mountains, with the hot tubs?"

"I'd really like that." She hugged me again, then let me go. "You have work to do."

I nodded reluctantly. "I have to call the Garmanian Prime Minister."

I saw her hand tighten on the doorknob at the mention of Garmania. "Give the bastard an earful from me."

When she'd gone, I slumped into a chair and picked up the phone. I stared at the old-fashioned receiver for a moment. I was exhausted, battered and in pain: I was in no shape to be attempting negotiations. But on the way down to the medical facility, Aleksander had shown me a report that left me no choice. I had to try to stop this turning into a war.

I took a deep breath and asked the palace secretaries to put me through.

"Your Majesty." The Prime Minister's accent took me straight back to the soldiers in my nightmares. "I'm relieved to hear you're alright."

"Thank you," I said carefully.

"I was concerned to hear about the attempts on your life. And the bombings. A terrible business."

I crushed the receiver in my hand, furious. I thought of Garrett's dad, of Caroline. *A terrible business?!* I knew he was a master politician, knew he'd been playing this game since before I was born. But how could he lie so brazenly? "Mr. Prime Minister... we know that the group responsible is led by Silvas Lukin, the Garmanian war criminal. We know that his men are Garmanian soldiers from his old squad—"

"Terrorists," said the Prime Minister calmly. "I assure you we don't support—"

"They're using Garmanian weapons!" I snapped, already losing my cool. "The rifle used to shoot my father! The mortar and incendiary rounds used to try to kill me in Texas! All manufactured in Garmania!" I snatched up the report Aleksander had given me. "I'm looking at a report on the bombs placed in our city: the explosives are the same type your army used in the war!"

He faked righteous indignation. "Are you suggesting—"

"Prime Minister, we know what you're doing. We know what you're planning!"

"Let me tell you what *we* know," he said coldly. "We see Lakovia close to falling apart, its people panicked, its leadership failing to protect them. You lash out at our country, accuse us of supporting terrorism in your media. We see Garmanians in your country persecuted, attacked in their homes—"

"We're already moving to stop that," I said quickly.

"Meanwhile, our satellites show activity at your airbases. You're preparing to attack. If you do, we'll have no choice but to defend ourselves."

What?! That's how he was going to play it, turn it all around and paint *them* as the victim? "Mr. Prime Minister, *please,*" I begged. "I—" I took a deep breath. "I *don't want a war.* But I'll do what I have to, to protect my people."

"As will I, Your Majesty."

And the line went dead.

I stared at the receiver, panting in frustration, and then hurled the thing across the room. I put my head on the desk and wrapped my arms over it. I just wanted to break down and cry. Whatever I did, war was coming. Millions were going to live or die based on what I did. *I'm not ready for this! I'm not a queen!*

Garrett's words came back to me. *I believe in you.*

I let out a long sigh, then swept my hair back from my face and sat up. I picked the phone up off the floor and called in General Novak and Aleksander. When they arrived, I filled them in on the phone call. Neither of them seemed surprised.

Aleksander sighed. "With this, the attack on the coronation and the evidence that the explosives they're using are Garmanian... Your Majesty, there's only one choice here. We have to attack."

I shook my head. "There must be some other way."

"Your Majesty, your father trusted me," said General Novak. "I ask that you do the same. War is inevitable at this point. We must attack first."

I wish Garrett was here. "How many?" I could only manage a whisper. "How many will die?"

"My latest estimates are two million of our people, over the course of the war."

"How many *in total,* General?"

"Two million of ours, Your Majesty. Eight million Garmanians."

The numbers were horrific, unthinkable. "And if I don't attack first?"

"Then their bombers will likely target our cities. Six to eight million of our people, a longer war: one I'm not sure we'd win. At least as many dead on their side, maybe more."

Ten million people. Dead. Or more than that if I didn't attack first. I wanted to throw up. They were right, there was only one decision I could make but that didn't make it any easier. "We attack," I said. "How does it work?"

General Novak nodded somberly. *Thank God he's here.* "The bombers will launch tomorrow morning at dawn, Your Majesty. They'll enter Garmanian airspace and start their bombing runs roughly an hour later."

"You'll go on TV and issue a formal declaration of war just before they cross the border," said Aleksander. "Also: the President of

Sorvatia is on his way. Once the war starts, we'll have to move troops and supplies through his country to reach parts of Garmania. He'll be here this evening."

I nodded. "I'd like to be alone now."

I managed to hold on until the door had closed behind them. Then I ran to my bathroom and threw up.

Kneeling there on the tiles, I started shaking and couldn't stop. *I've failed. I've failed my people.* My bathroom's not big, but the room felt enormous, a vast plain with winds whipping across it to chill me. I needed to get warm. I needed Garrett's arms around me.

But I couldn't have them.

Instead, I walked on shaky legs to the bathtub and ran a hot, deep bath. I dumped in some of the mandarin and patchouli oil I loved so much. I'd been dreaming about taking a bath ever since this whole nightmare started. But when I got in, it didn't relax me. I wanted *him.*

And then I heard his unmistakable, heavy footfall in the hallway outside my chambers. The thump of his knock, like a giant who has to knock with just one knuckle, or he'll knock down the door. That deep Texas rumble...but there was something wrong, a halting tension in his voice. "Your Majesty?"

Immediate, overwhelming relief. *He's here.* I needed him: God, I needed him. This rock of a man, the one person who wasn't all about double-talk and scheming. And right on the heels of that, the knowledge that we couldn't be together. *It isn't fair, damn it!*

I swallowed. "Come in. I'm bathing."

I heard the door to my bedroom open and then close. His footsteps approaching the bathroom door. My heart started to race: did he understand I only meant *come into the bedroom?* What if he just walks straight in here and sees me— My eyes went to the unlocked bathroom door and the lust slammed into me, pushing back my problems for a moment. The effect he had on me was physical, immediate. I could actually hear my breathing growing quicker and more ragged with each footstep that came towards me. Imagining his big hand turning the handle, the door swinging open, his eyes roaming over my body....

He stopped. I heard him hunker down and sit, right outside my bathroom door. I actually saw the door move a little as he leaned against it. I let out a long, heavy breath.

"The war's about to start," I told him through the door. "Whatever I do, however hard I try, I can't change it." I lay there staring at the door, wishing I could see him. "Garrett... did you ever send people to die?"

"No, Your Majesty. I'm just a grunt. I get the easy part."

He didn't try to tell me it would be okay. I loved that about him: the total lack of bullshit. But then he went quiet and I knew something awful was coming.

"Your Majesty," he said at last. "There's something I need to tell you."

Despite the hot water, a chill started to seep into me. "Go on," I told him.

"It's been an honor to serve you," he said. "But I have to leave."

47

GARRETT

"No," said Kristina. "No! I need you!"

I stared at the dark, polished wood of the door. I could hear her, hear the tiny laps and splashes as she moved around in the tub. I could smell the bath oil, like sweet oranges and flowers. Her skin would smell of it, if I ran in there and pressed my body against hers, her wet breasts pillowing against my chest. In my mind, I could see her, skin glistening, strands of her chestnut hair sticking to her pale shoulders.

My hand ached with the need to just grab the handle and hurl the door open. Sitting there was the hardest thing I've ever done in my life... which was exactly why I had to leave.

"You're safe in the palace," I said. "And I've heard the General, he's confident you'll win the war as long as we attack first. The threat against you will be gone."

"It's not just about needing your protection." The pain in her voice made my chest ache.

I closed my eyes. "I know. That's why I have to leave." I sighed. "You're a princess—Hell, you're the Queen, now. I'm—"

"I don't care what you are, Garrett!"

I opened my eyes and looked around at the huge chandelier and the four poster bed. At the solid silver chess set and the gold candlesticks. "We're from two different worlds, Kristina. You can't be with me. I thought coming here with you was the right thing to do, but it's just hurting you more and I never wanted to hurt you. You're the most special damn thing I've ever known in my life. I never wanted anyone so bad. But life ain't a fairytale." I pressed my palm against the door, wishing I could touch her.

48

KRISTINA

I WAS LEANING out of the bath, my hand pressed against the door. Even through the thick wood, I swore I could feel the warmth of him on the other side. "Stay," I begged. "Stay and we'll find a way!" My heart was pounding, my stomach a cold, dark knot of fear. Everything he was saying was true. We *couldn't* be together. But the thought of losing him forever made all those rules and traditions suddenly seemed so wrong. "*Stay!*"

The Texas rumble again, a vibration I felt in every inch of wet, exposed skin. "Even if we could figure something out, I'm not right to be with anyone. Got some bad shit in my head."

I needed to fix this before we tore apart forever. But I had to pick my way carefully or I'd shatter the slender bridge that still remained. My whole body had gone cold and I slid fully back into the bath and lay there in its heat and steam as I thought desperately. "Garrett," I said at last, "I know that things happened to you in the war. That's okay. I know what that's like. You know I do."

I heard his intake of breath, that protective rage as he remembered what happened to me. It warmed me inside. *I can't live without this, without him to make me feel safe.*

"It ain't just what happened," he said. "It's what I did."

And for the first time, I glimpsed the root of all that pain. *Guilt.* That's what he'd been carrying all these years. I had to help him, to save him. God knows, he'd saved me enough times. "Whatever it was, it's okay. I know you, Garrett. You're a good man. Tell me what happened."

But he was silent. He wasn't going to tell me. He was going to get up and go and that would be *it,* I'd never see him again. I'd be on my own forever. And *he'd* be on his own forever.

No. I wasn't going to let it end like this. I owed him too much. Even if we couldn't be together, I needed to help him before he left. I'd go out there and *make* him talk. *I'll stand up, throw open the door, wrap my arms around him and—*

But I couldn't get up.

At first it was funny: my legs had gone to sleep. But when I tried to wiggle my toes, they didn't respond. And when I tried to reach down and feel them, my arms wouldn't move. Something was horribly wrong.

I flexed my back, trying to sit up, but nothing happened. I was lying there helpless, chin a few inches above the surface. *What the hell?*

Through the door, I heard Garrett's body shift as he adjusted position. *Garrett!* I'd call to him. He'd help me. I inhaled... but my lungs barely moved. And my vocal cords wouldn't cooperate: I couldn't yell, couldn't even speak.

I was paralyzed.

For a moment, I just lay there listening to the faint sound of my own breath. And then something started to happen.

I was slipping.

I couldn't feel it because my legs were completely numb, but I could just see out of my peripheral vision that they were starting to flex as the muscles weakened. And as they flexed, my body was sliding down the bath...and under the water.

Oh Jesus Christ no.

I moved a millimeter at a time, the water rising up my neck. I was going to drown and I couldn't let Garrett know there was anything wrong. My only chance was if he spoke first. If he broke the silence and I didn't respond, and he realized something was wrong. *Please, Garrett! Talk to me!*

Silence.

The water lapped at my chin, then began to creep towards my lips. *Garrett! Talk to me!*

But the silence stretched on. I slipped down, down.... and then it happened: the water reached my lips.

Garrett!

A rivulet of sweet, scented bath water spilled over my lower lip and into my mouth. Then another and another. It became a flow, filling my mouth. And then it started to drain down into my windpipe. Inside, I was hysterical: I wanted to kick and thrash and scream. But my frozen body wouldn't move. I didn't even gag: the muscles no longer worked. The water just ran freely, filling my lungs. And I started to drown.

49

GARRETT

I WANTED TO TELL HER, but I couldn't. I couldn't go back there, to Baker and the house, the dust and the blood. All the pain and guilt rose up inside me and locked my throat down tight. Maybe if I had her calming touch, I could handle it... but if I ran in there and took her in my arms, we'd start something we couldn't stop.

I silently shook my head... and dropped my palm from the door. Then I got up and walked away. Through her bedroom. Out to the hallway.

But the further I got from her, the stronger the pull back towards her. I came to a stop on the threshold, the door handle gripped in my hand.

I couldn't shut the door.

I couldn't not be with her.

The instinctive urge to protect myself, to keep the memories sealed up tight, was strong... but the need to protect her, to be with her, was overwhelming.

I stomped back into the bedroom and over to the bathroom door. I stood there raging at myself, fists bunched, trying to get the words out. Eventually, I closed my eyes and laid my forehead against the cool wood. "I never told anyone before," I muttered. "But I want to...I *got* to tell you. And if you hear it all and you still want me...."

She didn't reply.

"Your Majesty?"

Nothing.

I raised my voice a little. "Kristina?"

Silence. A silence that made me go cold, right down to my bones.

I threw open the door. She was lying completely submerged, her hair sprayed out in a cloud around her head, her eyes open and staring at the ceiling. My stomach lurched. *Please God, let her just be lying there soaking. Her ears are underwater, maybe she didn't hear me.* That had to be it. I'd move into her line of sight and she'd jerk upright—

I loomed over her, but her eyes just stared sightlessly up at me. *Oh Jesus God, no—*

I plunged my arms into the water and scooped her up. She was limp in my arms: no breath, no movement. *What the hell happened?!* Had she slipped and hit her head? But I would have heard something and there was no blood.

Then I saw the rash. Very faint, like twisting pink snakes looping around her limbs and across her torso. *Something in the water.* I'd heard of stuff like that, in Iraq. Nerve agents: you didn't even have to breathe them in, just getting them on your skin was enough.

I ran. Down the stairs of the tower, through the palace hallways. Soldiers had begun to arrive to patrol the palace and I bellowed at them to *get out of the way!* The route to the medical facility was burned into my brain after all those hours trying to memorize the place. Down *this* hallway, into the elevator, four floors down—

I burst into the medical facility, hollering at the top of my lungs. "*Doctor! Need a doctor!*" A nurse screamed as she saw the naked, dripping princess in my arms. Doctors swarmed us and I told them about what I thought had happened. They snatched her from my arms and had her on a gurney inside of five seconds.

I raced with them into a treatment room. One doctor fed a tube down Kristina's throat while another readied a defibrillator. A third started hosing the stuff off her skin.

I stumbled back out of the way to let them work. I could feel the shock getting to me, now: my legs had gone weak and my chest felt numb. "Will she be okay?"

The doctor who seemed to be in charge, a big guy with a silver beard, was wiping Kristina's leg with a cotton swab. "I need to find out what she's been poisoned with. If you're sure it was in the water, then I have a suspicion...." He shoved the cotton into a test tube and filled it with a clear liquid, then shook it. The liquid turned blue. "There. We have an antidote." He grabbed a vial from a cabinet and started filling a syringe. At the same time, the guy with the defibrillator paddles shocked the princess for the first time. Her body jerked, but then fell lifelessly back to the gurney. *Please! Please wake up!* I couldn't lose her—

I fell.

It happened so fast, the first warning I had was when my ass hit the tiled floor. I hadn't slipped: my legs had just quit supporting me. *What the hell?*

I tried to get up. Couldn't. My arms didn't have any strength.

That's when I realized my clothes were soaked through with the bathwater, from carrying Kristina.

Some of the doctors broke off and surrounded me. "No! Save *her!*" My voice was getting weak. My lungs were barely moving air.

"No response!" yelled the guy using the defibrillator on the princess. "Charging, three hundred!"

"Get him on a gurney!" said someone else.

I was falling again, this time down a long, black tunnel. "Save *her!*" I croaked.

And then nothing.

50

KRISTINA

I opened my eyes. Blinding light seared into them and I screwed them closed again. When I moved my head, it set off a stabbing pain that jolted right down my spine and hurt all the way to my toes.

But I didn't care. The pain meant I could feel again, could move again. I was alive.

Dr. Glavnic filled my vision. "Your Majesty!" He said it as one long sigh of relief.

I tried to sit up and at first he winced and tried to coax me back down, but I kept struggling and he sighed again, put his hands under my shoulders and helped me up. "You've been unconscious for almost seven hours," he told me. "You were poisoned. Mr. Buchanan only just got you here in time."

I looked around. We were the only two people in the room. "Where is he?"

Dr. Glavnic looked at his shoes.

My stomach lurched. "*What?*"

"The poison was in your bathwater," he said. "Mr. Buchanan got soaked with it, carrying you here."

"He carried me all the way here?!"

"He's bigger than you and was in contact with it for less time, but

the increased exertion meant it hit his organs more quickly and..."—
he pressed his lips together—"we'd already used the antidote on you,
Your Majesty. We sent for more straight away, but—"

"You should have split it between us! How is he?"

"He hasn't regained consciousness."

"Where is he?!"

"Next door." His eyes bugged out as I tried to scramble off the
gurney. *"Wait!"* he said. I ignored him. "Your Majesty, your body's
been through a huge trauma—" My legs were like jello but I gritted
my teeth and stumbled on, clinging to the bed for support. The
doctor cursed, put his arm through mine and helped me along.
Together, we made it through the door, along the hallway and—

I drew in my breath. Garrett lay on a bed, his muscled form filling
it completely, his feet almost dangling off the end. Monitors beeped
in time to a slow, sickly pulse.

I grabbed onto the end of his bed. Someone was slowly crushing
my heart with freezing fingers. This big, honest, *good* man, one step
from death because he'd met me. And I couldn't even show how I felt
about him because Dr. Glavnic was right there, watching me.

"Could I have a glass of water, please?" I asked, fighting to keep
my voice level.

"Of course, Your Majesty." He paused and I could feel his eyes on
the two of us. "It may take me a moment to find a glass."

He knows. I wondered how many other people did. I nodded
gratefully and he withdrew.

I staggered around the bed to Garrett's chest and threw my arms
around him. I began to cry, tears dripping onto his cheeks. "Wake
up," I whispered. "Wake up *please* because I need you here with me. I
can't do this on my own, Garrett."

I buried my head in the crook of his neck and sobbed my heart
out, clinging to him. And then a big hand patted my back. I lifted up,
not daring to believe it. But he had his eyes half open. I gave a groan
of relief and pulled him close. We stayed like that for a long time. I
thought I heard Doctor Glavnic come in behind me... and then
quietly leave again.

Garrett slowly sat up, wincing with pain, just as I had. Then he started to swing himself out of bed. "Wait!" I yelped. "You're not meant to be—You got it worse than me, you shouldn't be on your feet!"

"No choice," he muttered. "Got to get to the evidence before someone gets rid of it."

He leaned on me and I leaned on him and, together, we managed to stumble to the elevator and then climbed the stairs of the tower. There were soldiers standing guard in the hallways, now, and they gawped at us as we passed in our medical gowns, but we ignored them. In my bathroom, the bottle of bath oil was still on the side of the bathtub and Garrett reached for it.

"Careful! Don't get any on your hands!"

He nodded gratefully, looked around, and then used a plastic shower cap to pick up the bottle. He turned it over a few times before showing me a pinprick hole in the neck. "Someone injected the poison into the bottle, so they could leave it still sealed."

My legs weakened and I had to slump against the wall. Someone had crept into my bathroom and done this.

My last safe place was gone. There was a traitor inside the palace.

51

KRISTINA

GARRETT WRAPPED me into his arms. I closed my eyes, put my head on his chest, and just let him hold me. I was physically and emotionally exhausted: having him almost leave, then almost losing him, now *this*....

One thing I knew: I needed this man in my life, no matter the cost. I ran my hands over those arms that made me feel so safe. I had to finish what we started, get him to open up so I could help him. "Look," I said. "We have to—"

There was a knock at my bedroom door. When I opened it, Aleksander was there. "Your Majesty," he said apologetically. "I'm so glad to see you're alright. And you, Mr. Buchanan. And I'm sorry to ask when you're still weak, but...."

"What is it?" I asked.

"The President of Sorvatia will be here in half an hour," he said. "I was going to take the meeting on your behalf, but I thought I should ask, now that you're awake...."

I nodded. "I'll meet him." I wasn't really up to it, but we couldn't win the war without Sorvatia's help and it was my job as Queen. "I'll need to change."

Garrett stepped outside with Aleksander. "Your Majesty, I'll be right outside your door."

My strength was slowly coming back but my legs still felt rubbery. I took a quick shower and then clumsily laced myself into a corset and gown: meeting with a head of state called for the full, traditional look. Normally, I would have got Caroline to help me, but I couldn't bring myself to call her, not when she was so upset about Sebastian. I did my make-up and pinned my hair up. The final step was to slide the crown carefully onto my head. Then I opened the door.

Aleksander was gone, but Garrett was right outside, just as he'd promised. When he saw me, his lungs filled, that strong chest rising. "... *wow*," he whispered at last.

I glanced down at myself. I hadn't thought there was anything special about it: he'd seen me in gowns before, though maybe never in red. This one was deep scarlet and deeply traditional, certainly not revealing or anything. If anything, with my hair pinned up and everything corseted and buttoned up tight, I looked super-formal. But the way he looked at me lit a warm glow inside me. "Thank you," I said.

He led the way downstairs and then Aleksander showed us to the Great Room. The dark oak table had been polished to a mirror-like shine and decorated with gold candelabras.

President Belliani, the head of Sorvatia, rose to meet me. He was in his late fifties, with a greasy, balding pate and a slight pot belly hanging over the front of his expensive pants. He kissed me on both cheeks and then took my hand. "I am so glad to see you've recovered, Your Majesty," he told me. "It's been too long. When I last met your father, you were just a teenager."

I nodded politely and we sat. As soon as I sat down, a wave of tiredness hit me. After everything I'd been through, I probably shouldn't have been out of bed, never mind negotiating. But I needed Belliani's help. I glanced over at Garrett, who'd taken up position behind Belliani. *He must be exhausted, too.* But he stood ramrod straight, hand clasped behind his back, ready in case I needed him.

"There is very little time," I told Belliani. "Tomorrow, soon after dawn, we'll attack Garmania. To defeat them, we'll need to send our troops through your country so that we can attack from the north as well as the south. Will you allow that?"

Belliani nodded. "Of course I will help you, Your Majesty."

I let out a sigh of relief. *Thank God.* "Thank you, Mr. President. Now—"

"I will help you as I helped your father," he said, "last time you had a war."

Had a war. As if it was some game we chose to play. But I nodded in thanks. "Now—"

"My roads will be bombed again," he said. "My infrastructure damaged... again."

I opened and closed my mouth a few times, caught off balance. "We are indebted to you, Mr. President," I said sincerely. "And of course we'll pay for—"

But he waved aside my offer and leaned forward. "I help you because our countries have always had a special relationship. A relationship I consider very important."

"As do I." I smiled gratefully, but I was flustered and confused. I didn't see where this was going. What the hell did he want?

"You will have my help," he said. "Your troops can pass freely through my country. And when you've won your war, I look forward to you visiting my country." He smiled. "Have you been to my villa in the mountains?"

I shook my head, smiling back at him. "No, but I'd lov—"

And then I froze. He was staring into my eyes in a very particular way.

"It's very private," he assured me. "A chance to get away from the public."

I'm imagining things. He's not—He can't be....

"Would you like that, Your Majesty?"

He was. I could see it in his eyes, just as clearly as if he'd been some drunk in a bar propositioning me. He was offering passage through his country... but only if I promised to sleep with him. And as soon as the realization hit, it was confirmed: a twitch, at the corners of his mouth. He knew that I knew. And it amused him to see me struggle with it.

My first reaction was shock. He'd gamble with my country's future, with millions of lives, just so he could say he'd bedded a queen? Then anger. How *dare* he? Of course I wasn't going to—

Then my stomach lurched. What would happen if I didn't do it? Even as a teenager, I'd followed the last war closely enough to know that moving our troops through Sorvatia had been vital to our victory. If I refused him, I was condemning us all.

This was my duty. I was asking my soldiers, male and female, to lay down their lives for their country. All I had to do was endure an hour lying on silk sheets in a country house. No one would ever have to know.

My mother was right. This is what she'd meant: a queen's relationships aren't for love. I'd sleep with Belliani and, eventually, I'd marry a man like him to prevent some future war, or secure Lakovia's safety for the future. That feeling I'd had, ever since the war... it would never go away. Because even when I married, I'd still be alone.

I swallowed and lowered my gaze. I could feel Belliani smirking. He knew what my answer was going to be.

52

GARRETT

I STOOD BEHIND BELLIANI, listening with growing disbelief. At first, I thought I must have gotten it wrong. I wasn't used to all this double-talk and subtlety. But when I saw the look on Kristina's face, I was sure. This bastard was talking about bedding her. He was the opposite of her: he was everything I hated about politicians, playing with soldiers' lives just to get what he wanted.

My hands curled into fists behind my back. I wanted to grab Belliani by the neck, ram his head into the wall, and shake him until he apologized. But she was The Queen. I had to let her deal with it her way. As soon as she'd given the bastard a dressing down, I could enjoy throwing him out.

But she didn't yell at him. She sat there staring... and then lowered her eyes. *She can't be....*

She was. She was considering it. She was going to sacrifice herself for the good of her country.

No way. No. Fucking. Way. I had to stop her, even if it meant we lost the war. I stepped forward to grab Belliani.

But then, suddenly, I didn't need to.

53

KRISTINA

It was the crown.

I'd been staring at the table. As I made my decision and lifted my head to look at Belliani, I felt its weight pressing down on me. I suddenly knew why they made it so heavy.

It was to remind you that you were *The Queen.*

I stood up. "President Belliani. If you think that I will spread my legs for you to—"

Belliani interrupted with smooth confidence. "Your Majesty! You are mistaken. I would never presume to—"

"I HADN'T. FINISHED. SPEAKING."

The room went utterly silent. I'd done the Queen voice for the very first time. It had been inside me all along. All the color drained from Belliani's face. "You will allow my troops to pass. You will allow me to save my people. You will do this without any sordid deal. Or you will make me into something you don't want: an enemy."

Belliani had to swallow three times before he could work up enough saliva to speak. "Of course, Your Majesty," he croaked. "It would be my honor. I apologize for the misunderstanding."

I glanced at Garrett and froze. The look on his face scalded my cheeks and sent a hot throb sinking down to my groin, where it detonated. *Oh my God....*

All of those rules and traditions, everything that had seemed so important, even his past: it had all just been overridden. He'd always seen me as a princess. He'd just seen me as a queen.

I had to get Belliani out of that room. I had to get him out *now*.

I walked around the table towards Belliani. He got up so fast, he knocked his chair over. "I'm sorry," he mumbled. He bumped into Garrett and then shrank back from his furious expression. When he looked at me, though, he looked even more scared. He backed through the door as if not daring to turn his back. "Sorry," he kept repeating. "Thank you, sorry."

I nodded coldly and pushed the door closed behind him. I just had time to turn around—

Garrett pinned me to the door with his kiss.

54

KRISTINA

BREATHLESS. That's the best way I can describe it. Breathless because it happened so fast. Breathless because neither of us wanted to stop to breathe. Our mouths were panting and desperate, our lips finding each other so easily, trained by countless hours of fantasy. Our tongues explored each other, finally free, and then danced joyously together.

All of my focus was on the kiss, on the way his lips sought and demanded, on the way they pressed and spread me just right. So it took a while for anything else to sink in.

I was up against the door. *Up* against the door. As in, my feet were actually off the ground. Those big hands were on my hips, just below the hard ridge where my corset finished, and they were pinning my ass to the door. My feet dangled but I didn't slip: I was held there as securely as if I was sitting on a seat.

He was pressed against me from groin to chest, his hard body pressing me tight against the wall and even tighter each time he inhaled. But it wasn't uncomfortable: I felt gloriously safe and protected. And... *small.* There was something about being held there so easily. After being The Queen non-stop for days, after all those huge decisions, to be... *manhandled* and kissed and just be passive was exactly what I needed.

My head was rocking against the hard wood of the door as he kissed me: luckily, my pinned-up hair at the back was a perfect cushion. He finally broke the kiss and drew his head back just a few inches so that he could look at me. He lifted one big hand to my face and took my chin firmly between finger and thumb. To keep me pinned there, he pressed his groin hard against mine and I swallowed as I felt the hard bulge of him through his uniform pants.

I searched his face. What had changed: what had finally broken through all the reasons *why not?*

His thumb and forefinger flexed in slow rhythm where they gripped my chin. I could feel the sexual heat, throbbing through him, almost beyond control. "Can't fight it anymore," he growled. "Not when you're...." He inhaled, his chest expanding with lust and pressing me even harder against the wall. His eyes flicked over me, telling me what he couldn't put into words.

When I'm so buttoned up and corseted and formal and imperious.

When I'm a queen.

He was the opposite of Belliani. That bastard had resented a woman in power. I threatened him. The only thing I was good for was being a trophy: he wanted me so he could strip me down to nothing, to make me come begging to his bed, to show that I wasn't *really* a leader.

But Garrett had wanted me when I was in jeans in a rib shack and when I was bruised and dirty and shivering in a sewer. He wanted *me.* Yes, all the formality turned him on and yes, he wanted to strip it all from me. But not to weaken me, like Belliani. To release what he knew was underneath.

I hesitated for a second. There'd be others like Belliani. There was my mother, there was the media, the people. None of them would like the idea of me with a commoner.

Garrett saw it in my eyes and his eyes grew stern. "Kristina," he rumbled. "For once in your goddamn life, do what *you* want."

I looked into those clear blue eyes...and kissed him as hard as I could.

He groaned in pleasure and pushed his body even harder against mine, freeing his hands so that he could run them up and down my sides. Then he suddenly grabbed my waist and lifted me, carrying me across the room. We were still kissing and the feeling of being carried, *floating,* almost, my feet kicking in the air while I hung from his hands, was heady and amazing. He walked me over to a wall and pinned me there, still kissing me. His hands roamed over my body, over my hips and thighs and breasts, until I was squirming and panting.

He broke the kiss and stared at me, eyes hooded with lust. My lips were throbbing, hungry for him.

He reached for the fastenings at the back of my dress. My eyes widened. "*Here?*"

"Yes, dammit," he growled "Here."

And he undressed me. Or tried to. The dress wasn't designed with quick exits in mind. "First you need to open the catch at the top," I panted. "Then there are pearl buttons that unhook, right down the—"

His big hands grabbed the fabric at the front of the bodice on both sides. *Oh.*

The sound of tearing filled the room. The cloth was thick and heavy, but in his hands it ripped apart like tissue. He tore it right down to my waist and then, with a shrug of my shoulders and a twist of my hips, the whole thing slithered down to the floor.

I stood there in just my cream-colored corset, panties and heels. And the crown, of course. My whole body was tingling and throbbing. The exhaustion had dropped away completely: adrenaline was flooding through every vein. I looked down at the dress on the floor. It was wrong and yet having it ripped off me felt so *right.*

He lifted me again and then laid me down on the table on my back. The polished wood was silky smooth and cool against my heated skin. He smoothed his hands over the lines of the corset: it was a fully-boned one in glossy cream, with gold trim. It started just at the waistband of my panties, scooped in at the waist, then blossomed outwards a little as it lifted and squeezed my breasts. I was covered... *just.* But without the dress there was a great deal of cleavage on display and that was where Garrett's eyes were now locked. His gaze was just feasting on me and I pressed my thighs hard together at the feeling.

He grabbed my ankles and pulled me to the edge of the table. He grabbed my panties and jerked them down my legs and off and I gasped at the sudden shock of the cool air. Then he was stepping between my legs, lowering his uniform pants and—

I swallowed. Stared at the thick length of his cock, heavy as it brushed my inner thigh. He rolled on the condom and—

I groaned, arching my back as he plunged into me. He grabbed my waist to stop me moving and looked down into my eyes, then pushed his hips forward. I drew in a shuddering breath as he hilted himself in me.

As my head rocked back, I glimpsed the huge oak doors. They didn't lock. And we were right in the heart of the palace, with servants and officials all around us in the hallways. *What if someone knocks? What if Aleksander just walks in?*

Then Garrett began to move and I just didn't care anymore. Each silken stroke of that hard flesh inside me sent ripples of pleasure right through my body. I grabbed hold of his wrists, squeezing him, needing to feel him. Our bodies were locked together, our breathing in time.

We didn't speak. We didn't need to. I gazed up into those clear, Texas-sky eyes and I knew how he felt about me. Knew that we were together, now: rules and traditions didn't matter and neither did his past. Both of us had let go of something.

He drove into me again and again, strong hips and muscled ass making him unstoppable. I gasped and clawed at his arms, heady from his size, from the feeling of being so completely filled, but wanting more of him. Both of us were breathing in quick, heated gulps as sensation took over. The delicious strength of his forearms under my fingertips. The hardness of his hips between my soft inner thighs. The hot stretch of him inside me, the glorious *push* of each thrust and the silken *pull* of my walls against him.

I caught our reflection in one of the room's big, gilt-framed mirrors. The rough, muscled soldier between the thighs of the princess. The image made me go weak. Each pump of his hips, each stroke of his cock inside me, sent another wave of heat rippling up through me to coalesce into a hot, tight ball at my center. Soon, I was twisting and squirming around it, frantic. I could see the pleasure in his eyes, too, hear it in his growls each time he plunged into my liquid heat.

"I never knew anyone like you," he rumbled.

His thrusts increased in force and pace, his strong thighs and tight core powering him into me. My back arched up off the wood, my ass and shoulders bearing all my weight. He hunkered low over me, his hands on my shoulders to hold me in place as his thrusts became faster and—*God yes!*—almost brutal.

The tight ball of heat inside me contracted and tightened and—

I knew I mustn't scream. So I grabbed his hair, pulled him down to me and kissed him, letting out my orgasm in a shuddering groan that vibrated against his lips. His hips kept pumping and it was a long time before I finally slumped down to the table.

When I opened my eyes, he was grinning down at me. Then he carefully picked me up again, his cock still inside me. That was when I realized we weren't done.

He used his foot to push a chair out from the table and then sat, carrying me down with him and—

Oh! God, I was on him, *impaled* on him, my ass against his muscled thighs. We were face to face and I sat there astride him, panting, eyes wide. He gave me a moment to get used to it, satisfied to just run his hands up and down my body for a while. I gradually settled, getting my legs under me and tentatively allowing myself to slip lower... right down to his root.

I put my hands on his shoulders. Even now, even after all this time, I still marveled at the size of him, at the breadth of those shoulders, at the hardness of his muscles under his uniform. I pressed down experimentally, pushing myself *up...*

... and *down.* Both of us caught our breath. I started to move again, but he put *his* hands on *my* shoulders to stop me. He reached behind me and found the bow where the laces of my corset were tied, and pulled it free. Then he hooked his fingers around the edges of the corset and pulled. The cords protested, holding firm... but his strength won out. The whole thing loosened and I drank in a huge, grateful gulp of air. Then it slid down and suddenly my breasts were free.

He leaned forward and I dug my fingers into the muscles of his back as he devoured me: first teasing licks, then using his whole mouth to engulf my breast. My eyes closed and I began to ride him, rising on my toes and then sinking down. Each stroke sent streamers of silver heat up inside me. They twisted together with the ones coming from my breasts, curling into a hurricane that spun faster and faster.

He reached up into my hair and pulled out the pins that held it. My hair spilled down my shoulders and back and he ran his fingers through it, delighting in it. He covered my lips and throat with kisses and then returned to my breasts.

I started to buck on his lap, my movements turning urgent. He could feel how close I was: his tongue lapped and flicked at me, then his teeth teased my nipples. I was out of control, now, twisting and circling my hips as I bounced on him, the heat inside twisting faster and faster, the huge room echoing with the sound of my pants. His mouth followed me, his lips and tongue always on one breast while his hand roughly squeezed the other. I moved harder, faster, desperate—

I gasped and cried out, tilting my head back as the heat exploded inside me. My hands clawed at his back and then buried themselves in his hair, pulling him to me as I rocked and shuddered against him for a second time. He gave a deep growl that vibrated against my wet breast...and then I felt him release deep inside me.

I slumped on top of him and we sat there, my head on his

shoulder, until I started to cool down. Then he took off his uniform jacket and wrapped it around me, and we called Caroline.

"I don't understand," said Caroline, when she arrived and Garrett met her at the door. "Why does she need a new dress? Did she spill something or—" Then she noticed Garrett's missing jacket. Then she caught a glimpse of me as I sheltered behind the door, naked except for jacket and panties. "*Oh!*" She handed over the dress she'd brought with a huge grin. I flushed... but I couldn't stop grinning, either.

When I'd dressed and done my best to make my hair look neat and formal and less... *wanton,* we hurried upstairs to my chambers and collapsed on my bed. After everything we'd been through that day, we were both exhausted, especially now the adrenaline had worn off. But neither of us could sleep. We stripped off and lay there naked in the darkness with the window open, looking out at the stars.

Garrett drew in a long, deep breath and let it out. "I like the air here."

"I thought it was too cold for you," I said. He was lying on his back and I was using his chest as a pillow.

"It *is* too cold. And wet. But... that's kinda nice, sometimes." He sighed. "Like now. It's different."

"To what?"

He drew in another long, slow breath. "To the desert."

I tensed, twisting around to look up at him as I realized what he was going to do. "You—Wait, you're sure?"

He nodded and reached down, wrapping his arms around my body. Not with a sexual touch, just smoothing his palms over my shoulders and arms and then my stomach. Drawing calm from me.

"You don't have to," I whispered. I could feel how his whole body had gone hard with tension.

"I want to."

I didn't want to hurt him... but the pain was inside him, just like mine had been. Getting it out would hurt... but it might be the only way he could heal. I rolled over onto my stomach and lay atop him so that I could hug him.

And he told me.

55

GARRETT

"I ENLISTED RIGHT OUT OF SCHOOL," I said. "My teachers said it was a good idea. What else was a big lunk like me going to do?"

Kristina squeezed me tight. "They shouldn't have just written you off! You're smart! Smarter than they knew!"

I shook my head. "Wasn't just that. I'd always wanted to serve. Saw my dad doing it, wanted to be like him. Wanted to be part of something bigger. Saw the flag at the recruiter's office and it just felt... *right*. First week of basic training, I realized I'd found something I was good at. I was bigger and I was strong and they just had to give me a mission and I wouldn't stop until it was done." I felt the rage inside me flare hot as I thought about how that loyalty had been betrayed.

"Anyway, I wound up in a squad with a great bunch of guys, all from Texas. Drummond, he was this tall, skinny guy, looked like he should be playing basketball. He could put a bullet through the O on a Coke can from half a mile away. Felton was our medic: he was the smart one. The marines had put him through medical school. Martinez always kidded around, but he always had your back. But the guy I got on best with was Baker, our squad leader."

"He was tough, but he was short: he always said he was 5'5" but we all knew he was 5'4". When he was giving me an order and there was gunfire, I had to hunker down so he could shout in my ear. People joked about it: the little guy and the big guy. But we just fought well together. And back home, it was Baker who helped me move into my apartment, Baker who had my back in a bar fight, Baker who was there for me when my mom died." I shook my head. "He was a *great* leader. Always looked after his people." I looked down at Kristina. "You remind me of him."

She blushed.

"In a squad you fight together, you eat together, you guard each other while you're sleeping. We went on too many missions to count, all over Iraq. When we came home to Texas on leave, we'd hang out. One by one, they got girlfriends, got married." I felt my neck color. "I didn't. Never was too good at all that stuff."

Kristina drew in her breath in sympathy, but I shook my head. "But it was okay, I didn't mind being the single one. We were one big family. The summers were barbecues and pool parties...." I trailed off, remembering. I didn't know how to put it into words, but those long summer days, sinking a cold beer and seeing the kids running around... it had reminded me what we were fighting for. "The squad was my life," I said simply.

Kristina tightened her arms around me. She could sense something bad was coming.

"Then one day, back in Iraq.... We're on a plane, flying back to base after a mission. Just the five of us, plus the pilot and co-pilot. A storm blows up out of nowhere. Worst storm I've ever seen in my life, the kind we used to get in Texas, where the whole sky's alive and best thing you can do is hunker down in the cellar. But we're right there in it, being hurled around, and there's no place to land. It goes on for hours, until the plane sounds like it's going to come apart. Then we lose both engines and after that we're just a twig in the wind."

Kristina was clutching at me, holding me as tight as I'd held onto my seat on that plane. "Don't remember the crash," I told her. "Just woke up in the wreckage. Pilot and co-pilot are dead, but my squad's okay, just banged up a little. We get outside and we've got no idea where we are: dawn's just breaking and it's just desert in every direction."

"We wait till nightfall for rescue: no one comes. We don't have much water so we decide we need to get moving and it's better to travel at night, when it's cool. So we pick a direction and we start walking. Mile after mile after mile, the sand coming over our boots. But it's okay: we're marines. Marching ain't gonna kill us."

"Then we come to the town. Abandoned, most of the houses just rubble. Takes us an hour before we find part of an old sign and Felton translates. That's when we find out that we're not in Iraq, anymore. The storm blew us over the border. We're in *Iran.* The only five US soldiers, at that time, in the entire goddamn country. And we're right out in the wilds, where it's just local militia who *hate* the US. We're... *alone."* I looked down at Kristina and she nodded somberly. She was the one person who could really understand what it had felt like.

"We hide out in one of the houses that's mostly still standing and get on the radio. We manage to raise a US airbase that's just over the border in Iraq, and everyone cheers. But then we give them our location... and it all goes quiet. We raise them again but we're told to wait for instructions. And then the local militia arrives and starts shooting. They'd found the plane and followed our tracks, I guess. And they're not going to stop until we're dead."

"There are way too many of them. We barricade ourselves in the house and try to hold them off. But they're calling their friends on the radio, spreading the word that we're there. All of us have been fighting in Iraq for years. We're not new to war. But this isn't war. They *hate* us. They're going to slaughter every one of us."

I'd closed my eyes. I could feel the heat of the desert on my skin, taste the dust in my mouth. I could see the abandoned house all around me: crumbling stone block walls, ragged mats on the floor, odd items that the family who'd fled had left behind: a jug, a plate, a kid's sweater. I knew that I was still in Lakovia but the softness of the bed beneath me, the quiet, even the cool, wet air from the window...

all of it faded away until I was crouched by a window, eyes straining against the sunlight as I watched figures creeping over the rubble towards us. Only Kristina remained real. Touching her was all that kept me grounded.

"It's hell: baking hot, dry and dusty, there's not enough water and we're all strung out from walking all night after the plane crash. We're trying to watch every direction at once: there's so many of them and they just keep coming. We can't take a break even for a minute to rest or drink. Then Martinez takes a bullet in the chest. A really bad wound. Felton, our medic, says he needs medevac, but we still can't get anyone on the radio. So Felton's got to treat him right there, in the damn dining room, as best he can."

"That takes us down to three guys guarding the house: Baker, Drummond and me. And we're running low on ammo, too, so we have to make every shot count. It's getting bad, but Baker, he just looks at the rest of us and he says, *we are going to hold this house.* We are going to *hold out* because that's what Marines do. And when he said it, we believed it." I stroked Kristina's hair. "Like I said, he was a lot like you."

"Night comes and we don't have night vision so it's just *black.* You see movement and you have to pray and fire. We're *begging* now on the radio, begging for someone to come get us out of there, but no one answers. And there's this moment when I look at Baker and he looks at me and we realize—" My voice grew tight, my throat suddenly dry. "We realize they're not coming."

"By morning, it's really bad. We're down to our handguns and we've been two nights without sleep. We're jumping at shadows, really losing it. Felton's trying to keep Martinez alive, but he's in agony." It was hard to speak, now. I could see the blood seeping through the bandages. "Martinez was the fun one. Like when we had the pool parties, he'd always cannonball into the pool. Or this one time, we were out there in Iraq over Christmas. So he puts on a Santa outfit—all he had was a Santa hat and a red shirt, but he stuffed a parachute up the shirt—and he goes around handing out gifts. It was only cookies from the mess hall and dumb shit like that, but... damn, if felt good, just to know we weren't forgotten. He had kids: two little girls. And he had this big, deep laugh, like he was laughing from the bottom of the sea." I swallowed. "Only... now he's screaming. So loud the walls are rattling with it. And he's pleading for something for the pain and Felton keeps telling him there's nothing left."

I could feel that Kristina had lifted her head and was staring up at me, but I couldn't look at her. If I did, I knew I wouldn't be able to continue. So I gently stroked her hair, stared at the ceiling, and kept going.

"We finally get someone on the radio. American, but no call sign. Some other grunt, probably disobeying orders just speaking to us. He just says, "Sorry." And that's when we know for sure: no one's coming."

"Just before noon, Drummond screams. He's at the window across the house from me: I turn around and there's a militia fighter right there, with a knife stuck into Drummond's throat. We were all so tired and strung out, he'd managed to creep right up to the window without Drummond seeing." I swallowed and had to stop for a second. "Drummond was the oldest. He had a stepdaughter who had something wrong with her spine, and he needed the pay for medical bills." I pressed my lips together. "I shoot the guy but it's too late, Drummond's dead."

"Now there's only two of us, Baker and me, who can guard the house. Felton's too busy trying to keep Martinez alive. There's no way we can watch all the windows and doors so we have to go outside, try and hold them off at a distance. But we're barely outside when it starts getting dark. At first, we think maybe we've lost track of time and it's dusk. Our watches are telling us it's noon, but we're so exhausted, we can't think straight. Then we see this... *thing* on the horizon. Not like cloud, or smoke. It's just dark brown *nothing,* you can't even tell how far away it is because there are no features. It looks like the goddamn edge of the world. And whatever it is, it's growing fast. Everything stops. Even the gunfire from the militia stops. Everyone's just standing there staring at it."

"People talk about the wind howling, but I never really

understood what they meant till right then. It was howling like a monster, like it hated us. That's when we figured out it was a sandstorm. Just before it hit us."

"We're swallowed up by it. The light goes out like someone hit a switch. You can see maybe a foot in front of your face, but that's if you dare open your eyes. As soon as you open them, even a crack, the wind rams sand into your eyeballs, cramming it up under your lids. So you screw your eyes tight shut, but you still can't breathe. The air's full of this dust, finer than the sand. It's like the air is solid: even if you catch some that isn't sand, it's this choking, heavy stuff that fills your lungs and turns to mud as soon as it gets wet: you cough on it, gag on it: your mouth is so dry that you can't talk or swallow."

"We somehow manage to stagger back to the house. For a while we just shelter there, coughing, eyes streaming. But we can hear the militia calling to each other and it's getting closer. They're coming, using the sandstorm as cover. Baker puts his hand on my shoulder and says we have to go back out there."

"We get scarves tied around our mouths so we can kind of breathe. We don't have goggles or anything so we can barely open our eyes. But we have to protect the other two. So we go out there, back-to-back, and start shooting at anything that moves. I manage to get three more of them, over the next half hour or so, but I'm almost out of ammo. I turn to Baker to see if he can spare a few rounds... and he's not there. I look around, but he's just... *gone*. I holler for him, but he doesn't answer, or if he does I can't hear him over the goddamn wind. I don't know if he's lost, or if the militia took him, or if he's shot and dying. He could be three feet away and I wouldn't even see him."

"So I do the only thing I can do. I put my head down and walk, in the last direction I saw him, and pray I'm going the right way. There are no landmarks, nothing, so I could be walking right towards the militia, for all I know. I keep hollering for him: I know it's going to bring them right to me, but it's the only thing I can think of. The wind's getting even stronger, it's blasting sand at me and it feels like my skin's being flayed off. I keep staggering forward, hollering, and then—" I sucked in my breath. "One of the militia fighters comes running out of the dust. I don't see him until he's right on top of me. I snap my gun up, put one in his chest and then my gun clicks empty. He's so close, he whacks into me as he falls and takes us both to the ground. I'm lying there under him, trying to roll him off me, and I recognize the gun he's gripping: it's one of ours. The bastard's taken Baker's gun. I finally manage to get him off me, tear off the scarf that's over his face. I'm going to ask him where Baker is, before he dies—"

I felt my eyes go hot. My voice fractured. "Only it *is* Baker."

Kristina gave a moan of raw horror.

"I lay him on his back and try and find the wound, praying I just clipped him, but—" I shook my head, the bitterness rising in me like vomit. "But it's a *great shot*. Best I ever made." I took a breath, but it turned into a sob. "Right in the heart. And he just lies there, blood soaking through his uniform, looking up at me with... *shock*. Shock and hurt, that I could have done this to him. And then he dies. Not a hero, not fighting the enemy: shot by his best friend."

Kristina didn't make a sound. She just laid her head on my chest, slid her arms as far around my chest as they'd go and hugged herself to me as tight as she possibly could. After several minutes, she spoke, her voice like silken glass, cooling my mind. "Garrett... it wasn't your fault."

I'd told myself that a million times, over the years. But you can't convince yourself of something like that. Someone else has to do it. Someone you trust.

I looked down and she looked up. Her eyes were shining in the moonlight, but her gaze was as steely as if she was commanding her army. I'd always trusted her and I trusted her now.

"It wasn't your fault," she repeated.

And for the first time, I believed it. I drew in a breath of cold, clean Lakovian air and it felt like my lungs properly filled, free of dust, for the first time in years.

I wrapped her in my arms and kissed the top of her head, then she tilted her head back and I kissed her long and sweet. I felt...

lighter, as if something had been crushing me down all that time. I held her close as I finished my story.

"I grab his body and throw him over my shoulder because no way am I leaving him there. I try to retrace my steps. When I eventually find the house, Martinez is dead. Felton's trying to hold off the militia on his own, but one of them picks him off just as I get there. Everybody's dead. Everybody except me."

"I run into the house and lay Baker's body down on the table, next to Martinez. The militia are coming through the windows, the door... they're everywhere. I make it into the back room, which is a dead end. I slam the door behind me but I know they'll follow me in, any second. There's no place to hide, all there is is an old stone fireplace, but I hunker down and get inside it. I don't know why: I'm dead as soon as they come through the door. Instinct, I guess. I'm not thinking straight: all I can see is Baker's face, over and over again."

"Seconds go by and nothing happens. I realize they don't know I'm out of ammo. They think I'm going to shoot them as soon as they come through the door. I can hear them muttering to each other about what to do. Then the door opens for a second and a grenade comes through. I remember closing my eyes and a flash and then... nothing."

"When I come to, I'm in pain like I've never known and I can barely breathe. There's stuff on me, crushing my chest, and I can't move. Eventually I manage to get one arm free and dig some of it away from my face."

"I'm in the corner of the room still, but the roof and half the wall has come down on top of me. The stars are out so I know I've been unconscious for hours. The militia are gone. I figure they looked at the pile of rubble and thought I must be dead."

"I almost *am* dead. Leg's broken. Ribs feel like a sackful of broken glass and every time I move, my head hurts so bad I almost pass out. But I'm alive. Then I see Baker's body and I don't want to be."

"I sit there for a while trying to figure out what to do. And eventually I just do what I've been trained to do. I figure it's about sixty miles to the border. I gather up what little water, ammo and rations we had left between us, make a splint from a piece of wood and some belts, and I limp out of there. When I put my foot down for the first time, I think I'm going to throw up from the pain. But then I figure, if I don't make it out of there, there'll be no one to tell anyone what happened. And I want answers. I want to know why they didn't come get us."

"It takes me the best part of three days. By the end of it, I'm sunburned, almost dead from thirst and my leg's infected. A US patrol finds me just over the border and gets me to a hospital and I spend a few days delirious before anyone can get any sense out of me. Then the brass haul me in. At first, I don't understand why they're mad."

My voice turned bitter. "See, we weren't supposed to be in Iran. When our plane went over the border, we violated about a thousand international treaties. When we got into a firefight with the militia, it became a political nightmare. The politicians in Washington wouldn't authorize a rescue op: it would have meant telling the Iranians we were there. Easier—cleaner—to just let us die."

"And then it gets worse because the military whitewash the whole thing. They get some special ops guys to recover the bodies a few days later, and they burn the wreckage of the plane until there's no evidence left that it's American. Then they tell me what the story's going to be: our plane went down on *this* side of the border and the others were killed on impact."

"And then the fuckers discharge me, and make it damn clear that if I say a word to anyone, they'll say I murdered Baker and put me in a cell. I'm shipped home with my leg still in a cast and my ribs taped up: no money, no future, no idea what to do."

I glanced down. Kristina was staring up at me, mouth a gaping black "O." She understood where my anger came from, now. Understood how I'd lost all faith in being loyal to anything... until she'd given me something to fight for again.

"There's one thing I have to do," I told her. "I visit Baker's widow, look her in the eyes and tell her what happened. I'm ready for her to slap me, to scream at me: hell, there's a part of me that's hoping she'll kill me. But she doesn't. She just nods and says she understands and that it wasn't my fault: all the right things. But there's this look in her eyes, just like Baker got: *why? Why would you do this?* And I get out of there. She tries to call me back, but I keep walking."

"I go home to Texas but I don't know what to do with myself. Ever since school, I always had the military. Always had a *mission.* Now there's too much time to think... to remember. And I've started having flashbacks."

"I try to get a job. Go to interview after interview. But as soon as they find out I'm a veteran, they get nervous. They think I'll get uppity with them because I used to have a rank, and now I'm a civilian." I gave a bitter laugh. "They don't get that I followed orders, not gave them. I'm *good* with following orders."

Kristina nodded sadly.

"And the flashbacks: that's even more of a problem. They're not allowed to ask about PTSD and stuff, but..." I felt the anger rising inside my chest. "But they don't have to, you know? They just say something like *it must have been tough, over there.* And they see me go tense and they *know.* And I want to scream at them, look, it comes back to me sometimes, but most of the time I'm *okay!* But I can't tell them what happened. Can't find the words. So they think I'm some psycho who's going to bring a gun to work and start shooting. No one'll hire me."

"I'm too ashamed to stay at the ranch, with my dad. He was a Marine his entire career. I've been discharged and now I can't even get a job. So I move to LA. Get a job as a doorman in a dive bar. But I'm too... dumb, I guess. Everyone else is on the take, like let one drug dealer in to deal, and stop all the others, in return for a cut. But I didn't want to do that. Didn't seem right." I sighed. "Like I said, dumb."

"*Not* dumb," Kristina said fiercely. "*Good.* What were you doing in New York?"

"Thought if I could get away from the desert, the flashbacks might stop. They didn't. So I was heading back to LA... when I met you."

Her eyes were shining with tears. There was so much I wanted to explain about what she meant to me: how meeting her had changed everything. She'd given me something to be loyal to, something I believed in. She'd made me feel happy for the first time since it all happened. And I loved her like I'd never loved anyone: she was sweet and special and bright and the most beautiful woman I'd ever seen. But my words had run out. I gazed at her, shook my head, and just said, "I know I'm not a prince. But you're right for me."

And she just nodded and kissed me. She scooched higher up my body, straddling me, and we lay like that in the darkness for a long time, our cheeks pressed together. I felt... *lighter.* Like something had released, inside me. "It's the first time I've ever told anyone," I muttered. "I mean, I told the brass how the others died. But not how it felt."

She nodded and the feel of her silky hair brushing my shoulders calmed the last of the anger inside me. It was weird: I wasn't used to feeling at peace.

"You know, there are people who can help you with the flashbacks," she said tentatively.

I shook my head. "Couldn't," I mumbled. "Tried it. Couldn't talk to them. You're different."

"Then will you at least let me share something with you? Something that worked for me, after the war?"

Just the reminder that she'd suffered made my arms tightened protectively around her. I wanted to kill every one of the bastards who'd imprisoned her. "Go on."

"I still get the flashbacks, sometimes. When it's really dark, or I'm alone. Sometimes they come as nightmares and those I can't stop...until I met you." She ran her hand over my chest. "But the flashbacks... my therapist taught me how to beat those. Maybe it'll work for you, too."

I nodded, but half-heartedly. "They're so real," I said. "And so *big*. And... heavy." I shook my head. "I know that doesn't make sense. It's just a memory. But—"

"But it feels like it's solid, like it weighs a thousand tons," she said.

I blinked at her, surprised. "*Yeah.* Like a freight train coming at me. I can't stop it."

She raised herself up on her arms so that she could look down at me. Her hair hung down, brushing my chest and, if I glanced down, I knew I'd see her breasts, pale in the moonlight. But I was so focused on what she was saying, I managed not to look. "That's because you're so big and stubborn," she said, mock-sternly. "You're trying to fight it."

I scrunched up my brow. "What the hell else am I supposed to do?"

She put those cooling, calming hands on my biceps. "You let it come, but you *get out of its way.* Like you're sidestepping."

"*Sidestepping?*"

"You don't have to move much. Just enough that it misses you. Just think really hard about somewhere you really like. A place you'd like to be, with a person you'd like to be with. You're *there.* And then the flashback still comes, but you're not *in* it. You're just watching it, like it's on TV."

I stared at her. If it had come straight from a therapist, I would have written it off as a load of horseshit. But I trusted her. Hell, there was no one I trusted more. "Somewhere I'd like to be?" I said slowly. *Texas.* "And someone I'd like to be with." I looked right at her, and she flushed, then cuddled down on my chest again.

I lay there feeling even better than before. I didn't know if it would work: it didn't seem like much of a weapon, given how powerful the flashbacks were. But just having *something,* after all these years... that helped.

There was a sound outside the window, very faint. I could barely hear it, but Kristina jerked to attention and listened and so I did, too. It sounded like bells.

"It's the clock tower in the city," she said at last. Her body had gone tense. "Midnight. Ten hours until the bombers launch."

"You did everything you could," I said. "Garmania started this. They pushed you and pushed you. They tried to kill you over and over again. *And* your dad. And planted bombs and—"

"I know. I just... I don't *feel* that it's true. I can't believe they want to go back to war with us. Not in my gut." She sighed and let herself flop on top of me. "I suppose I just don't want to believe it."

She lay there on my chest, defeated. And I frowned up at the ceiling. She'd done so much to help me. I wanted to help her. But I didn't know anything about politics, or being a leader.

So, I just told her what I *did* know. "Your instincts are good," I said.

She jerked up, startled. "What?"

"You were right about Emerik and Jakov. And Caroline, too. None of them were traitors. And you're smart. You're the smartest person I've ever met. If you say Garmania doesn't want war, I believe you."

She shook her head. "But they're behind everything! It all points to them!"

"OK, but...." I sat up, carrying her up with me until we were upright. She crossed her legs and sat on my thighs, our faces only a foot apart. "What if they're *not?*"

She shook her head. "Nothing else makes sense!"

I scrunched up my brow. This wasn't what I was good at. But this was what she needed me to do. So I *thought.* "The weapons the assassins used," I said at last. "All Garmanian. So if Garmania isn't supplying them, who is? Are there any other countries Garmania sells its stuff to?"

"No. They're highly secretive about their weapons tech. They're proud that only they have it." She shrugged. "Maybe the assassins bought it on the black market? There were lots of guns in circulation after the war."

I frowned again, thinking back to Texas. "I can believe that for rifles, maybe even the explosives. But not the mortar they used to attack the ranch. You can't buy *that* in the back room of a bar."

"So it *is* Garmania behind it all," she sighed and hung her head. "It has to be."

"No!" I tipped her chin up to look at me. We were onto something, now. I could feel it. The wheels in my head might turn slowly, but once they started...."Think! There must be someone else who has Garmanian weapons. Some other country, an ally...."

"There isn't! The only people who have their weapons are Garmania and—" She broke off and stared at me.

Even in the darkened room, I could see how pale her face had gone. "Who?" But she just looked ill. Something had occurred to her, something so horrible she didn't dare touch it again. *"Who?"*

She swallowed. "Us."

56

KRISTINA

THE WORDS CAME HALTINGLY. It felt as if I was lying on fragile ice above a deep, black lake and every word was another blow with a hammer. "We captured lots of Garmanian weapons when we won the war," I said. "But..." I shook my head. It couldn't be true. If it *was* true, that meant.... "No," I said. "No."

Garrett and I stared at each other, the implications running through our heads. Then, very slowly, Garrett picked up the phone and passed it to me. "Call the military," he said in that deep, Texas rumble. "Find out where they store captured weapons."

My whole body had gone cold, my skin clammy with fear. I didn't want to follow this idea any further. But....

Garrett took my hand in his big, warm one. I looked up at him and he nodded. Wherever this led, he'd be with me.

I dialed. It was midnight, but in the army there's always someone on duty. I got a series of supervisors out of bed, gradually going up through the ranks until I found someone who had the answers. "We do still keep Garmanian weapons in storage, for training purposes," I was told. "But as to exactly what and how much... unfortunately, Your Majesty, that information is classified."

"Not to your Queen, it's not," I said sternly.

I could almost hear him gulp. Then the tapping of computer keys. "Incendiary mortar rounds..." he muttered.

I held my breath.

"No, Your Majesty," he said. "We don't have any of those."

I let out a long sigh and leaned against Garrett for support. I was a mess of emotions: embarrassment, that we'd been wrong. Relief, that we had been. And despair that I hadn't found some last minute way out: we *were* going to war. I politely thanked the officer and apologized for being terse with him.

"That's quite alright, Your Majesty." I could hear that he'd relaxed. "Pity you didn't call a few weeks ago. Our records show we had fifty-two of those rounds then. But they were all signed out for a training exercise."

I jerked upright. "On whose authority?"

"General Novak."

I hung up the phone. Garrett and I stared at each other as ice water sluiced through my body. "Novak wants a war," I whispered. "He never wanted the first one to finish. He thought we should have gone ahead and wiped them out. It was only my father who stopped him."

"But how would he get in touch with Silvas Lukin?" asked Garrett. "He's Garmanian, he's the enemy."

My mind was racing. "Lukin was a war criminal. He was in a special military prison right here in Lakovia... until he escaped."

Garrett caught on immediately. He was a lot smarter than he thought. "And as head of the military, General Novak could visit Lukin in prison. The son of a bitch. He offered Lukin his freedom in return for helping to restart the war."

"Lukin agreed, Novak arranged the escape, gave Lukin captured Garmanian weapons and told him to put his old squad back together." My stomach lurched. "And then he sent them after me and my father."

I didn't want to believe it, but it made perfect sense. Lukin and his squad would assassinate my father and me and Novak would step into the power vacuum. With the royal family assassinated by

Garmania, the public would be baying for blood. They'd *want* war. And once we were victorious, Novak would keep the war going until he'd destroyed Garmania: every building, every child. The plan was elegant and perfect. And it would have worked, if Garrett hadn't been there to save me on the plane. He'd ordered Lukin to keep trying to kill me... and meanwhile, he'd convinced me to start the war.

I wanted to be sick. I'd completely bought the story he'd sold me about Garmania wanting to invade us. I'd been terrified we were going to lose. Now I was terrified we were going to win. Garmania was innocent: they'd been nothing but peaceful and now we were going to wipe them out: that would be the legacy of my reign.

I could hardly believe that the man I'd trusted so completely had betrayed me. What convinced me was that, in his mind, he was being loyal. Loyal to his country. To him, my father and I were the traitors for making peace. "We have to stop him," I croaked.

"That's going to be hard," said Garrett. "He's got troops all over the city... and in the palace."

I put my face in my hands, fighting the urge to scream. "I'm an idiot. I let him put troops on the streets! He's halfway to seizing power already!"

"We're going to need help," said Garrett.

He was right. We couldn't just accuse the General, not when he was surrounded by gun-toting troops. He might just take the final step and order them to shoot me, clearing the final obstacle from his path. For the same reason, I couldn't just stop the war, not until I'd removed him. "Aleksander," I said at last. "He'll be able to help." I dialed him.

Aleksander listened silently as I told him what we'd found out. "Novak has troops everywhere," he said, keeping his voice low. "Meet me at the dam. We can work out a plan there."

I hung up, jumped off the bed and started scrambling into my clothes. Then I cursed as the clock tower struck two. We had less than eight hours to stop the General... and stop the war.

57

KRISTINA

WE DIDN'T HAVE time to bother with armored SUVs and palace drivers, plus the less attention we drew, the better. So Garrett signed out one of the plain black Mercedes the guards used for palace business and we started up the twisting road to the dam. My phone rang: Caroline.

"Sorry to disturb you," she said, "But I didn't know who else to call and I thought you and Garrett might still be awake."

I glanced at Garrett. Even now, Caroline still knew how to make me blush. "We were. What's up?"

She sighed. "It's nothing, just...this guy's calling from New York and he's demanding to speak to someone in authority. He won't go away and he won't wait till morning. I can't reach Aleksander for some reason and Sebastian is...." She broke off, her voice beginning to shake.

"*I'll* take it," I said firmly. "You get some sleep."

She thanked me and a second later, my ear was assaulted by a gruff male voice with a New York twang. "*Finally!* About fucking time! This is Officer Tashiro, airport security. Am I speaking to someone high up?"

"You're speaking to the queen," I said politely.

His manner changed abruptly. I had to get through almost a minute of apologies before I found out what he wanted.

"It's your security passes. I need 'em back. I've been asking for days, but no one's got back to me and it's my fu—It's my job on the line."

"Security passes?"

"Two of your guys walked off with theirs after their inspection. God knows how they managed to get past my guys without handing them in, but they did, and it's my ass if I don't account for 'em."

I furrowed my brow. "*Where* did you say you worked?"

"JFK."

New York. Where our flight had taken off from. "And when you say two of *our* guys...."

"Two of your security guys. I issued five passes, so your security team could inspect the aircraft before it flew. But only three of them ever came back to me."

I went cold. The two assassins on the plane: they hadn't been smuggled on board at all. Five men from Lukin's squad had been welcomed aboard, posing as our security, and two of them had simply stayed on board. "Who organized this inspection?" I asked, my voice shaking.

He paused while he checked his paperwork. "A. Popovic."

Aleksander.

I heard myself thank the officer. I hung up and sat staring at the phone in a state of total shock. That made no sense, unless....

Something was forming at the back of my mind, huge and dark and cold, so horrific that I didn't dare look around and see it. But there were too many loose ends. And following each one suddenly seemed to lead me in the same direction.

We never found out who was leaking information to the assassins, when we were in America. I quickly dialed FBI Director Gibson. "Did you share your information with our military?" I asked breathlessly. "With a General Novak?"

"No, Your Majesty," said Gibson. "We sent all our information to your parents via the palace, but that's all."

"Via *who* at the palace?"

"Your chief advisor, Aleksander."

I thanked him and hung up. Ahead of us, the dam came into view. My mind was racing, now. A memory came back to me: Caroline, sobbing and hysterical, unable to believe her beloved Sebastian was a traitor.

What if he wasn't?

I called the dungeon and had them get Sebastian out of his cell. He was a quiet, slender man in his twenties with glasses, always polite, a little shy. But when he spoke now, he sounded as if he'd aged thirty years, his voice brittle with exhaustion and fear.

We were driving along the top of the dam, now. I could see a lone figure standing waiting for us, right in the middle. My knuckles went white where they gripped my phone. "Sebastian?" I asked. "Did Aleksander have access to your phone? Could he have read your messages?"

"We work in the same room," he said. "I leave it on my desk...."

My heart was thumping in my chest. "*Did he know you were sleeping with Caroline?!*"

Sebastian sighed. "I told her that no one knew, but... you know Aleksander. He knows everything that's going on. He guessed. But he said he wouldn't tell anyone. Your Majesty, what's going on?"

I could hear the confusion in his voice. He hadn't even considered the possibility that his boss, his friend, was a traitor. I couldn't believe it either.

I thought back to that night the lights went out, in my room. Aleksander sitting there, advising me to have Sebastian tortured. Could he really have done that, knowing that he himself was the traitor? *No. No way.* And *why* would he betray us? Money? Power? He'd never shown any interest in either.

I sighed. There had to be some other explanation. Aleksander, a traitor? He was practically family! I thought of him as an uncle. I'd felt sorry for him: he'd seemed so lonely, since his son died—

We pulled up, right beside Aleksander. He opened my door.

Since his son died. In the war. Oh Jesus. That was his reason. Not money or power. Simple revenge.

"Drive!" I yelled hysterically to Garrett. "Go!"

But Aleksander grabbed my shoulder and wrenched me out of the car. And behind him, Silvas Lukin and General Novak stepped out of the shadows.

58

GARRETT

I JUMPED out of the car and raced around, but Lukin was as fast as ever. He grabbed Kristina, slid an arm around her throat and rested the muzzle of his handgun against her temple. I skidded to a stop.

Aleksander was smart: he'd lured us where no one would see. The dam was deserted apart from our little group and it was pitch black: I couldn't see more than a hundred yards along the dam in either direction. The feeling of space all around us was unnerving: the sky high above, the valley sides far out of view on either side of us, the reservoir stretching out on one side of the dam and the sheer drop on the other.

Kristina was glaring up at Aleksander, too shocked and too mad to be scared. "You *son of a bitch!*" she breathed. "How could you—I trusted you! My father trusted you!" Her mouth fell open as she pieced more and more of it together. "You put the poison in the bath oil!"

I thought back to the day the King was shot. How Aleksander had been so slow to deliver the warning. "You didn't get stuck in the crowd that day, did you?" I growled. "You were giving them time to shoot!" I could feel the rage boil up inside me: anger at what he'd done, humiliation at being so expertly played. I took a step towards him, but Lukin pressed his gun harder against Kristina's head. I froze.

"You leaked the story about Garmania being behind the attacks, didn't you?" whispered Kristina. "You knew it'd cause violence and that gave the General an excuse to put troops on the streets."

Aleksander spoke for the first time. "I did what I had to do." The bastard sounded completely unrepentant.

"Think about what you're doing," begged Kristina. "This won't bring your son back!"

"It'll mean he didn't die for nothing," said Aleksander coldly. "When we wipe the bastards out."

I exchanged terrified looks with Kristina. With them in charge, it wouldn't be a war. It would be genocide.

"Let's get this over with," muttered General Novak.

One of Lukin's men grabbed me and pushed me towards Kristina. We stumbled into each other and I put my arms around her protectively. They pushed us until our hips were against the metal safety rail. Beyond it, the dam fell away into the darkness: I couldn't even see the bottom of the drop, just hear the water thundering down, hundreds of feet below.

"You can't just kill us," Kristina said desperately. "People will ask questions!"

"You came here to be alone with your American lover," said Aleksander sadly. "Love made you foolish: you sneaked out without your guards." He nodded at Lukin. "A Garmanian assassin had slipped past our security. You died in each other's arms."

She looked up at me, eyes full of hope. It made my heart twist because I'd failed her so utterly. "I'm sorry," I said.

She shook her head. But it *was* my fault. I was meant to protect her and I hadn't seen this coming: not General Novak *or* Aleksander. I took a deep, shuddering breath, trying to control my anger. I thought of all the times Aleksander had thanked me, lying right to my face. *I'm an idiot.* I'd let the politicians betray me all over again.

Kristina pressed herself to me and I pulled her close, as if I could stop what was going to happen if I only held her tight enough. She rubbed her cheek against my chest. "Please tell me you have a plan," she said, her voice cracking.

Think! But I didn't. I didn't have a damn thing. I shook my head and squeezed her even harder.

"Him first," someone said in the darkness. I think it was Novak. "Then her."

I felt cold metal against my scalp. The muzzle of Lukin's gun.

"You can kiss her, if you like," said Lukin.

I glared at him. The sick son of a bitch. All those children, *dead*. The FBI agents, the King... and now Kristina. All so he could get out of jail. Didn't he realize that Novak and Aleksander would wipe his country out? Or did he not care, as long as millions of Lakovians died as well?

And then there was my dad. A sweet guy who'd never done anything but fight for his country and try to protect Kristina and me. Lying in a hospital bed, barely clinging onto life. *All I need is one good punch.* But the gun was mashed right up against my head and the bastard was grinning. He wanted me to make a move.

And I had to kiss her. Just one last time.

She tilted her head back and those perfect, silken lips parted. To start with, the rage was pounding through me. I kissed her hard and deep. I wanted her, them, *everyone* to know she was mine, even in death.

But as always, she calmed me. As soon as our lips touched, it was like cool water running over my heated soul. It became about simple, sweet love. All the good she'd brought into my life, all the ways she'd changed me. I didn't give a damn, anymore, that I was just a grunt. We were right together. I lost myself in the kiss, running away with my princess—

"Enough," said Aleksander.

Cold reality returned. Kristina drew back from me, panting with fear, blinking back tears.

Lukin cocked his gun. The muzzle ground against my scalp.

And in that second, I saw it. Kissing her had cleared my head.

She'd taken away the anger and without it, I could think. I couldn't save myself. But maybe I could save her.

My arms tensed around her. I gave her a quick nod, the only warning I had time for.

And then I heaved us both over the safety barrier and off the dam.

The muzzle of the gun scraped through my hair. Lukin had been taken by surprise. Maybe there was a chance—

There was a boom as the gun went off. Blinding pain exploded across the back of my head.

And everything went black.

59

KRISTINA

I was falling, head first, into pitch blackness. I could feel the air rushing past me, faster and faster, the only evidence that I was speeding up—

And then, as my body spun, I glimpsed the wall of the dam, concrete blocks whizzing by just inches from my face, and I wished for the blackness again. If I clipped it, if I even brushed it with a hand or foot and went cartwheeling into it—

I tightened my arms around Garrett... but he was a dead weight against my body. I was too close to see his face and I didn't dare loosen my grip or we might be torn apart. And I wasn't brave enough to get through this on my own.

Clouds rose up to meet us: I could hardly see them in the dark, but I could feel them. First just a damp in the air, then a mist and then stinging spray as hard as pebbles. The roar of the water surrounded us, growing until it was deafening. My throat ached and my chest hurt: I knew I was screaming but I couldn't hear it.

And then we were down to where the water flowed out of the dam. I saw the geyser of water below us, as wide as a bus. If we touched *that,* its force would grab us and slam us down deep beneath the surface. I screwed my eyes shut—

We flashed past it, missing it by less than a foot. And then the surface of the river was rushing up to meet us—

We hit and the whole front of my body flared in pain: it felt like hitting concrete. Then, as we sunk, the cold hit me: the water had come down from the mountains and even in summer, it was freezing.

We went deeper and when we slowed to a stop it was utterly black. I knew we had to swim to the surface, but I couldn't tell which way was up and—

Oh God. Panic gripped me: Garrett wasn't swimming. He wasn't even moving. He was just sinking, dragging me down towards the bottom.

Keeping hold of him, I kicked for what I hoped was the surface, but my dress just ballooned and parachuted. I couldn't swim! I grabbed Garrett's belt and held on with one hand in a death-grip while I frantically clawed my dress off my shoulders and down my body with the other, then managed to kick it free. Thank God Garrett had torn the button-up one off me: if I'd still been in that, I'd be dead.

I got my hands under Garrett's armpits and kicked again, my lungs burning. For several long seconds there was nothing. Was I even swimming the right way?

Just as my lungs felt like they were about to explode, my face broke the surface. I hauled Garrett's head up too, and looked around. We were in the river and the current had already carried us half a mile from the dam.

The moon was behind a cloud and there was hardly any light. I shouted Garrett's name but he didn't respond. There was too much noise from the rushing water to hear if he was breathing.

I put my hand tentatively around the back of his head, where the gun had been pressed. Soft, shaggy hair. I explored, hardly daring to breathe. Hair, hair—

Hot wetness, sticky on my hand. *Oh Jesus, no!* I jerked my fingers away.

I was panting with cold and fear and desperation. I kicked for the side but the current was too strong and the banks of the river were too high: there was nowhere I could climb out. For now, I had to just focus on keeping Garrett's head above water.

A mile further on, we entered the city. By now, I was exhausted from supporting Garrett's body. My heart sank when I saw the deserted streets. Even this late at night, there'd normally be some people wandering back from bars and clubs. But the bombs had scared everyone off the streets. Even the late-night bars were shuttered. I twisted around in the water, looking for someone, anyone. "*Help!*" I yelled into the darkness. "*Please!*" But no one answered.

I was going to have to do this myself.

When I saw some stone steps that led up from the river, I kicked my way over to them. The current was so strong and Garrett was so big and heavy that I almost didn't make it in time. I reached the side as the water whipped us past and only barely got my fingertips hooked onto the bottom step. Then I had to haul us against the current until we were at the foot of the steps.

For the first time in what felt like hours, I stopped swimming and managed to put my feet down. I got Garrett lying on the bottom few steps and thought about just slumping there to rest. I was utterly exhausted, my muscles were on fire from fighting the current and I couldn't stop shaking. But I knew that if I stopped, I'd never get going again. A cold wind was blowing through the streets, knifing through my soaked clothes and stripping what little heat my body had left. If I lay down, I'd pass out and freeze to death.

Getting Garrett up the steps to the street nearly killed me. He weighed at least twice what I did and his soaking clothes made it worse. I had to heave him up one step at a time, shaking uncontrollably, being careful not to bang his head. When we finally reached the street, I knelt down over him and put my head on his chest. It was the first time we'd been away from the roar of the water, the first time I'd had a chance to hear—

Yes! It was weak and shallow, but he was breathing. I had to get him to a hospital.

Stumbling and slow with cold and fatigue, I went to the end of the street and looked around the corner. I recognized where I was, now. It was one of the city's main squares: a big cobbled plaza with trees and benches. Big animated signs line the buildings around it and advertisers pay huge amounts to advertise there because there's so much foot traffic. I'd never seen it deserted. A pair of soldiers were patrolling it. *Thank God.* They could take us to the hospital and then I'd have Aleksander and General Novak arrested—

I hurried across the square but they were facing away from me and didn't hear me approach. My teeth were chattering too much for me to yell: I'd have to go right up to them.

I was halfway there when I focused on one of the big screens. It was showing a news channel and—

What?!

I stumbled to a stop right in the center of the square, my face lit up by the light from the screen. I was staring at an image of *me*. And next to my photo, a headline my brain couldn't process.

Queen exposed as traitor.

60

KRISTINA

I STOOD there staring as the news ticker crawled across the bottom of the screen. I read about how my American lover had corrupted me and how we'd had the King shot so that I could steal the throne.

It got worse. I'd faked the attempts on my own life to throw off suspicion. And I was in league with Garmania: I'd been holding back our brave military, preventing them from saving us. My plan was to surrender the entire country, allowing Garmania to sweep in and rule, in return for wealth and a life overseas. Fortunately, General Novak and the military had discovered my plan and overthrown me, but I'd escaped the palace. Troops were now searching the city for me.

My eyes flicked to the soldiers I'd been hurrying towards. They were less than ten feet away, their backs still turned. I darted into an alley and stood there panting in fear, my back pressed to a wall. *How is this happening? How can anyone believe this?*

Then I remembered Aleksander and his close ties to the media. He'd known all of the news chiefs for years and he had the head of our military to back up his story. Why *wouldn't* they believe him?

And the public believed it, too. When I dared to peek around the alley, the news screens were showing interviews with furious, tearful citizens. *How could she do this,* they were asking. *How could she betray us?* The story had broken just an hour ago: Aleksander must have called the media as soon as Garrett threw us off the dam. But already, the internet was flooded with hateful comments, calls for my death and images of Garrett and me with cruel captions. He was being portrayed as an American spy who'd seduced me and corrupted me and I was the airhead princess who'd sold out her entire country so that she could run away and be with him. Tears were running down my cheeks. *No! It wasn't anything like that!* I'd resisted him for so long because I put my country first!

How do they even know we're together? Then I groaned. *Aleksander.* Sebastian was right: he knew everything that happened in the palace. Of course he'd noticed the way we looked at each other. He'd probably figured it out days ago.

I wanted to throw up. The whole army was searching for me. If they found me, I'd have no chance to explain my side. If they didn't shoot me on sight, they'd take me to General Novak and he'd execute me for treason. And the public would let him. They hated me.

I hadn't just lost the throne. I'd lost my people.

And Garrett—my chest contracted with fear. I'd left him lying by the river. If soldiers found him, they'd shoot him as a traitor!

I raced back to the riverbank. He was still lying there, but his breathing was weaker and, like me, he was getting colder and colder, his wet clothes drawing all the heat from his body. *What am I going to do?!* He needed a hospital, but I couldn't go to one, not now we'd been branded traitors. I looked around desperately. Being on the run was Garrett's department. *Think! What would* he *do?*

He'd get us *off the grid.* Hide out somewhere.

I heard footsteps approaching: the sound of heavy boots. I grabbed Garrett's shoulders and heaved—

He didn't move. I was too small and he was too big.

The footsteps had almost reached us. I hooked my hands under Garrett's arms, gritted my teeth and *pulled...*and managed to drag him into an alley.

A sign on a green wooden door said *Jarrow & Son, Electrical Repairs*. There was a window next to it that had been left ajar. Much too small for Garrett, but I could maybe squeeze through.

I heard the soldiers reach the riverbank and start to move down it. As they passed the alley, they'd see us.

I pried open the window as much as it would go and slipped a shoulder through, then jumped up and *squeezed*.

The soldiers were almost at the alley. Desperation gave me strength and I slithered through, picking up a few new scrapes and bruises. I raced around to the door, unlocked it and hauled Garrett inside, then shut the door and sat there in the darkness with him, holding my breath.

The sound of boots reached the alley...and continued on.

I looked around. It was a workshop, with shelves of TVs, toasters and hair dryers awaiting repairs. It was barely any warmer inside than out, but at least we were out of the wind.

I turned on a lamp. When I got my first look at the back of Garrett's head, I nearly threw up. His hair was matted with blood and some of it was scorched from the gun going off so close to him. But when I felt around, the wound was more of a furrow than a hole. The bullet had grazed him: it hadn't gone in. There might still be hope.

He was still bleeding and I couldn't find anything to use as bandages. Why couldn't I have found a doctor's surgery, or a vet's? I eventually found a pack of sponges in the kitchen and used one of them as gauze, then wrapped duct tape around his head to hold it in place and seal the wound. That at least stopped the bleeding, but I still couldn't wake him up.

I couldn't figure out how to get the heating on. I stripped off our wet clothes and used the tiny hand towel in the restroom to dry us as best I could. Then I rolled Garrett onto his side and cuddled into his chest so that my body heat would help to keep him warm.

I was alone again, just like during the war. Then, at least I'd still been a princess. I'd been on the side of good and known my country was searching for me. Now, I was nothing. I was a traitor on the run, hated by my people. Aleksander and General Novak were running the country and, in a few hours, the war would start and millions of people would die. I'd lost everything.

Exhaustion swept over me. With my tears wetting Garrett's chest, I slept.

61

KRISTINA

THE DAWN WOKE ME. I came awake slowly at first, wincing as I moved, stiff and aching from having slept on the hard floor. Then I remembered Garrett and grabbed for him, trying to shake him awake. Maybe now, after he'd had time to recover....

No. Nothing. He was breathing, but he was a limp weight in my arms: he wouldn't wake. My stomach twisted. I tried to shut out words like *brain hemorrhage* and *intracranial pressure.*

I stumbled over to the window and looked out. In the distance, I could just make out the palace's turrets. I almost started crying again. My whole life, everything I'd known, was there and now it was just... *gone,* closed off from me.

I suddenly drew in my breath. *My parents!* They were still in the palace, with Aleksander and General Novak! If my father ever woke from his coma, he'd try to retake the throne: the traitors wouldn't allow that. And my mother: she'd never stand for me being branded a traitor. She'd try to tell the media the truth. They'd have to kill her, too.

I had to save them. I had to get both of them the hell out of the palace... if it wasn't already too late.

I looked at Garrett, still unconscious. I had to do it on my own.

I hunted around and found a pair of dirty gray overalls and some work boots. With a lot of rolling up of sleeves and cuffs, I just about got them to fit. There was a baseball cap, too, with the name of the shop on it, and I jammed that on my head, stuffing my hair up under it. There was a cell phone on charge and I pocketed that. In the garage attached to the shop, I found the van the repairman used when he made house calls, and after a lot of searching I found the keys in a drawer. I wrote Garrett a note, folded it into his hand and closed his fingers around it. Then I kissed him gently on the lips and left, before I chickened out.

Driving was harder than I remembered it. Garrett had taught me on an empty highway and that was nothing like the twisting, narrow streets of the city. I kept stalling and had more near misses than I could count. But at last, the palace came into view.

There were even more troops stationed around it than I remembered, and General Novak had added armored personnel carriers and tanks, too. He'd turned the beautiful palace into a fortress. And the royal colors were no longer flying from the turrets. The bastard had taken them down.

I pulled over just before I reached the security checkpoint and dialed my mother. No reply. My stomach twisted. Had they just taken her phone off her, or....

I tried Emerik. No answer. Maybe they'd locked him up, since he'd be loyal to me.

Jakov. No answer there either. *Please!* I needed someone inside!

I called Caroline. It rang and rang and then, just as I was about to give up hope, she answered. She had to whisper down the phone to me. "There are soldiers everywhere! Everyone's looking for you! They're calling you a traitor!"

I calmed her and asked about my parents. My father was still in a coma in the medical facility. My mother was with him: they'd taken her phone and she wasn't allowed to leave his bedside.

I had to get them out. It was only a matter of time before General

Novak quietly disposed of both of them. But how? I wasn't a soldier, like Garrett!

But I had to try. I'd lost my country, and there was no way I could stop the war. I couldn't let them take my parents from me, as well.

"Okay," I told Caroline. "Here's what I need you to do."

62

GARRETT

I was floating in fuzzy black. The scent of her, the feel of a warm body pressed against me. Someone calling my name, but I was too deep in the blackness to reach.

Then a kiss. The brush of silky hair against my bare chest. That coaxed me up out of the blackness. It took a long time to reach the surface but—

I opened my eyes and immediately screwed them shut again. The daylight was painful. My head was throbbing. I made the mistake of probing the back of my head and the sudden agony almost made me pass out again. The room spun and blurred and there were two of everything. I lay there panting, trying not to throw up, and waited for it to pass.

Where the hell was I? Where was Kristina? The last thing I remembered was the dam. What was this on my head: duct tape?

Something was in my hand: a piece of folded paper. I scowled at it until I could see straight and then drew in my breath as I saw it was from Kristina. By the time I'd finished reading, I knew where she was.

And I'd had enough.

Those bastards had taken everything from her. Her throne, her beloved country... they'd even tried to take me, leaving her alone and unprotected.

Well, not anymore.

I dressed in my damp royal guard uniform and stalked outside. My head was still throbbing, but the rage was pumping through my veins, powering me forward.

Before I'd even reached the end of the street, there was a gasp from beside me. A guy on a motorcycle had slowed to a stop beside me, his eyes wide. From what Kristina had said in the note, my picture was everywhere, and with my size, I guess I stood out.

I didn't have time to argue with him. I grabbed hold of the bike, leaned in close and snarled in his face. *"Get off!"*

White-faced, he jumped off. I swung my leg over the bike and roared away.

I reached the palace just in time to see the van from the repair store pull up to the checkpoint. I ducked into some bushes and sneaked closer. My heart nearly stopped when I saw Kristina talking to the soldier manning the checkpoint, explaining that she was there to repair some medical equipment. *Are you nuts? Get out of there!*

The soldier stared at her... but her disguise worked. Everyone except me had only ever seen her in fancy dresses. In dirty overalls, with a baseball cap covering her long hair, no one would believe she was The Queen. The soldier wouldn't let her through, though. He said he had no repair visit down on his schedule: he'd have to call the palace to confirm. *Shit!*

At that moment, Caroline came sprinting out of the palace. She spoke to the soldier and I guess confirmed the story because he waved Kristina through. Relief sluiced through me...but now we were separated again. I needed to get into the palace to help her and I didn't have a clever plan or a disguise.

But I was a Marine. And we don't quit.

I went right around the palace to the gardens. They were still guarded but a lot less heavily than the palace itself. When a patrol had gone past, I climbed the wall and dropped down inside. Inside, the dawn mist was still creeping waist-deep over the lawns, and that helped to hide me. *God bless Lakovia's weird weather.* I started searching for the flowers Kristina had told me about. The gardens were full of all kinds of plants. *White camellia. What the hell do camellia look like?!*

I finally found them, growing in thick curtains over a dark, narrow opening. If the palace guards had still been in charge, it would have been guarded. But General Novak had put the palace under military guard instead and the soldiers didn't know about its secret passages.

I plunged inside. The passage wouldn't get me to the medical facility, but it would get me to the dungeon and I had a pretty good idea who I'd find there.

If I was going to save Kristina, I was going to need some help.

63

KRISTINA

CAROLINE and I hurried through the hallways. I'd found a toolbox in the back of the van and brought it along in the hope it would make me look more convincing. It seemed to work because the soldiers we passed didn't give me a second look. It was Caroline, with her long blonde hair and maid's uniform, who drew their eyes. My hopes started to rise as we neared the elevators. If we could just reach them and get down to the medical facility—

And then Aleksander came out of a doorway ahead of us.

I quickly stared at the floor. When I dared to look again, he was walking down the hallway, his back to us. Two of General Novak's soldiers were accompanying him.

We followed a few steps behind. Caroline looked as shaken as I was. If they looked round....

But Aleksander was busy talking on his phone. After a few moments, I realized it was General Novak he was talking to. They were planning a TV address to the nation. *They're going to tell everyone we're going to war!*

Aleksander and the soldiers reached the elevators... and instead of passing by as I'd hoped, they stopped and pressed the button.

Dammit! Caroline and I came to an awkward halt and tried to look inconspicuous.

The elevator arrived and they got in. I froze when I saw Aleksander hit the button for the medical facility. At the same time, I saw one of the soldiers check his rifle. Making sure it was ready to fire.

My stomach twisted. They were on their way to kill my parents.

64

GARRETT

THE SECRET PASSAGE took me into the dungeons, just as Kristina had said it would. It was part of the palace I'd never been in and the first part I came to was full-on medieval, the stone walls worn smooth with age and the iron bars crumbling. But further in, the cells had been restored. I crept through the hallways, keeping to the shadows. Praying that in one of them, I'd find—

There.

They were asleep, but there was no mistaking the huge, squat silhouette on one bunk, or the way the other occupant lay ramrod straight on his back, his hands folded neatly on his chest. I ducked around the corner and waited until a soldier passed by. I crept up behind him and slammed him into the bars, hard enough to knock him out. The two men inside the cell woke up fast.

"Where's The Queen?" asked Emerik immediately.

"Trying to rescue her parents," I told him, unlocking the door. "She needs your help." I looked between them. "*I* need your help."

Jakov bent, picked up the soldier's rifle and handed it to Emerik, then took the handgun for himself. He motioned me to lead the way. But halfway down the hallway, a voice stopped us. "Hey!"

I turned. A slender guy in a suit was gripping the bars of his cell. "Is Caroline okay?"

Sebastian. The poor bastard who'd been framed as a traitor.

He was shaking his head. "I swear, I'm not working for Garmania. Please, just tell her I love her."

"You can tell her yourself," I said, and unlocked his cell.

Together, we moved off through the hallway. We were vastly, comically outnumbered. But in a weird way... it felt as if I had my squad back.

I just hoped it was enough to save her.

65

KRISTINA

THE DOORS SLID CLOSED and Aleksander's elevator began its descent. I dropped the toolbox and sprinted for the door that led to the stairwell. Caroline caught on and raced after me. Our only chance now was to get there first.

The medical facility was four floors down. We pelted down the stairs, jumping the last few stairs of each flight. We raced straight past the nurse at the reception desk, turned the corner and burst into my father's room, breathless and frantic.

My mother was sitting on the edge of his bed, her eyes red from crying. Dr. Glavnic was there, too, and both of them looked up in amazement as we burst in.

"No time to explain," I snapped to my mother. "Aleksander's right behind me. He's going to kill you both. We have to get you out of here." I looked at Dr. Glavnic. "Is there another way out, big enough for a gurney?"

"There's a freight elevator. We use it to move patients down from the parking garage. Down the hall, to your left."

But there was no time. I heard the chime of Aleksander's elevator arriving. I wanted to weep with frustration. We'd been so close!

"I'll delay them," said Dr. Glavnic. He marched towards the door. "Get your parents out of here."

I grabbed his arm. "When he finds out what you've done, he'll arrest you for treason. Maybe worse."

Dr. Glavnic looked me in the eye. "I brought you into this world, Your Majesty. I'll be damned if I'm going to let that bastard take you from it. Now *go!*"

He hurried off down the hallway to intercept Aleksander. I stared after him, breathing hard. Not *all* my people had turned against me.

My mother was already freeing my father from the machines that had been monitoring him. I grabbed a gurney and helped her roll him onto it. Caroline held the doors wide and we silently pushed the gurney out of the room and into the hallway.

I could hear the doctor talking to Aleksander just around the corner. My mother, Caroline and I all stared at each other, our faces pale, as we pushed the gurney down the hall. If a wheel so much as squeaked....

I mashed the call button for the freight elevator and then we had to stand there waiting. *Come on. Come on!* There was a distant rumble of machinery. I could hear Aleksander growing impatient, demanding to see the King. *Come on!*

The elevator arrived and the doors slid open. We pushed my father's gurney in and slipped inside just as Aleksander came around the corner. I hit the button for the parking garage and willed the doors to close. But nothing happened.

I heard Aleksander and the soldiers march into my father's empty room. I hammered on the button. *Come on!*

Aleksander yelled a curse and they burst back out into the hallway. The doors finally started to close just as he ran past the elevator... and he saw us through the closing gap. His eyes widened in shock.

I tore off the baseball cap and let my hair fall free, staring back at him defiantly. Then the doors closed and we started to move.

I knew that he'd raise the alarm and that they'd lock the palace down in minutes. The instant the doors opened, we rushed out and pulled the gurney over to the electrical repair van I'd come in. We heaved the gurney into the back, slammed the doors and—

We froze. Four soldiers were approaching the van, guns pointed right at us. I closed my eyes and tensed, waiting for the bullets to hit.

There was a *wump*.

I opened my eyes to see one soldier crumpling to the ground and Garrett standing behind him, his fist still raised. Emerik stepped out of the shadows and slammed his rifle into another soldier's head. Jakov pistol-whipped the third one.

The fourth one had turned around to see what was happening. He turned back to face us, his rifle coming up—

My mother kneed him in the groin with the full force of her vengeful fury.

He hadn't even hit the ground before I'd slammed into Garrett's chest and wrapped my arms as far around him as I could. He crushed me to him and I pressed my face against him: he was the best thing I'd ever felt in my life. "I thought you wouldn't wake up!" I sobbed.

"Got kissed by a princess," he rumbled. "Figure there's got to be some magic in that."

Then Sebastian stepped out from behind the guards and Caroline let out a moan of disbelief and ran at him. He lifted her and swung her around, her blonde hair flying out. It was the first time I'd seen them together and, as soon as I saw the way he looked at her, I knew she'd been right. He *was* the one.

There were shouts from deeper in the parking garage. Caroline, Sebastian, Emerik and Jakov jumped into the back of the van. Garrett and I jumped into the front and Garrett slid along the bench seat towards the steering wheel. "I'll drive," he said.

My mother jumped in from the other side and pushed him out of the way. "*I'll* drive, Mr. Buchanan," she said firmly.

Garrett gaped at her. I could hear boots running towards us.

My mother gunned the engine with surprising aggression. "I wasn't always a queen, you know," she muttered. And we roared off into the streets.

66

KRISTINA

IT'S LESS than ten miles from the palace to our nearest border, with
the peaceful nation of Carlonia. For the first five or so, as we raced
away from the city and along twisting mountain roads, we managed
to stay ahead of any pursuit. My mother hurled the van around
corners far faster than its designers had ever intended: she seemed to
have an instinctual feel for just how far it would lean and skid
without flipping over, and she pushed it to the very limit.

But as the hills grew steeper, we slowed down and she cursed. I
could see military Humvees in the rear view mirror. Then the gunfire
began, bullets chewing up the road around us. We were too far away
and traveling too fast for them to hit us...*yet*. But they were gaining
fast.

I already had the cell phone to my ear and was desperately trying
to convince the Carlonian authorities that this really *was* the Queen
of Lakovia, calling the government's main switchboard on a random
cell phone number and begging to be put through to the Prime
Minister. "I need you to open the border and let us through!" I told
them. I had Garrett's hand in mine and was squeezing it hard. I was
pretty sure I was never going to let go of it again.

"Madam, we would need to verify your identity," said the civil servant I'd been put through to. "Then you'd have to apply for a visa. When do you think your delegation might be visiting our country?"

"In about thirty seconds!" I yelled. *"Open the border now!"*

We rounded the corner and I saw the border checkpoint with its red and white barrier still closed across the road. Carlonian soldiers ran into the road as they saw us screaming towards them and pointed their guns at us, yelling at us to stop.

My mother cursed and stood on the brakes. We slowed... and the soldiers chasing us surged forward in our rear view mirror. We jerked to a stop, the nose of the van almost touching the barrier... and the first bullet hit us. It went straight through the bodywork and out through the windshield, shattering it. Everyone screamed and hunkered down. Garrett threw himself protectively across me.

On the cell phone, a different voice came on the line. "This is the Prime Minister."

"Mr. Prime Minister, I met you at a garden party last year," I sobbed desperately. "You told me about your son winning the tennis tournament. You said I reminded you of my father. *It's me! Open the border, please!"*

There were muffled, urgent voices in the background. Two more bullets flew through the van. Then the barrier suddenly swung up and the soldiers dived out of the way.

My mother stamped on the gas and we shot forward just as bullets shredded our tires. We skidded, spun and finally lurched to a halt facing sideways...but we were in Carlonia.

The barrier swung closed. The soldiers who'd been chasing us were furious... but they weren't going to start firing into another nation's territory. We watched, panting, as they slowly retreated.

We were helped from the van by border security officers while two of the soldiers carefully unloaded my father from the back. Caroline and Sebastian climbed out hand-in-hand: *no one* was going to split them apart again. The officers were polite but cautious and we spent the next hour answering questions. Then some men from the Prime Minister's office arrived and everything became much more friendly. We were told that the Prime Minister had formally granted us asylum and that we could stay as long as we liked. An ambulance arrived to take my father to the hospital and my mother climbed into the back... but I held back.

My mother blinked at me, confused. Then she went pale. "You *are* coming with us?"

I shook my head and then nodded towards Lakovia. "My place is back there."

My mother stared at me with incredulity and then jumped out of the ambulance and rushed over to me. Her perfect black hair was being tousled by the mountain breeze, but she didn't seem to notice. "The people have turned on you!"

"That's exactly why they need me."

My mother shook her head, tears in her eyes. The mask she'd worn, ever since the war, was gone. "Please, Kristina! At least let's go to the Carlonian government. They can intervene, they can level sanctions—"

"We don't have time for any of that! The bombers are launching in a few hours."

My mother turned to Garrett. "Please, talk sense into her. We can live in peace in Carlonia." She glanced at me and then back at Garrett. "*All* of us."

I drew in my breath and looked at Garrett. He was staring back at my mother, his expression impossible to read. *This is everything he'd ever wanted.* I'd no longer be a queen, or even a princess: we could be together. My mother was willing to accept him. We wouldn't be in danger anymore. And I knew our family had overseas bank accounts we could access. We could live more than comfortably.

All he had to do was convince me to give up my country.

He looked into my eyes for a long moment. Then, without looking at my mother, he spoke. "I'll do what my Queen orders me to do," he said at last. "If she wants me to stay here, I'll stay here. But if she wants to go back, I'm with her to the end."

I threw my arms around him and hugged him close. I was trying to hold back a flood of tears and it was difficult to speak. "Thank you," I managed.

My mother stepped forward. "Mr. Buchanan...." It was the first time she'd said his name without that edge of disapproval. "I concede that I may have been wrong about you."

Garrett turned to her and bowed. "Thank you, Your Majesty." There wasn't a trace of bitterness in his voice.

"Please," said my mother, her voice cracking, "Take care of my daughter."

I hugged her goodbye and she got into the ambulance. I looked at Emerik and Jakov and then at the ambulance. I wanted to let them know that they were free to go with her if they wanted.

They each took a big, deliberate step towards me. I nodded my thanks, a huge lump in my throat. Caroline and Sebastian stepped forward too, and the tears welled up in my eyes: even after being accused of treachery, both of them were still willing to risk their lives. "No," I told them firmly. "You two have been through enough. And I want you to stay close to my mother and father, make sure they're okay." They reluctantly nodded and I embraced them, then watched as they walked off towards the ambulance hand-in-hand.

The Prime Minister's office lent us one of their Mercedes. Garrett got behind the wheel, I sat next to him and the guards climbed into the back. We drove back over the border and started along the twisting mountain road that led back to the city. "We better make a plan," said Garrett as we reached the outskirts. "They probably had a satellite watching the border. They're going to intercept us any time now."

I sighed and shook my head. Suddenly, this seemed impossible. "To stop the war, I need to get control of our armed forces. But they won't listen. They think I'm a traitor. Everybody does."

"Only because they've been lied to," said Garrett, his eyes on the road. "We need to tell them the truth."

"How? Aleksander is in league with the media. Probably promised them all sorts of things if they spread lies about me. They're not going to put me on the air."

"Then we'll have to persuade them." Garrett thought for a moment, then drove towards the center of the city. "We're going to need help. *Shit!*" He slammed on the brakes as two police cars skidded to a halt in front of us, blocking the street. He threw the car into reverse, but before we'd gone ten feet, a military Humvee blocked the street behind us.

Garrett went forward again and swung us towards an alley, but the Mercedes was almost too big. We all winced as we lost a wing mirror and scraped all the way down one side of the car... but we made it. "Where are you going?" I asked frantically. "Who's going to help us? We don't have any allies left!"

He didn't answer, but his jaw was set: he had a plan. We erupted out of the alley, then had to slew sideways to miss a pavement cafe. More police cars turned into the street ahead of us, and I could see more military vehicles, too. "Garrett," I said in despair, "where are you going? There's nowhere in the city that'll take us in!"

"No," he said, determined. "There's one place."

67

GARRETT

I SCREECHED to a stop in front of the big white building, grabbed Kristina's hand and hauled her towards the doors. The two guards followed. Kristina gulped as she saw The Stars and Stripes hanging overhead.

They gave me mixed feelings, too. For so many years, I'd been loyal to that flag... and then the politicians had abandoned us. Now I had to trust them again. But Kristina had convinced me that not all leaders are the same. And there was one man in particular I wanted to give a chance.

The US Marines guarding the embassy swung their rifles up as we approached. "Whoa!" I said, hands high, "Whoah, I'm an American. This is the Queen of Lakovia and her guards. Let us in!"

The marines hesitated. This was one scenario their training hadn't covered.

A Humvee screeched to a stop outside the embassy. Lakovian soldiers spilled out and sprinted towards us.

"Our countries have a treaty, goddammit!" I snapped at the marines. I pointed to Kristina. "This is this country's recognized leader! At least let her in!" I glanced at Emerik and Jakov and they nodded. We'd take our chances, as long as Kristina was safe. I gently pushed her forward towards the US marines.

"That woman's a traitor! She's coming with us!" yelled the leader of the Lakovian soldiers.

I shook my head and put myself between him and Kristina, shielding her with my body. He pointed his rifle at me. Then he made the mistake of pointing his rifle at the marines.

Faster than you can blink, every marine had their rifle leveled at the Lakovians and they let loose with the full force of their lungs. Other countries might think they can yell, but there's nothing in the world like a US marine at full volume. *"STAND DOWN! DROP YOUR WEAPONS NOW!"*

The Lakovians actually stumbled back a foot or so, intimidated. But they didn't lower their guns. They were under orders, just like the marines. Kristina was hunkering down, terrified. Any second, the bullets were going to start flying.

I ran at the leader of the Lakovians, grabbed his uniform and snarled in his face. "Those are *US marines!*" I yelled. "You fire *one shot* at them, Lakovia is at war with the United States of America. Do you want that?"

He stared back at me, torn... and then finally lowered his rifle. The Marines cautiously lowered theirs.

One of the marines must have been on the radio to their superiors inside because suddenly the embassy doors swung open and we were ushered inside. When the doors closed behind us, all of us went a little shaky-legged with relief.

A tall, thin man hurried forward. His suit was immaculate, but there was sweat trickling down the dome of his balding head. I figured he'd just watched the whole scene outside on a security camera. "I'm Raymond Hodge, the US ambassador to Lakovia," he told us. "I welcome you to our country, Your Majesty. But you've just put us in a very difficult situation."

"Yeah, well," I said, "we're about to put you in an even more difficult one." I glanced at Kristina and we exchanged a nod.

The ambassador paled. "If you're going to ask what I think you're going to ask... I can't possibly authorize—"

"I know," said Kristina, stepping forward. "That's why we need to speak to the President."

68

KRISTINA

THE CONFERENCE ROOM HAD SEATS, but I needed to stand, for this. I needed every bit of confidence I could get.

The big screen on the wall lit up and I saw the US President sitting behind his desk. "Your Majesty," he said. "I'm glad to see you're safe."

I swallowed. I had to be Queen now, more than I ever had before. I allowed myself just a single glance at Garrett. He nodded. *You can do this.*

"Mr. President," I began, "You once told me that if I ever needed help, I should come to you. Well, I'm coming to you now. There are US marines at this embassy. I'm asking you to provide us with as many as you can spare, to help us take the TV station and tell the nation the truth about what's going on." I laid it all out for him: Aleksander, General Novak, the assassination attempts on me and my father.

The President leaned forward, his face somber. "You're asking me to launch an attack with US troops in a foreign country. That's an act of war, Your Majesty."

"If you don't help us," I said, "there's going to *be* a war. The bombers are launching right now. They'll be in Garmanian airspace within an hour. Then the war will start and once it starts, no force on earth is going to be able to stop it. Millions of innocent people are going to die. Mr. President, five years ago, when Garmania invaded, we begged for help. Europe didn't do anything. The UN didn't do anything. The United States didn't do anything."

The President closed his eyes and nodded in acknowledgement.

"I don't blame you," I said. "I really don't. I'm just asking you to not let history repeat itself."

"And if we do this, and you don't succeed?" asked the President. "If US troops mount what's basically a coup against another country's leader and these people retain power? They'll paint us as conspirators with you and Garmania. No one will trust us again." He ran a hand through his hair and sighed. "Mr. Buchanan?"

Garrett stepped forward. "Mr. President?"

"You know the Queen. I'd appreciate an honest opinion. Can she pull this off? If the marines get her on TV, can she convince her people to follow her again? Can she stop the war?"

Garrett gazed at me for a few seconds, hunting for the words. Then, "Sir, this woman's only been in power a handful of days. But she's already a better leader than any I've ever met. I'd follow her to the end." I stared at him, overcome, my chest tight. "Sir, *we need to do this,*" he said. "We can't let politics get in the way." His voice was thick with emotion. "Not this time."

The President looked at me. "You're asking me to risk US lives. These are men with wives and children. Not all of them might make it back."

It was the part of being a leader I most feared. But I couldn't let that fear control me anymore. "I'm aware of that, Mr. President. And I accept that responsibility, if it's the price of stopping this war."

The President's face softened a little, as if I'd given the right answer. "Okay then," he said. "Let's get this thing moving."

69

GARRETT

KRISTINA WAS TRYING to do up the straps on her body armor, but her hands were shaking. I reached down, gently moved her hand out of the way and did them for her. But the truth was, I just wanted to tear the goddamn thing off her, pick her up and lock her in a room at the embassy. The idea of her walking right into danger terrified me.

But I couldn't see another way to do this. We needed her there, at the TV station, to speak to the people. I'd just have to keep her safe.

And that was another problem: was I up to this? I was worried I was going to have another flashback and if that happened, I'd be useless. This wasn't like the shootout on the highway, or seeing the blood seeping through the towel in the motel room. This was actual combat and I hadn't been in combat since I was discharged. Plus, I had a head injury. A medic at the embassy had unwound the duct tape from my head, taking off some hair in the process, cleaned me up and bandaged it. But he'd been very clear that what I really needed was some time in bed, not to go into action.

The leader of the marine squad, Master Sergeant Hadley, came over. His black hair was shaved in the classic Marine "high and tight" and he was tall, towering over Kristina. Given that he wasn't in the best mood, the effect was... intense. "Your Majesty, I want you to understand: we don't have the time or the manpower to hold that TV station." He was polite but his voice was tight with worry. "We're massively outnumbered. This is going to be an insertion, nothing more. We get you in there, but you have to work the magic once we do because we sure as hell aren't getting out again."

I understood that he wasn't being an asshole: he was just worried about his men. I turned to Kristina but she was already nodding. "I understand, Master Sergeant" she said. "And thank you and your men." She said it with such sincerity that Hadley nodded and calmed a little. I'd met two-star Generals who couldn't talk to the soldiers as well as she could. She was a natural.

Eight marines, Emerik and Jakov, Kristina and I all took our places in the back of a truck. Kristina looked tiny crammed between two marines. They'd found some military fatigues that just about fit her and a pair of boots, but by the time she'd strapped on the body armor and the helmet, it looked like the uniform was going to swallow her. I reached across the aisle and squeezed her hand. "You'll be okay," I told her.

She nodded, her face pale. I swore I'd protect her, whatever it took.

As we neared the TV station there was a rumble of aircraft engines above, heading towards the border with Garmania. We peeked out of the back of the truck and saw a formation of bombers, high overhead. I looked at Kristina, who was already doing the math in her head. "We've got twenty minutes," she said. "Maybe less."

Master Sergeant Hadley leaned over and showed us his phone. It was a live news feed, and Aleksander and General Novak were on screen, making the speech they'd wanted Kristina to make: the one declaring war on Garmania. "*Hurry!*" I said tightly.

The TV station was one of those super-modern places, all glass and white stone. We went around the back first, to drop off Emerik and Jakov. They had their own, separate job and it was crucial to our success.

Seconds later, we pulled up outside the front of the TV station. As we'd thought, there were soldiers guarding it: Aleksander knew the power of the media and he didn't want anyone telling the people the truth.

One by one, the marines jumped down from the truck and started shooting. I spun around and took Kristina's face between my hands. It made my chest ache to see her so scared. "Stay low," I told her, shouting to be heard over the gunfire. "Stay in the middle. Stay with us. I WILL protect you." She nodded. Then she grabbed me and kissed me hard, and the press of those soft, sweet lips made me light up inside. We took a second to enjoy it: both of us knew it might be our last chance.

Then we jumped down from the truck... and entered hell.

70

KRISTINA

IT WAS TERRIFYING.

The first floor of the TV station was one huge open plan area, filled with desks and glass partitions. The marines ran us through it towards the stairs at the back. *Ran.* I had shorter legs than them and I had to push myself to keep my place in the middle of the group. I didn't want to slow them down.

The noise was deafening. Soldiers yelling at us, marines screaming orders, glass shattering. And all around me, the constant clatter of gunfire. I wanted to clap both hands over my ears, but I couldn't: Garrett had told me to keep one hand pressed on his back the whole time, so that he knew I was still with him.

He was like a charging rhino in front of me, battering things out of the way. His strong back was my shield. But I still yelped and ducked as bits of glass and wood went flying on both sides of me. Desks were being shredded, glass was crashing to the ground, computer screens were sparking and tumbling as stray bullets caught them. The marines were incredible, whipping their rifles around and picking off enemies before I'd even seen them. But Master Sergeant Hadley was right, we were hugely outnumbered. There were only ten of us and at least three times that number of them. And this was only the first floor. *This is what it's like to be a soldier? How did Garrett do this every day?!*

The marine behind me suddenly yelled a warning and pushed me to the left. Then he cried out and spun around, falling to his knees. Hot red erupted out of the side of his neck and splattered me. Then he clamped a hand over it and I saw blood pumping between his fingers. *Oh Jesus!*

Another marine grabbed his arm and helped him to a side room. Our group reformed, with me in the middle again, and we moved off. But my eyes were locked on the open door to the side room as the marine's buddy struggled with gauze and bandages, trying to stop the bleeding. *He took that bullet for me! I'm getting people killed!* I wanted to weep. *I never wanted any of this!*

But if I didn't keep going, millions were going to die.

We reached the stairs and started up them. The studio Aleksander was broadcasting from was up on the fourth floor. The marines were far better trained than the Lakovian soldiers and at first we had the element of surprise. We made it up to the second floor, then the third. But then our momentum started to fade: the soldiers were organizing and holding their ground. Another marine was wounded as we tried to cross the third floor. Then two more fell. Our group had shrunk by half. I saw Garrett's face change, his jaw tight with tension. Our progress stopped completely. *We're not going to make it!*

Suddenly, something smacked me in the chest. It was as if someone had punched me right in the middle of my body but I hadn't seen anyone. I fell flat on my back.

I saw Garrett scream in rage and fire his rifle at someone on the other side of the room. I realized he was shooting the person who shot me.

The person who shot me. It echoed in my head. *Oh God, I've been shot!*

And then the pain hit me, spreading through my chest. I couldn't move, couldn't breathe.

Garrett turned, crouched... and suddenly I was being scooped up off the ground. He cradled me to his chest like a child, holding his rifle in his other hand, and ran with me through the room. I clung to him, my head on his shoulder, my whole torso throbbing.

There was a crash as he kicked over a desk. Then he gently laid me down behind it, where I was shielded from gunfire. The other marines fell back and joined us in our shelter.

Garrett hunkered down over me, searching my body armor for something. Then his big hands thrust underneath it and felt my body. I saw his shoulders slump in relief. "It's okay," he yelled over the gunfire. "It's okay, you're okay. The armor stopped it."

I was too scared and in too much pain to answer.

"I know, it hurts like a son of a bitch. But you'll be okay." He leaned down and kissed me. Even amidst the gunfire and the destruction, as soon as his big body pressed close, I felt safe. I closed my eyes and for one brief, glorious second just allowed his kiss to take me away from everything.

He drew back and spoke in Master Sergeant Hadley's ear. Hadley nodded in agreement and the two of them looked above us. The room we were in was double-height, overlooked by balconies on the fourth floor. And someone was shooting down at us from those balconies. That's who had shot me. That's why we'd stopped moving.

"Three men," yelled Garrett. "What's left of Lukin's kill team. I recognize one of the bastards. He's got them all up there, to make sure we don't get to the studio. Someone has to sneak up there and take them out, or we're stuck here."

My eyes widened as I realized who *someone* was. "No!" I had this horrible, lurching certainty that if he left, he wasn't coming back.

"I have to."

"At least take some men with you!"

He shook his head and glanced at the remaining marines. There were only three left. "We need them to protect you."

I gulped. The room had gone blurry. "Please don't leave me!"

"I promise I'll come back." He leaned down and kissed me. Then he turned, ran out from behind the table, and was gone.

71

GARRETT

I NEEDED to get back to her. Every second I was away from her felt like a year. What if she'd been shot again, and the armor didn't stop it, this time? What if she was lying there wounded, *right now,* and I wasn't there?

I growled and pushed on. To save her, I had to do this. I'd made my way up the back staircase to the fourth floor and now I was... I guess the word would be *backstage,* amongst all the electronics that made the studio work. It was like being in a forest, with thick trunks of computer servers and thousands of cables stretched between them. I threaded my way silently through and finally came out near one of the balconies that looked down onto the third floor. Right in front of me was one of Lukin's men. He was firing down at the third floor and—

My chest tightened. He was shooting at the table Kristina was sheltering behind.

I growled and ran at him like a charging bull. He heard me coming and turned around just in time to get my fist in his face. He staggered back against the balcony wall and I ducked down and grabbed his legs, helping him on his way. He screamed as he tumbled over the side and crashed to the floor below. *That's one.*

I disappeared back into the racks of computers and circled around to the next guy. But then it all went wrong. He'd been alerted by his buddy's scream and saw me as soon as I left the shelter of the computers and started shooting. I had to run for cover as bullets slammed into the computers all around, shattering plastic and puncturing metal. There was the sharp smell of ozone and then acrid smoke as things shorted out. White-hot sparks showered across the floor and I grunted as some of them struck my wrist.

I came to a stop hunkered down behind a rack of computer servers, wincing as the gunman pumped shots into them from the other side. *I don't have time for this!* I had to get back to Kristina. But the gunman was just waiting for me to emerge. As soon as I came out from behind the servers, I was dead. Brute force wouldn't cut it, for once. I had to *think.*

And then, glancing around at the server racks, I realized they were all on wheels, so they could be moved around.

I crouched down, making sure I didn't let anything poke out from behind my cover, and flipped up the little brakes that stopped the wheels from moving. And then I *heaved,* putting all my strength into it.

I heard the gunman falter as the server rack he was firing at started to roll towards him. I kept pushing. We started to pick up speed and I heard the gunman take a step backwards. He fired three more shots but they just sunk into the metal of the heavy computer servers. I pushed harder, almost running, now, nudging the thing left and right, aiming at where the sound was coming from—

I felt the impact as the servers thumped into the guy. Then a second later, a scream as they slammed him back against the balcony. I didn't know if he was injured or dead, but he was out of the fight. *That's two....*

A rifle butt caught me in the back of my bandaged head and I went down like a felled tree. My brain was suddenly one big, throbbing ball of pain. All I could see was white and all I could hear was a thin, shrill screech.

I nearly threw up. I managed to get my hands under me and tried to pry myself off the floor, but it felt like I weighed a thousand tons. I gritted my teeth and managed to turn myself over and looked up at—

I could see two of him, his face just an outline, black lines on blinding white. But I knew that slicked-back hair. *Silvas Lukin.*

He drew back his leg and kicked me in my kidneys. The pain rippled up my body and when it reached my head, it felt like it exploded.

I tried to get my feet under me but my head hurt so much, it wouldn't send the right messages to my limbs. I just lay there, slumped. Then he kicked me again and my whole body went limp.

I was done.

He could have just shot me while I was down, but no: he wanted it to hurt as much as possible. He raised his rifle above his head, ready to bring it down on me like a club. "We should have killed her in the war when we had the chance!" he spat.

And then I got mad.

I thought of my dad. I thought of the marines who'd been wounded, just that day, and the FBI agents back in America, and all the millions who'd die when the war started. I thought about those children he'd killed in the church. Most of all, I thought about Kristina, locked in that cell, filling with water. All because bastards like this decide some other race, or nation, or tribe, is inferior.

He swung the rifle at my head. My hand snapped up and caught the stock, stopping it an inch from my skull. His eyes bulged in sudden fear and he tried to tear it away from me, but I was stronger. Both of us heaved... and then both of us lost our grip on it and the rifle went spinning off across the floor.

I grabbed hold of some dangling cables and with sheer, stubborn determination, I used them to haul myself up, first to my knees and then to standing. I felt like I was on the rolling deck of a ship. The whole room was still throbbing white in time with my pulse. I could barely see or think. But I was going to stop him, no matter what. I was going to protect her.

I ran at him, staggering a little. I was still seeing double and I couldn't be sure of hitting him, so I spread my arms wide and charged, ramming him back into a rack of servers. Then I brought my fist up under his chin.

He stumbled back, bleeding from a split lip... and pulled out a knife. But I had this. I was angry, fired up. I'd tear him apart.

I stepped back a little, getting my balance... and went right into the smoke that was belching from one of the damaged computers. I blinked and coughed. And suddenly, I could feel it coming for me, bearing down on me like a runaway freight train. *No! Jesus, no, not now!*

But it was no good. I was frozen, the memory rushing towards me. A house in Iran, where my eyes were gritty with sand and my lungs were clogged with dust. Where everyone I cared about was dead.

"You can't protect her," panted Lukin. "Look at you."

I tried to hold it back. I used all my strength, but the memory had the weight of a planet, it would crush me when it hit—

Lukin kicked me viciously in the leg and I fell to the ground. I could barely see him, anymore. All I could see was the brown, swirling dust. The look on Baker's face when I shot him.

"You did us a favor," said Lukin. He fell to his knees astride me and raised the knife. "Killing's too good for a Lakovian bitch. You brought her right to us. Maybe we can take her alive."

Kristina. She needed me. And I remembered what she'd told me.

I closed my eyes and thought of her in plaid shirt and jeans. And the horses, snorting as she stroked them. I thought of fresh, clean air and a sunset in Texas. *That's* where I wanted to be.

I stopped trying to hold back the memory... and sidestepped, instead. I felt it pass by me, so close I could feel the wind on my face, and then slam home, heavy and real and terrifying. But I was outside it, looking in. Maybe for the first time, I could see it for what it was: the past.

My eyes opened and I surged up off the floor. I grabbed Lukin's throat in one hand and drove him back and back, then twisted and slammed him down on the floor. My fists hammered his face as I screamed at him in fury.

And then he groaned and went still and I slumped atop him, panting. It was over.

I heard a tiny noise behind me, almost undetectable. I opened my eyes and, on the computer screen in front of me, I saw the reflection of General Novak.

Then he brought his rifle down on my head and everything went black.

72

KRISTINA

THE GUNFIRE COMING down from the fourth floor had stopped and we'd made it to the bottom of the stairwell. We were nearly there! The studio was right at the stop of those stairs!

But every time we tried to advance, withering gunfire pushed us back. Master Sergeant Hadley shook his head. "There are too many of them," he yelled.

I was still hunched over: I couldn't straighten up properly without my chest exploding into agony. *Where's Garrett?* He should have been back by now. "We have to finish this," I croaked.

Hadley winced as bullets splintered the doorframe inches from where we were huddled. "It's too dangerous. I'm sorry, Your Majesty. We have to pull back." He turned and began looking for a route back downstairs.

Cold despair flooded through me, draining the last of my strength. We'd failed. We'd failed and millions of people were going to die.

I thought of Silvas Lukin and his hatred. Of Aleksander and his need for revenge. Of Jakov and his struggle to fit in. The last war was still claiming victims. How many generations would this next one condemn? We had to stop this now. Here. Today.

I gritted my teeth... and heaved myself upright. As all the bruised parts of my chest were stretched, the pain was so bad, I nearly passed out. I grabbed hold of the doorframe and squeezed it as hard as I could, determined not to scream. *"No,"* I told Master Sergeant Hadley.

The three remaining marines all turned to look at me, their eyes wide. They were scared. They just wanted to go home to their wives and kids. They'd seen their friends shot. They had Hadley to lead them, but right now, they needed something else. And I tried my best to give it to them.

I was smaller than any of them, but I stood as tall as I could. "I know that you're not from my country," I said, my voice shaking with pain. "I know this isn't your war. And I'm not asking you to fight because of some treaty, or because of orders, or because the President asked you to. This is about lives. Millions of people who are going to be killed." I drew in a shuddering breath. "So you can give up and go home or you can fight on but don't tell me it's too dangerous! Because those people are civilians and they're facing annihilation. And the only thing, the *only* thing standing between them and those bastards is *you.*"

There was utter silence for a few seconds. Then Master Sergeant Hadley said, "What do you say, marines?"

The other two responded immediately, with a yell they must have heard right through the building. *"Oorah!"*

And they raced up the stairs with me right on their heels. The soldiers who'd been holding us back sprayed bullets down at us, but they were firing in panic: they hadn't been expecting us to suddenly rush them. I felt the bullets hiss right by us, one barely missing my face, but none of them hit.

On the far side of the huge studio, I saw Aleksander standing before a semicircle of cameras, addressing the nation. If we could just cover the thirty feet or so of open space and get in front of the cameras, we'd be on the air.

We sprinted forward, but soldiers swarmed to intercept us, some rushing at us and some firing from where they stood. There were too many of them. *We're not going to make it!*

Twenty feet from the cameras, a soldier slammed into one of the marines, tearing him away from our little group and carrying him down to the floor. Master Sergeant Hadley and the other remaining marine grabbed my arms and hauled me forward, firing to clear a path. "Keep going!" Hadley yelled. But just a few steps further on, the other marine fell, clutching at a leg wound.

Hadley and I ran on. We were less than ten feet from the cameras, now. I could see Aleksander watching us out of the corner of his eye as he spoke calmly to the nation about how they must be brave in the coming war.

Hadley suddenly spun and fell to the ground, clutching at his shoulder. I grabbed his hand and tried to haul him along with me. "No!" he snapped. "Leave me! Just go!"

I looked up. A soldier was racing towards me, his hand already reaching down to grab me—

I ducked and scrambled between two camera operators and—

Everything stopped.

I stood beside Aleksander, panting. At least ten rifles were pointed right at me from behind the cameras, but no one was shooting. *They can't kill me,* I realized in shock. *Not in cold blood, on live TV, without a trial.*

"Cut it! Cut the broadcast!" snapped Aleksander.

A woman just behind the cameras, wearing a headset, shook her head, her face pale. She pointed to a glass-walled control room above us. Aleksander and I both looked.

Emerik and Jakov were in there, guns drawn, making sure the technical staff kept broadcasting. Emerik gave me a nod.

I stepped forward and looked right into the camera Aleksander had been talking to. "I need to speak to you," I said to millions of viewers. "I need to tell you—"

I broke off.

Silvas Lukin had just burst into the studio, behind the cameras. He was holding a bruised and battered Garrett in front of him, and had a knife pressed against Garrett's throat.

Aleksander stepped close to me and whispered in my ear, too low for even the microphones to pick it up. I froze and listened, still staring into the camera. "This would have been tidier if you'd just been killed," he said. "I don't want a trial and an execution. So I'm going to make you an offer, one that lets you fix everything."

I kept staring at the camera listening, my breathing tight.

"I'll let you and the American live and exile you," Aleksander told me. "You can go to Carlonia and be with your parents."

I drew in a slow, shuddering breath of hope.

"... all you have to do is tell the people that you were deceived by the Garmanians," said Aleksander. "Say you're handing power over to me and renouncing the throne."

It felt as if my insides had turned to ice. *No!*

"Or you can watch him die right in front of you," Aleksander whispered.

73

KRISTINA

I KNEW, straight away, what Garrett would want me to do. He'd want me to do the heroic thing. The brave thing. The *right* thing. He'd want me to sacrifice him.

But I just wanted *him!* I wanted the one man who made me feel safe, who wrapped me up in his strong arms and made the nightmares stop. The man I could trust, who'd stuck with me right to the end. Who'd never let me go. He'd saved me so many times. I couldn't abandon him now.

I looked at him. Our eyes locked.

And he nodded.

This went beyond love. He'd followed me because he believed in me. He believed I was a good leader. He'd trusted me and he was asking me to trust him, that he knew what he was doing.

I took a deep breath and looked into the camera. I still didn't know what I was going to say.

Then I saw my own reflection in the camera lens. My hair was matted and filthy. I was dressed in military fatigues, I was bruised and scraped. I'd never looked less like a royal.

But I still was one. And my father's words rang in my head one last time. *Being royal isn't about doing what you want. It's about doing what your people need.*

I knew what I had to do.

"You have been lied to," I told the cameras.

Silvas Lukin's face went wild with fury. He looked right into my eyes and I saw his forearm tense, about to slash Garrett's throat.

Garrett's hand flashed up under Lukin's armpit. The knife clattered to the floor and Lukin looked down in shock at his suddenly numb arm.

Lukin looked up just in time to get Garrett's fist in his face. A good, old-fashioned, meaty punch that had the full force of Garrett's anger behind it. Lukin crashed to the floor, out cold.

General Novak reached for his rifle, but Garrett snatched up Lukin's knife and held the tip to the General's throat. "*Don't,*" he growled.

The soldiers around him all swung their rifles to point right at Garrett. My heart nearly stopped.

I stabbed my finger at Aleksander. "This man has conspired with General Novak to assassinate my father and me, to overthrow our country and to start a war with Garmania." I wasn't looking at the cameras, anymore. I was looking right into the eyes of the soldiers. This wasn't about leaders and politicians now. It was about them: the grunts, as Garrett called them. It was what they did in the next few seconds that would decide everyone's fate. "He's willing to sacrifice you, and your wives and your children. He's going to *wipe out a nation,* but Garmania is not our enemy, not anymore." I took a deep breath. "There's still time to shut this thing off. But I need your help. I need you to arrest these two men and put me back in charge!"

"Shoot her!" snapped General Novak. "She's a traitor! Garmania's launched its bombers, they're already on their way!"

"I can save us," I told them. "I can save our country. But I can't do it alone."

"Follow orders!" bawled the General.

"Save those people!" I yelled.

"I am your commander!"

"*I am your Queen!*"

The soldiers all looked at me.

And then every one of them turned to point their rifles at General Novak and Aleksander.

I scanned the assembled military officials and found the one I needed. "Air Marshall Trathers!" I yelled. "Turn our bombers around!"

He whipped out his phone and started snapping orders.

"Someone give me a phone!" I said frantically. Emerik ran down from the control room and threw me one and I dialed the palace switchboard, then asked to be connected to the Garmanian Prime Minister. When he answered, the hate and distrust in his voice made my stomach twist. What if he didn't listen?

"Mr. Prime Minister," I said, "there is a great deal to tell you and very little time. We have both been the victim of a plot to spark war between our countries. I know now that the attempts on my life and my father's life were not your doing. The men responsible are in custody. I have turned around the bombers that were heading for your country. I ask you please to do the same."

There was no reply. I could hear his breathing, shaky with rage.

"*Sir,*" I said. "I know you don't like me. But I need you to trust me. I know I didn't trust you. I should have listened, when you called me. Everyone told me that you just wanted war and I believed it, I let them convince me that you were different to me. But now I think you're just the same." I looked at the soldiers. "You want to save your people."

Still only silence, but his breathing had changed.

"We have one chance to stop this, Mr. Prime Minister. One. Or our children will grow up hating each other."

There was a long silence. Then, "For a young woman, you have an old head, Your Majesty. I think your father would be proud." He sighed. "I have ordered my bombers home."

I closed my eyes. "Thank you, Mr. Prime Minister."

I ended the call and suddenly it all rolled towards me in a black wave: the days of barely any sleep, the emotional drain, the constant tension. I swayed and had to grab the podium to keep from falling over. "Is that it?" I asked weakly. I didn't even know who I was asking: I didn't have a lead advisor, anymore. "Is there anything else I need to do?"

And then a big, warm presence was behind me. My feet left the floor and I was scooped up into his arms. He turned me to face him and I looked up into those clear, Texas-blue eyes.

"Just one," he said. And he kissed me, long and deep and true.

EPILOGUE

Kristina

One Month Later

Cool metal whispered past my hair. There was an undefinable sensation of lightness. Freedom.

And that was it: I wasn't a queen anymore.

The official stepped back from my chair and bowed, my crown in his hands. He placed my crown in a velvet-lined box, picked up the King's crown... and placed it on my father's head. The thousands of people who filled the hall stood as one and cheered. The noise was deafening... and wonderful.

My father had woken from his coma four days after I'd retaken power, but he'd needed another three weeks to get back up to strength. Now—finally—my reign was over.

There was a knot of tension that had been right at the center of my chest, ever since my father was shot. It suddenly melted away and I wanted to groan at how good it felt. Instead, I leaned across to the chair next to mine, grabbed Garrett's hand and squeezed it, and he squeezed back. God, it was good to be able to do that with everyone watching.

A lot had changed, in the last month.

In the aftermath of the TV broadcast, my policy had been complete honesty. I'd told the media everything: how I'd met Garrett, how he'd helped to save our country, how I'd initially been forced to keep our relationship secret but how I now hoped my people would welcome him. And once they'd heard our story, they did. There was a little muttering about tradition and him not being a prince from the older generation, but they hadn't wanted to see their children sent off to war, so even they accepted him. And everyone else, especially the women, went nuts for him. I'd had to relate the part about him swearing his allegiance *four times* in interviews.

Now, as he sat next to me on the stage, he was wearing a gray tailored suit with a crisp white shirt and a blue tie that set off his eyes. He looked even better than he had in the royal guard's uniform. The tailoring of the suit showed off those huge, broad shoulders and his tight waist, while the white shirt was soft enough that it hinted at the strong curves of his pecs. The royal hairdresser had asked whether he could make Garrett look more "respectable" and I'd immediately forbidden it. Cutting his hair short or insisting he was clean-shaved would just be *wrong*. He was exactly as he was supposed to be.

And yet we'd both changed, in ways people couldn't see. There were no more nightmares for me, not when I had Garrett to cuddle up to in the night. And while he had a long way to go, he'd made the first steps to putting things behind him: the flashbacks were under control and he was talking to the therapist who'd helped me: gruffly and reluctantly, but they were talking.

Garrett was talking to his dad, too. He'd flown home to Texas as soon as the situation in Lakovia was stable. His dad had begun to recover and apparently the pair had had a serious heart-to-heart. From what Garrett said, his dad understood his problems far better than he'd expected. Turns out, he hadn't come through the marine corps emotionally unscathed either. Both of them were a lot happier for talking.

Something that helped both Garrett and me was riding. Once Garrett's wounds had healed, I'd re-opened the royal stables and we'd started going for long rides in Lakovia's cool, misty forests. Garrett was right: there was something incredibly calming about being around horses. Calming... and romantic. Both times, when we'd been out, he'd given me this sudden, heated look. I mean, I wasn't doing anything special, just riding alongside him in a long, white dress with a tight bodice, my hair streaming out in the wind. But suddenly he was sweeping me off my saddle and onto his horse and galloping deeper into the trees, where the guards couldn't see us. And then, up against a tree, my skirts hoisted up around my waist....

I flushed and grinned.

We'd have more time for that, now. I was looking forward to just being a princess again. For now, at least. Someday, hopefully far in the future, when my father grew too old, I'd have to reign again. The night before, in bed, Garrett had asked me, "Is it less scary, now that you've done it once?"

"Now, I know how much I still have to learn," I'd told him seriously. I'd survived a few weeks of being queen, but when it came time to do the job permanently, I wanted to do it well. I'd learn everything I could from my father, but I wanted to visit other countries, too, to see how they did things. And our country had been dangerously isolated for too long. I wanted to fix that. I wanted to build alliances, especially with the US.

Emerik and Jakov were still guarding me. For now, Emerik was still on active duty: after everything he'd done, no one was suggesting he was ready to retire. But I'd had a talk with him and reassured him that when that day did come, there was a position available training and supervising the next generation of my guards. It was Garrett's idea, and Emerik loved it.

Jakov, meanwhile, was helping to ease the tensions between our people and the Garmanian communities who lived in our country. He'd helped to set up a football league for kids, with Lakovian and Garmanian kids playing on the same team, and it was already getting very popular. If we could get them making friends when they were young, maybe we could inoculate them against hatred in the future.

We were making progress at other levels, too. The Prime Minister of Garmania was our guest of honor at this ceremony, the first time he'd made a state visit to our country since the war. We'd come so close to disaster, it had encouraged both countries to reach out. I caught his eye as the cheering finally died down and we exchanged respectful nods. Peace wouldn't be easy or quick but then nothing worthwhile is. It helped that Aleksander, General Novak and Silvas Lukin were all in prison and would be for the rest of their lives. People in both Garmania and Lakovia understood that this had been an attack on both our countries by people from both sides who couldn't let go of the past. This time, when my father talked about moving forward, they'd listen.

When the speeches were over, we made our way to the waiting limos for the trip back to the palace. A string quartet was playing in the lobby: my father had flown them over from New York and they were fantastic. They finished the Lakovian national anthem just as we walked past them. In the brief pause, I heard the violinist whisper, "Why *do* they speak English, here?"

"It's a funny story," said the cellist excitedly, and pushed her glasses up her nose. "Three hundred years ago—" Then she had to start playing as they launched into the Garmanian national anthem.

We walked on. Outside, Garrett held the door for my father and then my mother as they climbed into the first limo. She gave him a little smile—she smiled a lot more, now. "Thank you, Garrett."

Ever since that day at the Carlonian border, she'd really changed her mind about him. She'd even defended him: a few of the stuffier newspapers had dared to suggest that Garrett wasn't royal suitor material, and they'd suffered the full force of her wrath. When I'd asked her about it, she'd said, "You're like your father. I'm not sure I ever realized how much, until all this."

I'd frowned. "So?"

"So: when your father met me, they said *I* wasn't suitable, either."

I'd blinked at that. She was always so reserved: it was hard to imagine her as a disreputable wildchild.

"I changed, to fit expectations," she'd said, reading my expression. "Garrett won't. And that's a good thing."

And then she'd hugged me. A full-on, proper, motherly hug, even though it creased her suit.

We climbed into our limo, along with Caroline and Sebastian. The pair were inseparable and were enjoying not having to skulk around anymore. I'd ended the ban on staff relationships, which Jakov was also happy about. I'd finally brought out the cherry candy from America. I'd had to pretty much push him all the way through the palace to Simone's room in the maids' quarters and knock on the door for him. But, blushing and mumbling, he'd handed over the gift and asked her out. She'd said yes before he even finished the sentence.

The limo pulled away from the curb and we sped off towards the palace. There was a champagne reception for the Prime Minister of Garmania but, the second I felt I could slip away, I was going to whisper in Garrett's ear and we'd sneak off up to my bedroom. Actually, I had a feeling he might just pick me up and carry me all the way up the tower, when I told him I was wearing *that* corset underneath my dress. Then, tomorrow, Caroline, Sebastian, Emerik, Jakov, Garrett and I were all booked on a flight to Texas. Garrett's dad was out of the hospital and the rebuild of the ranch—paid for by the palace—was complete. A week away from the cameras, helping him move in and riding horses, was exactly what we all needed. Plus, I was looking forward to eating ribs and wearing jeans again.

Caroline held something out to me: a velvet box. When I opened it, my jaw dropped. *My tiara!*

"I saw it on the floor, after the SUV crashed on the highway, and I thought I'd better grab it," she said. "But then you were trying to be incognito and then you were queen, so I've held onto it ever since. I thought you might want it back."

Garrett picked it up and gently slid it onto my head. Then he just sat there gazing at me, and the look in his eyes made me melt. "What?" I asked shyly. "I'm back to looking like a princess again?"

"No," he said. "You never stopped."

And he put those big, warm hands on my shoulders, drew me close and kissed me.

The End

Thank you for reading!

You may also enjoy *Alaska Wild.*

Mason Boone. A former Navy SEAL who lives in isolation in the Alaskan mountains. He's rugged, untamed...and gorgeous. I'm an FBI agent; he's a fugitive on his way to prison. But when our plane crashes deep in the Alaskan wilderness, Mason becomes my only hope.

To survive the cold, the wild animals and the terrain, we'll need to stay close. But every time he touches me, I melt inside. He makes me feel protected like no man ever has and the way he looks at me, as if he just wants to push me up against a tree and rip my clothes off.... Could he be innocent of his crimes and can I help him escape the demons of his past? I'm a city girl but I'll need to learn to live as wild as him...because the other prisoner from our flight and his gang are out there...and they're hunting us.

You can find all my books at helenanewbury.com

Made in the USA
Middletown, DE
20 July 2023

35502478R00224